A Line in the Sand

The Twenty-Nine Series, Book 2

By J.M. Richardson

Winter Goose
Publishing

Winter Goose Publishing
2701 Del Paso Road, 130-92
Sacramento, CA 95835

www.wintergoosepublishing.com
Contact Information: info@wintergoosepublishing.com

A Line in the Sand

COPYRIGHT © 2014 by J.M. Richardson

First Edition, May 2014

ISBN: 978-1-941058-07-7

Cover Art by Winter Goose Publishing
Typeset by Odyssey Books

Published in the United States of America

For Melissa

Chapter 1

September in North Texas could be brutal, and this day was no exception. But the people came out anyway, even with their children. Men and women of all ages and socioeconomic classes herded themselves south down Main Street of the old cow town clad in sunglasses, flip-flops, and shorts. Sweat beaded on their lips and wet the hair on the backs of their heads as the charcoal pavement beneath their feet changed to red brick. Already half-empty water bottles swung lodged in hands. Behind, the old courthouse, a Fort Worth icon, shrunk away with the mountainous dome of the convention center growing taller ahead.

Kyle Perkins's right palm grew moist against Ashley's. Their locked fingers moved in unison between them as they trekked down Main Street toward the stage set before the convention center. He was trained to be aware of his surroundings at all times, and thus found his eyes always scanning. It was a hard habit to break outside of service, yet with Ashley Dykes, it was somehow easier. His head was fixed mostly forward, yet his eyes involuntarily shifted frequently to his right. He followed her tone, tanned legs upward across her tank-topped torso. He marveled at the way her long, shiny, deep brown hair flowed behind her like the train of some beautiful dark gown. Her equally dark eyebrows accented her perfect olive skin with mysterious brown eyes set like gems in a piece of exquisite jewelry. And when she glanced and smiled at him with those smooth pink lips puffed and puckered, he knew she felt the same way about him.

His hair was finally growing back, which he wore in an intentionally messy spike. It had been nearly a year and a half since basic training and the buzzed head. Until the last two months, he had just grown accustomed to keeping it short, but now with the cease-fire and the war seemingly over, he was attempting to transition back to the life of a normal young man. A t-shirt and shorts felt foreign. The skin of his feet meeting open air rather than encased in boots gave him almost a sensation of anxiety.

"Thanks for coming down here with me." Ashley looked over at him and smiled. "I know you're kind of tired of all this."

"Yeah, well . . ." He shrugged and smiled before directing his eyes ahead to the platform set with two podiums and the flags of the United States, the Republic, and the state of Texas. "The things I do for love," he smiled. "Besides, this is historic. Two American presidents on the same stage, finally at peace. I'm game."

She grinned, her dark eyes narrowed and arched with sweetness as she gazed up at him while they walked. The breakup had been a mistake. She often silently chastised herself in her own thoughts and emotions for leaving him without understanding why he had gone into the military and off to war. What a shallow and heartless thing to do, Ashley thought. And now, as sweet and loving as he still was, he had changed. Certainly there was a reason. He had seen and done some horrific things, no doubt.

"What do you want to do after this?" she asked as they drew closer to the stage and the crowd gathering before it. "Today is all we have. We have to drive back to College Station tomorrow."

"I know," Kyle nodded, disliking to be reminded. "These little whirl-wind visits with family—yours and mine—are going to be tough."

"It's a shame I don't get out of my last Friday class until four or we could get on the road earlier. I'm still tired from being on the road half the night." She shook her head. "I'll have to keep that in mind when I schedule for the spring."

"We could stay an extra day—head back Monday morning," he suggested with a grin, knowing she would never approve.

"Easy for you to say, Mr. I-don't-have-a-Monday-class-until-two-thirty," she smirked. "I can't miss that nine-thirty biology class."

"I know," he shrugged. "And I have a trig test on Tuesday I need to get ready for." He thought for a moment. "Well, when the speech is over, it should be about lunch time. Want to go to that awesome Mexican place over on University Drive?"

"Mmm, that sounds yummy." She almost licked her lips. "And drinks at Nichole's house tonight?"

"Sure." He fought the urge to wince. He loved Ashley, but her group of friends was popular in high school, and stereotypically shallow. He could think of more congenial company to get intoxicated with that evening.

The relatively open police-barricaded street abruptly turned into a traffic jam of flesh and bone. People were huddled in close to one another, and pushed ever further forward toward the stage in an effort to gain a better vantage point. The heat had already risen above one hundred and the addition of body heat, complete with accompanying smells of various kinds, made for severe discomfort. Kyle's anxiety levels rose. A stroller clipped the back of his calf with a sharp plastic sting. He turned his head around to find a nice woman's kind smile mouthing the words I'm sorry. As he swiveled forward, his left arm was brushed by the extra hairy, perspiring arm of a very large gentleman walking close to him. He wiped the sweat onto his shorts. Gross, he grimaced.

"What do you think Chandler and Davenport are going to say?" Ashley stood on the tips of her toes, trying to better see the empty stage.

"I don't know," he pondered the question. "It's got to be big for President Chandler to fly all the way down here to Fort Worth. This is enemy territory for her. I imagine it's some big news about the Taliban. I hope they got whoever is responsible for blowing the holy hell out of Dallas."

In an instant, as if Kyle himself had cued the beginning of the event, the sounds of the crowd grew from a baseline of jumbled conversation and complaints about the heat. It rose steadily, the decibel level a flash flood in a dry desert river bed during a summer shower. It crested to a thunderous peak with the appearance of Fort Worth Mayor Maxine Goodlife onto the stage. She certainly did not possess the shape or sexiness of U.S. President Cindy Chandler. She was shorter and slightly more rotund, yet had an unrivaled confidence and comfort in her own skin that made her appealing enough to win her office by a landslide some two years back. She floated across the stage with a Texas-size grin and too much rouge, waving to her cheering and adoring constituents as she reached the podium.

"How are y'all doin'?" she smiled as people cheered. "Y'all sound happy to be hot," she joked as she scanned the crowd.

Thousands of sweaty, weary people gathered in the middle of Main Street. They glistened and shielded their eyes from the vicious sun. Fort Worth police officers and Tarrant County Sherriff's deputies stood guard in the crowd while U.S. Secret Service agents in the typical black suits, shades, and ear pieces worked security on all sides of the stage.

"We've been through a lot here in Texas," she spoke again. "Shoot, we've been through a lot here in DFW. And I refuse to leave the D out of DFW!" People cheered as she spouted fire. "I'm proud of the folks here in Fort Worth. Our people and our community have been so welcoming and supportive of our neighbors to the east. And I know we will continue to be so until they rebuild." She paused again for applause. "It is now my pleasure to welcome to the stage two distinguished leaders who, despite obvious divisions, have been nothing but unified since this tragedy occurred. Please join me in welcoming United States President Cindy Chandler and Republic of America President Byron Davenport."

Cheers roared louder than before, echoing between the decorative sidewalk trees and stately downtown hotels. It rose above the dome of the convention center, carrying over across Sundance Square and even reaching Montgomery Plaza. Chandler strode with grace in her light gray skirt suit with her lavender blouse collar overlapping the lapel.

She donned her narrow business eyeglasses and her lightly-highlighted brown hair in a bun of power.

President Davenport followed her to the twin podiums, sure to let ladies go first. His gray hair had grown grayer and the facial wrinkles were more defined during the war. Losing thousands of young men on battlefields across America will keep a man awake at night. Hard-line Republicans criticized him deeply for losing so much territory to the United States. Even his own vice president openly challenged him. But now he gained surprising support from moderates in his effort to work with President Chandler to rebuild and find common ground.

They settled into their positions behind the microphone-rigged podiums as the Secret Service seemed to perk up and become more alert in an instant. The pair smiled their politician smiles, waving and absorbing the reception of the people assembled. They glanced and grinned at one another mostly out of respect, yet perhaps a bit falsely, as if they were forced upon the same stage out of convenience.

"Good morning." Davenport's voice echoed across the city and paused as he allowed cheers to rise and fall. "I want to thank all of the people who came out on this hot Texas day. I'd like to thank all the news crews from both sides of the border. Everyone in the Republic and in the U.S. needs to hear what is to be said today."

In Cleveland, Ohio, Derek Putnam trudged from the bedroom, stumbling with the intoxication of recent sleep. His eyelids remained heavy while he maneuvered through baby mats and rattle toys. He rubbed his eyes, scruffy cheeks, and Marine haircut attempting to awaken his nerves and shake away the slumber. He straightened his cotton boxers, his only garment, as he walked, in an attempt to become more comfortable.

"Are we ever going to get to sleep all night without interruptions again?" he called out to Carly back in the bedroom. "Geez, even the damned Reds let us sleep most of the night."

He was finally able to keep his eyes open for extended lengths of time, while he opened and shut the kitchen cabinets in search of all the necessary elements to produce a simple pot of coffee. He reached for the glass pot, taking it from its cradle, and poured the previous morning's post-coffee soak water into the sink. He then turned the knob of the aged faucet with a squeak, and filled the pot with fresh water. Fresh as it can be for Cleveland. He poured it into the coffee maker and replaced the pot on its cradle before he turned and filled the crinkled paper filter with grounds of cheap, mass-roasted coffee.

"Correct me if I'm wrong, Sergeant Putnam, but it sounds to me like you're complaining." She emerged from their room with a smile, their baby daughter on her hip. She pulled down her tank top after an obvious feeding, remnant milk soaking the fabric. "Because while you've only dealt with this a couple of months, this has been my entire life for ten."

"Well, excuse me for serving my country that whole time," he jabbed back with a smile, familiar with this usual playful banter. "Need I remind you that I got shot in the process?" He pointed to the lump of purple scar tissue which had finally formed along his chiseled torso and left shoulder.

"Need I remind you that while you were off playing soldier, your baby momma had her belly sliced open and a baby ripped out?" She lowered her panty line to reveal her C-section scar. "Major abdominal surgery," she taunted.

"Okay, you got me." He grinned and leaned in for a quick kiss. "Still, when are we going to banish this kid to the nursery I just finished out-fitting? She's ten months old. Even your sister said she should be ready to start crying it out and sleeping through the night."

"Well my sister isn't Olivia's mother, is she?" Carly snapped back. "I'll start putting her in her crib when I'm comfortable with it," she nodded. "I feel like she still needs me. Besides, she's growing so fast, she still gets hungry in the middle of the night."

"Do you maybe want to start her on some cereal?" he asked. "The doctor okayed it."

"Maybe." Carly shrugged and turned away, bouncing the baby slightly in her arms. "It's just that my milk is the perfect food. It's going to be hard to give that up."

"For your benefit or the baby's?"

"Both," she answered. "I feel needed and I like that."

"I like it too—trust me," he smiled, lunging in to grope her breasts.

"Hey, hey, hey." She swatted his hands away. "Those aren't yours. They're Olivia's," she smiled.

"Well, it's my paycheck that fills those babies up." He copped a successful feel. "Shouldn't I get to play with them every now and then?"

"Very funny, Mr. Provider." She swatted him away again with a playful smile. "Speaking of which, any word from the Marines?"

"Nope." He shook his head, quickly pulling the coffee pot from its station and pouring a quick cup before replacing it to allow for further brewing. "I would imagine that since North Carolina is now U.S. territory again, I might get assignment to Camp Lejune. It's either that or San Diego."

"I'd much rather San Diego," she said, her eyes upturned in a brief daydream of perfect weather and sunshine. "But really, I'm scared to move anywhere." She brought herself back to reality. "I mean, all my family's here. My parents get to visit Olivia all the time, and you know how my dad adores this child. Then there are my sisters—they're always around for motherly advice."

"I know. It's good to have family close by." He closed his eyes and nodded. "I've grown to really like your parents." He opened his eyes again. "But right now, I have to do what the Corps tells me and go where they send me. Besides, there's nothing here for me—nothing but bad memories." He looked over the place.

Little had changed in the house since his mother had passed, something he never stopped regretting. The only things that were different were the subtraction of cigarette smoke and the addition of baby gear lying around everywhere. The same outdated old cabinets, countertops, and linoleum kept the kitchen in the 1970s. Yellowed eggshell walls throughout the small house blended depressingly with the browns and beiges of the ruined carpets and furniture in each room. The place seemed at that moment the way it likely did when his mother and father brought him home from the hospital. It had probably been that way for a long time before that.

"I hate this house." He continued to glance around in loathing. "I don't remember anything really good ever happening here."

"Until now," Carly smiled, and held up Derek's smiling daughter as she gurgled and drooled.

"Yes," he grinned, reaching out to take his baby Olivia and hold her close. "Still, I think we're going to have a hard time selling this piece of shit if I get transferred. Oh wait. The speech. What time is it?"

He did not bother to check the time. He scrambled for the living room and searched the old end table near his mother's easy chair for the remote control. With the baby on his left arm, he brushed through junk mail and celebrity magazines, leaving his mother's old cigarette burn marks visible. Finally, he saw the controller wedged between the cushion and the side of the easy chair. He removed it with a swift and frantic tug, clicked on the TV, and searched for a news channel.

"Oh, good," he smiled with relief. "It just started."

"What's the speech about?" Carly slowly approached.

"It's both presidents in Dallas—well—Fort Worth," he explained. "They're making some big announcement. I want to know if it's going to affect me."

"About two months ago . . ." President Davenport stared confidently, but gravely across the crowd, "some thirty miles to our east, something unprecedented occurred. During the fierce Battle of Carrollton, while American killed American, a small thermonuclear weapon detonated, completely destroying downtown Dallas and everything in a seven mile radius. It is estimated that approximately half a million people who had not evacuated from the area prior to the siege's beginning lost their lives that day. Many other thousands were injured and have begun to develop radiation-related sicknesses and terrible, rare diseases. Prevailing wind currents from out of the northwest carried fallout into Mesquite, and to the southwest across Ellis, Kaufman, and Van Zandt counties. Radiation continues to poison the Trinity River—a river that provides water for drinking and crops from here to Houston. And why did this have to happen? Because some Shi'ite extremists hate the West? That's the reason hundreds of thousands must die?" Davenport stopped as he began to lose composure.

"We stand before you today still divided, yet united in a common interest," Chandler picked up, the softness in her voice a contrast to Davenport's crass emotion. "Our two nations have been faced with incredible adversity. Never did anyone think we would again be fighting among ourselves. Never did anyone think Americans would again go to war against other Americans. Still we endure. The contiguous forty-eight look a little different these days, but we're still here and now we have finally found something to unite against. Dallas may no longer be a city in the United States of America, but it is still an American city. And an attack against you is an attack against us." She paused for applause and cheers

President Chandler looked to her Republic counterpart to her left. He gazed back, solemnly nodding while his large Texas hands gripped the podium as if he were going to float away. He wondered in silence what the next part of the announcement would lead to. He secretly hoped it may someday lead them to unification; to a time when Americans may put their differences aside for the sake of unity.

"Citizens of the Republic," Davenport's voice rumbled down the street.

"Citizens of the United States," Chandler followed.

"The great Congress of The Republic of America . . ."

"As well as the Congress of the United States . . ."

"Has voted to issue a declaration of war against the Taliban-controlled state and government of Pakistan," Davenport announced, followed by cheers from the crowd. "We will avenge this attack and the people killed or harmed."

"And the U.S. vows to share the burden of this military action with the Republic," Chandler added. "Together we will prevent this threat from ever being of harm to another American ever again."

"Thank you and good day," Davenport concluded as both presidents exited the stage to the back left.

The crowd was a boisterous mess of support for the two politicians. Few of the presidents' outspoken critics would have bothered to brave the record heat to go down to the convention center to hear an announcement that they likely would have disagreed with. Each spectator bore a smile. Some hugged, mixing sweat without care. Arms stretched to the sky, capturing the moment on camera phones. Some talked politics and strategy right there in the crowd. The mood seemed victorious and blissful that revenge would be exacted.

But Kyle stood there with the sourest of looks, his arms folded while he shook his head. Ashley was not smiling, either. At first, her words failed to materialize. She dared not even hold her boyfriend close. She gently rubbed his back. The way he dealt with and expressed emotion had changed. He was once soft and patient. But after what he had been through, he lost his temper quicker and was harsher than ever before. She wished he would see a therapist as she suggested.

"So much for finishing my first semester," Kyle finally spoke.

"I'm so sorry." Ashley put her arm around him. "Maybe you won't have to go," she said, sure that was a lie.

"Bullshit," he said with a quiet voice "You know better. The Republic was losing the war because they had trouble finding personnel. They'll get a lot of volunteers to go off and avenge a terrorist attack, but they're still going to need all hands on deck."

"So what do we do?"

"Go about our lives until I get the call," he shrugged, as his mind swirled with thoughts of having to ship off to Pakistan. "It probably won't take long. I'll be contacted by my unit within the next week, ship off to assemble at Fort Hood, and after a couple of weeks, head for the sandbox."

"We've just heard from Presidents Chandler and Davenport announcing a unilateral declaration of war against Taliban Pakistan," the network news anchor debriefed the audience while Derek and Carly watched. "What do you think about the way they handled this speech, Chris." The anchor turned to one of the analyzing panelists.

"I think they did quite well," the panelist answered. "They tapped into the raw emotion that is still there over this attack. I think President Chandler did a particularly good job. She kept alluding to reunification with talk of all of us being Americans . . ."

Derek tuned them out, in no mood for the commentary. They were not going to express his concerns or the concerns of his young family. Lost now in his own world of disbelief and worry, he did not even see his fiancée and baby standing beside him. Carly's distraught expression was unnoticed by Derek. He did not see her or the outdated interior of his late mother's home. Only dust and spent bullet casings. Helmets covered in blood and pieces of human limb. He saw shredded Humvees and the bodies of young American men and women barely out of high school. Their eyes were closed and the blood had drained from their faces, spilling from some opening somewhere onto the dirt. The newscast was unheard, only helicopter blades chopping through the air. Rifles fired in anger and exploding RPGs saturated his thoughts.

Then he drifted to Carly here again by herself with the baby. He knew they would not be completely alone. As she had said before, her parents and sisters would be there almost constantly. She would have money and groceries. But she and Olivia would see no Daddy. Derek would again miss a giant segment of his precious daughter's life. He would return from combat—hopefully—and find that Olivia had been talking for months and did not yet know how to say "Daddy," nor would she recognize him.

"It's going to be all right, babe." Derek snapped out of it, reassuring Carly, who was at the edge of panic. "Maybe I won't even have to go," he said without believing a word of it.

He turned to look at the television screen. The anchor had directed the picture to display a reporter on the scene at the Fort Worth announcement. The redhead stood before a police barricade where spectators still stood trying to glimpse one of the two presidents. Policemen stood guard, their hands behind their backs, scanning the area from behind dark sunglasses.

"The energy here is joyful and hopeful," the redhead spoke into her microphone, turning to her rear as the cameraman zoomed in on a black Lincoln parked at a far-off section of the blocked circular street around the convention center. "You can see there down the street as U.S. Secret Servicemen are escorting President Davenport to his car and his police-escorted motorcade. The people's reaction to his speech was that he was sincere and ready to bring justice."

"Why is the President of the Republic of America using U.S. Secret Servicemen?" The anchor raised an eyebrow.

"Well, as you can remember," the reporter answered, "the war began relatively soon after the Republic was even created. With all of the other things a new government had to get into place, a system of protection for their president just simply doesn't exist yet. So President Davenport has had to rely on the local and state police everywhere he's visited away from and within Austin."

The initial flash was enough to momentarily white-wash everything from the capability of the camera to record and transmit. But the sound was unmistakable. The people in the crowd shuttered as they felt the wave of vibration and the immense increase in heat. From beneath the forearms shielding their brows, they watched as President Davenport's car launched into the air without effort. It rode an upward geyser of fire rivaling the height of the convention center's domed roof. It seemed it would never return to earth. Its ascent and descent were somehow slowed, defying the laws of physics.

It crashed to the scorched pavement, sending bits of metal and molten plastic away from the torched shell of a vehicle. Police squad cars immediately positioned in front and behind the Lincoln, which lay aflame on its side. Police officers and Secret Servicemen were burned and strewn about the scene, hapless victims of the act of terrorism.

Kyle clutched Ashley helplessly as the terrified masses scattered in all directions, nearly trampling one another as officers on crowd control were too distracted with securing the scene of the explosion. Kyle simply held his beloved as close as he could, cocooning her away from danger until the crowd had dissipated.

Derek sat on the armrest of his mother's old easy chair staring into the screen. He was numb; almost sedated. Scenes like this were not shocking. His heart rate never increased. But he lingered on future consequences. It would get worse, and he knew it would affect him and his family.

Chapter 2

The tall center window behind Cindy Chandler's desk may as well have been a feature film. She, still in the clothes she wore that morning, leaned back in her desk chair, and propped her chin upon her right hand. Through her small, wire-rimmed eyeglasses, she peered motionlessly out through the Oval Office window. Her face was sullen stone; contemplative.

"How long has she been in there?" Cindy's husband, Donny Chandler, asked the president's chief of staff, Sandra.

"An hour," she replied. "Just like that. Staring out the window. She's pretty shook up," she continued while they looked in at her through the partially open door.

"God Almighty." He clutched his temples with his thumb and middle finger. "I should have gone with her to Texas. I mean, that's enemy territory. I . . ." He paused. "If it weren't for that damned UN thing in New York . . ."

"She told you to go," Sandra reassured him. "It's not your fault and she knows that. She doesn't blame you for anything."

"I still should have been there," he stumbled, "to . . . I don't know . . . protect her."

"Go talk to her," Sandra nodded.

Donny pushed into the office without much of any sound. He ambled across the pristine gold and ivory carpet, past matching couches that hosted the posteriors of some the world's most important leaders and diplomats. Donny thought about that every time he saw the couches. Cindy surely heard him come in, yet she barely moved, still staring out across her own existential moment of humanity.

"How are you holding up, kiddo?" Donny planted himself to the side of her desk and plunged his hands into the pockets of his pinstriped pants with masculinity.

"Oh, you know . . ." She continued to stare out the window. "Just thinking about Kennedy."

"Cindy, come on." He shook his head with a smile. "You don't know if they, whoever they are, were gunning for you, him, or both of you. The important thing is that you're here and you're safe." He approached, placed his hand on her shoulder, to massage gently.

"What's the word?" She swiveled her chair, facing her husband. "What are they saying this was?"

"Honestly," he shook his head, "it's anybody's guess. The FBI isn't saying a word and the media is throwing around all kinds of speculations. Some are saying it was another Taliban bombing. Some of the more radical Republic newscasters are saying it was U.S. military-sanctioned."

"Jesus, that's all we need."

There was a pause. Donny continued to clutch his wife's shoulder while she placed her hand on his, silently communicating her appreciation for his emotional support. Turning again to the window, she went back to her staring into nothing. Time had slowed and sped up simultaneously. Up was down and nothing seemed familiar.

"Are you okay?" His eyebrows lifted and his eyes softened.

"Yeah, I'm fine," she finally said as she focused on a blue jay on a branch outside. "Contemplative. I'm growing a little tired of nearly getting blown up."

"We just got a call from the FBI," Sandra blurted as she burst into the room, oblivious to whatever the mood or moment was in the Oval Office. "They know who's responsible."

"Who?" Cindy turned her chair and perked up. "Taliban? Al-Qaeda?"

"ARA," she grinned, shifting her long, blond hair.

"Who the hell is the ARA?" Cindy tightened her brow.

"The FBI said the Texas news media started to get calls from a disposable phone about an hour ago," Sandra explained. "They said it was some angry guy who claimed to be the leader of a group called the American Reunification Army and claims responsibility for the car bomb that killed Davenport."

"Reunification," Cindy stated with simplicity.

"Yeah," Sandra continued. "The guy claimed responsibility and then started going off on a psychotic rant about stupid, partisan, Republican bullshit being responsible for the country's split and the war that killed so many people. He went on to promise more of these kinds of attacks until all the secessionist states rejoin the U.S."

"Well, how about that?" Cindy pondered in amazement. "Our very own terrorist group."

"And that is exactly what the Republic is treating the ARA as," Sandra reported, wide-eyed and serious. "The government in Austin is calling for blood, here. Davenport is going to become their Lincoln."

"It's a shame." Cindy closed her eyes and hung her head with a touch of sorrow. "I feel bad for his family. But most of all, I was beginning to feel like we were finally getting somewhere with him—on the path to a recovery."

"I'm sorry," Donny interrupted, "did I hear you say the FBI is giving us this information? What the hell are they doing down there?"

"Well, for one thing, we didn't yet know if they were gunning for our president, too," Sandra explained.

"Ah," Donny nodded. "Sorry, I wasn't thinking."

"And on top of that," Cindy added, "they were just offering their assistance as a good will gesture. They had just lost their president to an assassin. Besides, they don't have a federal law enforcement agency. There are several national services our government provides, but theirs delegates to the states. So it's likely that the highest squad they have on the case is the Texas Rangers."

"And let's hope they don't strike out." Donny giggled at his own joke, although no one else did.

Cindy again peered into an alternate dimension of thought. She gently massaged her feminine, porcelain chin with her thumb and index finger. Donny simply stood there in discomfort, knowing his wife was busy with her thoughts and all he could do was stare at her as if he were able to see her contemplation written on the outside of her body. Sandra could only clutch her clipboard with both hands near her chin, biting the inner lining of her lip while her eyes darted nervously between Donny and Cindy.

"But what if they did strike out," she finally uttered. "Don't get me wrong. I feel for the Davenports, but if the ARA undermines the already weak fabric of the Republic's existence, it could lead to the rebel states coming back into the fold."

"That's an interesting point," Donny admitted. "What does the FBI know about the ARA?"

"Nothing really." Sandra explained, "They did mention that because of the complexity of the plan and the device, someone involved must have been ex-military. But other than that, it's anyone's guess. They don't know the size of the group, how widespread it may be, or what kind of people are involved."

"So likely, authorities in the Republic are going to have a hard time finding this information, too," Cindy half grinned. "Express our support, but stay out of it."

"And the authorities there have already given the FBI the thanks but we'll take it from here," Sandra added. "It should be easy to stay out of it. I think it's important to make an effort to publicly denounce the ARA to keep the conspiracy theorists out in the boondocks down there from concocting some crazy-ass notion that you're behind it and that it's Pentagon-sanctioned."

"Good point," Cindy said thoughtfully. "Have my press secretary put together something vaguely disdainful, but not too harsh, about senseless violence and how it isn't the answer." She smiled, feeling better about nearly getting blown to pieces.

"I'll get on it," Sandra said as she walked to the office door. "Oh, and I'll go ahead and arrange your trip and accommodations for Davenport's state funeral in Austin."

Chapter 3

Kyle had been trained well at Fort Hood. He had learned to dress and equip himself for battle in a matter of a few short minutes. He had learned how to operate mortars and heavy machine guns. He had learned to fire at and hit targets with precision at over a hundred yards. He had learned how to kill another man and watch a friend die. He had learned to move stealthily into attack positions, but still had yet to master his parents' front door. With Ashley in tow, he tried to push the door open to slip inside without too much commotion. But alas, the expected squeak of the hinges had not been remedied. To Kyle's knowledge, it had sounded exactly that way since middle school. And then what immediately followed was the event he had wanted to avoid.

"Kyle?" his mother Angela cried out with nearly a squeal from the family room past the foyer and staircase. "Oh my God." She tore down the hallway, across the wood floors toward them, hugging and kissing both of them to compensate for all the worry she had experienced in the last few hours. "What? You can't call to tell me you two are okay?"

She still adorned the loose t-shirt and cotton shorts that she normally wore to perform her Saturday morning cleaning. She appeared sweaty, or at least she had been sweating earlier and had cooled. Still, she had obviously not showered. Her hair, newly dyed to its original medium blond, was tied up into some type of top-sitting ponytail wrapped in a bandana like she was wearing some ancient battle helmet. Moreover, she appeared frantic—emotionally taxed, as if she needed any more of that since the secession began. She shook, her eyes wide and spastic.

"We're okay, Mom," Kyle said as she moved in for another hug, just to make sure he was really there and okay. "We tried to call earlier, but there was this message that all circuits were busy. I guess there were too many other grown men out there checking with their mommies," he smiled as she backed up to shoot him a dirty look from under her lowered brow.

"Don't be a smartass." She shook her extended mother finger at her him.

Ashley stood to the side, away from the exchange. It had become somewhat commonplace of a scene in the Perkins household since he had been away from active duty; since the bomb. He had gone from living at home to boot camp and active combat duty as sharp as white on black. Then, instead of moving home for a while, he stayed only until he could go off to college while he still could. Ashley sensed that Angela wanted her baby back home, and while she sympathized with that, she knew Kyle had to be his own man. She liked Kyle's mother, and therefore stayed out of it. She would stand aside, arms crossed, looking away, and biting her lip. She remained neutral, going out of her way to make that obvious in her body language.

It was not something that Kyle and Angela really grappled with together and apart. It was not some dysfunctional relationship damaged in his youth where he was psychologically and emotionally inept. They had always had a healthy and normal relationship. So the reprimanding mother look and outstretched discipline finger only lasted for a moment or two, and then was sheathed. It changed into a smile as she led the young couple in past the oak wine cabinet and the stairs, finally emerging into the brighter area where the kitchen faded into the family room via the breakfast nook.

It was amazing to Kyle that with the changes all around him, the house he had grown up in had stayed the same. The cherry-stained hardwood in the front bore a small scar from the old broken oven he and his dad dropped on their way to the curb his freshman year. There was a penny-sized chip in the corner of one of the white ceramic tiles in the kitchen from dropping a hammer one summer. The cream-gold valences in the breakfast nook, the same old furniture, the tan granite countertops in the kitchen, and even his mother's favorite air freshener scent brought a flood of memories. They combined to make Kyle feel warm and at home. They ushered in a simpler time when innocence and joy murdered despair and uncertainty in their sleep. Kyle was unsure if it was the time period that was better or just a care-free age in his life when he had few responsibilities.

"Hey, hey." Kyle's father Drew smiled widely and stood from his spot on the couch while the news coverage still flashed from the television across the room. "Glad to see you kids are all right." He reached in to shake his son's hand and hug Ashley, kissing her cheek.

"I'm not gonna lie," Ashley admitted, half smiling. "It was pretty scary. There was this huge boom and all of a sudden, just a stampede of people," she recounted with wide eyes and a heart rate increasing all over again.

"It was definitely intense," Kyle agreed, though the thought of that day's event really held little excitement. He had seen worse.

"Well, I could have told you to stay away from that speech today." Drew started shaking his head.

"Oh Jesus," Angela commented from the kitchen. "He's gettin' out his soap box again."

"What do you mean, Dad?"

"I mean, first of all, you've got that damned tyrant socialist Chandler on the stage," Drew continued. "And then that traitor Davenport was going to try and make nice with her instead of doing what he should have and kicked her ass back up to Washington saying, 'We'll take care of this.' Hell, I'm not completely convinced she didn't order that nuke herself."

Kyle shook his head, saying nothing at first. He did not agree with his father, nor had he ever. He found himself at odds with the very idea of the secessionist state, yet he fought for it. He was pressured by his father to join the Republican Guard and had since forgiven him, but certainly had not forgotten. He tried to convince himself it was in defense of his home and his state, but ultimately he had been fighting for something in which he held no belief. He wondered how many ancestors had done the same thing.

"Come on now, Dad," Kyle chastised his father respectfully. "Don't tell me you're a conspiracy theorist like all the other bat-shit loonies posting videos all over the Internet. The Taliban claimed responsibility multiple times. They took over Pakistan, got access to nukes, and snuck one into Dallas. That's it."

"Well, I'm not totally convinced," he maintained. "Hell, I wouldn't be surprised if Davenport's assassination was a CIA hit," he declared.

"Drew." Angela tried to step in, but stopped as Kyle interrupted.

"Dad, the ARA already took responsibility for that one, too," Kyle said. "I heard it on the radio."

"And who the hell are those guys, anyway?" Drew said. "The news said they had to have had military training. Probably the CIA in ARA's clothing."

Kyle stopped for a moment to really take in the full level of craziness that was exiting his father's mouth. He had heard rants from his father, but it was getting ridiculous. He was pushing further and further right, growing angrier and angrier. Friends and coworkers he had known for years began to distance themselves. People made sure to stay away from political subjects when Drew and Angela attended parties and social events.

"Well, at least you've got Crane stepping up." Kyle shook his head in disgust. "That crazy asshole of a vice president is probably getting sworn in as we speak. He's more radical right than Davenport was, so at least you have that going for you, Dad. There's the silver lining."

"Well," Drew began, but stopped short with the interruption of his wife.

"Drew, I think we should stop there," she said with a gentle, but firm smile. She attempted to keep the peace. "You kids get to eat?"

"Not really," Ashley answered. "It took us so long to get out of downtown with all of the roadblocks, traffic, and cops everywhere. They were stopping random people and interrogating them. It was crazy. By the time we got on thirty-five, we just decided to come here."

"Well, you must be starving." Angela started to shuffle around the kitchen. "We've got plenty of bread and sandwich meat. There's also some leftover spaghetti and meatballs from a couple of nights ago that Dylan didn't eat."

"A sandwich is fine," Ashley politely chose as Angela gathered the required elements for her.

"Speaking of Dylan . . ." Kyle wrinkled his forehead and asked, "Where is he?"

"Studying at a friend's house if you can believe it," she replied.

"Are we talking about the same Dylan?" Kyle was surprised. "I haven't even talked to him. He wasn't here last night when we got in. I never get to talk to him on the phone. The same kid that wouldn't leave his room, his video games, or take his ear buds out has a study date? What's up?"

"He's changed," his mother stated, shaking her head with her own disbelief. "You going off to join the Republican Guard and then the nuke just changed him. He started this school year off with a new haircut, new clothes, and doing well in school."

"I guess some things were put into perspective," Kyle said in a lower, more somber tone as he stared into his own thoughts for a brief moment.

The pause was somewhat awkward. Everyone seemed for a moment to hang their heads and ponder the last two years. Emptiness replaced the Dallas skyline. Mortar craters still scarred roadways and shopping centers. Anywhere either of them went, the war and the bomb seemed to be the only thing anyone talked about. Most people would neutrally discuss their potassium iodide pills the government issued them as a precaution against radiation poisoning and how they had a funny aftertaste. It seemed polite conversation to talk about that, the disrupted traffic flow, or how many family members from the Dallas area were staying in their home. Of course a few would get into heated arguments over the politics and economics of it all, but either way, conversations always seemed to end in the same blank, silent awkwardness.

"Speaking of school . . ." Drew broke the silence with a smile. "How's A&M?"

"Good," Ashley said, speaking for herself.

"It's okay," Kyle replied hesitantly. "It's taking some getting used to. I'm in some abnormal classes because I got registered so late."

"I still can't believe they let you do that," Kyle's mother offered in disbelief. "They let you reapply and sign up for classes a month before they started. That's unheard of."

"What can I say?" Kyle shrugged. "That's one of the benefits of being a soldier. The admissions guy had a son that lost his life in the Siege of Houston, so he was sympathetic. I just had to take a couple of offbeat classes until next semester."

"That's some luck," Drew smiled. "I don't imagine there are a lot of veterans on campus."

"Very few," Kyle confirmed. "The Guard had a lot of trouble recruiting guys my age. That's part of why we were having such a hard time against the Blues. Still, there are more vets on campus than you think. I ran into a guy last week in one of the cafeterias with a prosthetic foot. He lost his own when the Marines landed at Mobile Airport. Mortar blast."

Angela and Ashley said nothing. Kyle flowed through conversations dealing with deaths and wounded soldiers with ease. He spoke of them as though he believed everyone within earshot was engaged and interested. And then, like clockwork, he finished with what he was saying, expecting everyone to feel enlightened, yet most people just felt uncomfortable or distanced from the topic. Either that or sometimes strangers would be able to tell of a neighbor or cousin that had fought in the war, but that was the extent of their experience and relation to the subject. In moments like that, Kyle longed to be again in the company of other soldiers.

"Wow, Dad," Kyle himself broke the awkward silence. "Is it hot enough in here for you?" He drew inspiration for the change in topic from the small droplets of sweat present on his mother's brow. "It's burning up in here."

"Those bastards at the electric company," Drew answered, welcoming the chance to rant again. "They went up on their rates by a good three cents per kilowatt-hour. It's ridiculous."

"That's fossil fuel for you." Kyle smiled as he nodded at his perplexed father. "The Republic's stuck back in the coal age."

"What do you mean?" Drew tilted his head.

"The U.S. Congress passed a new energy bill about six months ago," he explained. "I guess you guys couldn't get their news. I just found out about it a month ago. But since they didn't have Gulf Coast oil companies to cater to and be tempted by the campaign contributions to stay with the oil and coal standard, they're reinvesting in green energy."

"Shit, here we go again." Drew rolled his eyes.

"No, seriously," Kyle continued. "Congress saved so much money by not having to pay out oil subsidies to companies making tens of billions in profit that they were able to invest that money in stuff like wind farms off the northeastern coast. That and they've actually started a program where crews go in and clean out the buildup of crap in the sewers and cart it off to facilities to be burned and converted into energy like the British do."

"Huh," Drew responded. "No shit?" He giggled a bit at the pun.

"And they've subsidized the conversion of people's gas-run vehicles to full electric," Ashley added. "It's pretty cool."

"God, that must have cost the taxpayers a fortune."

"Actually," Kyle corrected, "it turns out that between at-home war production and the jobs that green energy has created, they've gone from recession before the war to an economic boom. Government's at a surplus. They're sitting pretty."

"Surely the cost of other petroleum products has gone up," Drew said, still skeptical. "As much plastic as people up there still use, and with so few refineries in the current U.S., the cost of consumer goods has to be eating people alive."

"You'd think," Ashley said. "But since they're not having to make gasoline, they're focusing the oil they do bring in on stuff like plastic and synthetics. And the value of the dollar is actually rising for the first time in decades."

"And the cost of energy has gone down?" Drew puzzled.

"Yeah," Kyle nodded. "They need to do all that here."

"Oh, I'm sure the market will balance out," Drew said confidently. "It's just strained because of the war and more resources going to that. It'll get better."

Neither Kyle nor Ashley said anything more. It had become impossible to argue with his father about politics, energy, or economics. He had bought into the rhetoric from the politicians at the capitol. He would simply spout the same talking points mentioned at press conferences and in the media, almost verbatim. There was no convincing him otherwise. There was another awkward silence. It pained Kyle for the home to provide such welcome, but the company to be so uncomfortable. *Jesus, where do I belong?*

"Spaghetti?" Angela asked, and moved toward the refrigerator with her son's polite nod.

But he still said nothing. He had lost touch with his father, and fought to regain it with each interaction with him. They had reconciled, but now they had grown so far apart that Kyle felt lost. They no longer spoke the same language or viewed things the same way. Even outside of his family's home, he was an outsider. He was a soldier for a secessionist republic that he did not believe in. He was a liberal in a land of conservatives. He was outnumbered and shut off. He was gagged and had no place. Suddenly, he felt gentle pressure from Ashley's soft, delicate hand around his. *This is my place.*

Chapter 4

Everything was washed in a pale, metallic blue hue. Nothing seemed its normal color. The trees and crumbling houses of the once proud industrial workers' neighborhood were more shades of gray. Working and nonworking cars lining the curbs were generic and anonymous. Nothing was lively, though it showed no liveliness even after dawn. Old hand-me-down big wheels and wagons sat unmanned in front yards in need of manicuring. Porches could use repairs and rust devoured holes in screen doors. Paint chipped from the rotting outside paneling. Derek sneered in memory of the decency this neighborhood held in his childhood. Though, things were turning around. A new car ahead in a driveway was a gleaming jewel of an indication that the factories had reopened and were hiring the unemployed.

The sky was just about to brighten with the first rays of daylight beaming in an upward arc beyond the eastern horizon. The morning air chilled Derek's sweat as he jogged along. He had lost some of his stamina while being laid-up in the house for over two months. His torso wound had healed but was still tender. Determined not to let that slow him, he continued on down his dusky street a bit winded, grimacing as he slowed to a trudge. The toe of his right sneaker caught an elevated crack in the neglected sidewalk, causing him to trip and almost sending him tumbling to the ground.

He struggled to regain his balance as he peered back at the menacing obstacle behind him.

As irritating as it was—as much as he longed for his neighborhood to return to its grandeur—he balanced his emotions, shedding the spike of mild anger as he jogged. He pushed on, the neglect on his fitness quite apparent. His stride had become a jangly bounce on the balls of his feet. His spring forward had lost elasticity and his clenched fists bobbled above his armpits, far above their usual waist-level. Through his squinted eyes, he spotted his saving grace ahead to the left. His house, as neglected as the rest on his street, beaconed with the front porch light, still able to outshine its dim surroundings. He felt his pace pick up as he tried to ignore the cramp in his side in favor of getting to his house and a glass of water.

He abruptly ceased his jog as he came to the old chain-link fence, lifting the aluminum latch to enter his small yard. There really was not much of a yard to fence in. A few steps forward and he was already up the flimsy, creaking wooden steps that led up the under-maintained porch. Splinters jutted up from the boards like a porcupine warning visitors. The old swing to the left had been in the same rotting position for years, piled beneath rusted chains and ages of dust. He had meant to hang it long ago, but it would not likely support a person who wanted to read a good book on a cool fall afternoon.

It was still early so Derek grasped the old doorknob with a rattle, and turned it slowly. He had learned the art of stealth better in his own home than he ever could in the Marines. Slipping out of bed before first light was a success. He had slid without detection off his left side of the bed, his body level and patient enough to make no sudden bed-shaking motions. He had opened drawers to retrieve shorts and his now sweat-drenched gray Marine Corps tank top without so much as a squeak of wood on wood. He had crept across the house, over the creaking linoleum-masked floorboards, and out the door unnoticed. Now he attempted to reenter his home without waking mother and baby.

All was quiet—even stagnant—as he opened the door leading into the kitchen. Lights were off. The shroud of darkness seemed to muffle sound. It was as if somehow it was opaque and soundproof, and as the shroud would lift with the rising sun, the volume knob would slowly turn with it. His mission was complete. He had exited and entered his house without waking anyone. That was what he thought until an increasingly familiar sound cut the silence and the soundproof darkness. It was the shrill, yet pleasing sound of his daughter cooing in her attempt to form words in vain. The sound emanated from somewhere in the house, glowing with beauty and warmth, an effect that reached Derek's cold soldier's heart in an instant.

"Derek," Carly shouted from the nursery, which was really Derek's old bedroom. "Derek, are you back?"

"Yeah, I just walked in," he stated as he moved, abandoning his stealth mode. "Good morning," he added as he took an orange plastic cup from one of the upper cabinets, opened the refrigerator, and removed the pitcher of filtered tap water.

"Did you get diapers at the store yesterday?" she called out.

"Um . . ." Derek thought hard, trying in his mind to make that an affirmative. His hand jolted, causing him to dribble a bit of water onto the kitchen floor. "I think I forgot," he winced, squinting his eyes to brace for the consequences.

"Damn it, Derek." She emerged from the hallway with Olivia situated on her hip. "This is her last one. Well—I take that back—there might be a couple in the diaper bag. But that's it."

He knew he deserved the response he was getting. That was a pretty big thing to forget. But as much as he should bulge his bottom lip and take his lumps, he could not help but smile at his little girl. She sat on her mother's hip with comfort and ease, sporting the little pink onesie while she gnawed as always on her saliva-soaked finger. She stared blankly at him though, and Derek's smile dulled. It still had not fully registered who this strange man was.

"I'm sorry, babe," he said as he scratched his head. "I guess I'm just not used to buying them."

"I know." She rolled her eyes, forgetting that he was almost alien, living for nearly two years in a different world. "I'm sorry. I know this is going to take some adjustment. I'll run up to the store in a little bit and get some." She still seemed irritated and stressed with yet another thing to have to worry about. She handed Olivia to him with a smooth, one-armed motion.

"Hey, baby girl," he beamed, taking her first under both underarms and then transferring her to his hip.

He looked her over as he often did, at times unable to take his eyes from her still-infantile radiance. She was beautiful—the most beautiful thing he had ever laid eyes upon. Olivia was something completely foreign, though a being that carried his genes and bore his history, as he has for his ancestors. Derek saw in her his brown eyes, brown hair, and complexion. She had her father's notches at the top ridge of her ears. She was sweet and soft. But mostly, she was getting big, and far quicker in Derek's eyes than in her mother's. Carly had spent nearly every waking moment with the child since birth, watching Olivia grow from a squirmy tube of flesh and cartilage into this being caught somewhere between an infant and a toddler. But for Derek, she shot immediately from the infant in a photograph that he had first seen on a Louisiana battlefield to this hulking, growing child upon his hip.

"Da-da," Derek slowly modeled for his daughter, bouncing her on his hip, swaying as he had seen Carly do, and nuzzling his nose lightly into Olivia's cheek now and again. "Da-da," he repeated. "Come on, baby. I know you can do it." He looked to Carly with worry. "Why—"

"It'll come," Carly reassured him. She knew that hurt Derek. It was hard to see this man—a man she was falling more in love with—hurting. "It will. I promise. She really hasn't been saying mama for very long, either."

"Mama," Olivia removed a slobbery finger from her ached mouth and gums and uttered as if mimicking on cue. She reached for her mother the same way she did when Carly handed her to a friend or extended family member. She leaned and whined, outstretching both little, dimple-elbowed arms until Carly took her safely into mother's arms.

Derek hung his head, curling his lips inward a bit in reaction. His gaze moved from his fiancée and daughter to random objects in the kitchen, and back to his young family. He said nothing, raising his shoulders as if he were protecting himself, and stepped back slightly. He was wounded, and though he tried to hide it from Carly, she noticed. She always noticed. She never said anything, but she noticed and she empathized in her expression.

"You, little girl," Carly said as she swept her little girl away to the living room, "need some playtime." She lowered her child to the floor.

Derek watched as the growing girl immediately directed her attention to something colorful and plastic on the floor near her. She, fenced in by a gray plastic collapsible baby barricade, crawled around within her cage, and bounced from toy to toy. Carly stepped away, joining Derek in watching her immerse herself in her own simple world of child's things and child's thoughts. There were no worries within her. Her concerns were shapes, sounds, and colors. She learned every second that she was awake, and truly, to Derek's mind, a wonder to observe.

"She's going to be walking soon." Carly nuzzled up to Derek, locking her arm with his as they watched their little girl. "I saw her try to pull up on the sides of the playpen yesterday."

"I guess I need to go get some baby gates for the hallway and our bedroom," he answered.

"Probably needed to be done a while back when she first started crawling," Carly jabbed.

"I know, I know," he admitted, rolling his eyes. "I should have done that already. I'm just now getting to where I can do more. This was the first morning I could actually go for a run."

"I know you'll get to it." She separated from him and moved about the kitchen, removing things from the refrigerator. "How about bacon, egg, and cheese biscuits for breakfast?" She smiled at him over her shoulder.

"My favorite," he grinned. "Sounds good." He walked toward the living room and plopped his tired body into his mother's old easy chair.

He sat, taking in family life. Within two years, he had thrown himself from working to support a sick, out of work mother into life in the Marines. Before he knew it, he found himself fighting in the war, and was snapped from that into the life of a father that had never met his child. Yet he marveled as he sat in his chair. He smiled somewhat as he heard the clank of skillets and the smell of scrambling eggs and sizzling bacon. He watched with ever growing delight as his oblivious daughter shook a plastic fish rattle over her head. But then anxiety began to set in. His smile slipped into a slight sneer. He rested his head against his hand, staring at nothing in particular. He felt he was supposed to be doing something other than sitting on the chair. He had been sitting for over two months. For a moment, he forgot where he was, as if he was living in someone else's life with someone else's family. He nearly panicked, his palms sweaty as his mind raced with fear.

"Good morning, Putnams!" The door burst open with shattering obnoxiousness that Derek immediately recognized. At first, as if by reflex, it threatened his temper, but then he knew who it was.

His life-long best friend Jake barged into the kitchen with his usual overflowing enthusiasm and energy. He was his perpetual tall, thick, furriness, smiling as always from beneath stubble and shaggy, blondish hair. His jumpsuit was stained with grease and oil, a uniform that he could be seen wearing the majority of the time. Derek sometimes wondered how much non-work clothing the man actually owned.

"Hi, Carly," he smiled as he stepped into the kitchen, giving her a light hug and simple cheek peck.

"Good morning, Jake," she greeted him. "Off to the garage?"

"Shit," he grinned. "Where else would I be heading?"

"Well, the biscuits will be done in a few if you want some breakfast before you go." She tended to the eggs, laying slices of cheese over the almost finalized golden morsels.

"I might grab a biscuit for the road." He pushed past the kitchen into the largely child-seized living room. "Hey, buddy," he boomed, and shook his friend's hand with a vice for a grip. "How are ya?"

"Getting there." Derek remained seated while Jake took a position on the old dusty love seat. "I finally got up and out of the house for a run this morning."

"Oh yeah? And how did that turn out?" he laughed.

"I felt like an old man," Derek grinned.

"Ah . . ." Jake reached over and back-handed his friend's leg. "You'll get it back. Don't forget—you got friggin' shot, bro. It's not your fault."

"Yeah," Derek nodded, "it's some greenhorn Dallas kid's fault. Little bastard. And now we're going to be on the same side in Pakistan? Freakin' crazy."

"Well, maybe it's the beginning of the healing process for the country, bro," Jake responded. "You know?"

"Maybe."

There was a moment of silent pause as both momentarily ran out of things to say. Those uncomfortable silences sometimes gave an illusion of awkward disconnect, yet it never felt that way between Jake and Derek. There was very little to talk about. Jake had been keeping his distance, to allow Derek time to settle into a new life. The rest was life as usual. Jake worked each day at the same old garage and went home to the same old girlfriend and beer-scented house. Derek spent his days imprisoned in a house of bad memories and a family that feels rented.

"Hey, you guys are coming to my party this weekend, right?" Jake broke the silence.

"If we can get a babysitter," Carly called out from the kitchen. "Babysitters have gotten expensive. I wish I made the kind of money these little broads are making these days when I was in high school."

"Babysitters," Jake laughed. "It's still weird to hear you guys talk about stuff like that. It's like you're grownups or something. But seriously, try to make it. Joselyn wants to see her cousin." Jake directed the comment at Carly.

"We'll try," she said.

"Well, I guess you'll at least be there, huh, buddy?" Jake said to his friend.

"Excuse me?" Carly gained a level of sass to her voice.

"Hey, I'm staying out of this one." Derek put his hands up to signal neutrality.

"I just figured if you don't have a sitter, at least Derek can come, right," he grinned sheepishly, knowing that may have been the wrong thing to imply.

"And why can't he stay here with Olivia?" Carly placed a hand in contempt upon her hip. "It's an equal household. I'm not little miss kitchen slave wifey," she half joked with a playful smile. "Yeah, he can probably go," she admitted. "But I'd like to come too."

"Maybe you can bring 'little-bit' with you," Jake laughed.

"Shit," Derek burst with laughter. "To a house full of multiple types of smoke and people doing keg stands?"

"And enough drunken hoes flashing their tits to confuse the poor child," Carly added. "No thanks," she grinned.

"Don't knock it, Carly," he fired back. "It wasn't that long ago you were one of those hoes. In fact, if I remember, that's how you two met." He slid off the love seat to crouch in front of Olivia playing on the other side of the playpen wall. "Hear that, little Olivia?" he cooed. "Mommy and Daddy made you at one of Uncle Jake's parties."

Derek first grinned at the joke as he watched Jake now sitting on the dated, dingy carpet before his daughter while she played by way of outstretched fingers through the holes in the playpen. He observed as his friend cooed and smiled, taking to the child with ease. Perhaps it had become common as much time as he had spent there taking care of Derek's mother in the soldier's absence. But as he saw Olivia gravitate toward his friend, cooing back with glee, his heart soured and his smile faded. He wanted to cry but could not. His eyes squinted and hands trembled. He focused on the Purple Heart cradled in its open case upon the bookshelf. It sat accompanying his Marine Corps graduation photo that his mother had framed almost two years before. He stared at it without interruption as Carly caught on and watched helplessly as her man no doubt prayed for the phone to ring from the Department of Defense.

Chapter 5

Joe Crane stood tall with every bit of authority bestowed upon him with the swearing of his oath. His chin was elevated and nose turned upward as if radiant showers of God's blessing were poured onto him through the lone star upon the ceiling of the capitol's rotunda. He peered through his dark eyes out across the dignitaries seated across the marble. He was somber and cold. No grin or light expression gave even a hint of formation. His tailored black suit and royal blue tie were the classic presidential look of power completed by a crowning head that was as bony and distinct as the lack of hair atop it.

The small stage and florally enclosed podium rose above the people. It stole focus from the Republic flag-draped silver coffin in the center of the five seals and emblems of Texas emblazoned upon the marble floors of the rotunda. Just a couple hundred select dignitaries, including U.S. President Cindy Chandler, sat in a semi-circle around the opposite side from the stage. No one cried; faces were stone and dress was black. Davenport's ex-wife and grown children sat sadly in the front, backed by countless Texas legislators and Republic senators and congressmen and women. It remained quiet. None said, or even whispered a word, for every squeak of a shoe or movement of a chair echoed from the polished marble floors and spiraled upward through the rising rings of the capitol's dome.

President Crane was confident and stiff-backed. His shoulders were back as he drew strength from dozens of portraits of former governors of Texas positioned on the walls circling him. It was as if their power beamed forward from the columned ivory walls to empower the new president. He glowed with authority as he cleared his throat to begin.

"Close family and friends of the deceased," he started with a nod to Davenport's grieving children. "Distinguished Republican elected officials and lawmakers. Other visiting dignitaries," he motioned toward President Chandler to the side. "We are gathered here today under the saddest of circumstances, to mourn the passing of a revolutionary leader. But today, we instead should celebrate the life of this visionary named Byron Davenport. I knew him well. We had been colleagues for nearly twenty years. I was elected into the U.S. Senate from this great state of Texas the same year he was elected from Wyoming. We worked together, he and I, to follow the Constitution in the way that the founding fathers intended it. We fought for the interest of the average hard-working American. President Davenport was an outspoken critic of the over-taxing, over regulating strong central government. He worked hard to free the American people of red tape and tyrannical overreaching of the government in Washington. And when the U.S. Federal government had finally failed to serve its people, Byron Davenport led the charge in reviving the true vision of our forefathers and reinventing America for future generations. I was honored when he asked me to run with him for President of the Republic." He paused for a moment.

"I can promise you one thing in the time that I will spend in completing the term of my predecessor. His martyrdom for the cause of freedom will not be in vain. We will carry on his work. We will carry this hallowed Republic into the future and strive to restore the nation to its rightful greatness. We will avenge the devastating attack upon millions of innocent people, again making Americans a people to be feared and respected. And we will bring justice to the people who would murder the father of our great country." He paused again before he brought up the next speaker. "With that, I give you Pastor Jim Johnson, our late president's own personal minister, to lead the service." He stepped aside, shook the hand of the kindly, aging pastor, and approached his seat at the back of the stage next to his new vice president.

"Well said," Vice President Douglas Sims told the president as he sat down.

"Too bad it's all bullshit," Crane whispered back. "He got weak. He should never have cozied up to Chandler after the bombing in Dallas. It showed he was weak. Now anyone with a liberal bone in their body—ARA, or whoever—is going to think we're dead in the water. They're going to try to pick at us and get us to reunify with the U.S., and don't think those bastards aren't still gunning for us." He watched Cindy Chandler in the crowd with an eye of impunity. "We need a win in Pakistan," he said decisively. "Gotta show the world we're here to stay."

"Might as well use the Blues' resources in the sandbox to help us with that," Sims commented.

"Then dump 'em first chance we get."

The back entrance of the Texas State Capitol opened with a wall of black suits and spiraled earpieces, surrounding President Chandler and keeping a watchful eye for anything amiss. But immediately, the Secret Servicemen had the added and unexpected stress of the encroaching press. The president, her husband, and her chief of staff, Sandra, reeled from the sudden tide of flash photography, news cameras, and microphone-bearing reporters. Chandler's head snapped around in shock as she blinked rapidly in reflex. Her guards did their best to form a perimeter, but the president stopped for a moment to appease the pack and give a statement.

"President Chandler, how will you remember President Davenport—friend or foe?" one clean-cut reporter asked over the low roar of the others vying for attention.

"Well," she paused and planned her response with a politician's care, "I've known Byron for quite awhile—we were in the Senate together. We've had triumphs and we've had rough patches, but all-in-all, he was a good man, and I was looking forward to negotiating a truce with him."

"And what do you think of working with President Crane?" a woman blurted, not letting Cindy finish with her earlier statement.

"I . . ." She again paused to think, looking skyward at first. "I haven't worked with Crane in a couple of years—not since he was a U.S. senator. And even then, I really hadn't worked directly with him. Things have been so hectic with the aftermath of this horrible attack on President Davenport that President Crane and I have barely spoken. Surely, we'll get back on track soon," she concluded, and then signaled to her entourage that she was ready to push forth.

Several Secret Service agents plowed almost brutally through the crowd of reporters, leaving the Austin police officers on duty to form a protective wall for the escape. The president, her husband, and her chief of staff descended the stone steps of the capitol building without further pause or pursuit and headed for the barricaded street far across the capitol's lawn.

"Whose bright idea was that?" Sandra griped irately. "Nice of those assholes to let the press swarm the doors."

"Makes it difficult to protect you, ma'am," one of the agents commented. "Can't be too careful with the car bombs and nukes in this state lately—and you're public enemy number one to a lot of these people." He continued to rush the president across the lawn, while he searched and scanned the area for gunmen.

"I'm sure that was the point," Donny scoffed, keeping the pace.

Secret Service had always been very good about positioning the car very close to exits, planning exit strategies to keep the president shielded. There was too much distance between the exit and the capitol's driveway, a stressful situation for the president and her guards. The car, surrounded by Austin police cruisers and SUVs packed with Secret Service agents waited along the curb while all crowds of mourners and onlookers remained barricaded across the streets and intersection. Nervousness set in.

"You cleared the driver?" Chandler asked the agent.

"Yes, it's one of our guys," he replied.

"And you're not parked over a sewer manhole?" she worried. "That's how they got Davenport. An ARA member parked the car over a manhole and they set the bomb using the sewers."

"We prepared for all of that, ma'am," he assured her. "And we got clearance to put a few sharpshooters up on some of these buildings, too." He nonchalantly nodded his head in those directions.

"Good." She felt almost relieved. "Public enemy number one," she said in disgust.

She rolled her eyes as they neared the car, allowed the agent to open her door, and stepped inside with the rest. "Just get me the hell back to the airport and steer clear of the clock tower at UT."

Chapter 6

The ground was cold and gray. The dust was lighter, as were the long bits of dry, dead grass, with darker shadows between. It was like ash without the powdery incinerated matter. It was dry and bland with a single, central splash of color. Thick red blood pooled with smaller droplets spattered outward from the central crimson gore. Big blue eyes stared lifelessly toward heaven, projecting perhaps. The whitening lips gaped apart with relaxation, breath no longer moving in or out. The Kevlar helmet lay haphazardly away from the head and the arms flailed outward from the torso. The torso was now Kyle's focus—the torso of his best friend.

The camouflage fatigues, though earth tones, were brilliant against the dullness of the ground. The glistening, bright red blood was piercing to the eye. It soaked most of the fatigues covering what was left of the torso. Remains of vital organs, tissue, and bone fragments littered the hole blasted through him. His body was shredded and drained. His spirit was gone. His being was cold. The sum of his eighteen years of experiences and knowledge, multiplied by decades more lay erased and splattered across the ground, lost forever.

As his gaze arose to the colorless grass, mesquite trees in the distance, and sprawling horizon. Kyle felt dismay and dread. Terror permeated his emotions while he trembled at the sight of hell's most furious fire pluming upward with hate and brilliant orange and yellow billows. The heat radiated against his skin, light warm at first, but with greater intensity. The trees in the distance spontaneously flattened and then incinerated as quickly. A wall of radioactive menace hurdled his way, burning him alive as he screamed in agony.

The screams echoed from one wall to the next in a room designed for superior acoustics and the carrying of sound throughout the lecture hall. Kyle woke himself and lifted his head suddenly with a jerk. A thin stream of clear saliva flowed from the corner of his mouth where it pooled on his open notebook, soaking the paper to bleed the blue lines. His eyes darted from side to side as his head followed, with an attempt to reconcile the place his mind believed he was with the place he actually sat.

A hundred pairs of eyes were upon him. His fear and anxiety drifted and his heart rate slowed. It faded into embarrassment. The stares were accompanied by giggles and smiles. He wondered how loud he was, truly weighing the pros and cons of remaining where he would be ridiculed for the last twenty minutes of the class. The giggles, stares, and smiles won, sending Kyle into a flurry of assembling his notebook, pens, and textbooks. He stuffed them violently into his backpack, old papers falling to the side. He zipped with force, threw the pack over his shoulder, and shuffled down the row, bumping into people along the way. He stumbled clumsily into the side aisle and made his way to the front as best he could in flip-flops, jolting past the white-bearded professor along the way with an apologetic expression as he plunged through the door.

The professor stroked his beard, narrowing his eyes in thought and observation of the large survey class. He panned across the multitude of kids mostly just out of high school. Giggles and judgment still floated upon the air, finding their way to the aging professor's ears.

"Y'all keep laughing," he finally spoke in his calm professor voice cutting through all sound, and brought any snickering or whispers to a halt. "You don't know that young man. While you were sittin' in the comfort of your homes drinking energy drinks and playing some war video game for fun, he was gettin' shot at. He was servin'. He watched close friends die at his feet. He saw, first-hand, that mushroom cloud rise over Dallas. He was witness to hundreds of thousands of deaths in an instant. You have no idea what he's seen—why he has nightmares. He sacrificed." He met the eyes of a few previously smiling young students, now regretting their actions. "But I guess your generation wouldn't know anything about that, would you? Now if you don't mind, let's continue with class."

Kyle stumbled through the doors and into the fresh, hot air. The sudden brilliance of the sunlight was blinding, a brief white shroud over his eyes. He hung his head as he slowly tripped along, rubbing sleep from his eyes with his palm. He was caught between the realm of reality and the slumberous dream world of terror from whence he came, still unsure of what was real. He found himself in the quad where he was surrounded by civilian clothing, book bags, school buildings and an imposing library at the far end. But directing his eyes to the northeast, he could see the semi-circular segment of Bizzell Street that separated campus from the golf course. United States military vehicles from Humvees to personnel trucks, painted camouflage green, travelled the College Station streets still keeping close guard over the territory they had conquered less than a year before. The golf course was a city of tents housing thousands of U.S. troops that occupied the location.

Kyle trembled and his legs faltered. His body longed to rest and properly transition from sleep to consciousness. He positioned his body before a bench and allowed his legs to give. He plopped down, first staring at the ground and then back off toward the occupying force to the northeast of campus. He felt no hatred. There was no malice. These were men he, only two months before, called enemy. They would likely still treat him as such—a traitor and a rebel. These were men he may have well shot at in the recent past. But there was no grudge. Instead, he harbored a lingering fear and haunting memory of death and decimation symbolic in this occupying force.

He tried to breathe slow and deep, digging in his pocket for his phone. He removed it with shaky fingers, careful to search for Ashley's number before pressing the correct button. He lifted the phone to his ear and listened for the tone to end in a voice.

"Kyle?" she answered, surprised. "Aren't you supposed to be in geography right now? What's wrong?"

"Happened again," he sighed, frustrated and embarrassed. "You know . . ." He stood up, becoming angry. "If I could get a decent fucking night's sleep for a change—at least six hours without a nightmare—I wouldn't fall asleep in class and this shit wouldn't happen!"

"It's okay, baby," she sympathized in a whisper, gently shutting her eyes. "I'm so sorry. Calm down. You're okay."

"I'm calm." He immediately shut down the frustration. "I'm good." He closed his eyes, swallowed, and nodded. "Why are you whispering?"

"I'm having coffee with some friends," she replied. "I wanted to be discreet. Hey, since you're probably not going back to class, you want to come join us?"

"That place just off campus? The place you always go?" He scanned around as if he could see it from where he was, yet knew he could not.

"Yeah, Jimmy Java's," she said. "Come on over. Meet my friends."

"Okay," he grinned, moving that direction. "It's about a five minute walk. I'll be there in a few."

"See you soon." She smiled wide. "Love you." She hung up as did he.

Kyle put one foot in front of the other, beginning with a slow trudge as he stuffed the phone back into the depths of his pocket. He felt it settle as the pace increased and his head lifted. He was thankful that A&M was such an easy campus to navigate. He had but to follow the general grid of streets and cut-throughs between the buildings, still wishing there were more trees along his cross-campus treks to shade him from the devilish Texas sun.

In the distance he could see another Humvee cruising University Drive, and in the foreground young students from all walks of life strolled along with their backpacks, hardly paying attention to their paths as they remained sucked into their phones. Not a mortar crater blemished the campus grounds. Not a crack or bullet divot scarred the building facades. No casings could be found randomly in the bushes, nor were there any tales of student civilian bloodshed in the wake of U.S. invasion. College Station fell easily and the campus had been evacuated. But as soon as the cease-fire had been announced, American attention spans faded, and school was resumed as if the occupying force camping on the golf course did not exist.

He continued ahead, drawing ever closer to the edge of campus. The smell of vehicle exhaust became more evident and pungent. He could see heavier traffic and gas station signs approaching, symbols of commercial envelopment of the school. He stopped at the intersection and peered across the traffic while he waited for the little white man to appear on the electronic screen. College-cheap restaurants mingled with convenience stores that seemed to always have a beer delivery truck next to them. Residences lay in the backdrop of the college town scene. And there in the middle, directly across the hot, paved lanes, was Jimmy Java's.

It was a dingy, seedy-appearing place that, should it have existed in an impoverished neighborhood, could have easily been a crack distribution center. The white-washed cinderblock exterior was smudged and caked with gray road dust and grime. The concrete's exposed gravel cracked and crumbled, aged and weathered by brutal Texas summers. Yet to offset the discouraging appearance, a new-looking, crisp burgundy and white "Jimmy Java's" sign hung over the entrance, inviting in only those who would take a chance on the place after judging its cover.

Kyle started through the white-striped crosswalk, a lone pedestrian somehow closely watched by spectators in their halted vehicles. His head was down and his gait was unsure. Comfort escaped him. He was almost in a foreign land, surrounded by the unfamiliar. He was homing in on a beacon of comfort when he stepped into the coffee shop.

The heavy wooden door screeched open, a resistance in the spring-loaded hinges. The small three-inch-by-three-inch white tiles, laid in an era long forgotten, were dingy. Black smudges across the little squares matched the unclean grout between and grit ground beneath his flip-flops. A wall of thick aroma met him as an invisible, yet completely tangible resistant field. The smell of darkly-roasted grounds blended with hints of incense poked at his nostrils with intent to harm. Throughout the shop were scarred and stained old square tables with wobbly chairs positioned at each side. The 1940s stucco walls were hard and cold, stained yellow by decades of allowed smoking, though now it was banned. The employees behind the counter, and poorly cleaning the tables, trudged lazily about in baggy black jeans, Rasta beanies, and death metal t-shirts. Employees and customers alike wore shaggy beards and dreadlocks, smelling of cigarettes and marijuana. Most of the eyes in the room were heavy and bloodshot, the strong coffee fighting the good fight against the relaxing THC in their blood.

None of the obvious regulars bothered to look up from their laptops or magazines. No one seemed to even notice him. Kyle pivoted his head from left to right, scanning the quiet congregation of independent thinkers for someone he surely knew would stick out as badly as he did. Then he caught sight of Ashley. She sat upon one of two tattered old couches in the far right corner. Light cascaded in through the large plate-glass windows, bathing her dark hair and olive skin in wholesome, natural light that danced beautifully with her features. Coffees sat positioned on the cheap, rectangular table at the center of the L of couches. She occupied the crook in the center, flanked by two male students to the right and a young woman to the left.

They were all trendy, and even preppy by comparison with the rest of the clientele. No one minded, or even noticed. They were absorbed in coffee, media, and their own altered states. The preppies in the corner were prim and trim. Hair was perfect and skin clear and shaven. Their attire was mall-originated and overpriced. Teeth were white, flossed, and free of tar stains.

Ashley's face brightened to a flash of luminance, her eyes softening and mouth gaping in happiness as she spotted her boyfriend uncomfortable in the entrance. She waved him to approach, eager to introduce him to her friends, all of whom remained stone-faced and expressionless. They teetered upon the edge of smiling along the jubilee sparkling in the eyes of their friend. But they were cautious, unwilling to put away poker faces, hunched forward in the anticipation of meeting the slightly awkward, yet fit-looking young man.

"Hey, baby." Ashley sprung to her feet, arms outstretched, and pulled her man in for a tight embrace and short kiss. "These are my friends," she motioned around. "This is Moira." She stepped aside to allow Kyle to shake the hand of the trendy short-haired brunette. "And this is Brice and Jeremiah." She again allowed them to shake. "Guys, this is Kyle."

"Nice to meet you," Kyle said before sinking into the deceptively comfortable old couch at the center of the group next to Ashley.

A very long moment passed. Kyle began nodding nervously, fidgeting with his hands and staring into Ashley's black coffee steaming on the table. Not a word was spoken for some time, and even as something to say came to someone's mind, there was doubt that it would sufficiently break the awkwardness. Lips moved, but no sound escaped. Eyes scanned around as nervous smiles became contagious.

"Just continue," Kyle said, his hands tracing connections in the air between the group of friends, "with . . . whatever you guys . . . were . . . you know, talking about." He did what he could as the members of the group smiled and nodded, thankful that they were over that hump. Wow, look at the pedigree sitting around me here. I'm surprised they're allowed to talk to someone like me.

"So anyway, my professor finally calls me into his office," Moira continued her earlier conversation with the well-born group. "And he asks me if I'd ever thought about the Republican Guardsmen that fought or died, or their families, blah, blah, blah, before I wrote my paper." She rolled her eyes, ridiculing her professor with a smile that dripped with mockery.

"And you told him to go fuck himself, right?" Brice glowed with amusement.

"Well, not in so many words," she giggled. "I just told him that it's my opinion that the Republic is open rebellion, the war is illegal, and so many of those Guardsmen are criminals. And I'm entitled to my opinion."

"Yes," Brice laughed. "That's awesome."

Pressure had been building behind Kyle's increasingly malicious eyes. Fresh on his mind, lingering images of his best friend's mangled body flickered in and out. He sat in the vortex of fiery opinion, heated by it as he simply closed his eyes and tried to ignore those words. He shook his head as if what he heard would somehow fling out from his ears and he would no longer have to endure it. He opened his eyes and turned his head to see Ashley wince with apology for her friends. Kyle felt his mouth open and words bulge from his throat like a bubble ready to burst.

"What can I get you?" A jittery and highly caffeinated female voice appeared almost out of nowhere.

Kyle's mouth, gaped in preparation to unleash a hail of soldier's wrath, closed. His eyes lifted to a new focal point. Ripped black fishnet hose rose to an extremely short bright purple skirt and finally to a black-metal band t-shirt torn around the collar for a neo-eighties off-the-shoulder effect. The mess of tussled black hair and extreme amounts of eye makeup made him brighten. He looked into her widened brown eyes with thanks while she fidgeted and waited for his order.

"Yeah, what kind of regular coffees do you have today?" Kyle asked, sensing that this was a connoisseur's coffee shop, likely with various types of brews from various countries.

"Um, yeah," she answered, her brain trying to keep up with her rapidly moving mouth. "We have a mild-roast Brazilian and a bold blend of Indian and Congolese coffee."

"I'll have that last one," Kyle said. "That sounds good."

"I'll have another, too," Jeremiah added, tapping the rim of his cup, to which she just nodded and then scurried off across the seating floor, disappearing behind the counter. "So what's your story, man?" He lightly backhanded the side of Kyle's leg.

"Huh?" His mind was elsewhere.

"What's your story?"

"Yeah, did you guys just start dating?" Moira joined the conversation, tying in each end of the group and integrating Kyle fully into a serious conversation.

"No, we've been together awhile." Kyle smiled shyly, dreading the direction of this exchange.

"Really?" Moira and the rest of the group paused, thoughts tumbling freely behind contemplative eyes, trying to develop at least the semblance of logic and sense in the matter.

"We first started dating in high school." Ashley sensed the confusion and attempted to explain before it came to interrogation. "We were just on a break for part of last year—"

"And I took a break from academics after high school," Kyle interrupted, taking part in the explanation.

"And of course the school year got cut short last year with the invasion," Ashley continued. "That's when we rekindled." She smiled sweetly, the way girls do in recounting their own love stories.

"Very cool," Moira, the only other female beamed along with her friend's apparent happiness.

"So what did you do before enrolling at A&M?" Brice inquired.

There was the moment that Kyle and Ashley dreaded. He first pretended not to understand the question. His face said, "Hmm?" with an honest hope that the interrogation would stop. The rest of the group, however, was captivated and silent. Everyone heard the question quite clearly and they were waiting. It was no use pretending. But the savior had returned, stealing attention away with a hot cup of coffee for Kyle and Jeremiah.

"Thank you," Kyle communicated almost in excess, wishing he could say more to further the attention and conversation away from himself. Then, he thought, they may lose interest. And they did as Brice's phone chimed from within his pocket, which he snapped out as if by reflex.

"That's awesome," he blurted as he read the text message that appeared on the screen and then looked up to share. "My friend Pitt—his last name was Pittman, so we called him Pitt," he explained to an audience that couldn't care less, "he goes to UT in Austin, and he's organizing a massive protest tomorrow at the state house."

"Just a . . . protest?" Ashley asked. "Or is there something special going on that they're protesting?"

"Well you know they're having a big ceremony there outside on the grounds," Brice explained. "Crane is giving all these special medals to 'war heroes'—these asshole traitor soldiers. So Pitt and all his friends are going out to the state house with signs and shit to remind everyone that the government and the soldiers are all just that—traitors to the United States."

"It's only a matter of time," Moira said with a sad expression on her face. "It's a wonder UT, as liberal a place as it is, has been allowed to coexist in Austin since the secession. So it's only a matter of time before the government cleans out the campus and eighty-sixes free speech rights—you know the Republic's constitution doesn't specifically mention that . . ."

"I say we go," Jeremiah nearly leaped with excitement. "I'd say we could do one here but there aren't any of those coward Republican Guardsmen anywhere near here," he laughed. "Austin's what, an hour and a half away? We could make a day trip out of it."

Ashley was quiet, nibbling on the inside of her lip. She regretted inviting Kyle to the coffee shop to meet her friends. She knew this exchange would eventually take place, but now that it was happening, every ounce of her being willed it to stop. She waited for a response, as she watched the ever dynamic expressions on her boyfriend's face. She could see pain build in his eyes.

"Why would you protest the soldiers?" Kyle finally spoke up. "Protesting the secessionist government, I get. Rallying outside the capitol building, I see. But why target soldiers who are just following orders?"

Ashley closed her eyes, as if to brace for the coming swoon of heated debate. Her liberal friends were fire-breathers, often outspoken and radical. She heard nothing for a moment, opening her eyes to take in the full span of expression in the absence of speech. Eyes were wide and mouths were ajar, shocked that an apparent wolf had infiltrated their flock.

"Because, dude," Brice scoffed in disbelief over the question, "those assholes signed up to protect what this illegal rebel government stands for. They're traitors."

"Ever met one?" Kyle asked.

"Who?" Brice replied. "A Republican Guardsman? I had a few classmates from high school join—"

"Did you ever ask them why they joined?" Kyle interrupted.

"No, I . . ." Brice stumbled.

"What does that matter?" Moira sneered. "They signed up nonetheless."

"And so every one of them is the same, right?" Kyle fired back. "That's like assuming a Mexican guy is a painter."

"That's not even the same—" Moira was cut off.

"Yes, it is," Kyle rebutted. "What about the Oklahoman who signed up for the U.S. Army before the secession? The guy that didn't want to end up part of the brigade that storms his own mother's neighborhood. He couldn't bear going to war against a state he grew up in or shooting at a guy he played t-ball with. What about the kid who needed the college money, so he signed up because he was out of options—like my best friend Ryan? I watched him get blown in half in training at Fort Hood and all he wanted was a ride to college."

"Wait, you're a Guardsman?" Jeremiah's eyes widened as the rest of the group made the same realization. "Jesus, I feel so betrayed."

"Yeah, I'm a Guardsman." Kyle stood and nodded, pulling a wallet from his back pocket. "Pressured into joining by my father, when all I wanted to do was go to A&M with my girlfriend. And I lost that in the decision, too. We didn't all join out of rebellion and Republican pride. I don't agree with the secession, either. So don't lump all of us into the same fucking category you silver spoon-carrying prick. And until the day you come into contact with the business end of an assault rifle or have to take the life of another American . . ." his voice cracked. "Until you're staring down a mushroom cloud forty-five miles from your house, you might want to think hard about what you say about those 'traitors' in the Republican Guard and respect what they've gone through and what their stories are." Kyle retrieved five Republican dollars from his wallet and slapped them down on the table to pay for his coffee. "I love you. I'll see you after a while," he leaned in and kissed Ashley.

The group was silent as they watched the young soldier storm away, turn the corner, and exit the building. Ashley grinned as she watched him through the window, stood without a word, picked up her school bag, and started out the door after him.

Chapter 7

The presidential office, still a temporary one, flooded with the uninhibited daylight of yet another scorching, cloudless Texas day. Joe Crane glanced about the room, not smiling; not content. This office was familiar. It belonged to Byron Davenport, and he hated it then, too. It was not suited to such a powerful executive. He had been in the Oval Office twice in his time as a U.S. senator, but the small taste of such a room dripping with all the clout and might of the highest office in the land was like a nectar of the gods, promising to elude forever. This tiny office in the Texas State Capitol seemed something more suited to a high school football coach.

"I had a better office in the private sector," he lamented with a sneer as he recalled his old position as a bank executive before running for senate.

He slowly stepped across the small office affront his oak desk, as he tugged and straightened his heavily starched white shirt collar before fastening the top snugly around his neck. He stretched and moved his torso in exaggeration against the conflict with his hips, while he allowed his gleaming, tucked shirt to find its comfortable position to let his body have fluid movement. His gait was precise and calculated, approaching a lovely old armoire his predecessor had moved into the office after his wife left.

Crane opened the right-hand door, to reveal a small mirror and a rod in the back where his gray coat hung crisp and clean. He lifted a thick, almost armor-grade burgundy silk tie to his neck and crossed, looped, and pulled the serpentine accessory into a dense, tight Windsor, which he adjusted and straightened into position at the crook of his collar. He tucked his smoothly-shaven chin into his chest, to observe the length. He then lifted his head and his gaze again, making eye contact with himself in the small mirror hung on the inside of the armoire door. He lifted his protruding chin of power, pursing his lips like an eighties punk rocker with a chip on his shoulder. He moved his head from side to side, to admire his own menacing political look before he reached in to grab his coat and don it with satisfaction. A knock on the door startled him a bit from his exercise in self-absorption.

"Yes, come in," he gurgled a bit, immediately clearing his throat after.

"They have us all set up down the hall," Crane's chief of staff, Zach Wallace, opened the door just enough to fit his slender frame between it and the door jam.

He had youth. That was one of the biggest contributions the new executive chief of staff added to the Joe Crane team. He almost always seemed to be missing the coat portion of his suit, setting Joe to often wonder if the young man even knew where it was half the time. His tie was always tight, though crooked, and his sleeves seemed permanently rolled up. He had the appearance of a go-getter; someone who got his hands dirty in the political sense. His eyes were cunning and blue, beaming from his symmetrical face beneath stylish, trim blond locks.

"All right, then." Crane finished straightening his coat. "Let's git." His slight country drawl seeped into his speech a bit. "Lay some numbers on me, Wally." They began down the hall and the row of offices leading to the conference room. "What are my approval ratings looking like?"

"So far, so good," Zach shot back. "Your basic, across-the-board conservatives love you. They love you to the tune of about ninety-three percent. I think they grab on to your speeches—they believe what you say and seem to view you as charismatic. The people of the Republic have been dealt blow after devastating blow, and they know you are the hardline guy who is going to exact their revenge for Dallas and for Davenport."

"Good," Crane answered, as he strolled with confidence down the hallway. "They would be right. And now that Davenport—God rest his soul—is out, we can finally handle this the way it should be. We're gonna kick ass in Pakistan and we're gonna get our domestic territory back in this meeting with Chandler." He pointed down the hall, squinting as he said the U.S. president's name.

"You're going to have to put on your game face," Zach advised. "Chandler's no joke. She's one tough bitch, and you're certainly going to have to have your wits about you."

"Oh, I can handle this woman," Crane smiled.

"Well don't handle her too hard," Zach warned. "The governor of Maryland tried to stonewall her a couple of years ago in a secret negotiation to get him to rejoin the U.S. He pissed her off, and a few days later, Maryland was occupied and the governor was under arrest."

"The first act of aggression," Crane added in disgust. "She should have left well enough alone, but she had to start a war and set us down the path of death and destruction."

"Either way," Zach continued as he tried to process the last statement, "don't piss her off too bad. Be firm, but respectful. We need her in Pakistan. She'll pull her troop commitment in a friggin' heartbeat."

"Noted," Crane nodded as they reached the conference room door. He paused for a moment, his shoulder resting against the door, smiling at his bright chief of staff. "Let's do this." He turned the doorknob and the two of them lunged through.

"Morning, Mr. President," Vice President Douglas Sims greeted Crane, standing in unified respect with the other half dozen staff in the room.

"Good morning, guys," Crane smiled with a polite political nod, as if they were the press. "Are we almost set?"

"Pretty much," Sims confirmed, sitting back down as the rest followed suit. "The equipment is almost set up." He motioned to an IT worker putting the finishing touches on the setup of a new laptop and accompanying state-of-the-art webcam at the nearest end of the table.

Aside from the vice president and the young man from the technology team, positioned around the long rectangular wooden table were other close members of Crane's staff. A young political strategist sat on the other side of Sims, her eyes fixed upon a few pages of notes that she had compiled for the president to use, fingering through them to double-check her work. The secretary of defense, Jay Gaines, sat across from her, his stubbled chin resting upon his open hand. General Dale Weaver, Davenport's old Armed Forces Chief sat naturally close to Gaines, ready to offer support on military issues. Another two interns were at the far end of the table, out of the way, but available should the officials in the room need anything else.

"We got a message from the White House just a minute ago that Chandler is in the situation room and ready when we are," Sims added, with a nervous stroke to his mustache.

"Well . . ." Crane sat at the head of the table like a father at Thanksgiving dinner. "Let's not keep her waiting. But first, would you join me in a word of prayer?" He bowed his head, as did the rest of the congregation. "Dear Heavenly Father, we bow our heads today in praise of you. We thank you for such a great nation to be a part of, and I thank you for such a great team. Bless our lawmakers and guide them in matters of legislation. Bless our troops and their families as we seek to avenge the actions of heathens for the harm of so many of your faithful children. And please guide us during our actions here today. Help us to make the decisions that would be your will, and please do the same for President Chandler. Open her eyes that she too would see your will and make wise decisions. We ask all of these things in Jesus' glorious name. Amen." He lifted his head, grinning smugly as he observed his staff's reverence. "Gosh, I feel like Captain Jean-Luc Picard about to hail a Klingon Bird of Prey," he said, with a nod to the tech worker to begin the call.

A strange electronic tone chimed as the secure conference call began. A light appeared on the front of the mounted webcam, indication that the video and microphone were indeed active. As the chime continued, a spiral graphic on the screen turned, signaling that the call was made and a small, dark box appeared where the U.S. president's face was to appear. Suddenly, the box was filled, and there within it was the choppy and pixilated face of President Chandler.

"Good morning, President Chandler." Crane plastered a wide false smile on his face.

"Good morning, Mr. Crane," she snubbed, returned the fake smile of politeness, watching him smirk as he realized how she had addressed him.

"Can you make that full-screen?" Crane asked the IT guy in a lighter tone. "Great, thanks." He then returned his attention to Chandler. "Boy, this is somethin' else, ain't it? Web conferencing," he chuckled. "Even less than a decade ago, we were still sending diplomats to meet up, work out details, and report back for approval and maneuvering. Now we can do our own dirty work."

"Dirty work," she grinned. "What a truthful way to put it."

"Indeed," he chuckled. "Well, let's get down to business, shall we?" He shuffled through a few sheets of paper in front of him, and briefly studied the content before he continued. "The war is over—" he began, but was cut short.

"Not really," Chandler chimed in. "Last I checked, we just had a really firm cease-fire. Until we get each of our foreign relations teams together and work out a solid treaty, the situation stands as-is."

"Oh, come on, Madam President . . ." Crane leaned back in his chair, relaxing in protest. "You know dad-gum good and well that's what we're here to talk about. I thought we could come to a truce now that we're about to go to war with each other, instead of against each other."

She fought off a sneer and showed her agitation with politeness. She had a feeling it would come to this conversation, and she was prepared.

"I'm not going to sit here and work out something as huge as a peace treaty over a video conference call, Joe." She lifted her head, somehow now deformalizing. "As I said, that's a job for our diplomatic teams, and that's likely going to take days or weeks to negotiate."

"I understand." Crane leaned forward and pressed his hands together as he carefully constructed his next set of statements. "But I have to bring back normalcy to my people."

"Normalcy?" Her eyebrows raised. "We just spent a year and a half fighting a civil war." She laughed in astonishment. "Things will never be as they were."

"What I mean, Cindy, is that people in the Republic need to get back to normal," he pushed on. "The only way for that to happen is for you to withdraw your troops from Republic territory."

Chandler just stared for a moment, unable to react. Blankness shined from behind her glasses and her mouth hung slightly ajar. It was not something she quite expected for him to so blatantly ask for, and so she was unprepared.

"You want me to withdraw U.S. troops occupying Republic territory?" she finally restated. "That's something you do when you're losing. Remember, we were winning this war. You know as well as I do that if it hadn't been for the Taliban smuggling a Pakistani nuke across your Mexican border and deciding to barbecue Dallas, we'd have the Metroplex by now and we'd be closing in on Austin. You're the one who's occupied. I don't believe you have much of a bargaining chip."

He said nothing for a brief moment, his face a testament to his struggle to remain composed. She was blunt and had struck a nerve, one that was attached to the truth. It stung and throbbed in his ego. His lips puckered and his eyes narrowed, managing his discontent before he responded.

"This is true. You are absolutely right." He leaned forward, politeness gone and some form of malice his new expression. "I just wonder, with your government's commitment to our coalition and future invasion of Pakistan, how will you be able to send a sufficient number of troops? I think you pledged something like fifty thousand. You still have men and women holding the fronts in Texas, the northern areas of the Gulf states, and the Carolinas, not to mention the occupying forces in our ports—New Orleans, Mobile, Houston . . ."

"You're right," she admitted after a long pause. "We may have to pull some personnel off of occupation duty, but don't think that we're going to withdraw. Thousands of U.S. servicemen and women did not bleed and die so we could just give you back territory. Your twenty-nine states are still, as far as the United States is concerned, in rebellion. And the territory we have regained is now U.S. territory—period. But as a show of good faith that we are committed to the coalition in Pakistan and that we are still interested in negotiating further down the road, I will authorize the reducing of occupying personnel in areas that have been less problematic in terms of resistance, and in states that we hold and you have no more troops."

"Fair enough," Crane nodded and smiled again. "Hey, it's a start."

"Now if you'll excuse me," Chandler said, "I have another engagement."

"Thank you, Madam President," Crane grinned. "A pleasure as always. Good day," he ended, as they both clicked out of the session.

"Pompous ass." She dropped the politeness in exchange for a more genuine look of disgust. "Can you believe he actually wanted me to just withdraw all troops out of the goodness of my heart?"

"Madam President . . ." General Harlan Bates, seated between Sandra and Secretary of Defense Jay Shields, buried his face in his hands. "I really wish you would have consulted with me before promising Crane you would withdraw some of the troops." He looked up at her, smiling respectfully, but stressing within. "This is going to be a logistics nightmare."

"We were going to have to pull troops off the front lines anyway," Chandler replied. "We're sending fifty thousand to Pakistan and we only have—what—a hundred and twenty thousand in the field right now? There's no way we're going to just recruit fifty thousand new soldiers on such short notice."

"I understand, ma'am," Bates said. "I just would have liked to have assessed our situation a little better first. We're going to get troops for Pakistan in a number of places. There have been a lot of new personnel enlisting out of sheer patriotism in response to the Dallas bombing, despite the fact it's technically not a U.S. city. Maybe some with kin down there. We also have a lot of soldiers sent home from the front lines with minor wounds that should be healed by now. If they haven't been discharged and they have to serve the rest of their four years anyway, we can call those people back out for a tour in Pakistan."

"I see. I understand," Cindy responded. "Well I didn't give him a number of troops we'd pull from occupied areas. Let's just play it by ear." She began to stand up, followed by everyone else. "Update me on personnel later on, General, and we'll touch on this again soon. If you'll excuse me, I have to get ready to go down to the Rebuilding the Capitol ribbon-cutting thing up on the hill." She nodded to her staff, turned, and exited the situation room.

Chapter 8

The eyelids slowly lifted like curtains in a high school drama production to reveal painful brown irises that seemed engulfed by a sea of fire. A few blinks confirmed the end of the night's sleep, however short. Derek rolled lazily between the sheets and the mattress to place a lumbering, lifeless arm around Carly's waist. She squirmed beneath it, unsure of whether to invite it or reject.

Saturday morning meant no alarm clocks, not that they needed one. The dim light of dawn was just beginning to allow objects in the bedroom to be silhouetted against the illuminated walls. The big red digital numbers of the clock were fierce in the twilight. They were the eyes of some evil beast that threatened to devour what flesh he may find in the room. They stared a menacing 6:07, laughing as the two of them groaned against the wailing of their daughter Olivia across the house.

A child's morning cry, one of both hunger and fearful parental detachment, is piercing and vicious. Worse is when that cry is converted from warm, natural fleshy vocals into something almost metallic and artificial. The super-sensitive microphone resting atop Olivia's girly white dresser transmits that sound over the radio waves into the little plastic receiver, squawking it loudly and irritatingly throughout the bedroom for a near daily rude awakening.

"Jesus, the kid's almost a year old," Derek squirmed and groaned. "When is she going to learn about Saturday mornings?"

"Never," Carly barely annunciated. "But we need to learn it's not smart to be up until three a.m." She slowly lifted her torso and placed her feet on the bed, looking back at Derek who was beginning to snore again. "Hell no. You're getting up with me."

"What?" he protested, opening his eyes with pain. "I got up with her in the middle of the night and rocked her back to sleep."

"I did too," she fired back, now on her feet. "So we're even. If I'm getting up, you sure as hell are too."

"All right, all right." He pulled the covers off to the right and sat up, watching the room spin.

The blood in his head felt as though it sank to the bottom of his skull, sloshing around like water in a bucket, awkward and heavy. His eyes were aflame and lungs felt clogged from massive smoke inhalation. Crust and mucus obstructed the flow of air through his nostrils and his mouth tasted like asphalt. He sat unmotivated, listening to Carly consoling their daughter through the baby monitor.

His feet finally touched the floor, flat and unsure as he stood, his body creaking all the way. He kept waiting for a cold sweat and a churning of the stomach to send him kneeling before the toilet, but it never came. A yawn and a headache were enough. He ambled for the bathroom, lazily flipping the switch to ignite the bulbs above. The light hurt his eyes for a short moment while his pupils rapidly tightened.

His first and most important mission was to go for the old mirror-doored medicine cabinet, which swung open with an irritating screech. It was a treasure chest of medicinal goodness, stocked to the brim with anything one could need. Various muscle relaxers and experimental drugs with his late mother's name printed on the orangish-brown containers were a sad reminder of her painful last days with Lou Gehrig's disease. There were leftover painkillers from his battle wounds. Flu powders, decongestants, laxatives, and the pink bottle all had their place. But what Derek needed was the simplistic wonder of ibuprofen. A hospital dose of six hundred milligrams would force that headache to its knees. As long as he could nap later when Olivia did, he would be home free for the rest of the day.

He lunged for the white plastic bottle of generic ibuprofen, his hand heavy like a sandbag nearly knocking it and other bottles off the shelf. His fingers, tight and bloated, could barely be coaxed to grip the container and finally retrieve it. His eyes drifted closed while he pressed down and twisted the childproof cap until he could remove it. The little brown pills rattled like a baby's toy while they slid across the plastic, spilling into his open palm.

"Shit." He realized that perhaps a dozen pills filled his hand.

He set aside three for himself and another three for Carly, knowing she would be in need, and dumped the rest back into the bottle. He scooped his share of the pills up and popped them into his mouth like peanuts. Frantic to swallow before he began tasting the bitter coating, he flung the faucet handle around, releasing a stream of water forth into the sink. Derek cupped his right hand to capture as much as he could, and swigged it up, grimacing at the swimming pool-flavored city tap water. But water was water, and after the amount of beer imbibed the night before, toilet water might have been welcome.

Somewhat refreshed and with renewed spunk in his step, he palmed the remaining three pills and exited the bathroom and bedroom into the dimly-lit family room. The overhead range light, a simple appliance bulb, served as a weak beacon in the house. It was a nightlight of sorts that stayed lit throughout each night, serving them well when Olivia awoke sporadically during the wee hours.

Derek made his way through the labyrinth that was now his family room, dodging the playpen and scattered toys, large and small, attempting to avoid the often sharp-cornered plastic whatever into the tenderest parts of his foot. Carly scooted from the hallway and bedrooms to the left, Olivia upon her hip, surely on a mission to dispose of the nasty diaper in her hand. Her brown ponytail, filled with straight, shiny hair swung like a metronome above her little gray tank top. Her hips, covered in comfortable, cotton pajama pants, swayed naturally, something that put an inevitable smile on Derek's face.

"Ibuprofen?" He strolled up to her in the kitchen.

"Oh God, yes," she said with almost exaggerated relief. "Here." She handed Olivia to her father.

The child had no choice but to be passed, but she certainly was not happy about it. Her tiny eyes squinted and her bottom lip curled down. She began whining, leaning, and stretching her arms out for her mother. Her tiny fingers, complete with dimples at the knuckles, opened and closed as she tried to grab for Carly. Derek never grew accustomed to it. His face lost what little color it had and the corner of his lips drooped low, clearly hurt. Still, he clung to his little girl, watching Carly open the refrigerator and remove a green plastic workout bottle. Condensation formed on it immediately, and though Derek knew it was filled with tap water, it appeared somehow more refreshing and pure pouring into Carly's mouth, washing down the ibuprofen tablets.

"Why do you always keep a bottle of nasty tap water in the fridge?" he asked.

"The cold kind of cancels out the nasty tap taste," she shrugged, opening the refrigerator and replacing the bottle.

"We need to get one of those tap purification things. I don't trust Cleveland water."

"I don't care what it is," she winced, and flared her nostrils, "as long as it gets this beer taste out of my mouth. I just don't think we can keep partying like this. It's not worth it." She reached back into the refrigerator for a small, yellow-capped bottle of breast milk.

Derek stood and watched the master of motherhood bounce around the kitchen knowing just what she needed to do. He was in awe. He himself could move a squad into position, put artillery pressure on the enemy, and launch a small ground offensive. Even after a few months, caring for a child was still an unknown. He admired as Carly warmed the milk a bit under the hot water from the faucet. Satisfied with the temperature, she poured some dry cereal flakes into a small toddler bowl, mixed in the milk, and began to stir, finally finishing it off with a bit of pear baby food.

"You used a bottle from the fridge," Derek noticed aloud.

"Yeah." She looked up at him from her stirring. "So?"

"Don't I normally see you squeeze your boob or go pump to get the milk for the cereal?"

"Oh." She understood the nature of the question. "Yeah, usually. But I pumped a bit before going to Jake's last night so I would have milk for this morning. And when she wants to nurse in a little while, she's going to have to just settle for the rest of this bottle because I still need to pump and dump. The alcohol won't be out of my system until . . ." She turned her eyes upward, silently mouthing numbers as she did the math in her head. "I guess around ten."

"You know that actually looks appetizing," he smiled, glancing down at the baby's breakfast.

"It does, doesn't it," she smiled back. "Too bad it tastes like breast milk."

"Wait, you've tasted it?" He turned his nose up. "Gross."

"Why not?" she laughed. "I deal with it every day. Olivia drinks it every day. I had to know what it tastes like. You know you've tasted it."

"Yeah, but that was an accident. That was during sex and I will never make that mistake again."

They both laughed, something Olivia surely picked up on. She had ceased whining for Carly, somewhat warming up to her daddy. Yet as much as he loved that, he still felt awkward holding her and somehow could not wait to put her down. He finally sensed his opportunity, moving over to the cheap, plastic high chair near the table. He took the child under the arms, lowering her into the seat and strapping her in before adjusting the tabletop attached in front.

"You want to feed her?" Carly asked, setting the bowl in front of him with a little plastic spoon. "Good. Just try to scoop the stuff that comes out of the side of her mouth back in," she instructed, giving Olivia a bite and exhibiting the routine.

"I think I can manage," Derek grinned nervously.

"Good, I've got to go pump." She began to move away. "My boobs are killing me," she said as she rubbed them in pain.

He sat before his daughter, for the moment content in the highchair. His head was turned all the way to the rear, watching Carly head for the bedroom where she kept her pump, continuing to rub her engorged breasts. As he became satisfied, seeing her disappear from sight, he turned his head back to its most natural position, gazing into his daughter's big brown eyes. She just looked back, fidgeting with her clothing or her ear; making eye contact and then not.

"You hear that, kid?" Derek smiled. "Just you and me for a few minutes. Is that going to be okay with you?" He dipped the little plastic spoon into the breakfast mush, scooped, and began placing the food into the eagerly-waiting mouth before him. He grinned at how cute she was when her whole head moved to position her open baby bird's mouth just right for the coming cereal. "I am your daddy, you know." He paused for a moment, thought, and shook his head. "Oh, who am I kidding? You don't know me from Adam. I don't blame you for not ever wanting anything to do with me. You're not used to me. I'm just this dude that showed up one day. You see, partly I have to remind myself that what I was doing all those months was important. But another side of me tells me that the only thing that's important is you and your mommy. I should have been here for you." He looked into her eyes, continuing to feed her the mush. "I'm sorry. You needed your da-da."

He stopped talking, somewhat satisfied with the apology to a child that couldn't possibly understand what he was saying. It was not a matter of Olivia forgiving him, though. It was a relief to unload that burden. He had said it; made the statement to at least someone. But all the relief in the world could not make any of it less true. It would not simply vanish. His feelings of regret haunted him still. He could not imagine Carly in the delivery room without him. He could not bear the thought of her having to care for both his disabled mother and a child he had never met. He felt he had inflicted a wound that may never heal.

Derek could hear the whirring of the pump motor and the vacuum action in the pump's cups cease in the next room. A few moments passed with the frequent checking, glancing over his shoulder to see if she was yet coming forth. Then he saw from the corner of his eye as she again entered the room. He turned his head and in an instant, through his left ear, a sound was made that he had never heard. It was foreign but sweet, and it planted a seed of love in his heart.

"Da-da," the sweet voice uttered amid playing with cereal spilled on the chair top. "Da-da," it chimed again, more sweetly than before.

"Da-da?" Derek lit up, his face barely able to contain his smile. "You said 'da-da.' Ha. That's—that's right." He placed a flattened palm over his chest. "I'm your da-da."

"Oh honey," Carly gleamed, rushing to Derek's side and staring down lovingly at her precious daughter.

Derek was focused on one thing only in that moment. He still held the spoon, but it went unused. His gaze was locked and lost on his child; his own flesh and blood. She played and fidgeted sweetly in her chair, really unaware of the impact of her newest word. She was repeating. She was simply learning speech. But to Derek, she was making him a father. He just stared and smiled, unable to break his transfixed eyes from the child. But a rude, electronic tone began cutting through the confections in the air. His eyes broke away as Carly shifted over to Derek's phone on the countertop. She picked it up, trying to make sense of the display and who it may indicate was calling.

"Restricted number." She handed it to Derek.

"Oh . . ." He received the chiming device from her, a frown forming. "Hello?" He put it to his ear, and began a series of nods that surely the person on the other end would not see. He listened, an almost metallic squawk was all that was audible to Carly. "Thank you. Yes sir. Goodbye." He pressed end and set the phone on the table.

"Was that . . ." she started to ask, but hesitated.

"The Marines." He returned his disappointed eyes back to his beloved daughter. "I'm to report to New London NSB—a base in Connecticut—a week from today. They already have my plane ticket ready. I'm going to Pakistan." He glared at Olivia and her playful and oblivious gurgles.

Chapter 9

Cindy Chandler's pumps knocked stylishly against the pristine polished marble of the West Wing corridor. The sound was one of femininity, yet of power in the presidential mansion. She wore the sound like a medal or symbol of supremacy. She flaunted it and accentuated it, always secretly trying to make the sound of her heels echoing between the elegant ivory walls even more menacing.

The exit to the West Wing carport was in sight, the door already open for her, allowing cutting beams of sunshine past flanks of Secret Service agents and into the dim hall. Staffers bustled as agents finalized the sequence of exit and the motorcade instructions and planned route. Intersections were blocked by Secret Service and DC police personnel, the strobes of their patrol units flashing rapidly. Snipers and agents clad in black fatigues accessorized with assault rifles secured the perimeter, all while Cindy strutted confidently toward the door and the cars, almost oblivious to the care and planning it took for her just to leave the building. Donny, the first gentleman, followed, loyally escorting her as usual while Cindy chatted into her cell phone.

"Julie . . ." She rolled her eyes, her tone set deeply in mother mode. "We've discussed this. You're not going back to Tulane. New Orleans isn't safe. You'll have to make due here in the States." She paused for the usual rebuttal. "I know the city's occupied by our military—I gave the order to invade it, remember? Don't try to act like you know more about this than I do. Just because it's occupied and the campus has reopened doesn't mean it's safe down there. Gang activity is picking up, the city is shot full of bullet holes and mortar craters, and there's an insurgency of rag-tag Red loyal terrorists bombing security checkpoints." She paused again. "Look, you're not going to change my mind. No means no. I'm on my way out the door to go address Congress, so I have to go . . . okay . . . b-bye." She pressed the end button and climbed into the black presidential limousine with her husband. "That kid . . ." She shook her head in frustration as she scooted and positioned her rear end on the leather upholstery, the rubbing sound drawing a sophomoric smile from her husband.

"She's headstrong." He continued to grin as the car began to move forward. "Like someone else I know," he said as he nudged her arm. "That might serve her well, too, later in life."

"Or get her into trouble." She leered out her tinted window as they neared the heavily-guarded gate to the White House grounds. Kept at a distance by DC police, a moderate-sized crowd of protesters held up signs that read phrases like "FINISH THE JOB" and "TAKE OFF THE LIP-STICK AND PUT ON THE WARPAINT." Barely audible through the thick bulletproof glass and heavy armor were chants about their unhappiness with their president. "I'm starting to doubt my decisions."

"To go to war with the Republic?" He raised his eyebrows in shock.

"Of course not." She continued to stare out the window at the passing DC buildings. "I'm doubting my decisions to agree to a cease-fire. After the Reds were reeling from the Dallas nuke strike, General Bates wanted to use the opportunity to take Austin."

"And you regret not doing so," he nodded with understanding.

"All those people back there," she referred back to the protesters, "think I should have gone after Austin, too. I can't blame them. I thought I was being compassionate for the people in Texas. It was an outside terrorist strike on an American city!" She finally looked into her husband's eyes. "What was I supposed to do? I thought it would bring Americans back together. We'd go after Taliban-run Pakistan together and reunite as a country."

"You can't beat yourself up." He placed his hand on hers, caressing it. "You're not a soothsayer. There's no way you could have known Davenport would have been killed. This could have brought our country back together. You didn't know you were going to have to deal with this Crane maniac."

"Did you just use the word soothsayer?" she said with loving ridicule. "Am I in a Shakespeare play or something?"

"Smartass," he grinned, placing his arm around her and pulled her close.

But her eyes had already wandered back through the dark glass, peering out into the city as it passed rather slowly. Washington was not the same. Though activity in the city was beginning to pick up with people returning from evacuation, it was a virtual ghost town by comparison. Cindy and Donny could see the National Mall to the south. Surrounding the crumbled pile of stone that once stood proud as George Washington's obelisk-shaped monument, naval shells had cratered the grounds into something that resembled a sponge. It was battered and beaten, and along with the rest of the capitol, resembled something more like Berlin in 1945.

The motorcade traveled along E Street, approaching its eastern transition into Pennsylvania Avenue and the Federal Triangle, Donny peered in silence at the bruised, partially crumbling Treasury building. It wore repair scaffolding on the exterior like a cast or a splint, still a symbol that the structure was injured, yet bore the promise of healing. It was the same with all of the federal buildings that approached. While some outer-lying private buildings housing stores and businesses remained badly damaged or a shell of a structure gutted by fire, most showed signs that repairs had begun. Giant holes blown into the sides and roofs of the old postal building, the IRS, The National Art Gallery, and the various museums of the Smithsonian Institute were covered in giant sheets of plastic and temporary wooden structure. Metal construction scaffolding now obscured the extent of the damage to the crumbled majestic federal columns and maimed roofs and rotundas. Lofty crane arms shadowing much of the city and signs of reconstruction brought mixed emotions for the Chandlers—symbols of a city brought to its knees that would never be the same again. Yet, they were also symbols of hope and rebirth. They were, in a sense, inspiring.

The motorcade, a caravan of black agent-filled vehicles, exited Pennsylvania Avenue and began to circle Capitol Hill to the north. The once manicured and stately green grounds were a phantom of their former self. The concrete surrounding the Capitol's reflecting pool was mangled, massive chunks still waiting to be hauled away. The lawns were deeply ulcerated, leaving once regal trees splintered or uprooted.

The procession of executive vehicles came to a halt, one by one, at the north end of the Capitol, just outside the Senate wing. Cindy waited as Secret Service agents filed from within their respective SUVs, dressed typically in black suits and dark shades. They scurried like worker bees around their beloved queen as she patiently sat with her husband in the presidential limousine. She could see down the length of the intimidating expanse of steps that led up into the Senate, the central rotunda, and at the far end, the House, where she normally would have addressed the whole of Congress. Scaffolding and orange caution tape enveloped the outside of the House of Representatives, a foreboding sign of the near destruction of her Capitol, her government, and her country as she knew it.

Her door popped open as a sharp blade of vertical sunlight sliced into the dimness of the interior of the car. She looked up at her bodyguards, their eyes elsewhere. They were perpetually scanning for even the slightest inconsistency in plan or surroundings. They guarded the president, yet seemed to hardly ever look at her. She began the delicate art of a female in a skirt exiting a limousine. She swung her legs out toward the opened door, pressing down on the front of her skirt and keeping her knees as tightly pressed together as she could before taking an outstretched hand and planting her heels on the pavement outside. Standing erect, she locked her knees, brushing any wrinkles from her blouse, jacket, and skirt. Donny followed as he slid out of the same door, stood tall, and fastened the top button of his coat.

"Right out in the open as usual, huh?" Cindy smirked as she started for the Senate steps.

"I'm sorry, ma'am," the lead agent apologized. "We'd prefer the tunnels and the Capitol subway too, but after all the shelling, the Army Corps of Engineers isn't one hundred percent convinced of the structural integrity down there. So for now, it's off-limits."

"You don't have to apologize, Dean," she smiled. "It's not your fault. Who do I look like? Stalin? I'm not going to have you hauled off to Siberia and shot over it."

"Yes ma'am," he smiled. "I mean, no ma'am. I mean, you're not Stalin . . ." he stumbled nervously.

"Again," she soothed, "you're stammering. Relax. I know it's your job to be high-strung, but it's really okay. Besides, this way was good enough for my predecessors."

"I think it shows courage and strength." Donny trailed her only slightly.

They approached the imposing structure as dwarfed mortals encroaching on the territory of the gods. Olympus cast its shadow over them, insignificant in comparison. The interior could be menacing, and its inhabitants, at times, vicious and judging. The columns glowed, but were cold. The flag at the crest cracked like a bullwhip in the wind. It was always a humbling experience for Cindy to visit the houses of Congress, and her anxiety began to mount, shrouded in an ever-calm and confident façade.

The entourage ascended the steps as if it were to the throne room of the universe, a lofty temple beaming its power. They reached the top of the steps, and the cool of the shadows, winded and aching in the legs. An agent pulled at the door, greeted by two security guards on the other side. They stepped aside at the sight of the Secret Service agents and approaching president, and the entourage met the cool of the interior hall.

Ivory walls and polished marble floors were immaculate and glowed with as much nearly supernatural power as the exterior. The air vibrated with it. It shook the soul and rattled blood vessels. Shivers moved in waves from the spine, across the skin, and into the extremities as Cindy again began to hear her own heels knock against the floor and challenge the very power of the gods of Capitol Hill.

The heavy wooden doors were opened, unleashing a tidal wave of thunderous voices. Conversation, laughter, and all manner of communication and emotions mixed together and burst from the Senate chamber as a singular roar. At first, no one noticed the open door or the agents flanking the doorway. But as a few senators and representatives began to catch sight of the peach-colored suit, others followed in a wave across the Congressional body, causing first a lull of silence and then a burst of respectful applause. She smiled, waving presidentially as she strutted down the aisle toward the central podium, her husband staying back to take a seat in the crowd.

The regal blue carpet almost felt more cushioned under her feet, giving the illusion of walking on air. She ascended to the podium, behind which was seated Vice President Coffman, and the new speaker of the House, Bobby Dixon, watching and waiting in fervent support. The imperial walls accented in gold and marble were crowned by decorative florals around the lighting, haloing the recessed center of the lofty ceiling.

Cindy stepped up to the podium, calm outwardly, but bustling within. She breathed deeply and slowly, allowing more oxygen to reach her brain so that she could think quickly and clearly. It calmed her as she watched the storm in the room, once flashing with lightning and rumbling with thunder, roll past and silence. The eyes of both houses of Congress were upon her, a body now small enough to fit in the much smaller Senate chamber while the House chamber was being repaired. It was nothing like the Congress she addressed shortly after she took office nearly two years prior. That Congress was bitterly divided along party lines. It was polarized. This was an all-Democrat Congress, but something dangerous was happening and Cindy could see it as she scanned over the assembled body.

"Ladies and gentlemen of Congress," she began, glancing back down at the speech prepared for her. "I come to you . . ." She paused, closed her eyes, and started again. "I come to . . ." She paused again, and then grinned, shook her head, and folded up the pages before her. "Boy, I bet you're wondering why I've come to you today." She stuck out her chin. "I'm not pushing any major bills. We already have a declaration of war against Pakistan. In fact, we've had really no problems getting anything done in nearly two years. It's sad, though, that we basically became a one-party government in order for that to happen. Truly, I wish we still had that diversity—the devil's advocate—in this room. Too many like-minded people in the same room can be dangerous. But what's more dangerous is what I'm beginning to see happen in this building and in our country as we speak . . ." She paused as a low rumble rose from the floor.

"Division." Her tone became one of calm, but angered disappointment. "Again. After all we've been through, we still can't stand united. Do you not see the things we've done?"

"Like start a civil war?" a male voice echoed out from the crowd, followed by elevated rumble.

"Would you rather have been the Congress that presided over the splitting of the United States?" Her booming, yet feminine voice calmed the waters. "That fight is not over! I can promise you that this country will again be united. But I need you to stick with me. We can't lose focus." She paused a moment before returning to her point. "Since the beginning of this conflict, as horrible as it may be, we have done great things. We've brought unemployment to the lowest point in fifty years.

We have our financial sector on Wall Street working with us in replacing the safety nets our economy once had and still needs. No longer can the most powerful businesses and banking institutions have such control over the economy—the consumer does. You've done that in the legislation you've passed here! You've brought jobs and manufacturing back here to the U.S. You've knocked the rust off of the rust belt and revitalized our heartland. You've reinvested in our infrastructure and our education. Banks are loaning money. We are rebuilding our crippled capitol city. And yet you still feel the need to squabble!" She pounded her fist on the podium, a sound that thundered over the dead silence.

"And for what?" Her voice softened. "Because some of you believe I've been too soft with the Republic as of late? Been too much of a 'woman'? Pardon me for having compassion for what I still consider an American city filled with American people! I saw an opportunity to work through the conflict peacefully—to forego the sending of more young men to their deaths. It is my hope that this still can be achieved, perhaps through cooperation in Pakistan. But if not, trust me—we will reunite this country. But I need your help. All of those people out there protesting our perceived weakness in resolve—the ones who say we're going too soft on the Republic. We need to stand united and win those people back over. We cannot afford to divide in this governmental body! We cannot allow our people to divide, either! Disunity is our demise, ladies and gentlemen! And only you can prevent it. Thank you and good day," she finished, and before a response immediately stepped down from the podium.

The applause began as a low clap that grew in volume and in decibels. Soon came the cheers and the standing of every person in the room. Smiles graced their faces, which spread to Cindy's. She stopped, nodded in appreciation, bowed slightly, and left completely ecstatic that she had again won them over . . . for the moment.

Chapter 10

Kyle Perkins was not Catholic. He did not necessarily believe in a purgatory or a limbo dimension of any kind, so he had never really thought about what it may feel like to be there. Somehow, he now had somewhat of an idea. He was caught somewhere in between layers of existence. Life went on around him in his family home, and though he saw it, he felt as though he were in some parallel plane of being, able to see all that happened, but no one could see outward at him. It was like the two-way mirror one sees in police drama shows, only he was not attentively observing some interrogation of a suspect. Everything almost blurred like time-exposure photography, making all that he saw morph into some sort of strange cross between impressionism and the surreal.

He was numb, staring forward, yet not really at anything in particular. The television in the family room was on. His mother had changed the décor again, this time ditching the gaudy Easter-like pastels for more elegant shades of burgundy and aged gold. It was a nice change, he had thought earlier, but now eclipsed by other things. The television flickered at the focal point of the small family room. To Kyle, it was something in the distance that shimmered with the sun, but was too far away to be of any consequence. Angela had reentered the room, rejoining her son after taking a quite lengthy phone call from a girlfriend. She seemed winded; overexerted. Some of her friends could carry on about insignificant things for hours. They had no substance really, but they were always loyal and dependable, so she maintained the friendship. But again, Angela's entry barely drew Kyle's attention. She simply slipped into the room and took her seat on the far end of the couch from him where she had been before. Out of the corner of his eye, he could see her lay down her smartphone and pull her shoulder-length, highlighted hair back into a ponytail, yet just let it fall again, draping around her neck.

He paid attention to nothing. His thoughts were scattered like the ashes of a loved one spread over a mountainside and caught in the winds that howled above. They coursed erratically with currents of love, hate, and regret, but free of really any of those emotions. His hand still clutched the letter he had just opened a few minutes before. From the time he looked at the top right corner of the envelope, he knew that anything with his name on it and processed initially in Austin, Texas, was going to ruin any decent mood he may be enjoying. Joe Crane's name beside the twenty-nine-star flag on the letterhead represented the materialization of everything he feared might happen. Yet, somehow he paid the letter no attention, nor the television. He showed nothing regard.

He was ablaze with random thoughts that suddenly appeared to him, and each new revelation or epiphany brought a different emotion that still never seemed to manifest in his expression. Would the college hold his spot or give him credit for the little bit of work he had done in his classes so far? Damn it. Finally get to start college like I was supposed to and I get deployed again . . . to Pakistan. I'd rather be back in Carroll-ton. What will I tell Ashley? She'll be devastated. I've barely been back two months. He wondered if he would have to serve with U.S. troops, and how hot Pakistan might be, even in fall and the approaching winter. Would the locals be friendly and supportive?

"What's that?" Kyle's mother broke his trance. "A letter?" She peeked over finally noticing the letterhead. "Oh Jesus." Her expression turned somber.

"It's fine, Mom," he blinked and reacted, but opted out of eye contact. "We both knew this day was coming. The Republic has always been short on personnel, so they need all grunts to the front."

"But we just got you back," she protested in more of a whine than an argument. "What about school? Ashley?"

"I know, I know." He rolled his eyes with the beginning signs of frustration. "Trust me, I've been thinking about all of this. School will always be there. Ashley is going to be tough to deal with, but I think she knows it's coming."

His thoughts lingered on his girlfriend. His mind wandered back to the day on that very couch when he broke the news to her that he had enlisted to fight in the Republican Guard. He remembered so clearly the pain in her eyes. Tears leaked her anguish and her words poured her anger. Her devastation was something he never wanted to see again. Ashley had finally come to terms with his role in the military, and that he didn't really agree with the ideology of the Republic. She envisioned his contract running its course and his parting ways with everything the Republic stands for. But what if I die before than can happen?

"At least I can be proud to fight this time," he added after several moments. "I mean, I convinced myself of the need to defend my city when I was back in Carrollton, but I really didn't think the secession and war and everything should have even happened." He stared into nowhere as he rambled. "At least I know I'm going to be avenging all those people who were killed in Dallas. At least I know I'm fighting people who truly hate who we are, blue or red. I can pull the trigger with ease," he half smiled. "You know?" He looked at his mother.

"No, I don't really," she answered honestly, and shook her head.

"I wonder what Dad will say," he jumped to the next random thought.

"Surely he'll be proud you're going off to bring justice to the people responsible for Dallas," she smiled.

"Of course he will." Kyle rolled his eyes. "Typical Republican. Where is he anyway? I come in to visit for the weekend and he's not around?"

"Golfing with his boss," Angela answered. "You know, that whole keeping-up-appearances thing."

The conversation stopped as Kyle's attention was grabbed and directed toward the flickering screen. He first was unsure of what he was looking at. It was a nice, shaded lawn with some people—it made no sense. He had not been paying attention until then. He had no clue what channel it was even on. But as he continued to watch, he started to understand. Medals were being hung around tightly-collared military necks. President Crane smiled like a jester at court while he bestowed honors while legislative onlookers clapped alongside proud parents of Republic heroes.

"I know what this is," he smirked. "A bunch of Ashley's friends are there in Austin to protest the troops."

"The troops?" She raised her eyebrows. "Why the troops? They're just following orders."

"I know," he nodded. "They're stupid. I tried to explain to them that not every soldier agrees with the government. They just do what they're ordered. Hell, look at me—about as liberal as you can be, but I'm loyal to the idea of serving my country."

"Are you really?" she squinted. "Your country? Somehow I don't believe you."

No answer came to his lips. He had never hesitated to express his liberal, anti-Republic views, at least to his family or Ashley. He would never try to fight that battle amongst other soldiers. The soldiers' bond was important to keep intact. On the battlefield, one needed to know that the man beside him had his back. A liberal in the platoon could undermine that, so he kept his mouth shut. One thing that he maintained, despite his political views, was his loyalty in that when he committed to something, he stuck to it until the end. But as he looked into that flat television screen, the cameras beginning to shift and focus on the rallying protestors in the background, he began to see the point Ashley's friends had made in the coffee shop. Perhaps every bit of this was wrong. Perhaps loyalty to his duty was the same as loyalty to the cause and the ideology to everything he despised.

No longer did the cameras covering the scene pay focus on the young men and their medals. No longer was the story one of bravery and loyalty to the cause of the Republic. It was not about those who fought and sacrificed to the conservative cause. The images flashing across the television were that of disdain and discourse. They were chants of anger. They were signs of discontent. The youthful masses that gathered behind metal barricades across the street had chased away sympathetic and patriotic families and benevolent onlookers. Over the smooth, politically seductive voice of President Crane, Kyle could hear indistinguishable, yet profoundly provocative chants of the disgruntled youth of Texas. Signs rose above the heads of the crowds. They carried bold, hand-drawn messages like "CRANE = PAIN," "END THE WAR; END THE REPUBLIC," and "SOLDIERS, THINK FOR YOURSELVES," just to name a few of the generics.

The rally seemed to have structure and order. The chant, though not completely audible, seemed as though it was in unison. Any anger was bridled and channeled toward a common cause. It was a vibrant, grassroots demonstration, shrouded by the ominous presence on the other side of the barricades. The few Austin police officers originally on the scene had become accompanied by black fatigue-clad soldiers of the Republic. They proudly adorned menacing Kevlar helmets and assault rifles, a silent threat to anyone who may think of stepping out of line. Kyle knew what kind of soldiers these were. He knew the kind of ferocity that was building.

In an instant, the camera jumped erratically with a few unforeseen pops heard over anything else. Kyle's heart seemed to stop momentarily, his stomach twisting and bladder filling. The cameraman finally settled, finding the images of a section of crowd across the street from the capitol grounds. A section of metal barricade lay toppled forward in the direction of the Republican Guardsmen. Screams pierced the fall air, echoing off the downtown buildings and the trees on the capitol property. The crowd scattered in each to the left and right of the barricades that still remained. They had few options in direction, unable to move perpendicularly away from the barricades because of the buildings. It was a terror-stricken stampede of people bottlenecked into a small area, desperate to get away from the center of the confusion. The awards ceremony began to disperse in a panicked fashion while in seconds, the conditions deteriorated.

Angela gasped, covering her mouth to see that where the barricade had fallen, a few human bodies lay upon the asphalt and even on the barricade itself. They did not move as a thundering herd of the scattering protestors frequently obscured them, and even seemed to stomp over them. Then the cameras zoomed more to show the bodies lying still on the ground, their heads jerking sharply with each new set of feet that strode across them. Their limbs jumped and kicked as people trampled every inch of their bodies.

Soldiers shuffled backwards, their rifles raised and their eyes peering down the length of the barrels. They were in defense mode, the insurgence of people seeking another direction of escape from the crowded bottleneck between the barricade and the buildings enacted sleeping bits of training and conditioning in the troops. They had been standing at the battle lines, tensely waiting. And now the enemy was surging, sending survival instincts to the forefront of soldierly thinking. Trigger fingers became tightly pressed against the deadly slivers of steel and now adrenaline was filling their blood.

Kyle could hear a few more pops barking from the speakers next to the television, but now he could see the muzzle flashes. Fire erupted from the deadly openings of the soldiers' assault rifles. It was as if the gods were unleashing the punishing fury of the heavens upon these scared and fragile mortals. Bodies of students and other young demonstrators fell lifelessly to the pavement, their blood spilling onto the street in growing crimson pools. It followed the flow of gravity, resting briefly in the angled gutters below the sidewalk, and started for the storm drains further up at the corner.

"Cease fire," Kyle could hear someone order hastily after just a few seconds, which brought an end to the gunfire, but certainly not the screams or the confusion.

"Oh dear God," Angela sobbed. "Oh my God. That's horrible," she chanted.

Kyle just stared into the screen like he would be pulled in; transported to that place through his thoughts. He did not blink or cry. He did not frown or wince. There were no gasps from his mouth; no tears or ill feelings. His breaths somehow slowed and his heart rate was calm. In his right hand, his index finger and thumb still clutched the letter calling him to serve The Republic of America yet again. Organized emotion failed him. His sense of duty battled fiercely with his sense of identity and morality. But while his heart questioned, his eyes were fixed upon the blood in the streets, and he was at peace.

Chapter 11

"Damn it." President Crane stomped and paced around his office in the Austin, TX, State House.

He was unable to stop moving. Anger stirred in him, continuing to rev his heart rate and chill his skin as if he were in the throes of man-to-man combat. He paced about his cluttered office, his hands firmly planted upon the border between his suit pants and his stiffly starched white shirt. His head shook and jaw jutted forward feigning a nasty underbite while his bottom lip threatened to totally consume the upper one. His fair-skinned face was beginning to turn as red as the blood that was boiling within him.

Periodically, he stopped by the window overlooking the Capitol lawn below. He paused only a moment, but long enough to glare out over the scene of chaos that took place only an hour before. The crowds were long gone—protestors and spectators alike. Iron barricades, mostly standing, stood almost as a memorial. Remnant bits of trash were symbols of desolation, and even occupation. What remained and replaced them were the camouflaged servicemen they had all come to demonstrate against. They patrolled and loomed over the scene, keeping watch over the quiet, somber streets. They paced surrounding areas with full gear and rifles at the ready, as if they were occupying some enemy ground in a distant land.

"Can you believe this shit?" Crane ranted again, seeing that Zach Wallace, his chief of staff had entered the room. "Still can't believe those damned hippies ruined the ceremony. Who does that?" he blurted as he threw his hands up in the air. "Have they no respect? Serves their asses right," his said with his drawl becoming more apparent.

"I'm afraid this is going to be bigger than that, sir." Zack stood aback, withdrawn in the face of such an angered Commander-in-Chief.

"I know, I know." Crane calmed and closed his eyes. "It just pissed me off, you know?" He looked at Zach. "We were just honoring the bravery of our servicemen, and these yahoos . . ." He did not finish the sentence. He only glared back out the window.

"Something is changing in the Republic." Zach clutched his legal pads and his electronic tablet to his chest. "The people are fickle. They aren't the same unified, straight-party Republicans that flung up a middle finger at Cindy Chandler and the United States when we seceded."

Crane said nothing, only listened. His eyes were fixed upon the street and the troops outside. He was attentive to his chief of staff, though somehow distant and lost in his thoughts. He soaked them in, allowing more to come as Zach continued to speak, taking Crane's silence as a signal to continue.

"The latest polls are in." Zach tucked the tablet under the legal pad and rolled the front page back. "These were polls across the board—pretty much about everything. Approval ratings are down everywhere, and these were taken, of course, before today."

"For me or for the government in general?" Crane turned his attention to the young man.

"Both." Zach's eyes widened. "That's not to say you don't have supporters. There are some hard-core Republicans you'll never lose no matter what, but approval ratings for the government, the cause, the war with the U.S., and for you are all down. That protest out there is just the cherry on top of a big shit cake."

"So we're losing that unity," Crane nodded in thought.

"A bit," Zach affirmed. "I don't think we're beyond getting it back, though. What's hurting us is people tired of getting sons and fathers back in a pine box. And then there are the super conservatives that think we shouldn't be allying with the United States when we're still technically at war with them. So you're getting it from both ends. What may save us is a victory in Pakistan. That's the only positive thing we've found in the polls—people are unified throughout the Republic on one thing. That's justice for the Dallas blast."

"So we have to win in Pakistan," he repeated, again staring out the window and crossing his arms. "And I don't think we can do that without U.S. coalition forces."

"You're probably right, sir," Zach agreed. "And I don't think today's events helped us win sympathy in the U.S."

"What do you mean?" Crane snapped from his trance, and raised his voice. "You saw what happened. Those damned hippies from UT charged the barricades. They attacked our troops."

"I don't know how true that is, sir." Zach withdrew a bit, almost cowering behind his legal pad in preparation for what he was about to say. "This video has already popped up on the Internet." He started his tablet and walked over to allow his president to see. "Somebody in the crowd a while ago caught this footage on a camera phone."

"And it's already on the Internet?" Crane was surprised.

"Ten thousand hits in just the last hour," Zach replied, and started the video.

The shaky footage was digitally crisp, though the chants of the crowd and noise level overwhelmed the small microphone in the device. The sound shifted from peak decibels that distorted inaudibly to the following lows before ascending back to distortion. The footage darted around, the person holding the phone nudged lightly from side to side by the crammed, crowded conditions. The shot briefly diverted to the pavement and an array of shoed feet and then up to capture people near the metal barricade ahead and the nervous, tense troops on the other side.

The footage experienced two heavy jolts as the videographer lunged forward with the heavy pushing originating from behind. People near the barricade lost their footing and were rammed against the metal bars, sending them toppling forward with a surge of people involuntarily pushing forth. The footage showed a few helpless protestors lying face-down across the upset barricades and then darted upward to record a young soldier frantically falling back, his weapon shouldered, and the muzzle flashing with a couple of short bursts into the crowd. A couple of victims fell to the ground, accompanied by frenzied screams of the onlookers. As people scattered forward and to the side, the shot darted all over before finally cutting off amid the confusion.

"Oh dear Lord . . ." Crane buried his eyes beneath his thick, masculine fingers.

"Sir, this doesn't do a lot for winning hearts and minds," Zach commented, and put away his tablet. "Can't spin this. There's the smoking gun, so to speak." He cringed at what he said, too soon and in too poor of taste.

"See, I thought the protestors charged the line. But really it was an accident and a greenhorn young Guardsman with an itchy trigger finger. The soldiers next to him hear the shots, see the stampede, and they follow suit, firing into the crowd like they're being attacked."

"Exactly," Zach agreed, and paused as both contemplated the magnitude of the situation. "We're not going to win the wayward Republicans here in the twenty-nine, and we're certainly not going to gain any support across the border. All sympathy over Dallas—out the window. We need a unified front."

"Christ . . ." Crane became agitated. "This video is going to go viral. People are going to think we're oppressive. They're going to think we're intolerant of other people's political opinions."

"And it's already hit the media in New York," Zach dropped the worst bit of news yet. "I checked before I came in. With the wartime media ban lifted at the moment, this video is popping up all over the U.S. and the liberal media in New York is already broadcasting. They're calling it 'The Austin Massacre'."

"Oh sweet Jesus," Crane snapped his head back in disbelief, and paused for a few moments in thought. "Okay, you go and grab my press secretary. Do some damage control. Let the media know I'm preparing a statement. Have my press secretary put one together assuring that my administration does not condone this action and that the soldiers involved will be reprimanded."

"Will they?"

"Of course not, but we'll tell the media we are—we'll just ship 'em off to Pakistan and hopefully this goes away."

"Yes sir," Zach answered, and headed for the door.

"Let me know when the statement is ready, and I'll prepare to go before the cameras." He turned his gaze back to the window and the scene of the violence as the office door shut.

Chapter 12

Late September

Derek's mother's old station wagon screeched from roaring, illegal speeds to a rubber-burning halt along the cool, shaded concrete curb affront the airport. Derek, calm and in good spirits, glanced over at the nonchalant driver, his best friend Jake. Jake's overgrown stubble and curly, dirty-blond hair was ill-kept as usual. His gleaming white smile was permanently plastered across his face while he looked around at his passengers.

"First time riding with Jake?" Derek peeked over into the back seat at Carly.

Her eyes were wide and lips puckered as tight and tense as the rest of the muscles in her body. Her left hand appeared fused and bonded to the blue plastic armrest and handle of her door, while her other hand rested nervously across the body of her baby in the rear-facing child seat beside her.

"Jake?" she finally spoke, as she shifted her eyes to the driver. He smiled, sure of what was to come. "Would you mind terribly if I drove on the ride back?" she asked as the two men erupted into laughter.

"That's a good idea, Jake," Derek said in agreement. "I'd like for my daughter to live to see a day when she doesn't shit her pants."

"Jesus, you're lucky I didn't shit mine," she commented as they all continued laughing.

Everyone felt positive. They needed that, considering the circumstances. The laughter ran its course, as it tapered off to a stifled chuckle and then faded into a fleeting smile. Each of them stared at his or her own lap, out the window, or at the ceiling. They knew what was on the horizon, and they did not want that positivity and happiness to end. But it was, however, something to savor, so perhaps it was the right moment.

"Well, here we go," Derek uneasily broke the silence, pulling the shiny metal handle and cracking open the heavy station wagon door.

Everyone followed suit, opening their doors and stepping out while TSA parking Nazis eyed them menacingly. Jake and Carly slammed their doors and rounded the front and rear of the car while Derek circled back to open the hatch. He hoisted his olive drab duffel bag, stenciled with his surname, over his camouflaged shoulder and straightened his government-issued cap. He grinned uneasily at Carly as he closed the hatch and accompanied her up to the curb and dropped his bag to the concrete to pull her close.

"I'm gonna miss you, baby," she sighed, her voice muffled while she buried her face into his chest.

There was no answer. Her face lifted and her sad, glazed eyes followed his neck upward to his sympathetic, somber face. He said nothing. His posture was strong and masculine. He held her with his solid Marine arms, shielding and protecting her. He needed not say a word. His body said everything, and so did his eyes.

"I love you," he finally spoke, and then planted a massive kiss upon her lips.

"I love you, too," she replied as she caught sight of Jake as he approached in her periphery. She let go to allow them to say goodbye.

"Where's my hug and kiss?" Jake opened his arms as he crept forward.

"You can have a hug." Derek embraced his friend. "You have to wait until my coming home party for a kiss—a few drinks should do it," he laughed, and then released Jake. "Seriously, look after my family," Derek implored his best friend.

"Don't I always?" Jake smiled.

"Yeah, you do," Derek nodded. "Thank you."

"Don't mention it bro," he said. "Your family is my family."

That statement struck Derek like a bullet to the chest. He fought hard to hold back tears, and then glanced over to see that Carly was removing Olivia from her child seat, hoisting her from the back seat of the car and setting her finally on her hip. Derek smiled as he struggled with the ever threatening tears. Olivia glowed like the brightest summer morning with Carly thrusting her hip and the baby toward her daddy. Derek extended his hands for her, and for once, Olivia reached for him with her gaping, infantile smile burning across her face.

"Say bye-bye to your daddy, Olivia." Carly sniffled and wiped away a tear from her nose.

"Oh I love you so much, Olivia." Derek nuzzled his nose to her soft, cool cheek and then kissed it. "Daddy's gonna miss you."

"Da-da . . ." She grabbed his nose and smiled as she playfully studied his face. "Da-da," she said again before a tear ran down Derek's face and he handed his daughter back to her mother.

"I love you both, and I'll call you as soon as I can." He kissed Carly again, and then his Olivia before stepping back, grinning in a forced, sorrowful way, and heading for the entrance to the airport.

As he approached the glass and metal of the doors, Derek briefly cast one last glance over his shoulder to see Carly, his child, and his best friend Jake peering back at him. He turned his eyes forward again, and a multi-layered veil of sadness fell over him. The three looked so much like a family. I wonder if we look that much like a family when I'm with them. Hell, Olivia has spent more of her life around Jake than she has me. He hated to leave them. He wanted more time with Carly and Olivia. He wanted to get to know them. But it would have to wait. He pressed the metal latch release of the airport door and pushed it open. Suddenly, he was in soldier mode, ready for rank, chain of command, dirt, MREs, and gunfire. At that moment, he was at peace.

Chapter 13

The main parking lot of the Will Rogers Coliseum bustled, alive with vehicles and people. It was not uncommon for the nineteen-thirties art-deco event center. The coliseum held circuses, gun shows, and rodeos on nearly a weekly basis. The surrounding stables were host to the annual livestock show drawing crowds of thousands from all over the Dallas and Fort Worth area. The Depression era icon was nestled securely within the warmth of the cultural district, engulfed by museums, theatres, and some of the best local restaurants in Fort Worth.

On the air, Kyle could almost smell the permanent odor of livestock manure, even if it was indeed absent. He had been to Will Rogers many times, and it was just what he expected to smell while he was there. It was a phantom smell in the absence of actual dung. He scanned the parking lot. The scene was different. Though in camouflage, these people were not here for a hunting expo. Several large charter busses grumbled, filling the lot with the noxious fumes of exhaust. Soldiers of the Republic, clad in fatigues and toting duffel bags, held their fretting mothers. They kissed their tearful wives, most of whom had somehow convinced themselves their husbands were done with the business of serving and risking their lives. The men lifted their small children into their strong soldiers' arms and stole a few last hugs; enough to last them for perhaps months in the barren wastelands of Pakistan.

Kyle's booted foot nudged the thick, stuffed duffel bag on the pavement to his right. It gave resistance, heavy with clothing and belongings. His fingers fidgeted as he nibbled the inside of his lip, becoming ever more impatient. He lifted his head again, his eyes shifting from one end of the lot to the other, only to be disappointed again. His eyes, slotted and squinted from the glare of the bright September sun, turned from keen to disappointed and rounded.

"He's not coming," he admitted, as he pulled his lips inward and nodded with acceptance.

"Your father's been," Angela, Kyle's mother, paused, thinking before she chose her words wisely. "He's been under a lot of stress." She gave a slow exaggerated nod. "Work and such, you know?" she tried to explain as Ashley held to his hand and gripped it tighter to signify that she sympathized. "Trying to keep the firm afloat with all these unsure economic times—"

"That's bullshit, Mom," he blurted as an angrier tone infected his voice.

"Language, Kyle Jeffrey," Angela scolded.

"But it is, Mom," he defended. "I wouldn't have even joined the Republican Guard if it weren't for him. I'm shipping out half way across the world where I could easily get my ass shot up, and he can't even make it to the parking lot to see me off?" he fumed.

"I know, Son," Angela agreed. "I don't understand him anymore either. I haven't had a normal conversation with him in months. He's fanatical and angry. He's distant. He's gone a lot." She became sad as she spoke, something Kyle picked up on.

"Mom, are you and Dad having trouble?" His anger turned to soft-hearted worry for his mother.

"I don't know," she shook her head. "I'm hoping it's just some sort of midlife crisis that he'll grow out of or something." She seemed exhausted by the mere talk of it. "But don't worry yourself with this stuff. You worry about you for the time being." She reached forward and firmly patted his chest.

"Yeah, focus on getting back safe to us." Ashley gazed lovingly into his eyes, their hands clasped.

"Hey, hey, cowboy," a male voice boomed from nearby and blind-sided them all with a fury of masculine country drawl.

Two firm, coarse hands slapped both of Kyle's shoulders with the weight of blacksmiths' anvils. Kyle's survival instincts, jolted and shocked, sent him reflexively spinning around to face the unidentified foe, only to find a familiar, smiling face under the same camouflage that he himself bore. Without a word, Kyle closed his eyes for a moment, secretly regretting his initial instinctive defense preparation with a grin. Instead, all rage and aggression was channeled into a tight, manly hug with a dear friend and fellow soldier. It lasted several seconds, each glad to see the other, and then, finally, a release, accompanied by the warmth of friendship.

"Mom, Ashley, this is Dwayne . . . er . . . well . . . Okie," Kyle said. "He doesn't even answer to Dwayne anymore. You have to say 'Okie' to get his attention. Okie, this is my mom, Angela, and my girlfriend Ashley."

"A pleasure." He shook both of the women's hands, his black hair, tan skin, and white toothy smile gelling into his own brand of charm. "I've heard so much about both of you. Before the nuke, we had really nothin' to do all day up in Carrollton but talk. So I feel like I know you already."

"Okie, huh?" Angela prepared to age herself to the young man. "Okie from Muskogee?" She quoted the old song lyric from her Texas youth.

"Broken Arrow," he replied. "But close enough."

"Hey . . ." Kyle turned his attention away from his beloved women for a moment. His temperament changed, becoming more rugged. His voiced deepened and his chest puffed out. His body language became more choppy and forceful, something neither Angela nor Ashley had ever really seen in him. "Any word on where the hell we're going?" he asked his friend.

"Pakistan, I'm pretty sure," Okie grinned devilishly.

"No, douche bag." Kyle rolled his eyes. "I mean where are we shipping out of? Can't ship out of Houston. That's Blue territory."

Ashley watched as her beloved man took on a new persona. She had always known Kyle as a liberal black sheep in a very conservative world, something he had always described as hostile to change and difference. In the presence of a proud and conservative soldier of the Republic, her boyfriend almost seemed to immediately transition into a completely different personality. His voice took on a slight drawl and testosterone dominated his stance and demeanor. He spoke like the liberals were the enemy, though she knew he did not feel that way. Was it brotherhood? Was it the soldiers' mentality? Was it possible he was much more complex than she realized?

"Yeah, I was thinking it might be Corpus or somewhere like that," Okie said with more of a serious tone. "But word around the campfire is Cameron, Louisiana—down south of Lake Charles."

"No shit," Kyle shook his head. "I guess the Marines skipped Lake Charles for Houston, so that's the next logical, decent seaport. That or Galveston."

The conversation was rudely interrupted with the screech of a bullhorn as it was switched on and an old gunnery sergeant began squawking orders. The shrill, metallic voice was amplified and sharply echoed from cars to the walls of the stone museums all around.

"All right, men," the sergeant announced. "Time to finish up your goodbyes and load up! Stow your duffel bags in the luggage compartment on either side of your bus and begin filing in. Load up these busses, boys. Time to go off and kick a little Taliban ass." A small cheer surged from the crowd in the lot.

"That's our cue." Okie began to walk away. "It was nice meeting y'all. I'll keep this boy safe," he smiled with reassurance. "I'll save you a spot," he told Kyle before he joined the other soldiers in heading for the busses.

"I love you." Angela hugged her son tight and kissed his cheek. "You be safe and come back to us in one piece."

"I will, Mom." He hugged her one last time before he turned his attention to Ashley. "I love you."

"I love you, too." She kissed his lips passionately, her soft hands caressed his smooth, baby-like, blushed cheeks. "Please be careful, baby. I'm going to miss you soooo much."

She pulled close to him and felt his strong arms wrap around her in a tight and warm embrace. She loved feeling that. It felt safe and secure. It felt like true love. But alas, it had to end and his arms went slack. His lips again met with hers before he pushed away and backed up.

"I'll call the first chance I get, I promise," he said. "And I'll try to keep you updated as to where you can send mail. I love both of you." He turned and headed for the bus. The final image of them, set burned into memory, was their proud and loving faces. It was all he could ever really hope for, except for not having to board the bus. But like the others in the line of army ants, he filed upon the bus and joined the ranks of soldiers destined for combat in the name of revenge.

Chapter 14

October

"Anti-war demonstrations continue here in our nation's capital on the eve of war with Pakistan," the black-haired, olive-hued reporter plugged one ear and almost yelled into her microphone over the background protestors. "The White House announced yesterday that U.S. forces are finally, after nearly two weeks of positioning, ready to strike. No one knows how closely U.S. troops will be working with Republican Guardsmen, all too recent foes, and there seems to be no word from the Pentagon about that, though it does seem to weigh heavily on people's minds."

"It's frightening," a middle-aged woman stated as the shot cut to a previously-recorded street interview. "My son was fighting the Reds less than a year ago—helped conquer St. Louis. And now he might be fighting alongside them. I mean, who's to say some vengeful Red soldier doesn't kill my son and try to chalk it up as an accident?"

"Many others I talked to had similar fears," the journalist continued, the camera back on her. "But as you can see, the story of the day is the thousands of American soldiers on the brink of entering yet another war, and the U.S. citizens frankly unhappy with that." She pointed behind her at the picketing multitudes rallying along the Pennsylvania Avenue fences and the majestic White House in the background, its appearance golden in the afternoon sun.

The cameraman began zooming in on the crowds of angry demonstrators shouting slogans in defiance of the president's decisions and foreign policy. Picket signs were hoisted high above fuming heads bearing slogans like, "SLEEPING WITH THE ENEMY," "WRONG WAR," and "KEEP YOUR EYE ON THE BALL." Shouts and screams elevated as they saw the media attention. Signs shook overhead like the angry display of a weapon at war. The shot zoomed back out, again with the reporter in the frame as she continued.

"As you can see, quite a few people are unhappy with the decisions made here," she said. "Leaders here cite the uneasy alliance with a rebel nation and losing sight of the goal of true unification. Many feel that the U.S. government should leave the Republic to fight their own fight and that it is not our responsibility to retaliate for Dallas." She was interrupted by the shutting off of the television in the Oval Office.

"And what do you know, bitch?" Cindy Chandler threw the remote control onto the sofa as she stood and straightened the wrinkles in her skirt suit. "I'm getting sick of this negative press and all these people that think it's so easy to make these decisions," she vented to Sandra, her chief of staff.

"I know, I know," Sandra nodded, forever attached to her clipboard and her smart phone. "Everybody's an expert. For a general public that's so used to letting others think for them, you'd imagine they'd let their leaders do their job."

"This is such a shitty situation," Cindy sighed, and hung her head. "This kind of disunity is exactly what we don't need. It's why we're in this mess in the first place."

"At the same time . . ." Sandra chose her words and spoke slowly, as she searched through the murkiness of tact. "You can't force unity. The USSR tried that already. It didn't work out too well. We live in a country founded on the ability to speak out against your government if you disagree with its policies. We thrive on difference of opinion. You can't please everyone. Just do the best you can." She paused as they both silently reflected.

"Jesus," Chandler joked, "why aren't you president?" They both laughed. "Hey, at least I'm not catching the kind of heat Joe Crane is over the 'Austin Massacre.' If he's not careful, he's going to lose his country in a big way."

"Absolutely," Sandra agreed, and then segued into business at hand. "Let's get to the situation room, Madam President. General Bates wants to brief you on the plan of action before your conference with President Crane."

Sandra's suggestion prompted the president to begin moving for the door, stepping aside in an almost bowing motion to allow the regal stateswoman passage between her and the sofa. A nod said everything as Cindy walked with confidence, forged ahead, and opened the door to the Oval Office herself. Sandra, as usual, was no more than a few steps behind her, again on her smart phone to check the remainder of scheduled events for the day.

The two women moved about their royal court, commanding the environment and the mood with lifted chins, keen eyes, and blistering strides. Their heels moved with a glide over the red carpets as they lorded over the staff and interns. Upper-level members of the White House multitudes could not help but glance and glance again, yet continue their work without interruption. Cindy always smiled, however, as younger interns, without fail, stopped everything, their mouths gaping like a star-struck teen glimpsing an idol at the mall. And Cindy whipped by them with a nod, Sandra in tow.

Chandler, having traversed the busy West Wing halls and their bustling offices, arrived at the situation room door, pausing a moment to breathe deeply and adjust her collar. She used her index finger to push her light wire glasses back up the bridge of her nose where they belonged. The tightness gave her comfort. Her muscles loosened and the momentary strike of anxiety and doubt melted away. She released the tension as she turned the knob and pushed through unannounced. That was something she loved—being important enough to not have to knock, call ahead, or make a reservation at a restaurant. It emboldened her. She strutted into the situation room with a bounce and a smirk, her staff eyeing her with admiration.

"Hello, everyone." She started for her seat at the head of the long, dark wooden table around which everyone rose, while Sandra closed the door behind them. "Sit, sit," she motioned, palm downward as she occupied her seat.

She scanned the familiar figures around the table, all with their business faces on. Files, reports, and legal pads were positioned affront most of them, ready for the briefing. The aging General Bates and Vice President Coffman sat nearest to her, while Secretary of State Jessica DeLaune and Secretary of Defense Jay Shields remained further down the length of the table. She had spent the better part of two years entering this room with these people at least once per week, constantly requiring updates on rebel territory gained and casualties lost. She tired of it. She often wondered how something that had become so natural, comfortable, and common could feel so loathsome to her. She had come to dread entering the situation room. It was difficult at one moment to receive a report that half of the state of Tennessee had been conquered, but then be told it cost another three thousand casualties. These were young men and women who loved and were loved by someone, and now they were either dead, or would in some way never be the same again.

"Madam President," General Bates greeted his Commander-in-Chief in the usual deep, gruff voice, something that seemed to perfectly match his increasing wrinkles and gray balding head.

"General." She looked back, always at ease around him, even when he had bad news. She had grown to trust him. He was her greatest confidante, aside from her husband. "Do we have a finalized plan before my conference with President Douchebag in a little while?" She glanced toward the large screen at the other end of the room.

"We do," Bates replied confidently. "We just require your approval, and I'll start filtering it down the chain to the commanding officers getting ready for invasion."

"Fire away," she invited, and prepared to offer her undivided attention.

"Here are our forces." Bates picked up the remote control in front of him and switched on the screen to show a map of South Asia and some digital markings to note the position of U.S. forces. "They're all still here aboard ships in the Kutch-Bugten Gulf of India, some eighty miles or so from a little-known disputed border between India and Pakistan."

"Geez," Secretary of State DeLaune spoke up, "I thought they only disputed Kashmir."

"Indians and Pakistanis don't really agree on much," Shields interjected, allowing the general to continue.

"We finally, just a few hours ago, got permission from India to land near the coastal city of Mandvi," Bates went on, but was again cut short by DeLaune's information.

"That was pretty easy, by the way," she informed the president. "I know you had apprehensions about steaming the full invasion force all the way to India without confirmation, but the State Department was sure India would cooperate. They've been looking forward to this for decades."

"The opportunity to assist someone else kicking some Pakistani ass? Sure." Vice President Coffman chuckled, and leaned back comfortably in his chair.

"Continue, General." Chandler wanted to get back to the nuts and bolts of the plan.

"It's worth saying," he began again, before clearing his throat of phlegm left over from a nasty chest cold he had just recovered from, "that the navy is going to have little to no problem here." He used a laser pointer to emphasize points along the coast on the map they all looked toward. "Our troops and landing craft are in the gulf here, ready to go. But the rest of the navy is in blockade position along the coast of Pakistan. We have aircraft carriers here in case our troops need air support and we can also launch drones from these carriers. Pakistan doesn't have much of a navy, so I don't see much action here. We're there to cut off what little international trade they have—part of an overall plan to beat these guys by cutting off resources."

"What about an air force?" President Chandler asked. "Pakistan has an air force. Surely they will try to go after our troops and our ships."

"Correct," the general responded. "They will. And they are operating with American-made F-16s sold to the pre-Taliban government there. The aircraft we have are much more numerous and our pilots better-trained so I don't think we're going to have much of a problem here. I doubt most Taliban operatives have flight training of this caliber, although there may be a few former Pakistani pilots now willingly fighting for the Taliban. We plan on conducting some preliminary air strikes anyway. One objective is to destroy as many airfields and aircraft as we can."

"Okay . . ." Chandler paused, obviously thinking it over. "So blockade, air support, and troops landing in India. Go on," she urged.

"Yes, so we land here, and unload," he explained as he pointed to the Mandvi vicinity. "From there, we will run massive convoys of personnel, vehicles, weapons, supplies, and whatever else we need north along this five or six hundred mile border with Pakistan from the coast here to the Punjab region. This won't be hard militarily. We're not expecting to get a lot of resistance here. But because of distance and terrain issues, this might take up to a week to move everyone into position, set up several base camps along the border on the Indian side, and prep the troops for their missions. Everybody got it so far?" The general scanned around and searched faces for uncertainness and confusion.

"Okay," he continued, "the plan is to move in a simultaneous push across the border into Pakistan. For the troops crossing the border south of the Punjab region, this initial invasion will be a breeze. There isn't much out here in the Thar Desert, and I doubt Taliban is going to have anyone out there to greet us. But for these troops moving in through the Punjab region to the north toward the capital of Islamabad, it might get a little hairy. This is a much greener and milder climate, and it has plenty of water sources. For that reason, it's more heavily populated."

"Is it more heavily fortified?" Chandler asked, her chin resting upon the pedestal made by her propped arm.

"It used to be." The general fingered through a few files and looked up. "There were some Pakistani military bases up here—remember, this is the area where the hottest border disputes are between India and Pakistan. But since Taliban took over the capitol and government last year, things changed. The regular army seems to have been disbanded, I guess as an attempt to rid themselves of any loyalists. Surely, they have recruited some ex-army regulars who lean extremist, but try to remember that the Taliban doesn't wear uniforms or fight using conventional tactics. They wear plain clothes and blend into the population. That's how they infiltrated the capitol. They took it from within."

"So this is going to be difficult," Vice President Coffman threw in with grimness. "That's what you're saying. This is going to be real damned difficult."

"Yes, unfortunately." Bates returned the somber frown. "They are going to have to be sharp. That's why I think Marines and Rangers need to be deployed in these areas. They have had more rigorous training. And it's going to help, as much as I hate sending veterans back into the lions' den, that we'll have some experienced boots on the ground here."

"So what exactly is the objective, General?" Chandler sought the point.

"Conquer and occupy until Islamabad falls," Bates shrugged. "The capitol is way up here, nestled up next to these low mountains near Kashmir," he pointed with his laser. "It's further north from the accepted Indian border in the Punjab region, and there's a lot of populated, Taliban-filled ground to cover in between. In the meantime, major cities will be held and tightly policed. Further to the south, all along this green Indus River valley, troops will seize and do the same for the few small trading cities like Hyderabad and Khairpur. By doing this, we control the collecting and transporting of food grown in the valley up and down the river. We can basically starve out the Taliban especially further up, closer to Islamabad."

"War of attrition." Shields crossed his arms smugly as he quoted his high school lesson on the Civil War from years before.

"All wars are," Bates quickly added.

"One problem," DeLaune protested. "If you starve out the Taliban, don't you starve out regular people, too? Kids? Families?"

"Unfortunately, yes," Bates nodded, pausing for a moment to think before he continued to justify the position. "As was said earlier, the Taliban likes to blend into the crowd, so first, who knows who is Taliban or a local goat herder? Second . . ." He touched his right index finger to his left middle, and indicated another point in a list. "If we're serious about winning this thing, we have to do this right. War is hell. I'm not sending our people up there to be humanitarians. We have a job to do, and if we're going to do the Pakistan thing and do it with conventional warfare, this is how it's done. Besides, if you start starving out the oppressed masses, they might start turning against the Taliban and helping us out," he concluded.

"Lower morale," Shields commented again.

"So we choke off the food and supply lines," Chandler vocalized her personal review of the plan, "occupy the river valley, and inch our way up toward Islamabad." She stared into thin air for several moments, running over all of it in her head. Her chin bobbed up and down while her eyes remained fixed upon someone's pencil; just a random object that caught her attention. "Fine," she broke her silence. "But one question—where does the Republican Guard fall into this plan? Sounds like we're taking charge when really we're supposed to be simply assisting the Republic in this invasion."

"You're right, Madam President," Bates said. "We are kind of taking the lead. That's only because we haven't been able to plan in conjunction with the Republic's military leaders. So we planned it like we were going in alone, and hopefully their plan is along these lines."

"Okay," Cindy said. "I'll hash that out with President Thumb-dick." She motioned to the screen. "If this is it," her eyes implored a nodding General Bates, "go ahead and get Crane's people on the phone and see if he's ready to chat."

The room began bustling as her staff and cabinet members began talking amongst themselves about whatever. Cindy sat, the only one not talking to anyone. She looked about the room at mixed emotions and expressions. Hands flailed around, accenting speech for emphasis. No one talked to her. She frowned, but remained silent, wondering why no one wanted to talk to her. A few IT staffers moved about, making sure the connections were right and ensuring the camera was in place so that Crane would see Chandler alone.

"Ready, Madam President?" a young male staffer asked as she confirmed, and then clicked the appropriate button, initializing the conference call to Austin.

Her stomach quivered for a moment. It always did anytime she spoke to the President of the Republic or was around him. She hated that. It made her feel weak; sucked back into a world of aproned housewives kissing their husbands off to work and spending the day dusting and cooking. Normal thoughts and conversations about Joe Crane gave her no anxiety. She was not intimidated by him or the idea of him. But for some quirky reason, a conversation with him gave her a momentary instance of panic.

As the digital tone rang, mimicking a telephone but more pleasant to listen to, Cindy prepared herself. She wiped away worry and anxiety, straightened her clothes and posture. She was as a football player sitting alone in the locker room before the game. She narrowed her awareness of sensory things, unable to hear any low, droning conversation in the room. Her vision focused primarily on the screen ahead of her, tunneling to exclude all others. An unofficial and unorganized mantra flowed through her thoughts—incoherent jumbles of confidence and defiance of gender roles. And then the screen changed, and Crane's perfect hair dominated the picture, followed by his snaky grin and slick greeting.

"Hello, Madam President," Crane spoke, the sound not quite perfectly matching the movement of his lips.

"Hello back," she smiled with confidence, and took on almost a manly posture. "It's good to finally get in touch with you, being that we're on the eve of a joint invasion," she snarked.

"Yes, well," he maneuvered. "It's been busy on my end."

"Surely." She grinned in a way that sugar might cover garbage. "I'm assuming your forces are in place and ready?"

"They are. In fact, my commanders say that we're in position in that . . . gulf." He obviously either forgot the name or had no idea how to pronounce it. "Within sight of some of your ships. Seventy-five thousand troops to start with."

"Splendid." She entered business mode. "And I'm assuming you have a plan of action. We haven't seen anything from you, so we've had to plan as if we were going this alone. Really, we would have loved to have planned together, but I guess that time has passed."

"Again, we've been busy with this whole thing," he deflected. "But yes, we do have a plan to land and enter from the Indian side. We will do a strike that covers the length of the Indus River, and head to Islamabad. We just don't yet have permission from India. They don't yet recognize our sovereignty."

"That's pretty much our plan to a T," she nodded. "And we have procured India's blessing. I can agree with their lack of recognition of your country's sovereignty, but I'm sure it will be okay if you tag along," she jabbed smilingly.

"Wonderful," he grinned, resisting her attempts to cause him to lose his cool. He paused for a few moments, peering silently at her from his desk in Austin. "Are we going to discuss the eight hundred pound gorilla?" he finally asked.

"What is this gorilla's name?" She folded her hands and laid them on the table before her.

"His name is 'U.S. troops were just murdering Republican Guardsmen in the streets of their own sovereign nation a few months ago and now they're suddenly allies,'" he spouted cleverly.

"Mr. Crane . . ." Her eyes almost glowed red and she growled a little as she bit her upper lip. "Unless you want me to pull my entire commitment to this cause, you will retract that ridiculous piece of propaganda and rephrase the statement. My men and women are not murderers and your country is not sovereign in our eyes," she fumed.

"My apologies," he said, slightly taken aback. "I retract. But that doesn't change the fact that Republic and U.S. troops, just a few months ago, were killing each other in the streets. I think it's best to keep our respective forces at a distance from each other."

"I agree," Chandler was quick to respond. "There may be some bitterness, although I can't imagine why . . ." She rolled her eyes. "It appears we have roughly the same plan and objective. We move across the Indian/Pakistani border simultaneously and go for the capitol."

"So I think what we can do is coordinate locations of command centers," he nodded. "And then coordinate which cities and towns along the river are Republic or U.S. objectives. From there, we could easily move on Islamabad in a two-prong attack."

"We can take the east and you can swing around from the west," Chandler interrupted.

"Fair enough, but this is primarily our fight," he fired back. "We lead the charge, and the kill shot in Islamabad is ours."

"Deal," she agreed. "Let's set up a conference like this between General Bates of the Joint Chiefs and your top commander for later today. The two of them can talk about the logistics."

"Sounds good," he said. "I'll make it happen. If there's nothing else, I have some other things to attend to."

"Nope. Until next time." She nodded and then the video feed was killed. She buried her weary face into both palms for a moment or two, and then emerged with laden eyes and stress. "This is going to be a fucking fiasco. Can't we just destroy their whole military while we're there? Surprise attack? Just get this shit over with?"

"Not advisable," Bates discouraged. "Believe it or not, they're likely looking for that. Expect them to be on their guard. Besides, Taliban is the common enemy to both of us. They do not discriminate. They likely had that Dallas blast planned long before there was a Republic of America. They hate all of us. So there's nothing stopping them from hitting Milwaukee or Boston. We have to take the Taliban out of power in this nuclear country."

"If we start fighting each other right there in Pakistan," Shields added, "that gives Taliban the upper hand. It's the same distraction that allowed them to get a nuke onto American soil in the first place."

"Point taken," she conceded. "We'll deal with that in due time. General Bates, keep some planning simmering for when this Pakistan thing is over."

"Yes, ma'am. Two steps ahead of you."

Chapter 15

The seas were calm enough. Skies were clear and wind was at a minimum and made for an ideal day for an amphibious landing. Still, the landing craft's bow was rising with the high-speed sliding across the Kutch-Bugten Gulf waters and periodically dipping back down to produce a light spray of salty water that misted over tan camouflage fatigues, helmets, and assault rifles. It was humid and warm, though not particularly close to the equator. Moisture was still rising from the Indian Ocean and filling the air with a sticky quality that made comfort something that one could only dream of.

Derek felt cramped, as if he could somehow feel the collective body heat of his brothers and sisters in arms through the air whipping past his body. Most, he could tell, were veterans of the fighting back stateside. They, like him, were strangely calm. The muzzles of their weapons were steady. Their faces were not flush. No silent prayers of protection for their bodies and souls were uttered. They were focused; sharp. The new recruits that had never seen combat, especially an amphibious landing, displayed all of those signs of anxiety and near panic. But they were few, at least on Derek's boat.

The high metal sides of the landing craft, a slightly more technologically advanced version of the ones used at Normandy in 1945, always made it hard to see what was happening on the outside. It never failed to churn and twist Derek's stomach. Though not every landing he had been a part of was that deadly, he always thought back to his first at the airfield on Mobile Bay. Sharp, vivid images of shells exploding in the waters surrounding his craft raced across his thoughts. Memories of fellow Marines and bullets passing through their bodies clung to him like parasites. They would receive no resistance on the beaches outside of Mandvi. Still, the brisk air currents, the smell and spray of salt water, and the growl of the landing craft's engines caused him to tense and grip his weapon, ready to defend his life with the sum of all the rage in his heart.

What the hell is wrong with me? He began to grapple with a sudden epiphany—something he was surprised to have never thought of before. This was comfortable. It was almost exhilarating. He felt at ease and even excited to be on this craft surrounded by cold metal and deadly weapons. He could not wait to hit that beach head and begin moving inland. He almost fantasized about the first major engagement. He eagerly awaited his chance to see if he'd lost his touch. Amid mental preparing for combat, thoughts of Carly entered his mind. He thought of how she and Olivia were doing back home. He could picture her packing his baby upon her hip, moving about the kitchen to prepare something for Olivia to eat. Anxiety washed over him as he thought of that environment. He pushed it from his thoughts, and went back into combat mode.

He felt the throttle ease back as the landing craft slowed to a crawl. The bow dipped back into the water and they were now more at the will of the gently-swelling waves. They rocked, slightly rose, and fell again with sounds of lapping and swishing. The exhaust fumes from the massive inboard engines were now able to envelop the boat and fill the nostrils of the soldiers, sharing the smell of the sea. They crept forward in their approach with no need to hastily hit the beach and begin fighting.

"This is going to be cake, boys and girls," Derek yelled out to his multi-gendered platoon, proudly feeling the loftiness of his sergeant stripes. "But when we hit that beachhead, and this ramp comes down, you file out like the whole Republican Seventh Guard is right on the other side. You file out like you mean it. We will convene at the top of the beachhead and wait for the gear to hit. At that point, we will assist in the offloading of equipment before preparing to head inland."

"I know the Reds are going to be landing, too, sir," a private spoke up. "Are we going to have to deal with them?"

"Let's hope so," Jay "Queens" Daigle shouted out with a chuckle in his heavy New York dialect.

"I wish," Derek smiled back at Queens, one of his closest comrades from the gulf coastal invasions back home. "Maybe when we get home. But here, we have to behave ourselves!" he still shouted over the boat's engine. "The Reds are scared we're gonna take care of unfinished business, so they're landing about thirty-seven clicks to the east at a place called Mundra. You won't have to deal with those sons of bitches, hopefully the whole time we're here."

"We might not get shot at today," Queens added. "But don't expect a party welcoming us in."

"That's right," Derek confirmed to his troops. "Be on the lookout for Taliban sympathizers. This is far western India—close to the Pakistani border. It's enough of a concern that the Indian military has apparently sent a small security force down here to make sure we don't get any trouble out of the locals, which I don't anticipate anyway. But stay away from them and they'll stay away from you. Don't give yourself any reason so have to kill anybody before we cross the border. Everybody get me?"

"Yes sir," the soldiers chanted, and then went back to chatting amongst themselves.

A young private stood silently swaying toward the front of the landing craft. Most of her fellow soldiers faced forward, transfixed upon the ramp ahead. Some chatted about menial things or about what units they previously were with and where they had fought or trained. Private Kendra Voss was transfixed upon Derek Putnam. Her face was expressionless, or perhaps with blank wonder beneath the heavy Kevlar helmet strapped to her head. Her greenish-blue eyes were stuck to him like he was some sort of idol for all to view.

"What's his story?" Kendra asked the Marine next to her. "You know anything about him?"

"Who? Derek Putnam?" Alex Jasper grinned, struck by the humor of the enamored young woman. "Yeah, I know him. I know him very well," he said. "We've been friends since Camp Lejune . . . before the war even started."

"Well then you must know something about him," Kendra pressed. "I heard he charged the guns on the Mobile airstrip by himself."

"You don't say." Alex burst with laughter. "I don't know about all that, but he was definitely there. He painted the target so the airstrike could blow in and take out the airstrip gun emplacements. Him and Queens over there were at the strip together. I was across the bay at Daphne." He stopped there, Kendra left imploring for more.

"Well?" her eyes widened. "What else?"

"He was at New Orleans," Alex continued with reluctance. "We served there and at Baton Rouge together. Hell, he carried my wounded ass off the field in Baton Rouge—saved my life. Um . . ." he thought. "Houston, the I-35 crawl, and then Dallas—"

"Dallas?" Her jaw dropped. "He saw all that action and then survived the nuke?"

"Even got wounded," Alex nodded. "Shit, that was only a few months ago, and here he is." He paused for a moment, looked down, and became slightly more serious. "Look, don't go to him like this is all a big deal. He hates that put-me-on-a-pedestal crap. If you ask him, he's just doing what he's supposed to do. The reality of it is, though . . . he's the finest soldier the Marines could ever ask for. He's tough, he's smart, and he's a born leader. He is one bad-ass Marine."

"Yes he is." She looked him up and down with hunger in her eyes.

"Don't get a lot of bright ideas, Private," Alex advised. "He has a girlfriend at home—mother of his child."

Her mind remained unthwarted, and she was about to rebut with something feisty, but she was derailed. The landing craft jolted to a halt, sending her, unprepared and unsteady, backward into a sturdy fellow soldier. He gave only a brief, smirking glance back at her as she regained her posture, and at that moment, the ramp screamed and ground down along its tracks, plunging into the shallow water and digging into the sand. Suddenly, soldiers filed out ahead of her and the eager masses behind pushed her to escape the craft and splash into the warm waters.

She shifted to combat mode, all other thoughts far away. Her head checked from left to right. She could see hundreds of landing craft lining the beach unleashing thousands of soldiers onto the course, heavy sands. She had never seen such a thing. She had been in the presence of thousands of soldiers before, but never in this type of setting. She burst with pride, a joyful smile on her face as she took in the sights. Down the shore in the distance, slightly inland from the sand, she could see a strange clump of wood surrounded by wooden scaffolding. Her eyebrows tightened and her eyes narrowed in an attempt to improve her view and determine what it was.

"It's a ship being built," Derek's voice came from nowhere. "They have a thriving ship-building industry here." He walked up next to her and watched her tremble with his movement closer. "Now get your ass up that beachhead," he ordered as she snapped back into combat mode, held her helmet tight atop her head, and ran up the beach to the rendezvous point. Derek just shook his head as the timid young private scurried away with the rest of his platoon.

Chapter 16

"Ever think about doing that for a living?" Sarah grinned as she watched her sister Carly slip the red and black jumble over Olivia's little body.

Carly wrangled and wrestled with the frilly puff of red and black tulle cut into long strips and sewn to a black elastic band. She slid the band down over her child, letting it rest around her mid torso before taking hold of two longer black strips and tying them in a bow around the back of her neck. She teased and puffed out the tutu-dress covered in little black dots and plastic ladybugs, and then crowned her little head with a black headband made into a set of black velvet antennae.

"There." Carly soaked in the cuteness. "There's my little ladybug," she marveled for a moment, and then finally acknowledged her sister's question. "What, this?"

"Yeah." Sarah took another sip of energy concoction from the tall aluminum can. "Hell, I should have had you do my kids' costumes." She peeked over into the living room at her four-year-old daughter and six-year-old son, who had somehow regressed into infancy with the discovery of Olivia's toys on the living room floor. "Aubrey would have loved to dress up in this little tutu costume thingy you've made here." She took a strand of her niece's tulle in her hand and allowed the length of it to slip gently from her fingers. "Braeden, of course, is going to be a Jedi for Halloween. So much like his father," she sneered. "Jesse's a Star Wars freak—can't even give up that gaudy-ass Millennium Falcon replica in our living room. So Braeden becomes his Jedi pupil."

"Oh, how funny," Carly laughed. "Nah, I don't know about doing this for a living. You should have told me, and I would have made something for Aubrey. It's too late now. Halloween is tomorrow night."

"I didn't know you had this talent," Sarah gaped. "Seriously. I would have hit you up. I had to settle for those crappy ones at the store. You seriously could run a business like this out of your house," she continued, watching Carly continue to fiddle with the costume.

"You think?" Carly grinned with skepticisim. "I don't know . . ."

"Oh yes," Sarah nodded, gushing on. "You just wait and see how many people you bring your daughter around to, whoring her out for your own candy needs, love this costume. Moms who love their kids and what they look like will go nuts over this stuff. They get tired of the cheap-ass costumes in the stores. This is yuppie stuff. People will pay top dollar, especially since the economy's doing better and people are finally going back to work."

"Maybe." Carly blushed a little, never really thinking of this as more than a hobby.

"Oh yeah," Sarah continued. "Jesse could help out with your website—domain names and hosting are cheap—and you could just do this out of your house. Surely you have plenty of time on your hands, especially with Derek overseas."

"I don't know . . . maybe." Carly's ears perked up as she heard the dull rumble and screeching brakes of the mail truck outside. "Will you get the mail real quick while I pull this costume off of Olivia?"

"Yeah." She turned for the door leading out from the kitchen, squeaking the floorboards with each step.

The door closed, which always seemed to threaten to bring the whole kitchen down around her. Carly directed her attention back to her innocent daughter, untying the bow and tugging on the elastic band. She glanced over at the television as scenes flashed from the news program out over the ill-illuminated living room. She kept it on, as wars were now broadcast in real-time. She somehow kept hoping to get a glimpse of her

Derek on the news. The children flickered in the light of serious things, yet oblivious to the negative goings-on in the world. A corner of her mouth rose with the beginnings of a smile. She envied them. They could ignore all that was wrong with the world, and even see through that to find the hidden jewels. Even her own Olivia was too young to really miss her daddy. If he were to be killed in action, she almost hoped it would be now so her daughter would not have to deal with the grief in this stage of life.

"And as troops are surely moving into position to attack Taliban-held Pakistan, back here at home, unrest is mounting as protests have popped up all over the loyal twenty-one," the pompous, aging anchor read. "But are we really in that bad of shape? New information today sheds new light on the Republic's social and financial problems. Joining us today are our chief economic correspondent, Al Delmonico, and personal financial guru Dana Russell," he continued as Carly peered over her shoulder, trying to imagine what could be taking her sister so long in simply getting the mail. "So what do you think? Do we really have it that bad?"

"Well first, to be fair, even with protests all over, as you say, something like sixty percent of U.S. citizens still are okay with assisting the Republic in invading Pakistan, mainly because they still view Dallas as one of their own cities, and they want justice." Al smiled, a bright decoration to accompany his shiny, completely bald head. "But yes, we are in a much better situation than the media is making us out to be in. First, let's look at the facts." His hands seemed to do the talking, animating him more fully. "We are no longer in a recession. Our GDP has grown by leaps and bounds since President Chandler took office."

"Hasn't the war done that for us just as it did with World War II and The Great Depression?" the anchor inquired.

"To some degree," Al responded. "But think about what happened to bring us out of the depression then. The government needed things for the war effort, and so manufacturing ramped up, and people got jobs. People went to work. Then they spent that money on groceries and things. Stores hired, and more people got jobs. Money was flowing through the system. It was like a defibrillator to the economy's chest. But back then, everything was manufactured in the U.S. By contrast, Afghanistan and Iraq some years back did not do the same. The government spent money, and so much of it and the manufacturing jobs went overseas. That could have been our situation with our civil war and now this action in Pakistan, but Chandler really made a brilliant stand in pushing through resolutions to only allow the government to buy American-made goods. Essentially, that has brought back our manufacturing base."

"And the jobs . . . oh the jobs," Dana shouted dramatically, looking to the heavens. "Before, we were at an unemployment rate of over eleven percent. Now we're down to five in record time! So many Americans are back to work. They're not relying as heavily on credit cards and are finally showing some signs of getting out of their mounds of debt. It's really an exciting time."

"You mentioned The Great Depression, Al," the anchor further examined. "Do you think Chandler has been almost Rooseveltian in the legislation she's pushed and dealing with such political upheaval and war? This resolution for the government to only buy American, removing many of the tax loopholes that hurt the government's revenue stream, revamping the tax code to favor the middle class over the richest five percent, cutting corporate welfare, cutting fossil fuel subsidies . . . the list goes on. These are bold steps."

"And they're working," Al chimed in with his usual gleaming smile. "The deficit has turned into a surplus, the debt is projected to fall by five trillion over the next ten years, unemployment is falling, the government is putting its investments into greener energy and infrastructure— it's drastic. And that's where we come to the Republic. They've got this thing all wrong. Finally, they have the opportunity, these conservatives, to put their money where their mouth is, and they're failing."

"Failing big," Dana interjected. "Their people must be miserable. Sure, taxes are low—their lawmakers insist that next-to-nothing tax rates solves all their problems, and maybe it gives the average Joe more money to spend and helps create jobs, but their government is being so cavalier with spending and debt, it cancels that out."

"That's right," Al added. "The Republican dollar is already weak in its infancy, and backed by, as far as anyone can tell, no gold whatsoever—so it's all confidence-based. But with the low tax rates for individuals and corporations alike digging into their government's budget, they are left with massive foreign borrowing and simply printing more money. The value of the currency goes down, and prices go up. So while their people have money to spend, it's taking an increasingly high amount of it just to live. Econ 101."

"And they simply can't come off this tax cuts thing," the anchor shook his head. "Their government needs revenue, but they refuse to tax the oil produced in Louisiana and Texas or really anyone who makes any money in the Republic."

"And really, they could have more jobs and an even larger workforce paying income taxes," Dana added, "if they would manufacture for the war effort right there in their borders, but most of that goes to China and Taiwan. And most of the other major corporations still operating in Atlanta, Fort Worth, and Houston are banks and service industries. Shaky stuff when it comes down to it."

"So is it any wonder people are upset down there?" The anchor started to read through some statistics off of the laptop before him on the desk. "Forty-three percent of people in the Republic support rejoining the U.S. They not only have protests, they have riots. And this American Reunification Army keeps setting off bombs and such. It really seems like the whole thing is coming unraveled."

The door swung open into the outdated kitchen, the squeal of the hinges drew Carly's attention from the droning of political analysts. She had no real interest in "why." Statistics and the inner-workings of economics were not her focus. What interested her was what the government was going to do for the wellbeing of the common person, and especially she was interested in where her Derek was going to be and how safe. The talking heads became a mumble as her attention shifted to her preoccupied older sister entering the kitchen clutching a small stack of mail in one hand and her work phone in the other. The light from the screen lit her face and sparkled in her eyes. She was transfixed, moving slow and blind into the kitchen.

"Jesus, what took you so long?" Carly leered at her sister as she hoisted little Olivia to her hip. "You only went to get the mail."

"Huh?" Sarah finally broke from her trance. "Oh, sorry. My work phone dinged. I got this e-mail from this dumb bitch I work with. I swear she's been getting by with people doing everything for her all her life. She just uses her bubbly demeanor," she batted her eyes mockingly. "And that cute little figure . . . makes me sick. She doesn't know how to do anything."

"My mail?" Carly blew off the usual corporate workplace rant.

"Oh, yeah." She handed it over. "Here you go."

"Thanks." Carly rolled her eyes and began flipping through the bills and junk mail. "Holy shit! Why didn't you tell me there was a letter from Derek?" she exclaimed, sending a splatter of shock and surprise across Sarah's face, but no words.

She recognized the sloppy, almost illegible handwriting that was unmistakably Derek's. It was as if a fourth-grader had addressed the envelope, yet in this moment, it was the most beautiful thing she had seen all day. Waves of irregular heartbeats fluttered in her chest as her skin felt as though she had been wrapped in a heated blanket. A smile raised her cheeks into her eye sockets and her thin, feminine fingers fumbled to turn the envelope over to see that the letter had already been opened once and then taped back over.

"Has that already been opened?" Sarah moved closer to her sister to peek over her shoulder with a level of concern.

"Standard procedure," Carly shrugged as she tore off the tape and removed the letter. "The military people have opened and read every letter I've ever gotten from Derek. I've gotten a couple with lines blacked out for security reasons. Derek basically gave too much information about where he was and what he was doing."

Though the paper appeared somewhat normal, with no signs of unusual wear or any black permanent marker ink soaking through to the back side, it seemed as though it had been through a lot. Perhaps it was her mind attaching some kind of personified dismay to it. She knew where it had come from, and maybe even a sense of what Derek had been seeing or doing when he wrote it. She imagined bombs exploding around him on some battlefield as he sat and wrote, though she knew that would never have been the scenario. Then he would sign his name with a smile and a kiss, folding the pages and placing them carefully into the dingy, dirty envelope. He would then pick up his gun and strap the Kevlar helmet to his head, and begin fighting as he did best. That letter would then trek across Pakistan, end up on a military transport plane, and fly half-way across the world, only to be ripped open by people at the Pentagon and then sent on to her mailbox. But it was likely only the most mundane events of that imagined sequence really happened. It was nice, though, to think of her husband-to-be in that heroic state. She grinned and then read.

Dear Carly,

We made it here safely. Seas were a little rough, though. Lots of guys got seasick with all the rocking back and forth, so the bunk rooms now have this sort of permanent smell like your bathroom has when you have the flu. That took some getting used to. But we're here and finally unloaded. That took forever—a lot longer than we were told at briefing. It feels great being back in the saddle, only this time it's weird because I'm heading up a platoon of my own. They all answer to me, which is taking some getting used to, but I'm managing. I've got a lot of good Marines with me, so I'm happy. Many of the people I served with before are back in my squad, though we have lost some. They've been replaced with these kids that don't have a clue what they are doing. But it's good to have guys like Alex and Queens back with me. I haven't been in the field with Alex since the Battle of Baton Rouge about a year ago.

The people here are strange, but I guess that's to be expected. They have a different lifestyle, which comes with a whole different set of habits, customs, and smells. Every night, I can smell people's cooking. It drifts in from just outside of camp. It smells nasty. Thank God for MREs. I'm glad they're not making us eat this local shit. And they're not friendly—well, most of them. They're mostly Muslims, persecuted by Hindu Indians all the time. They kind of seem like they have a chip on their shoulders. They definitely don't like us here in their town, and they don't like us, period, I think. I think they're sympathizers with Pakistani Taliban—well, not all of them, but a lot, you can tell. We'll be out of their hair soon, though. I hear we're pushing out tomorrow. I can't tell you where, but I can almost surely tell you it's north. I don't know how easy it will be to get letters from you, but please try. It would be great to hear from you and maybe a new picture of Olivia? I'll write again when I get a chance (I don't know when that will be). Give Jake a hug and Olivia a great big kiss for me. And for you, kisses in all the right places! I love you!

Derek

Carly smiled warmly, blushed a soft mauve color as she pulled the letter to her chest, and stared off into nothing. Then she looked lovingly at her darling daughter and laid the letter on the counter. She picked up Olivia and gave her the big kiss willed by her father as she gurgled. Sarah grinned without a word, seeing her happiness with this life, and that ejected any fears she had for her sister.

Chapter 17

November

Zach had never seen General Dale Weaver loosen his posture, even now in this black luxury SUV. It was the best that money could buy—hand-selected for only the upper echelon of the Republic's military and diplomatic cream. The leather bucket seats were quite comfortable, making it very easy to relax. Zach drove the massive vehicle like it was his own, occasionally fiddling with the air conditioning and the radio, something he suspected had begun to irritate the coarse general. Admiral Denton Haskell was Weaver's naval equivalent, he too clad in all his colorful and shiny decorations, and even he was taking advantage of the plush comfort, lounging wide-kneed in the back. Still, Weaver could not bring himself to shed the formality or his stern face.

The SUV see-sawed back and forth from each of its four corners, bouncing with the occasional crater in the dirt-and-gravel road. A peacock's plume of light tan dust trailed the vehicle like a central Texas comet blazing through the vast rolling hills over thousands of acres of land only accented by small patches of trees, especially mesquite. Clusters of prickly pear cacti grew in patches along the ditch and by the rocks up on the low ridges. Black Angus cows grazed lazily up on the distant hill of a pasture. For those from the teeming metropolises claimed by the state of Texas, it was a potent reminder of how untamed and untapped the Texas (and Republic) countryside was.

"How long have we been on the road?" the admiral whined from the back seat as would a child on a road trip.

"Almost an hour and a half," Zach smiled, taking in these sights, something he always enjoyed about driving in Texas. "We're almost there. Don't worry."

"Who takes a vacation during an invasion of a sovereign country?" Haskell muttered after a few more minutes.

"The Commander-in-Chief does," Weaver's gruff, deep military voice shattered the air inside the SUV. "The Commander-in-Chief can do whatever the hell he wants."

Haskell felt reprimanded. Though he was technically a peer in rank, Weaver outranked him in the since that he was President Crane's top military advisor, a title that trumped all others in the hierarchy of the Republican armed forces. Haskell pouted, returning his gaze to open spaces that he was growing tired of.

"I get it," Zach offered in an attempt to smooth out the tension. "He's had a lot on his plate. It's got to be stressful when you're juggling falling approval ratings, losing whole states to the U.S., and a new invasion of Pakistan. Hell, that will send a sane person to the loony bin. I'm grateful he's just on vacation." He glanced over to see that Weaver was still emotionless. It was tense again. He had failed to lighten the mood or spark comfortable conversation. Several dreadful minutes passed until something caught Zach's eye. "Ah, here it is." He pointed to the right side of the road.

Zach removed his foot from the gas and lightly applied the brake, slowing to cautiously approach the two Republican Guardsmen and their Humvee parked at the entrance to the ranch. It was almost a gaudy monument, completely out of place here. Wire fences and their steel posts ran on for miles in either direction, but converged at this giant iron gate linking two pillars of natural Texas stone, mortared finely together as a solid mosaic of an entrance. Zach approached cautiously, slowing to a gentle stop before the two young soldiers tightly clutching their rifles. He had seen enough instances of nervousness and trigger-happiness in these young troops to fear for his life.

"Can I help you?" The pale, freckled soldier approached in full fatigues and helmet, his heavy drawl accompanying the unique Texas breeze. He peered in at Zach with almost menacing, gung-ho eyes, a twinge of a prayer for the excuse to blow this SUV away at any moment.

"Zach Wallace," he replied, leaning outward a bit, but not as much as to startle the soldier. "I'm the president's chief of staff." He tugged at the lanyard around his neck and lifted an identification badge to show the guardsman. "We're here to see President Crane."

"For what?" the soldier mocked, his voice dripped with military attitude.

"Soldier, open the fucking gate," Weaver shouted from the other side of the cab.

"Who's that?" The guardsman, backed by his counterpart, squinted his eyes and tried to look deeper into the vehicle, but in vain with the glare of the brutal Texas sun.

"That would be General Dale Weaver, private," Zach smirked as the soldier finally was able to make out the face in the passenger seat.

"General Weaver." His face looked panicked as he and his fellow guard snapped to attention, the stocks of their rifles to the dusty ground and a stiff salute whipping to their brows. "Sorry, sir."

"It's all right, private," Weaver finally loosened. "You boys are doing a great job. Can't be too careful these days," he told the young man. "But I really do need you to open that gate."

"Yes sir," he nodded, as the other soldier raced over to the callbox and keypad and began typing numbers.

After a few electronic tones, out-of-place in this environment, the guardsman had finished typing in the combination and the gate began to retract with a hum of the motor accented by the occasional squeak of the metal gears on metal gears. Zach shifted back into drive and moved the SUV past the stone pillars. Slowly, they snaked down the winding dirt road past a lonesome hardwood tree of some sort. To the left, a pond, littered with fallen branches inhabited by turtles sunning themselves in the fleeting heat, sprawled before a patch of woods above on the ridge. The vehicle continued up the road, rising to the crest of a dusty hill until they at last could see the ranch house below, nestled among a fenced-in riding yard, a corrugated metal shed, and a stable.

The black SUV skidded to a stop in the gravel, followed by the tan cloud catching up to them just as they all began stepping out onto the running boards, and then the ground. The general and admiral looked about, taking in smells and sights. They removed the stiff officers' caps from under their arms and placed them squarely upon their heads, still squinting from the glare. Zach's polarized sunglasses gleamed with a bright circle on each lens, warding the harmful rays away from his tender eyes.

"Officer on deck," a distant cry was heard, and then a small detachment of men lazily assembled beneath the shed was spotted, scurrying to their feet and saluting at attention. They were dressed down, Weaver and the officials could see, as they walked around the back of the house toward the riding yard. A Humvee was parked under the shade of the metal building. Smoke and the smell of smoldering charcoal coursed on the air. Beer bottles cluttered up the wooden picnic table near the grill.

"As you were." Weaver smiled with unease at the men and their unorthodox behavior, something he would never allow under his direct command. They must have known that. They went back to their activities, but with newfound dullness since Weaver arrived. Laughter no longer burst from their mouths. They sat in silence, sipping their beers and tending to the grill.

"Today's their barbecue day," the men heard after a short gallop. "They get to grill and drink beer once a week. Of course, it's only their second, and well, last time," President Crane called from up on his thoroughbred before flinging his booted right foot around the rear and stepping off of the stirrup. "Thank you boys for coming all the way out here to chat me up and update me." He handed the reins to his Mexican ranch hand, who led the animal off. "I know it's far. That's why we can't video conference or talk on the phone. I purposely don't have an Internet connection and cell phones don't work that well out here. It's my refuge." He tipped up his cream-colored cowboy hat.

"Our pleasure, sir," Zach said with enthusiasm, and gripped Crane's hand for a genuine cowboy handshake. "It's great to finally get to see . . ." He paused to look around with bewilderment in realizing that he had never heard Crane mention the name of the place.

"Eagle's Nest Ranch," Crane filled in as he opened the small gate to step out of the riding yard. "You boys come on into the house." He led them around front toward the screen porch. "Allie's got some biscuits baking for the boys to have with their barbecue out there, and I'm sure we can scare up a beer or a drink if you like."

"Thank you, sir," Weaver replied, following his leader up the slight incline toward the house.

Crane stepped up onto the first, and then the second worn, wooden step and yanked forth the screen door to produce the ever-expected tingling, stretching sound of the spring that would soon snap the door back shut. He entered the porch, holding the flimsy door open for the General. Each paid forward the favor to the one behind until all four men had plunged themselves into the cool, breezy shade of the screened porch. Zach was a city boy, quite unaccustomed to sights like old, rusted saws and farm tools, mingled with dry, lifeless deer antlers hanging on the wood paneled outer walls.

He was equally unnerved with the interior. It was dimly lit, most of the light coming from the kitchen where Allie tended the baking. The smell of biscuits swirled in the thick, warm air. Full-head mounts of whitetail deer hung on the walls along with that of a few rams, a wild boar, and a mounted wood duck in flight. Preserved deer hides were draped over the backs of the couches and a rather impressive glass-door gun cabinet in the corner held the hunting arsenal that made all of the décor possible.

"Nice place." Zach looked around with unease as the men circled the coffee table.

"Thank you," Crane nodded, his eyes canvassing the walls while he sat back in his favorite leather easy chair. "My granddad built this place back in the forties. He started out with twenty acres he bought at auction with his GI Bill money and within a decade had the full twenty-one hundred and forty-five acres it is today," he touted proudly. "Allie," he called to his wife with a slight raise of his voice.

"Yes, dear?" She stepped in wearing her apron.

"You remember General Weaver and Admiral Haskell." He motioned toward the two officers.

"Yes," she acknowledged as her bright red lips curled upward into a big Texas grin. "How are you gentlemen?" she greeted as they each half stood to gently take her hand.

"And this is my chief of staff, Zach Wallace," he motioned again.

"Pleased to meet you." She extended her hand in the same way.

"We've actually met." Zach took her hand with a polite smile. "It was the state dinner about a month or so ago."

"Oh yes, of course," she said with widening eyes, though Zach got the feeling that she had no memory of him, and why would she?

"Would you gentlemen like anything to drink?" she offered. "We have some beer, scotch, bourbon, iced tea," she listed. "I could brew some coffee if you like."

"Oh, don't go through any trouble with the coffee," Weaver said. "I'll have a scotch and water."

"Nothing for me, thank you," the Admiral declined.

"Just an iced tea is fine," Zach replied.

"And a beer for me, babe," Crane said as she scurried off to the kitchen and began making drinks. "So what do we have, gentlemen?" He leaned back in the easy chair. "Troops in place yet?"

"Almost," Weaver confirmed. "We're spread from the coast all the way up through Punjab. Right now, we're setting up command posts before we get ready to push west into Pakistan."

"Any trouble? Snags?" Crane implored as his wife fluttered in with drinks for everyone and disappeared in a flash.

"All has been smooth," Weaver replied, leaning forward at first, and then took a sip of his scotch before reclining. "Our boys have barely seen any U.S. personnel. No fights or skirmishes. They're all staying pretty far away from one another."

"Good." Crane seemed relieved. "That one was worrying me. We need positive news to give our citizens."

"And it's going to be." Zach sipped his iced tea, and then set in on a coaster before him. "This is still our rally issue—vengeance for the Dallas bombing. The people are still, for the most part, on board for us to kick some ass over there. Hell, they'd really rather see us fighting Pakistanis than fellow Americans anyway."

"You got that right," Haskell spoke up. "People are just kind of getting tired of war, I think."

"I know," Crane nodded, staring blankly into the top of his brown beer bottle. "But we have to push on." He lifted his eyes. "And when we're done in Pakistan, we still have things to work out here. Hopefully, things go swiftly in Pakistan so we can get back to that." He eyed his chief advisor.

"I don't know, sir," Weaver answered the implied question. "We don't really know what difficulties to expect in Pakistan. And then after that, we'll have to occupy the country for a while and make sure Taliban doesn't make a comeback and take over the government again. I don't know how quickly we can get the full force of troops back here. Then there's recruitment and re-upping contracts to worry about—people getting tired of fighting . . ." He seemed weary about it all.

"It's going to be all right," Crane stopped him there. "At least we know the U.S. is going to have an occupying force there too, and have the same issues."

"But not the money issues," Zack spoke boldly, hushing eyes thrown from the military men.

The commanders slunk back in their rustic leather cushions unsure of what reaction there may be. The air was still—no movement, nor sound, except for light clanging and typical kitchen noises produced by Mrs. Crane. The president rocked back, his beer resting on his knee. The young man's words had mass. They struck Crane physically, dumbfounding a man who usually knew just what to say. At first, there was but a sigh from him, and an expression of contemplation.

"Yeah," he finally spoke, and then paused for another few moments, shaking his head a bit. "Countless sleepless nights . . . I have no idea how to make that work. We've barely started our new country, and . . . the debt . . . the inflation." He tripped on his words, at a loss.

"War ain't cheap," Weaver slouched. "Sure, we started with, and still have, a great economic base, but when you're forced into war from the get-go, before you really get on your feet, it's hard not to devaluate your currency and go into debt." He tried to reassure the president with the truth.

"That doesn't change the fact, though," Crane raised his voice with frustration. "That doesn't make me feel better. We have to figure out a way to reduce our deficits."

"Raise taxes," Zack suggested with a shrug. "At least for the wealthiest."

"Are you out of your damned mind?" Crane narrowed his eyes. "That's the kind of thing we seceded over—unfair tax practices. Punishing success of the rich. That ain't the American way! I simply won't raise taxes . . . for anyone."

"Then you have to cut," Zack replied. "You either have to make it up with revenue or do some serious cutting, and the biggest thing we spend on is the military. And I know that's not what we're going to do."

The men sat there for a few moments, silently kneading the heavy notions in their minds. This was a difficult issue. It baffled Ivy League economists, and these men were nothing close to that. Yet it was up to politicians—lawyers, fortune heirs, and real estate developers—to save their country's economy.

"Remember the Reagan years?" Crane finally spoke. "The early eighties when he pulled the U.S. out of a recession."

"Voodoo economics?" Weaver puzzled.

"Yeah, didn't lowering taxes bring us out of a recession?" Crane speculated and repeated what the party had always claimed, but really unsure of the facts.

"Not really," the well-read chief of staff politely corrected. "Technology and innovation helped bring us out of a recession. And sure, lowering taxes helped—gave people extra money to burn. It gave cash flow to the system and created jobs. We're dealing with massive inflation—people have little buying power with their wages. Businesses are failing. People are getting laid off. And we have mounting government debt and spending. Reaganomics might have helped with a recession, but contrary to popular belief, it didn't help raise government revenue. We went from surplus to massive deficit by his second term."

"So what then?" Crane threw up his hands in frustration.

"If you're dead-set against raising taxes, you've got to cut some things," Zach leveled.

Tension returned, and with it the tense silence. The military commanders said nothing. This was not their area. They had not studied the economy at some prestigious university. Little of this was understood by two men who had as average of an understanding of the economy as any common American. They had spent their lives protecting the nation and trying to stamp out terrorist groups that threatened American security and peace of mind. Their contribution would remain in the way of helping to win battles and kill enemies. Crane, however, had begun curling his lower lip over the top one and scratching his chin with his thumb. He was thinking and young Zach Weaver was wide-eyed in anticipation of his response.

"Then that's what we have to do," he said. "Tighten our belt. That's what the average family would do in a financial crisis."

"No, they'd probably just run up the credit card," Zach blurted before he could stop it, but Crane's mind was elsewhere.

"Get together my economic team," Crane ordered Zach, who had retrieved his smart phone from his jacket pocket and begun to type in a note. "Tell them I want them to figure out what we can start cutting and be ready to present to me by the end of next week."

"Yes sir," Zach nodded, and placed the phone back into its rightful place.

"If that's all . . ." Crane stood up. "Follow me and we'll see if those boys out there have a few extra steaks."

Chapter 18

The hot wind on Kyle's face had a sharpened nature to it, as though it had been honed purposely for maximum discomfort. It was not even refreshing in this desolate, arid environment. Sweat seeped from every pore in his body's attempt to keep him cool in conjunction with the wind, but it was no use.

His baby-smooth face and naturally rosy-cheeked complexion was slathered with sun block. The Irish in his DNA needed a bit of help in the unrelenting sun. His Republican Guard-issued polarized sport sunglasses helped, casting a slightly gray shadow over the endless tan around him. A scowl formed on his face. These aren't the ones I would have chosen. He felt they made him look too much like an insect or a jock, two things he had never been. But they protected his eyes. And the helmet did the same for his head. But for all the keeping of his shorn-headed scalp from evil UV rays, sweat poured in waterfalls from beneath the protective material, mixing with sun block to fill his eyes with a bitter stinging unrivalled by chopped onions.

He let go of the fifty cal mounted atop the Humvee's weapons plat-form, and lifted his sunglasses a bit to wipe his eyes and forehead. He readjusted the glasses and his helmet and began to again take in the sights. The barrel of his automatic fifty cal extended out from him into the wild like some dreadful appendage. It was as some death-making third arm; cold, metallic, and nightmarish. It was lifeless and odd sur-rounded by the warm and organic, yet it commanded and lorded over the surrounding beauty.

Kyle had never really been in a desert. Fort Worth was his hometown, and though he had been all over the eastern United States even in his youth, he had never been much farther west than his home. The Thar Desert they had been crossing all morning was and was not what he was expecting at the same time. They had crested dune after wind-blown yellow dune since crossing over the Indian-Pakistani border. That, he had expected, based on every wind-swept, camel-crossed desert he had ever seen in a movie or a book. What was unexpected was the vegetation. Slow, rolling waves of sand were patched and dotted with various clumps of grasses, small trees, and shrubs. It was some sort of unorthodox grassland coexisting with a classic, sandy-duned, typical desert. To Kyle, it was like seeing a sandy, tropical beach in Antarctica or a polar bear in New Mexico. He enjoyed it. It was the most unique place he had ever witnessed.

And as it turned out, it was quite difficult to cross. There were no real roads to go by, only sandy terrain dotted with inconvenient shrubs and brush, none of which was problematic for the four-wheel-drive, hard-bottomed Humvee he poked his upper torso out of now. It was likely that the tank battalions, with their heavy-duty treads, were chewing up the ground as well, but the other vehicles Kyle could see mingled among the Humvees in the invasion force struggled a bit more. The personnel trucks, especially, were having a tough time. The distance between the Indian border and their first objective at the eastern edge of the Indus River valley was only about sixty miles, but they had been moving across this desert the better part of the morning and were probably, by Kyle's mind, only about halfway there. They moved with the speed of the blitzkrieg for a bit, and then the entire invasion force would have to stop because a truck had gotten stuck in the sand, or there was sand getting into the transmission. Everything had to stop while the engineers and mechanics came out to remedy the problem.

They were way behind schedule, not that Kyle really minded. He was not looking forward to firing this rifle in anger or taking a human life. He was not yet prepared for facing mortality again. Bullets whizzing by his head were a thought that he tried to keep far from his mind. He was enjoying the delay. He relished the time spent popped out of the top of the Humvee, enjoying the scenery, the warmth, and the nasty piece of weaponry he wielded. Chatter and banter rumbled between his friend Okie and the other few guys below. Laughter and testosterone were pungent in that Humvee, no doubt. They were, as a group, coping with their position—as men. Kyle was doing the same alone, towering about the desert like a god.

They were moving swiftly. It had been several minutes since the last bog-down. Kyle could see no enemy, or any people at all for that matter. That was in the briefing. This portion of the Thar Desert was sparsely-populated; a few small villages here and there. Surprisingly, certain fall-harvested crops were grown in the region, but he had seen no fields. A few miles back, he had seen a distant village beyond the other scores of military vehicles to his right. But at that distance, he saw no indication of bustling, and no one stopped to disturb it. They had been told that the way to the objective would be a piece of cake. There was likely not going to be a struggle for every yard of dusty ground. The enemy would pool its resources in securing the most important towns and cities in the fertile Indus Valley.

The vehicles around his began to slow. Unbelievable. This is going to take all day, he half chuckled. He scanned the area as his Humvee rolled to a stop and watched the others do the same. At first, he paid no attention to what was ahead; only the other trucks and Humvees. But something caught his eye, somewhat nearby his own vehicle and to the right.

Three camels stood gangly and awkward before the convoy, stopped and exuding iconic completion of what the men in this Republican Guard battalion expected to see in the deserts of southeastern Pakistan. But they were not wild or alone. Bags hung from the camels' sides, full of whatever. Colorful blankets were draped over the humps and reins drooped from their mouths, held securely by a rider for each of them.

Typical off-white and brown flowing garments fluttered in the wind. Head wrappings were wound around each head, leaving only small slits for dark eyes and a bit of caramel skin to peer through.

All military vehicles had stopped, and for a long while there was movement from neither American, nor from Pakistani. Nothing was uttered. Nothing was gestured—just staring. Behind Kyle, a sound was made. He pivoted to see the door of a Humvee further back open and a rifle-wielding soldier emerge alone. He trudged across the loose, moving sand below his feet. His gait was shaky, but his look certain. Kyle noted the soldier's tan complexion. Ah, an interpreter, Kyle realized. Surely he's going up there to tell these guys to kindly get the hell out of the way.

He sat and watched as the interpreter approached the men on camelback, stopped, and began speaking to them. He could hear the voices, but unclearly. Of course, that was of little consequence since Kyle could barely speak crude Spanish after two years of it in high school, much less some Pakistani language. But he watched gestures on either side, and after a few minutes, there was frustration on the face and the swinging hand of the interpreter. A lieutenant had emerged from some vehicle, outside of what he was paying attention to.

"What's the problem?" Kyle could hear the lieutenant yell. "You tell him to move his ass yet?"

"I can't talk to this guy," the interpreter yelled back, flustered. "I only speak Urdu, the national language."

"Well wouldn't they speak it, seeing as they live in this country?" the lieutenant rationalized.

"Apparently not, sir. He seems to only speak some rural dialect of Sindhi, I think," the interpreter replied. "I can't understand this guy. I can make out a few things, but it's not enough, sir."

The lieutenant looked at the interpreter, and then at the men on the camels who were frozen in the sand, and perhaps a bit overwhelmed and frightened by the unexpected encounter. The lieutenant's arms began to wave, erratically and exaggeratedly for the men to move, but to no avail.

"You know, I've seen this shit back home in Arizona," the lieutenant said. "Goddamned Mexicans do the same thing to get out of shit. They pretend not to speak English so they can get away with whatever. I bet these sons of bitches understand Urdu. They're faking it."

At that moment, Kyle was startled by the sudden rattle of gunfire. To his right, he saw the muzzle of a fifty cal like his flash and burn with its frightful brilliance. The sound was loud and unmistakable; piercing. It echoed like thunder in a cloudless sky. Kyle watched three seemingly civilian traders or farmers dismantled piece by piece in a gory show of brutality. They and their camels were cut down mercilessly by another young man atop his Humvee. And in a few short seconds, there lie only a bloody mess in the sand. It was like a horror film, its accompanying score the laughter and cheering of men all over the convoy, including within his own vehicle. Disgust gnarled his face and penetrated his gut. He was nearly nauseated as he watched the smiling lieutenant and interpreter move gaily back to their vehicles and signal for the convoy to continue.

Humvees and trucks shifted into gear, and there was a chain of clicks like an entire army locking and loading assault rifles, and cocking them to prepare for action. The familiarity of exhaust fumes rose with the desert convection as big, off-road tires began to slowly roll. The breeze picked up on Kyle's face, his Humvee moving forward with the pack. He looked off to his right, catching sight of the pile of flesh frying on the hot desert sand. The lifeless clumps of slaughtered animal and flowing robes were drenched in crimson blood. It spilled about them on the sand, flowing from gaping body cavities torn apart from fifty caliber bullets.

He took his eyes off of it. He could feel his stomach churn as he tried to ward off any nausea by clenching his eyelids and mouth shut as tightly as possible. That image, like others he had seen back in the Battle of Dallas, was there permanently. Now he could only hope that he would see more atrocities to numb him of it. He could not get nauseated like this every time he saw a dead body. He could hear the laughing below. Sickness became anger, but he held his tongue. Nothing he could have said would have made much of a difference. There were no other sympathetic bleeding hearts here. There were no TV cameras covering their advance. No one would find out, or even care back home. And so those three men would lie there until the scavenger birds and wild dogs pick their bones, and their families would likely never find out why they never returned home.

The parade of monstrous military beasts continued on, pushing through the sands and brush of the Thar. No more stops were made to gun down farmers on camelback or to spin wheels helplessly in the sand. They droned and growled ahead with blood-thirsty vengeance and a fury that Kyle could feel in his bones. It was the same feeling, he knew, that most of the other men were experiencing, too. They had Dallas on their minds; revenge in their trigger fingers. Kyle was prepared to ring justice to the wicked and punish the Taliban, but there was conflicting emotion. The images of the three men on camels perpetuated. The thoughts of their families and loved ones remained. Do I really want to kill anyone else? he asked himself.

Then, perhaps, he would have no choice. A distant, but crushing boom sounded in the distance. Kyle perked his eyes, suddenly in target acquisition mode, and he could see short, stuccoed buildings near on the horizon. They had reached Umerkot, the first objective on the eastern edge of the Indus River Valley. All hopes for a relatively peaceful city invasion bitterly faded with sand erupting in dreadful yellow geysers ahead and amongst the vehicles. Each thunderous boom in the distance came with a corresponding burst of sand around them. Kyle's heart began to race. He searched for someone to fire back at, clutching the handles of his fifty cal rifle. There was nothing; no one to shoot at. The cannon fire was distant—way back deep in the down, likely. It was like a beach invasion. They experienced fire from afar, but simply had to endure until they were close enough to engage the enemy. Kyle felt helpless as he looked about himself on either side to see the occasional Humvee flung twisting and hurdling in the air, and fall dead and aflame, digging into the dust. Personnel trucks met the same fate, leaping upward or halted in their tracks as men were launched about in pieces. Those surviving the initial blast were sometimes flung into the path of other vehicles and run over.

Kyle could feel that churning in his stomach again. It sickened him, but anger soon overpowered it. He was beginning to find that familiar mindset that he had experienced back in Carrollton, Texas, when he first saw U.S. troops crossing the desolate interstate and descending upon his position. He remembered that feeling of being shot at for the first time. He was again experiencing that flushness of face and tightening of muscles. His teeth clenched and grip noosed the rifle's handles. Rage cancelled all other emotion or compassion for man, and he was ready to kill.

Endless sand became civilization, first with a few small homes and buildings lying outward from the city, lonely and ostracized. Clusters of houses and sheds behind short walls huddled near small plantations of some kind. And as they neared the city's edges, the cannon fire ceased. They were too close. Yet small explosions in the sand and steel continued, but Kyle could finally see the culprits. Men in various local civilian robes crouched beside homes and walls. There were no muzzle flashes or firing noises—these were mortar squads. He grinned, finally having someone to target. He gripped the fifty cal, swinging it to the right as the Humvee continued to barrel along, and squeezed the trigger. Frightening and surprising rounds burst from his muzzle in a deadly display of might. He clenched one eye shut as he loosed his modern-day arrows and watched as brick and stucco popped in bits from the building's walls and ended with two dead men beside their mortar tube.

A rare menacing smile gaped across his face, somehow happy that he had just taken two men's lives. He watched as other mortar squads met similar fates along homes at the edge of the city. He joined them again, sending shattering fifty caliber bullets to easily break the stronghold's second line of defense.

Kyle's Humvee was still moving and the mortar fire had stopped. They no longer could be of use. The Republican Guard was beginning to percolate into the city. It had become urban warfare. The terrible, explosive power of mortar shells faded to a sound almost of microwave popcorn popping. Muzzle flashes could be seen where the city met the desert, a deadly shoreline awaiting the troops. The olive drab-painted ammunition box mounted to the left of Kyle's rifle shook violently with his rapid fire and the massive bullets being fed into his weapon from within. Small clouds of dust popped up from the unpaved streets and enemy defenders fell into the grit under heavy barrage from the approaching Humvees. Abrams tanks moved up along the Humvees, helping to spearhead the assault as troops filed out of the personnel trucks and behind the cover of their mobile artillery.

"What now?" he heard the driver of his Humvee ask as the vehicle slowed at the edge of the city.

"We get out, and follow along behind you, you dumbass!" Okie exclaimed, his drawl somehow more prominent than ever. "Jesus, didn't you pay attention in briefin'?" He and the other soldiers began to climb out with their rifles. "Just keep movin'. Rendezvous is the old fort on the other side of town," he finally said, and closed the door behind him.

"You better be a good shot, Perkins," the driver called up at him. "I'm a sitting friggin' duck up here." And the Humvee started moving at a much more steady pace, entering town carefully.

Enemy fire had slowed. Eerie silences contrasted with the commotion of the assault before. An occasional pop or two was heard, usually responded to with another burst of rifle fire. It was ghostly and still. The crunch of the Humvee's tires and boots could be heard in the gritty street. Kyle saw no civilians, not that he would be able to tell. The men he had shot a minute ago were not in some army-issued uniform, carrying standard infantry gear. They looked like anyone else in this area, only with assault rifles.

The Humvees crept down the street, ever aware of their surroundings. Kyle clutched his menacing weapon with anticipation. He was careful not to move his head too quickly, somehow ridiculously convinced that it would unsettle the air or make some sort of sharp sound to alert the enemy and send a barrage of fire. But what made the infantrymen on the ground trailing his Humvee so nervous was the lack of cover. There were a few doorway recesses along the street. Occasionally, there would be a narrow alleyway between otherwise connected houses and shops. But there were very few cars parked along the streets. That would be better cover. It was surprising how little motorized transportation this seemingly thriving old city had.

A few pops pierced the silence, echoing from wall to stuccoed wall with a strange and horrifying reverberation that nearly vibrated the hot desert air. Kyle could feel his fifty cal rattle with a ricocheted bullet off the protective metal plate attached to it. He instinctively ducked partially back into the Humvee like a frightened prairie dog, and popped back up, ready to target the source and protect himself and his driver. But as he swiveled the mighty rifle and scanned for someone to shoot, muzzle flashes multiplied, deadly daytime fireflies twinkling from ahead in the major three-way intersection.

"Shit," Kyle yelled, and began unleashing a hail of high-caliber volleys into the enemy defenses.

Kyle's surroundings clinked and sparked. He could feel the terrifying vibrations with every enemy bullet that hit his Humvee—bullets he knew were meant for him. He continued to plunge rounds into the intersection until his ammunition box was empty. He released the trigger and frantically began removing the empty metal box from its position mounted on the side. Below him, he reached and then hoisted up another hefty box of rounds. He fed the chain into the receiver and again cocked, looking about him to see how his men fared. He came, at that moment, to a realization that he was the most important man on the street. In the mere seconds it took for him to reload, fellow soldiers to each side of him on the ground were being hit. He watched in horror as a man next to Okie took two rounds to the chest, spraying thick red spatters onto the Humvee and men around him.

As the man fell to the dust, Kyle's brows lowered and his lips clenched in rage as he reached for the grenade launcher trigger and loosed an explosive projectile into the intersection. Dust and brick erupted into the air as it destroyed anything and everyone in the immediate vicinity. Still, the enemy fired from within the safe confines of homes and buildings on the other side of the intersection.

Kyle yelled out, "Somebody blow apart those walls. Get in there. I can't tear 'em up myself."

Cold ran over Kyle's hot, sweating face as he was again affirmed as the one man responsible for his unit's success. He again took aim and began firing a rapidly-moving set of unending fifty caliber bullets into the walls separating his men from the enemy. The large projectiles chewed the brick into bits as he attempted to poke holes in the enemy cover and allow his men to assault the position. But he was beginning to feel hopeless. Bullets continued to ricochet around him. Men fell to the ground in pools of human essence. His head was jolted, snapping back rapidly and leaving him dazed. The street blurred for a moment and he was disoriented. He had stopped firing and was wobbling from side to side, unsure for an instant where he was. And when he had returned to normal, the feelings of futility also returned until a building across the intersection exploded into bits of clay and plaster. Several more explosions followed and a smile formed on Kyle's face.

"Abrams," Kyle heard Okie shout from below. "Abrams tanks one street over. Cool, let's move."

Kyle was still a bit disoriented, his head bobbling around. What had happened? He reached up and felt around on his helmet, knowing something was amiss, and found a nick in the Kevlar. The bullet had not penetrated the material, nor was it even a direct hit. From what Kyle could feel, it seemed to have caught his helmet at an angle in the upper left side, and deflected off. Jesus. Lucky break.

"Come on. Move it." Okie's voice snapped Kyle out of his trance.

"Yeah, let's go." Kyle slapped the roof of the Humvee. "Intersection's clear." He ducked into the interior of the vehicle to see the driver slumped over in the seat. A few holes in the windshield and blood spatter all over the dashboard were all he needed to see. He stood up, emerging again from the hole in the roof. "He's dead," Kyle announced with disappointment in himself.

Okie cursed under his breath and peered back up at Kyle. "Dude, it's not your fault." He looked around, trying to figure out what to do, and realized there was but one option that no one else was volunteering for. He circled around the Humvee, opened the driver door, and pushed the unfortunate soldier unceremoniously from his bloody seat. "All right, here we go." He put it in gear and the convoy began to move again. "Almost half way to the rendezvous point, so keep your eyes peeled."

Again, it was quiet. There was no traffic on the street. Now and then, a door would open with gunfire, and the Guardsmen would cut the man down, rush into the building, and clear it of any other enemy defenders. That was the good thing about having no element of surprise. Everyone in the city knew the attack was taking place. It kept the civilians inside. Only those with a mind to die for God and cause would risk it with an assault. It was easier to discern between friend and foe. Even that, though, was lighter than he had expected. He assumed resistance would be heavy at the first line of defense. On the other hand, however, Umerkot was not the primary objective of this prong of the invasion. Hyderabad, across the fertile river valley, was the real target.

Gunfire erupted ahead, and Kyle was back into kill mode. He pointed his heavy rifle again down the street across a main intersection where men on the street and in windows fired at the advancing troops. He took aim and fired fifty caliber bullets that cut through men and walls behind them. There were many, though—much more than in the previous skirmish. He just kept firing, as did the men on the ground, Okie defenseless in the driver seat the only thing on his mind.

"The fort's right there." Okie hopped out with his rifle, and fell back around the back of the Humvee for cover. "I can see the walls." He took a few shots as Kyle again changed the ammunition box. "We're almost there."

"That's why the defense is heavier," Kyle commented. "Last line. I bet their big cannons—the ones that were pounding us when we rode in—are right back there. Problem is we're bottlenecked in this street, and they have men feeding in from either direction. And they have plenty of cover."

"I wish everybody would catch up," Okie yelled, still firing. "Most streets converge here. Once everyone else moves up these streets, it will all come down on those boys."

The fighting continued with fire blazing from muzzles on either side of the intersection. Men fell and blood spilled. Shell casings were piling around Kyle's feet. He kept shuffling his feet, kicking them around, but now and again, he would step on a few, roll, and lose his balance. He would have to release his trigger and grab the roof of the Humvee to brace himself. He regained his footing, took hold of the gun and peered forward, only to be stunned with a horrifying sight.

"RPG!" he screamed, and opened fire.

Everyone seemed to take aim at that one defender. Everything about him was terrifying—the bulbous projectile at head level, the kneeling down, the malevolent expression on his face. The most frightening thing to Kyle was knowing there was but one target in sight for the man—the

Humvee with the fifty cal. The defender was struck with bullets, though it was impossible to tell who got him. He loosed the RPG as he fell lifeless, sending it whizzing in a trail of sparks and smoke just over Kyle's head. It flew to the rear, well past any Republic soldiers and exploded somewhere, probably into the home of some innocent civilians taking cover.

Finally, the gunfire seemed to amplify from all directions. Other teams were moving down the other streets, applying greater pressure to the heavily-defended intersection. The enemy weakened. Fewer shots were fired. Fewer robed men were seen, and then all shots died. Okie opened the door and hopped back into his bloody driver's seat, shifting into drive pushing forward. They crossed the intersection, piled with corpses. It was impossible to move forward without running over a few. Kyle cringed a bit as he felt the vehicle bounce on its shocks like they were crossing a speed bump. The sound of bones cracking and tissue squishing made him nauseated.

As they drove forward with no more resistance, a sense of relief and pride washed over Kyle and the rest of the men. The Humvee moved a bit faster and less cautious. The foot soldiers trotted with confidence and smiles. It was a victory lap for all teams—all Humvees, tanks, and men that entered the old fort to take possession of the city.

Kyle ducked into the Humvee as it came to a stop, and jumped out to shake hands with Okie in a masculine, jerking fashion. Their dusty faces mixed with sweat to form a thin mud coating. Their white teeth shined in contrast. Kyle turned to face the city they had just plowed through, patting his friend on the back. It was wet. He looked to see blood on his hand and all over Okie's back. He knew who it belonged to. His smile turned to a sour frown and he looked back at the city. He heard more gunfire, knowing that a second and third wave was moving in to secure all major intersections and ensure possession of Umerkot. They had not killed all defenders. They were popping out of windows and doorways, killing unsuspecting Americans who thought the fight was over. Still, the position was won, and the guns would be silenced soon, but at the cost of how many lives? Kyle frowned and thought. What in the hell am I doing here?

Chapter 19

"Reports are coming in from correspondents in India and Pakistan this morning that while America slept, her armed forces and that of tens of thousands more Republican Guardsmen began their first strike at Taliban-controlled Pakistan." The news anchor finessed the words with skill that came from years of experience. "Reporters were not allowed among the first waves of troops that crossed the Thar Desert or Punjab region due to safety reasons, but soon we will have live reports on this massive unilateral invasion that has been so controversial here in the United States."

Cindy Chandler sipped her coffee carefully as she watched the newscast with her husband on the plush, pristine sofa of the Oval Office. She was always nervous about eating or drinking anything in the office, especially on this furniture. She was sure that if she did spill something on the sofa or the carpet, the government could deploy some sort of Pentagon-grade, top-secret cleaning force with stain remover developed by NASA. Yet, she was reluctant to chance it. She carefully sipped and set the cup back onto its saucer before her on the coffee table.

"Nervous?" Donny glanced over at his wife as she adjusted her little cat-like wire eyeglasses and fidgeted with her fingers.

"No, I'm fine." She faked a brief smile and turned her eyes back to the television. "Okay, a little. There's already enough pressure with this being a very unpopular decision, so I'm hoping casualties are minimal. Americans are tired of hearing casualty numbers and getting their loved ones back in boxes."

"It's going to be okay." Donny rubbed his wife's shoulder. "Whatever happens, you made the right decision and it's all going to work out okay."

"I hope so," she replied. "When I gave the orders to send men and women into battle against the Republic, it was hard, but at least I knew it was in the interest of saving the country—it was a cause everyone could get behind. But I find myself wondering if the men and women dying in Pakistan . . . is it going to be worth it? What are we going to get out of it?"

There was a knock at the door that seemed to fill the room, followed by a sinking feeling. Cindy's stomach moved some two inches lower and nervous shivers rippled through her muscles. But they were barely noticeable to Donny. She thought they were, at least. Then she suddenly and briefly thought it sad that she had come to hide vulnerability from even her husband, the most supportive spouse anyone could ever ask for.

"Come in," Cindy called out, taking another sip of her creamed and sugared coffee, and then setting it back in its saucer.

The door swung open and General Bates's commanding presence was known. He had loudness to his being, even in quiet. When he spoke, the world listened, hanging on to every brick of speech. Yet, even when he was quiet in every way, he emitted waves of silent boisterousness that caused one to stop and take heed. He carried his usual folder stuffed with a few sheets of paperwork and reports, peering down at it and then to the president.

"Good morning, Madam President," he said in his normal gruff voice as he shut the door. "I do have day one reports for you. I even have some intel about how the Reds are doing."

"Should I go?" Donny half stood up awkwardly as he realized this was privileged information, and he had no real official position.

"No." Cindy motioned for him to sit. "You're okay," she said as Bates glanced over at him with a look that seemed to disagree, but nothing was uttered.

"Well . . ." Bates sat stiffly on the loveseat opposite the president and first gentleman and opened his file. "The strike went off without any major complications to timing and effectiveness. The Reds were able to move unilaterally with us, and there have been no known clashes between our boys and theirs."

"And girls," she corrected with a smile, knowing that irritated him.

"And girls," he nodded briefly and went on. "The southern half of Pakistan is going beautifully." He closed his eyes and smoothed the air with his flattened hand to add some emphasis. "All the places our forces hit—Rasoolpur, Cheelh, Kaloi City, to name a few—all big successes. We conquered those in a day. We were able to really thin the heavy defenses with drone strikes so our troops just kind of waltzed right in."

"How did the Republican Guard do?" Cindy was curious.

"A little tougher time all around," he said. "They don't have the drone support, so they had heavier resistance, and of course, heavier losses. But all in all, they pretty much did their part. But as far as the southern half of Pakistan goes, we're golden. It's just phase one. We're on the outskirts of the more densely populated river valley. It's going to get a little harder as we move into the heavier urban areas. The only city we don't completely hold yet is Bahawalpur—that one has been tough."

"And the north?" Cindy asked.

"The north is a completely different animal." The general leaned forward on his knees and back. "The resistance was much worse. You have to understand that the southern two-thirds of the country is a fertile river valley that cuts through desert, so the only place where people live is right there near the river. The move through the desert was only about a sixty mile trip for most, and then they hit their objectives. Up north, it's more of a humid subtropical climate that becomes green hills and mountains the further north you go. These areas are just naturally more densely populated, and being closer to the capital of Islamabad, they're more heavily defended."

"So is that translating into heavier losses?" Cindy kept her composure, though becoming uneasy.

"A bit," he replied. "Drones have done some good, but even the smaller towns we're hitting are resisting harder than their southern counterparts. And it's hard to do drone strikes here. It's hard to tell civilian from militant, so when in doubt, we don't use them. The biggest city we're hitting this early is Lahore. We've focused most of our personnel and attention there. It's huge, and densely populated. And it's rough, urban warfare. They're making progress, but they're maybe a fourth of the way into the city, up from the south."

"Overall losses?" Cindy asked, straight-faced.

"A few hundred so far," he said as he looked at his file. "Total. That's dead and wounded."

Cindy stared down at her coffee, thinking. She was pleased, overall, but she hated hearing of losses. On paper, it wasn't so bad. It was a report. She tried to separate herself from the realities of those numbers and statistics. She tried to be strictly analytical. It made decisions—tough ones that she absolutely had to make—much easier. A few hundred was not so bad. But as hard as she tried, she could never keep that mindset. Even one casualty meant that some poor young man or woman had lost a leg or was lying dead in the dust. This was someone's son or daughter, or someone's parent, and it was because of a decision she had made from an office. Her hands trembled. Her lip quivered, and then she stopped, forcing strength from the inside out.

"Thank you, General." She looked at him with her president's eyes and smiled. "Is there anything else?"

"No, ma'am." He stood, as did she, and shook her hand. "I'll keep you updated." And then he turned and marched forward, and then out the door.

Cindy collapsed again into the soft sofa, her tearful face buried in her hand. She sobbed and sniffed while a torrent of tears rolled down her face. Donny wrapped his arms around her whole body and took her safely into his chest. She let herself be shielded, though there was nothing to shield against.

"Dear God," she sniffed, her face still buried. "What have I done? What have I done?"

Chapter 20

Derek lounged in the normally uncomfortable metal chair. At the moment, sitting was the best thing he had ever felt. His legs were gelatinous and weak. His head still pounded with every push of blood from his heart into his brain. His eyes pulsed and neck bulged. It had been hours, and still, he had not recovered from the push into Punjabi, Pakistan. The ten miles from the Indian border to the Lahore airport was the longest ten miles of his short life. To spend all day fighting just to have the leisure of slaving away unloading trucks of supplies and munitions was a harsh reality of war.

And it was business time again. He sprawled about, legs stretched far in front of him. His head hung cocked back behind his shoulders like a candy dispenser. Then the dozens of other metal chairs began to fill with soldiers. He straightened himself, almost annoyed by the crowding space closing in around him. For a moment, the air tightened in the gutted-out hangar. Boots knocked against the concrete floors, and echoed like gunfire across the corrugated metal walls and ceiling. Tanks and trucks were a rumbling thunderstorm in the dimming sunlight outside. Fellow soldiers were camouflaged walls closing in, causing Derek's nerves to crinkle and fray until he felt another body slide into him from across the seat to his right.

"Sergeant Putnam," Kendra Voss called, her piercing blue-green eyes wide and attentive to him.

Derek had no response. He tried, but nothing would pass his lips. He just stared at her, and she was obviously waiting. Her light-brown natural curls were a bit matted with sweat in the absence of the Kevlar helmet that too recently capped her head. The nearly porcelain skin was unblemished, though smudged with dirt and grime. But her glow came from within, shining outward to engulf and obscure all imperfections.

"Private Voss," Derek managed, struggling to think of something else to say. "Um, you did well today."

"Oh," she seemed surprised. "I didn't know you had even . . . um . . . seen me."

"Yeah, yeah," he nodded, looking away bashfully. "You were clean and concise. You followed orders. You were steady. You did well."

"Thanks," she smiled back at him sweetly. "You were . . ."

"Hey buddy." Queens popped up and heavily fell into his chair beside Derek, Alex right behind him. "Some friggin' day, huh?"

"Yeah, the CJs had it in for us." Derek shot another quick glance and grin toward Kendra before he deepened his voice and dove head-first into guy talk.

"CJs?" Kendra puzzled.

"Camel Jockeys," Alex chuckled, and then proceeded to ignore her.

The boys continued in the usual way. Testosterone burst around them like fireworks. Kendra looked around to see that most of the growing congregation was male, only dotted now and again with the occasional woman soldier. She grinned at the male-dominated crowd, confident, rather than meek. Derek and the other men joked and poked at each other; a mixture of praise and playful insult.

"Jesus, I don't know why we didn't surround the city and choke it off like we did Houston," Queens pondered.

"Yeah, this would be a perfect siege city," Alex added.

"Shit no," Derek said. "You saw how heavy it was just getting the airport today. We would have spent weeks and countless casualties just trying to surround the city. It's too heavily-defended. Brass figured that the airport is on the eastern side of the city—the India side—so we just take it, build a base of operations, and hit the city head-on from there," he explained. "You'll see. That's just what we're going to do."

"Houston, huh?" Kendra bit her lip coyly, smiling and unable to sit still.

"Yeah." Derek's voice lowered and softened as he grinned back at her. "Me and Queens here were in the unit that controlled the I-10 corridor crossing the bay into Houston during the siege."

"Hmm," she said. "Impressive."

Again, he was speechless, unable to imagine a response. It seemed like nothing he would say would match. He was not even sure how he felt about her transparent intentions. He was taken aback; attacked by surprise, and without defense. Finally, there was something to distract him. Captain Jacobi approached, fresh from his briefing and ready to address his own troops about the days to come.

"All right, people." Jacobi strolled up swiftly and confidently and stood overlooking his company. "Just got out of division briefing with Major General Wright, and as was to be expected, Lahore isn't going to be a leisurely stroll in the meadow. That resistance we took on the way in was just an appetizer. The main course is the Thanksgiving dinner of urban warfare. Lahore is the second largest city in Pakistan and one of its economic centers. And being that it's only about eleven miles from the border with Pakistan's enemy, India, there's a long history of defending it. At the same time, it seems that Lahore is one of the more liberal cities in Pakistan. That doesn't mean, necessarily, that there are strip clubs and liquor stores for when we finish the job. It doesn't mean they enjoy all the freedoms you do. All that means is women don't always have to wear a burqa and people don't subsist on dirt." He paused as a low rumble of laughter rose from the troops ahead of him. "It's the educational center of Pakistan and it's full of shopping malls, boutiques, and high-end restaurants. A lot of these streets, surprisingly, are going to look a lot like home."

He paused again, peering out from his keen eyes framed by deepening crows' feet. His men and women were tired and dirty, yet they were attentive and eager. For them, there was no political agenda. They simply did their job, and that was something he was always proud of.

"So here's the plan," he continued. "We're going to use the airport here as a base. We're setting up a perimeter of defenses around it now. From here, we will fan out into the city and take it in sections," he said as Derek nudged Queens in the side to illustrate that he had predicted the plan of action. "Each section will likely take several companies—it's that big of a city. We will be moving first due north into Al-Faisal Town as part of a larger maneuver to capture the entire Ghazibad district of the city between here and Canal Bank Road. You will have Humvees and tank support for sure, and possibly Black Hawks and Apaches in certain situations, but don't count on air strikes—it's too densely populated, and there are a lot of civilians. Drones are out there constantly gathering intel, and the Predators are hitting the big cannon defenses that they can find. Other than that, because it's hard to discern civilian from foe from the air, there's no real possibility of thinning the herd before we go in. Taliban guys are going to look a lot like civilians in some cases. Guerilla tactics. You're not used to these people's culture or habits. You won't see the subtle differences in people. A guy holding a gun is going to be your tip-off, so keep your eyes peeled. Any questions?" He looked over the quiet audience of troops, unsure if they fully understood or if they were just too exhausted. "Okay then, get some rest and I'll see you in the morning," he dismissed, and they rose and scattered slowly in a growing buzz of voices. "Putnam, come see me," he shouted over the crowd.

Derek heard him, his head lifting to view the captain over the crowd. Jacobi was looking right at him. He had indeed heard correctly that it was his name called over the one hundred and fifty other men and women. He broke with his friends, nodding to them to indicate that they would catch up later, and pushed through the thinning crowd toward the front. He stumbled a few times, his foot catching the leg of one of the folding chairs and knocking it crooked. He felt like a blundering fool in the watchful eye of Captain Jacobi.

"Yes sir?" Derek reported, standing at attention.

"Shit, son," Jacobi said with a chuckle. "You know better than to give me that formal call-you-into-my-office crap. We've fought and bled with each other. At ease."

"Yes sir." Derek smiled and hung his head a little, loosened up, and then returned his attention to his commanding officer.

"As always, you showed today that you're a great soldier and a talented warrior," Jacobi began. "This is obviously what you were born to do. And you have the superb leadership skills to go with it. I see what Captain Andrews—rest his soul—saw in you when he promoted you during the Texas campaign." Jacobi saw a flash of sadness across Derek's face as he hung his head briefly. "So I'm promoting you to First Sergeant. I need a competent and trustworthy right-hand NCO to help me command these troops. We're going to have a rough day tomorrow. Okay?"

"Yes sir." Derek did his best to hide his excitement. "Thank you, sir." He shook the Captain's outstretched hand.

Kendra watched from a distance, leaning with her back against a parked Humvee and her arms folded. She grinned, capturing his every move as he released the Captain's hand and turned away to catch up to his friends. His step had a hop in it. A smile was permanently fixed upon his face. He overlooked her, but she was okay with that. She felt that she could just watch him all day and be happy.

But she would have more than that. Alex opened his eyes that night and without moving on his cot, followed two silhouettes tiptoeing across the moonlight-bathed hangar floor. They raced into the shadows, disappearing into perhaps an office in the corner of the hangar. He simply shook his head and closed his eyes again, for he would need his rest for the coming day.

They all did, rising in the morning's pink hue glowing from the hangar's open portal. Muscles ached and tightened from a day of fighting and a night on a stiff cot. Backs popped and joints cracked. Yawns gaped open mouths and arms stretched from contorted bodies. The sounds of vehicles began buzzing around outside the military hive. Soldiers were scurrying to dress and move along at the prodding of their superior officers. Within minutes they were clad in full regulation fatigues and ready for the chow line.

"What took you two so long?" Queens's head popped up from his breakfast as he looked with a twinkle at Derek and Kendra seated across the table.

"Had to run to the head." Derek slapped his plate down next to Kendra's and hopped across the bench.

"Both of you?" Alex chuckled.

Derek and Kendra looked into each other's eyes playfully for a long moment. Grins formed on their lips without quite turning to laughter. There was language in their eyes—the widening of the sockets and arching, then lowering of the brows. But nothing was spoken, and they abandoned the silent banter before they perceived that the others would notice. Derek's head swung forward and locked eyes with Alex across the table from him. As much as he wanted to look away, he could not. He was trapped and Alex was no longer smiling, though he was not frowning, either. He just leered and chewed, his chin propped lightly upon his hand and fork dangling under. Again, there was silent language. Derek's childlike playfulness quickly soured into the vinegar of self-shame. Breakfast was therefore very quiet and reserved.

Troops were beginning to assemble and breakfast had to be shoveled into mouths as quickly as possible. Plates and trays were left on the tables, some with food left unfinished. The crowd was moving; a deadly herd of personnel preparing for a tough day. Derek and his friends left the mess tables, following the others to their company's preparation area to gear up. He fell back, allowing Queens and Kendra to gain distance from them.

"What was that look?" Derek asked his friend, his brows tightening. "What look?"

"Back there at the table," Derek pressed. "You gave me a shitty look. What was that about?"

"Man, it's none of my business." Alex threw his hands up in the air. "Do what you want to," he half grinned, but without much candor.

"See, I don't even know what you're talking about," Derek disclaimed. "What do you mean, 'do what I want to'?"

Alex laughed a little as they continued to walk slower than the other Marines. The two were playing dumb, and in competition with regard to how dumb they were playing.

"Look, I saw you two last night." Alex watched Derek's face change, almost feeling the cold wash of nerves that surely covered his body. "I saw you run off to the corner of the hangar. I know," he smiled.

"You did?" Derek's faced showed a slight panic. His eyes darted around as he began to tremble with every thought of losing friends, loved ones, and falling out of favor with anyone.

"Yeah, I saw you," Alex reaffirmed. "I'm not judging, buddy. Your life is your life. Your needs are your needs. I'm sure you know how to do what's best for you."

"You mean you don't hate me?"

"Hate you?" Alex reeled. "What? Of course not. I think it's a mistake. It wouldn't be my choice. But as I said, that's all on you. I know you'll still have my back out there, and I have yours. That's all that matters." He briefly placed a hand firmly on Derek's shoulder, gave him one strong look in the eye, smiled, and picked up his pace, pulling ahead of the lagging Marine.

Derek geared up by himself, without the usual banter and light-heartedness of his friends. He could see the guys laughing and poking at each other across the way. They stuffed pockets with extra ammunition and hooked grenades to their utility vests. Derek valued that time to strengthen bonds with those in whom he trusted his life. He relied on it to keep his mind clear before going into the fight. He was reserved and sullen, his face sour with contemplation. He tried to focus on his tasks at hand, trying to stock up on what he needed without overburdening himself.

He glanced up to see Kendra also alone to his left. She often looked up and smiled at him. He could manage one to return, but only for a brief moment. She noticed. His mind was elsewhere. He could not stop thinking about Carly and Olivia at home praying he was okay, yet he was in another country, intimate with someone else. The thought of that sent a stabbing pain into his chest and jolts sprang out from it, crackling across his torso. It brought pre-tear bulging under the eyes, but stopped with that. And then it was time. Packed and fully-armed Marines picked up their rifles and began filing out into the Punjabi morning, ready to meet the enemy. Derek swiftly rejoined his guys, but he felt Kendra's presence right behind him. He glanced back and there she was. She would have loved to be arm-in-arm, or to receive a pre-battle kiss, but she knew it was not coming. She knew what he had at home, and she knew what she had chosen with Derek Putnam.

Soon, they were marching across the tarmac, companies of soldiers with accompanying tanks and Humvees fanning out into the open area. Some moved south, prepared to assault the affluent DHA neighborhoods, while others headed due west into the lions' den—the heavily-defended center of downtown Lahore.

Derek felt secure, surrounded by grunts he could trust. He looked to his left briefly, and then to his right, observing the narrowed eyes and determined expressions on the faces of his men and women. They grasped their rifles, fingers on the triggers, with malice leaking onto the weapons in their palm sweat. He felt safe, somehow.

Shell craters dotted the grass and pavement of the Lahore International Airport. The occasional body of a forgotten enemy lay cold and stiff in the cool morning air. They neared the Pakistani Army Officers'

Housing Complex. It once held some of Pakistan's best military leaders and their families, but since the Taliban had driven out any remnants of the old regime, it had become a stronghold for the Taliban to protect the airport. Now it smoldered, smoke still billowing up into the pastel sky. It loomed like a black cloud of hate, casting a grim shadow over the abandoned playground where the children of officers once played. The swings no longer squealed. Laughter no longer bloomed flowers in the air. The soccer nets blew frayed on the breeze. Basketball and tennis courts lay neglected and quiet. The once plush green grass had wilted and yellowed, overgrown with weeds.

And now hate. It coursed in veins throughout the air all around. It smelled of smoke and death. Derek began to feel that same familiar sensation; one he had felt in Mobile, New Orleans, and even the previous day. He loved it; invited it. It threatened death and made him feel alive. His chest tightened and a cold wash of adrenaline spread across his skin, leaving almost a burning sensation. His bladder suddenly felt full, and then it subsided. He shivered only once, and then steadied. His brow lowered and lips tensed together. All other thoughts left his mind, his only goal to vanquish the enemy and conquer the sector given his company.

"All right, guys," Derek spoke to the troops immediately around him. "Keep your eyes peeled. That's Amjhad Chauhdry Road up ahead. All those houses on the other side—actually this whole area—are former army officer housing. We don't know who in these neighborhoods are former military, who joined the ranks of the Taliban, or even who lives in those houses now."

"Flying blind," Alex said, scanning actively.

"Is that a golf course?" Queens gazed out to his left.

"Garrison Country Club," Derek grinned, remembering the briefing. "For the officers that lived here."

"After we take the city," Queens said in his usual loud, boisterous manner, "I say we play a round to celebrate."

"You play golf?" Alex reacted with surprise.

"What, that surprises you? A former New York hoodlum like me can't be a golfer?" Queens feigned offense.

"I could see you stealing golf clubs, but not using them." Alex laughed at the thought as the troops began crossing the silent highway at the perimeter of the airport and headed into narrow residential streets.

"I ain't no Tiger, you know?" Queens added. "But I can play . . ."

The neighborhood was quiet. Small, fuel efficient cars lined the streets, a noticeable difference between this place and the giant SUVs of back home. Houses, most of them two-story, stood behind often brightly-colored concrete walls with iron gates. Balconies protruded from the white-washed exteriors held by sometimes Greek-style columns and were laden with patio furniture. It seemed like a nice neighborhood, but again, quiet. It was hard to tell if it was abandoned or if people were cowering inside.

"Still trying to picture it," Derek chuckled. "It's like trying to imagine my grandmother running hurdles or something." He looked to the right so see blood explode from the chest and back of another soldier.

It came almost simultaneously with the sound of automatic gun fire. The young soldier fell to the ground as Marines reeled, searching for cover. No one saw the muzzle flashes. Derek and Queens crouched behind a parked hatch-back as Kendra ran up to join them. Her eyes were wide and breath labored. She stared into Derek's stone-cold, calm soldier's face and marveled, somehow feeling more confident herself.

"Anybody see him?" Derek called out.

"Nope," someone answered.

"I only heard one gun," Alex added. "But that doesn't mean there aren't more of them."

The platoon was paralyzed, all seeming to have a safe spot. There was no more fire. All had cover from the shooter's sight. No one could move, nor did they dare to. But they had to move on. Derek stared into the dusty pavement. He was a leader. He knew he had to come up with something.

"I'm about to do something stupid," he quietly told Queens, and then motioned to Alex and some of the other troops across the little street to keep a close watch on the buildings around them.

He jumped up and ran across the street to another parked car that provided cover for Alex and a couple more Marines. His heart raced as shots rang out again, echoing from concrete wall to concrete wall. Alex saw two muzzle flashes from upon a balcony across the way. Several Marine guns began firing into that location, chipping away bits of concrete and stucco. Amidst the fire, two Marines pulled the pins from their grenades and tossed them up past the ledge. After a few seconds, they exploded with a deadly pop and all fell silent for several moments. Derek stood slowly, carefully scanning the balcony for the return of rifle barrels, but none returned.

"I think we got 'em," Queens nodded, also checking for movement.

"Jesus," Derek finally exhaled. "It's going to be a long day."

Chapter 21

November

"This one's clear," Alex called out as he and two other soldiers trudged out from within the walled yard.

The neighborhood was a shadow of its former self. Sections of concrete wall that once provided solace, comfort, and privacy were blown apart by RPGs and tank fire. The air seemed permanently steeped in smoke rising from various burning abodes in the area. Chunks of concrete littered the narrow streets like an ancient Mediterranean classical city, but without the same charm or beauty. Shots echoed across the city, often sporadically, though no one really noticed. Choppers flying overhead either patrolling the conquered portions of Lahore or bringing wounded back to command were almost a permanent sound that became more like some sort of white noise. It was lulling.

"We're getting more and more empty houses." Queens sat on his helmet and leaned against a wall on the opposite side of the street. "Maybe we've got 'em runnin' scared," he remarked, and then took a sip of water from his canteen, dribbling a little down his chin and neck.

"Who knows." Alex stepped past the gate into the street. "I'm just glad all the old officers' families and civilians are out of here. This is no place for a child."

"Most of these places still have clothes and kids' toys and shit." Queens took another sip and then closed his canteen. "Looks like they got the hell out of here in a hurry. I just wish they had left a beer in the fridge."

"It's illegal," another voice sounded, and Derek walked out from another house on the street, followed by Kendra who was straightening her pants and gear and walking funny. "Pakistanis aren't allowed to drink alcohol. Even foreigners would have a hard time finding it around here. Oh, and this house is definitely clear," he smiled deviously.

"How the hell do you all of a sudden know so much about Pakistan? Did getting promoted come with a bigger brain or something?" Alex joked.

"I read." Derek marched out through the open gate. "I talk to people—people who know more than me. How else do you learn new things?"

"Took you a while to clear that house," Alex smirked as Queens and half a dozen other men raised an eyebrow at their first sergeant.

Derek could find no words. All eyes were on him, and that came with a certain level of discomfort. He could handle that when others were being fired upon and desperately needed direction. But these piercing, judging eyes were far deadlier than enemy bullets.

"We're thorough," he smiled, half innocent, and half crediting the implications. "Jesus," he blurted as he nearly tripped, neglecting to see the body bags at his feet.

They were lined up in the dust along the off-white walls at the edge of the street. The black bags were ominous. Most tried to ignore them. Many were desensitized. They had become a common sight over the last week that they had spent trying to neutralize Ghazibad. Seeing even a loved one—even a close uncle or grandmother—in a casket at a wake was easier to handle. They lay surrounded by flowers and caked with essence-faking makeup. They looked well and peaceful. It was harder to see the body of a young man or woman with gaping holes in their torsos or missing limbs. They were caked with dried blood and bluish with the chill of death upon them. They often stared lifelessly into nothing. And then they were bagged and hauled off.

"It's been four hours," Derek continued to complain. "And still, no one from command has come to get these guys?"

His conversation with his comrades ended, it seemed, abruptly. Things had become awkward with people he considered closer than most people in his life. He could not quite pin-point what was happening. He was moving up in rank. Suddenly, they had to follow his orders—at least more so now than before. There was a stiffness in chain of command. It had become too formal. Had his promotions changed the friendships? Or was it the other thing—the obvious thing? He trudged lazily alongside Kendra further up the street away from his friends and sat in a tuft of grass against the wall. Kendra took a similar position beside him. Nothing was said for a few moments. It was just a series of looks and awkward gestures that reminded them both of junior high. There was somehow a lack of maturity here.

"So . . ." she began aimlessly.

"So," he returned fire, waiting for a long while before speaking again. "Hell of a week, huh?"

"Derek," she almost giggled. "That can't be what you wanted to talk about."

A slow and steady smile formed up on his face as he stared into the dust beneath him. "No, I guess not."

"Then shall we talk about the eight-hundred-pound gorilla on the battlefront?" She looked up suddenly as a pair of navy jets screamed overhead.

There was a pause—no answer from Derek immediately. He was unsure how to proceed. He imagined that she was prepared for the next line of conversation, but what if she wasn't. What if he offended or upset her. He thought for many moments, listening to sporadic clusters of gunfire echo across the city somewhere far off. He could not simply shrug it off and say "never mind." He was invested, and had to carry on the rest of the conversation. Perhaps if he offended her and the affair ended, the conflict would be resolved that way.

"Look, I know what the deal is." She removed her helmet and let her long tresses cascade down.

"Yeah?" He was somewhat surprised that she had broken the ice, and actually glad.

"Yeah," she nodded sympathetically. "I know what you have at home—your girlfriend; your baby. And I'd never ask you to give any of that up."

"I just . . ." He stopped, thought, and began again. "I just don't want to hurt you. I love them, and every day I feel like I'm betraying them."

"Any pain for me that comes out of this, I brought upon myself," she said. "I'm the fool that let myself fall in love with a taken man—from the first time I laid eyes on you actually. You don't have to worry about me."

"And my family?" He looked away, ashamed. "My guilt?"

"It's done," she said. "If you're going to feel guilty from what we've done already, might as well enjoy it as long as you can. You're a man. You have needs, whether it comes from brotherhood with your buddies over there or through affection with me. You need something to cling to in this place. I don't think you have anything to be guilty over."

"I still feel guilty," he fidgeted. "And my buddies over there," he continued as he shot a glance that way, "well . . . things aren't the same with them, either."

"I think that's more because you're moving up in rank," she said. "Your relationship with them has changed."

"I didn't want that to happen." His face soured.

"They're still your brothers; your friends." She put her hand on his shoulder. "They'll always be there for you."

"And you?"

"Me?" She placed her hand over her chest. "I'll be fine. I'll be here for you through thick and thin."

"And after we leave?"

"We'll go our separate ways," she said. "You'll go back to your family and I'll go back to my life."

"Do you have someone to go back to?"

"No," she shook her head. "Not like you do, at least. Mom. Dad."

"Oh, now I do feel bad." He threw his hands up. "Like I'm taking advantage of you."

"Don't . . ." She put her hands on him. "I chose this. I chose you. I knew what I was doing. Even if we won't ever live happily ever after, I got to have you for a little while, and that's enough to last me a lifetime."

He smiled with sweet affection and allowed his gaze to penetrate her very being and absorb every drop of her love for him. He basked in it. He soaked in its warmth and enjoyed its light. He could not take his eyes off of her smooth, yet dirty face. All else stopped in the world until he heard his name.

"First Sergeant Putnam!" some anonymous corporal from command called out. "Mail."

He jumped up from the earthen seat he had taken, and with a long, painful, and guilty look back at her moved slowly toward the corporal to receive from him a letter from someone else that held his affections. And the pain set in again. The joy he had felt faded into bitter guilt, and then love of a different kind as he looked at the distinctive handwriting on the envelope.

Still staring longingly at the small envelope, a little bent and creased from so much handling from half a world off, he drifted over to the side of the street and leaned against the white concrete wall. Distant explosions rumbled and choppers flew overhead while he flipped to the back side where it was routinely taped back together. He shook his head at the thought that the Pentagon had to read every letter from his girl-friend, but he was used to it. It no longer felt so invasive. He tore above the taped seams and removed the little letter, unfolding and turning it so that he could read to himself.

Dear Derek,

Your daughter is driving me crazy!! A couple of weeks ago, she was pulling up on the furniture or her play pen, and I knew she was close to walking. But I didn't know she was going to skip it altogether! She went straight from standing to running, and now she's into EVERY-

THING! I'm so sorry you had to miss her first steps. But don't worry. I shot some great videos of it on my phone. She is so funny and so sweet. She misses her daddy. She says "da-da-da" all the time. And when I ask her where "da-da" is, she looks around for you. We can't wait until you get home.

Things have been a little crazy around here. I still get a little help from my sister, but you know she has her own family and she can't be coming over here every day. I guess I'm having to learn to be more independent and do without the help. The hardest thing to get used to is Jake being gone. If anything broke or was too heavy to lift or something, he'd come by to help, but he's not around anymore. I hate for you to find this out from me, but Jake enlisted last month. In fact, it shouldn't be long before he's done with training. I'm sure it's likely he'll be heading to Pakistan, though everyone is hoping he just goes to Mississippi or somewhere to hold a line that no one is fighting over anymore. He is so proud of you and so inspired by you. He talks about you all the time and how you're a hero. He wanted that for himself. He wanted that same brotherhood you have with the other Marines. I think he wants for you both to come back from the war and be able to swap stories.

Anyway, I miss you so much, and I love you so much. I can't wait for my hero Marine to come home to hold me and our baby in his arms. Be safe, babe, and kick some Taliban ass! ☺

Love always,

Carly

He carefully folded the letter back into its original configuration. He always did that. It was important for him to preserve every letter he ever got on a battle front just the way he received it. As he slid it back into its envelope, he looked around, partially in abstract thought. He was elsewhere, but also very present and actively scanning his surroundings—the smoke billowing in the distance, the body bags, the rubble in the streets, and his brothers in arms. He peered up the street at Kendra still sitting against the wall where they had been talking. She smiled gently and acceptingly at him. He felt at ease, and with a burst of confidence, he left his position against the wall, joining his friends in the usual boyish banter and laughter. Kendra just sat there, watching the man she loved and willing him to be happy at all costs.

Chapter 22

"How the hell did we end up drawing market patrol?" Kyle ambled along next to his friend Okie, toting his heavy weapon and keeping a keen eye peeled. "So many friggin' people."

"I don't know," Okie shrugged. "Did you piss on a colonel's shoe or something?" The comment sparked a giggle amongst other men within earshot.

The Republican Guardsmen fanned out evenly throughout the public square framed by two-story whitewashed homes and businesses. It was hard to hear each other speak unless one yelled a bit. The invasion was over and in the occupation stage of American presence in Umarkot, the people of the city were now comfortable carrying out their daily lives. It made the soldiers nervous. At least during the invasion, only enemies emerged from the buildings. Those who wished to keep their lives stayed huddled indoors. Now, the men had to pay much closer attention to their surroundings.

At the center of the square, poles extended up from the dusty ground. Large white sheets hung draped about, tied to the tops of the poles, and fluttered in the breeze. Beneath the shade, vendors stood behind their tables and stands peddling various recently harvested fall crop items. Others held up cloths for sale or caged chickens, the smell of which made market duty even less appealing. The rather large bazaar was teeming with people kicking up a constant thin cloud of dust. Men in flowing traditional robes contrasted with those in trousers and loafers. An occasional woman walked quickly and fearfully through the scene in a full burqa, terrified of any perceived contact with a man in the square.

"God, these markets stink," Kyle grimaced. "I'd breathe through my mouth if the dust didn't make mud in there."

"Smells like home to me." Okie grinned a cowboy's grin.

"I see why you left," Kyle poked as his friend responded with a lewd masturbation-like gesture.

Pay attention, Kyle thought to himself. Bad things happen when you're distracted. He moved slightly apart from the rest of the guys; enough to matter but subtle enough to not be obvious. His eyes narrowed and vision somehow became keener. He often found himself trying too hard. It was noticeable. He would squint his eyes like this as if he had super-human powers to scan for miles around. He imagined it also formed a facial expression that exuded an "American Bad-ass" look. He would clench his weapon with white knuckles and puff out his chest. He was sure that all of this, combined with the military gear he adorned, made him appear menacing. But inside, he wished he was at home in Ashley's bed sleeping late. He wished he was back in school.

"Fan out," his commanding officer ordered from afar. "Spread out into the crowd and actively monitor."

Now Kyle had an excuse. He shrugged at his best friend and increased his pace to move out away from the rest of the Guardsmen. At the same time, he wanted to keep his distance from that market. It was centered at the heart of the square, but there was plenty of open and unused space elsewhere. The crowds became denser near the market, and thus dispersed further away. He tried to appear to move into the crowd, yet keep a distance from the bustle, monitoring from the perimeter while other soldiers plunged into the thick of body odor and manure smells.

A familiar sound cut through the jumbled noise of chatter and haggling in a Sindhi language. But all that stopped by the second time the sound occurred. Screams of terror, a language Kyle could certainly understand, became the dominant noise dotted with pops of gunfire. He immediately dropped to one knee and raised his rifle to his shoulder, scanning for a target. He felt himself become a little more frantic by the second as he desperately searched for the source of the gunfire. The mob of men and women scattering in all directions obscured everything from his line of sight. He moved his head from side to side, trying to get a clear look.

Finally, as the crowd thinned, he could see three shooters firing from underneath the market awnings, their muzzle flashes heralding pain and death. Kyle quickly and as calmly as he could, took aim at one of them, and squeezed the trigger to send a hail of bullets that killed his target with impunity. The other two dropped to the dusty ground soon thereafter as the other Guardsmen neutralized the threat.

Kyle extended his legs with a quiver and stood erect, trying to control his erratic breathing. He had been in several firefights, yet he still had a hard time managing the surge of adrenaline that came with it. He looked around to assess the aftermath, aside from the three gunmen he knew were dead. Most of his fellow soldiers were rushing to the aid of two of his men lying and bleeding in the dust. His commanding officer called on his radio for a team of medics to come at once.

Kyle roamed the square almost in slow motion. He looked around with emerging panic to make sure his friend Okie was all right, and then was soothed to see him standing. Kyle approached the market at the center of the square, taking in the horrors. Several Pakistani men were growing cold in terrible, deathly poses on the ground. Blood poured from their torsos, soaking their shirts and trousers. He could see lifeless clumps of frumpy black burqa material blowing in the silent breeze. He walked up on a young girl, still in the dirt. Her innocent eyes were closed as if she were peacefully dreaming in her bed. No bullet wounds. Kyle's eyes welled with tears as the thought of the poor child trampled by panicked market-goers. He violently fought back the urge to sob, imagining that soon, her frantic mother, who had sent her for bread that morning, would be emotionally destroyed. He knelt down to begin collecting her or moving her without really knowing what to do.

"Leave her, private," his sergeant commanded. "These people will take care of their own kind. We don't know their beliefs or rituals. It's best to just leave them alone."

Kyle stood again and continued to wander aimlessly and numb. He gravitated toward the market some more, perhaps to get a better view of the evil men who caused this pain and death. He looked around, shaken by the sudden, uncanny silence. He scanned every inch of the perimeter for other possible shooters until he neared the abandoned market. A few other soldiers approached as well, eyeballing the dead enemies that bled onto the ground.

"Rot in hell, you sons of bitches," one of the men, unknown to Kyle, screamed in his rural southern dialect, and then spit on one of the bodies.

Kyle concurred with the sentiment as he looked over the scene once again, taking in the sights of dead women and children, as well as fellow soldiers. From the corner of his eye, he noticed an odd set of actions. They seemed unnatural, though blurry, so his head whipped back to the direction of the dead enemies. The sound came before the sight. It was the familiar sound of liquid splattering. He found himself witness to a soldier who had taken his penis from his pants and begun urinating onto the lifeless corpse of one of the gunmen.

His immediate and automatic response was shock, and even disgust at the sight of a relative stranger urinating in plain sight. But somehow, it sharply switched to amusement. The soldier was urinating on an enemy corpse. He deserved it. Besides, he's dead. He can't feel it. He experienced no shame. Without realizing why, his thoughts switched to that of his friend Ryan, dead on that training field at Fort Hood. What if someone pissed on his corpse? Kyle loved him. It would have angered him on Ryan's behalf. Suddenly, his amusement in watching warm yellowish urine wash over the face of his enemy was no longer amusing. He turned away, a scowl across his face, and pushed through the gathering crowds of soldiers enjoying the show.

"Hey, man." Okie jogged up to catch him. "You all right?"

"I'm okay." Kyle glanced back and kept moving.

"Yeah." Okie looked over toward the spectacle, aware of how Kyle felt, but unwilling to say anything. He smiled, finding the scene a bit humorous to him personally. "I'll be glad when we finally get out of this God-forsaken place. These friggin' insurgent hits just keep coming."

"Tomorrow," Kyle said with relief. "We'll be out of here tomorrow, headed for the river and Hyderabad. That's where the real action is."

"Let the damned greenhorns they're bringing in to replace us with deal with this shit." Okie swatted in the direction of the market as they both walked away from the scene.

Chapter 23

Knuckles solidly rapped against the large, solid oak door. It was stout and unmoving as it was when it still ran with the essence of life. It did not feel cheap, hollow, and manufactured like so many of the front doors across America. It stopped General Weaver's fist cold, sending almost uncomfortable vibrations up his wrist and forearm. His bulging, aged veins stung with the jolt of the stalwart door.

He stood before the main entrance of the new presidential mansion looking around at the gleaming splendor. The expansive yard and gardens affront the massive building were pristinely manicured, though yellowing in the dropping fall temperatures. The columns and bricks all around were constructed into a marvel of classic architecture, but surely with the finest of modern technological advancements. Yet, it was strange for a presidential abode. Security was tight around the perimeter. Soldiers patrolled the fence lines and grounds. But he was sent to walk right up to the front door. It opened.

"Hola," a meek Latin voice squeaked from behind the opening door.

The middle-aged Mexican woman was shy and apprehensive. She kept her head down but her dark brown eyes remained sharply transfixed upon this uniformed man. She had experienced uniformed Texans many times, and they always made her nervous. She clung to the door with both soft, wrinkling hands, pulling it slowly further ajar.

"Gracias, Yoheris." Allie Crane strode forth from within the confines of the massive home, carrying herself with every bit of first lady stature. "General Weaver, it's great to see you again." Her southern dialect sweetened her words almost beyond palatability until sticky like rock candy. "Come on in." She shooed the housekeeper along back to her duties.

"I'll show you back to the study where Joe is. He'll be happy to see you."

"Thank you, ma'am." Weaver followed, taking in the sights.

Just as the outside, the interior of this new presidential residence rivaled that of the White House. It was majestically decorated with bold, elegant colors in the carpets and art. The chandeliers emitted just enough light for a comfortable place between bright and dim. It gave the feeling of warmth and home amidst the air of a museum. Weaver could still smell the newness of the paint, varnish, and carpet. They twisted down multiple hallways decorated with imitation paintings of leaders like Jefferson and Jackson. Framed "Don't Tread on Me" and Texas Revolution battle flags hung amidst the portraits. This was truly the home of the President of the Republic of America.

"Go on in." Mrs. Crane opened one of the tall double doors, allowing him to pass.

"Thank you," he smiled with politeness, nodding as he passed and left her in the hallway.

"Hey, General Weaver." The president looked very excited, rising from his leather chair. He was not dressed for business—jeans and a button-down. But after all, this was his home. "What do you think of the new digs?" he motioned around him.

"Nice." Weaver glanced around at the same kind of rustic décor that characterized his ranch house, yet more professional. The wooden walls were dark. The furniture was all brown leather and was accented by various items of decoration and art that used black wrought iron. "I've been to the White House once . . . back when Clinton was president. It definitely holds its own, though I seem to remember entering the White House through a side entrance . . . not the front door," he smiled.

"Ha," Crane burst. "That's exactly what I wanted to change. The White House is a tourist attraction now. Comings and goings of officials like you and Zach here," he motioned to the chief of staff on one of the couches, "are spirited in and out through secret doors and such . . ." He paused to shake his head in disapproval. "This is the way things were done in Jackson's day. He had an inaugural party when he was elected and the public was invited. This place is built with taxpayer money and I'm their servant," he exclaimed excitedly.

"Didn't the public nearly destroy everything in the house at that party?" Weaver recalled.

"Yeah, well, that's not my point," Crane replied. "This is my home, not a tourist attraction. But this is also a place of business paid for by the taxpayer. I think people should be able to access it and walk through the front door, just like they would any other person's house."

Weaver had no answer. His sour scowl was a permanent fixture on his face. He rarely displayed much emotion. He was an aging, ornery army lifer set on getting things done. With that, he followed the president into this masculine lodge and sat upon one of the leather-upholstered sofas across from the much younger Zach Wallace.

"Okay, gentlemen . . ." Crane sat, his tone draining of its liveliness. "I know this is not going to be all peaches and cream, so let's get it over with."

"Well, sir," Weaver said. "It's pretty much the same as every week. We're having a lot of success in the lower half of the country where it's sparsely populated. Really it's not more success," he clarified. "We're just moving more quickly than in Punjab. The north, closer to the capital of Islamabad, is heavily populated and defended. It's taking us weeks to accomplish what we do in days in the Sindh region to the south."

"Gotcha," Crane nodded. "Casualties?"

"This week?" Weaver conjured up figures he had read the previous day. "About seven hundred forty-nine this past week. Most of those are injuries. I think only two hundred or so were actually KIA."

"Okay." Crane lounged in his comfortable leather chair. "And how many of the other injuries require the soldier to be pulled from duty and sent home? The reason I ask is that recruiting, as you know, has drastically slowed. Tours are going to just have to get longer for each soldier."

"Yes sir, I know," Weaver accepted. "Three hundred and something, I think, sir. The rest are minor things that can be taped, wrapped, and bandaged and sent on their way." He paused a moment, noting that the president was still silently listening and nodding; taking it all in. "Aside from the heavy defenses we're getting in Punjab, the other thing that's giving our guys headaches throughout the Indus valley is the damned insurgents. The Guard will take control of a city and lock it down. But the Taliban doesn't wear a uniform. It's easy for those guys to wear the same thing as every other rag-head in town, and then the white boy from Kansas sticks out like a turd in a bowl of cereal! So our boys are patrolling the city and coming up on small pockets of un-uniformed fighters. They don't mind dying as long as they take a few Guardsmen with them. And if it's not that, it's IEDs—just like Iraq back in the Bush era."

"I see," Crane said contemplatively. "So what's going on this week?"

"Moving out across the valley," Weaver replied. "We're moving first wave people out of our objective towns and cities on the east bank of the river, and having them invade the other side of the river valley. It's phase two of controlling the river. A new batch of greenhorns will come in and take over the occupation of the cities we already hold. Hyderabad is a big one we're going after this week, but as I understand it, there's resistance in the rural agricultural areas in the valley."

"Good," Crane said. "Sounds like you have it all under control. Aside from recruits, what do you need to make this work better?"

"Well," Weaver folded his hands and paused. "We need supplies of all kinds."

"My God," Crane slumped, tired of the issue. "We've been over this. The money—"

"I know, sir," Weaver continued. "But if you want to be successful, my boys need simple things like ammo and armor. We're not getting the new recruits we need, so we have to keep who we have as safe as possible."

"General," Crane said. "I know you need supplies. I know this . . ." He paused a moment. "I'm fighting with the legislature on this. Our Constitution mandates a balanced budget, and it's November, so budget issues are hot. We have to work all this out for the coming new year. It's hard to do when you're fighting a war overseas."

"Sir, our guys can't fight effectively without proper equipment and support," Weaver reiterated.

"It's going to take pulling funds from somewhere else," Crane said. "That's the price of national defense. I've been preparing the legislature for the possibility of propositions that pull from other programs like education and healthcare."

"That's going to be tough," Zach chimed in.

"Well," Crane rationalized. "This isn't a socialist country. People are going to have to learn to make their own way, and stop living off the government. Besides, if they want us to defend them by destroying the Taliban in Pakistan, they have to know that there are things we have to sacrifice."

"Healthcare and education are huge services people depend on for wellbeing," Zach commented again. "I'm not saying not to do it. I'm just saying it's a tough sell. The legislature is easy. It's the public you're going to have to convince. If you don't get their blessing on this, we may be in trouble."

"You're right," Crane agreed, as did Weaver. "I think we need to pray on this." He reached for the hands of his chief of staff and military advisor. "Dear Heavenly Father, we ask you for your guiding hand today. Please direct us on the right path—the path that's best for our people and our good Christian fighters out there toiling in their great crusade. We ask you for the blessing of Heaven and your divine guidance as we enter these murky waters. In Jesus' name, Amen."

Chapter 24

"What?" Cindy Chandler shouted into her trendy smart phone. She stood from her well-lit chair where paper bibs sprouted from her collar like she was Queen Elizabeth I, sending her team of hair and makeup experts reeling away. "What do you mean you're not coming home for Thanksgiving?" She shot a look of disbelief at Donny.

"I'm sorry, Mom." Julie paced around her single-student dorm room, still in her flannel pajama pants and t-shirt. She took in the sights of her room, creaking the old floorboards of Ware College House beneath her feet. It only vaguely resembled a normal college room. It was classy; free of piles of dirty laundry and empty beer cans. There were no posters of a collegiate or heart-throb nature. Big, fluffy pillows of bright, blinding colors heaped on her bed. Nice, brown wicker storage bins and shelves added a homey feel to the plain, dreary, off-white plaster walls. The morning light glared off of the minimal dusting of snow on the University of Pennsylvania upper quad, brightening the already inviting space.

"What on earth could possibly keep you from spending Thanksgiving at the White House?" Cindy nagged.

"Well . . ." Julie continued to pace in her small area. "My Women in Leadership organization is working down at the food bank and then serving the homeless at a shelter on Thanksgiving Day," she said meekly.

There was a pause. Unbeknownst to Julie, her mother had opened her mouth and was poised for the counter-offensive. Her finger was positioned above the phone like a cobra ready to strike, yet words would not leave her mouth. She blinked, and lowered her serpentine hand, relaxing into a reluctantly accepting state. She glanced at Donny, who having heard Julie's reason to stay in Philadelphia, was grinning with ease.

"Can't argue with charity," he said as Cindy scolded him with her eyes for not helping.

"All right, all right, fine." Cindy finally closed her eyes briefly as she caved and sat back down to allow her cosmetics staff to continue to work on her. "Just be careful. We've been getting a lot of hate mail lately over Pakistan. Stick close to the agents there with you. I have to do a press conference, but call me later."

"I will," Julie smiled, and bounced happily. "I'll call you guys on Thanksgiving Day. Love you." And she hung up.

"I meant later today," Cindy found herself saying into an inactive phone. She shook her head in disappointment. "That girl . . ." She paused. "When we had to take her out of Tulane because New Orleans became Republic territory, I figured Penn is just a short plane ride from DC and we'd see her all the time. Is this the beginning? Is this where she outgrows us and stops visiting? We'll be in a nursing home in no time."

"It's going to be fine." Donny offered only those words as he walked up behind her chair and placed his hands on her shoulders. Those were the only words he could muster because as comforting as he could be, he had the same feelings that his little girl was growing up and would soon be her own woman. Yet, his smile remained and was there for the purpose of consoling his overstressed wife.

Julie removed the phone from her ear, holding it low and staring before she pressed the touch-screen button to end the call. A smile formed slowly under her untethered brown curls. She bit her lip with the giddiness of a child, bouncing as she darted across the room toward the door. She twisted the knob and pulled, revealing the usual black-suited Secret Service agent standing sentinel. Julie's smile quickly snapped into a pitiful pout just as she caught his attention.

"Good morning, Miss Chandler," the broad-shouldered agent greeted with the slowness of standing guard all night. "What's wrong?" He had seen that pout before.

"I need your help." She backed into her room, still puffing out her bottom lip as he followed her in. "I want to move my bed here and my dresser here . . ." She pointed out the switch. "But it's too heavy for me."

"All right," the agent sighed and moved for the bed without much energy.

"Thank you." She bounced with a renewed giddiness and clapped her hands in excitement. She then walked across the room and picked up a plastic basket full of soap, shampoo, and other shower paraphernalia and headed for the door. "I've got to go get a shower."

"Wait." The agent stood up from trying to move the heavy bed. "I need to—"

"It's just down the hall," she interrupted. "The bathroom's, like, two doors down. I'll be okay."

The agent relaxed and accepted the first daughter's rationalization, turning his attention again to the heavy oak bed while Julie slipped out of the room with a click of the doorknob. All bouncing and childishness ceased sharply. Her gait turned from the bouncing of a ten-year-old to a steady, confident stride down the old hardwood planks, veering left into the hall's communal bathroom. On the far end of a line of sinks and mirrors stood another girl smiling nervously and fully dressed, including a coat and scarf.

"Thank you so much for stashing this in your room for me." Julie took hold of one of the two roller suitcases at the young woman's side, opened it, and dumped in her shower toiletries. She removed a pair of jeans, a shirt, and underwear from the suitcase and quickly got dressed, then brushed her teeth.

"No problem," she answered, watching Julie brush her teeth feverishly. "You've been slipping me clothes a little at a time for weeks," she laughed. "I was kind of afraid your bodyguards were going to get suspicious." The friend handed over a gray wool coat as they pushed into the other hallway opposite Julie's, their suitcases rhythmically bumping over the creases between wooden planks like the bumps on an old vinyl LP.

"No," Julie half chuckled. "The guys that guard my mom are super perceptive and detail-oriented like that, but not these agents. They do a good job—don't get me wrong. But let's face it. It's highly unlikely anyone's coming after me. So these guys don't pay all that much attention."

"Ah, gotcha," her friend nodded. "It's nice to know you're important. Is your door guard the only one on duty?"

"Yeah, on a weekend like this, I usually just have the one that guards the door and follows me around shopping and such," Julie said, her curls bouncing around. "Is Joey downstairs in the car?"

"Yes, and sooo excited," she answered as they turned and began down the stairs. "All he keeps talking about are the gay bars on Bourbon Street, so we have to hit some of those."

"Oh we will," Julie nodded. "They're so much fun. I can't wait to show you guys New Orleans. I can't wait for you to meet some of my friends down there. Off to the airport."

Chapter 25

Flashes of bright digital color reflected in the stylish, almost catlike eyeglass lenses set before the presidential eyes. Her eyes jumped sharply in short movements, bathed in artificial light. They followed slight changes represented in ones and zeroes—pixels dancing across the screen as she manipulated the happenings on her touch-screen smart phone with the tip of her index finger. Now and again, she grunted in disapproval or broke into a brief celebratory smile before again entering into intense concentration on what she was doing.

"Damn it," she suddenly belted from behind her Oval Office desk. "What do I have to do to get the stupid glass thing to fall down?" She looked up from her game with a moment of paranoia, just to assure she was indeed alone in her office.

She looked back down at the phone, her eyes glancing over the watch secured around her dainty, feminine wrist. Oops, she grimaced with the realization that she had killed a little too much time. General Bates is going to be here any— There was a knocking at the door, interrupting her thoughts. She quickly tapped the home key on her phone, ending her refreshingly mindless game, and laid the device on her desktop.

"Come on in," she had to call out so she could be heard through the thick old door.

"Good afternoon, Madam President," the general greeted in as cheery of a way as the aging curmudgeon could muster, pushing through the door and closing it behind him. His gait had changed over the past two years. War had aged him. His joints, Cindy could tell, were stiffer. The wrinkles were deeper and what hair he had left was further whitening. He walked across the office with almost a limp, meeting the president at the sofas in the center of the office. He plopped down on the comfortable cushions with relief, his usual files in his hand.

"How are you, General Bates?" Cindy asked sweetly, eyeing him up and down with empathy.

"I'm sorry?" He heard her, but could not recall a time when she had ever really asked him how he was doing on a personal level.

"How are you doing?" she repeated. "I mean . . ." She sort of shrugged and made some kind of unintelligible hand motions. "How are you . . . you know . . . doing?" She did not want to seem as she was prying into his personal life.

"Oh." He was still caught off-guard. "Well . . . I suppose," he began, "I'm doing okay. Just business as usual, you know?" He paused for several moments. Cindy, perhaps, was waiting for a little more without trying to force it. She also did not want to cut him off if he were to say more. "Speaking of business," he continued, and opened his file. "Here is the update from my generals in India."

"Okay." She quickly abandoned her small-talk lightness. "Let's have it."

"Well . . ." General Bates opened his folder and removed a sheet of paper on top, and then handed it to the Commander-in-Chief. "Casualties are up this week," he said gravely. "But we're making progress."

"Wow." She read, and then looked up at her military advisor. "Still in Lahore."

"Heightened casualties, unconventional tactics . . . We're doing all we can, but the Taliban and other terrorist network operatives are dug in pretty deep. We're overpowering them, but they don't fight like us."

"What do you mean?" She seemed agitated. "We're the largest, most powerful military force the world has ever known. We crush them with sheer might."

"With all due respect, ma'am, that's slightly inaccurate." He leaned back and closed the manila folder. "History tells us otherwise. In 1775, the most powerful military in the world belonged to Great Britain.

And they sent thousands of troops and a massive fleet to put down this little rebellion in the North American colonies. Had most of the colonial militia formed ranks and fought the Redcoats in open field the way everyone else did, we'd still have tea time every day at four p.m. But no. Instead, we fought them with guerrilla tactics and unconventional strategies. Why? Because our forefathers wanted to win. If you want to win a bar brawl against a bigger guy, you might have to kick him in the nuts or grab a pool cue. That's why we were unsuccessful in Vietnam. That's what happened in Afghanistan after 9/11. And guess what. In every instance, the bigger nation with the bigger military went broke fighting with outdated tactics against an unconventional army. Want to destroy your Goliath opponent? Hit him where it hurts—his pocketbook."

A moment passed as Bates continued to recline, almost smug with the righteousness in his speech. He was confident and the president was contemplative. She leaned forward, the status sheet in her hand and her elbows on her knees. She stared into the ornate carvings of the coffee table, considering what he said.

"So what are you suggesting?" she finally said, looking at the general.

"Let's start thinking about adapting." He leaned forward again, propping himself up on his knees. "Maybe we don't need tens of thousands of troops and ultra-expensive weapons. Maybe we don't need to lose so many young men and women. Give me the order, and I'll start running heavier drone recon on enemy activity and top Taliban hideouts. Maybe we can do this much more surgically."

"Even in Islamabad?"

"Wherever you want," he answered.

"That would violate our agreement with the Republic," she said. "It might be overstepping."

"But maybe," he countered, "we'd get out of Pakistan and cost fewer lives."

Another moment passed as the president's wide-open eyes darted and jittered in thought. She continued to nod in silence.

"Let's stay the course for now," she finally said, looking up. "I don't want to tell you one hundred percent yes just yet. But you make a valid point. We have troops in place and a solid plan in progress. It's slow, but it's working. However, I don't want to rule out the possibilities of what you're saying. Start compiling intelligence. Send in more drone attacks to thin what defenses you can. Run the recon and explore the logistics of more surgical tactics. We'll revisit this later."

"Yes ma'am." He slowly stood with a creak in his bones.

"If there's nothing else," she said as she stood with him, "I have other business to attend to."

"Thank you." He started for the door. "I'll keep you updated with what I find," he finally said, and then exited with a gentle shutting of the door behind him.

Chandler sighed and strolled across the room, deep in thought about what the general had told her. She rounded the enormous desk and plopped herself into the chair as before, thinking for another few minutes and finally picking her phone back up to resume her game.

Chapter 26

Brilliant and beautiful star-shaped bursts of fire erupted from the menacing ends of assault rifles, accompanied by the deafening pops and brass casings ejecting and jingling on the ground next to beige combat boots. The unit was fully engaged, using two parallel buildings in the school complex as cover while they peeked around and fired at a rarely seen enemy further into the school grounds. The yellowish orange paint of the buildings glowed in the unabated sunlight, almost as if they emanated their own luminescence. Bullets buzzed through the air like a swarm of gnats, but more than just annoying. They struck the concrete walls, blasting bits of gritty material away and leaving divots and craters as permanent evidence of the malice that occurred there.

"Can you see how many?" Derek Putnam yelled over the boisterous echoing of gunfire. He continued to fire his weapon as sweat streamed from underneath his helmet, cutting channels into the dirt and grime on his face.

"Not really," Alex yelled back as he peeked briefly around the corner and fired a burst of three shots.

"It's at least two—dug in deep," Kendra yelled.

"Gotta be more than that," Alex replied as he glanced around to see a few team members lifeless in the dust with fresh blood welling up from holes in their bodies.

"Surely we've gotten a few of these assholes," Queens chimed in.

"I don't think we have," Derek answered. "And don't call me 'Shirley.'" He smirked and looked over at the others in the unit. He expected all of them to be doubled over in laughter, but only Queens seemed to have gotten the joke. "What?" Derek half shrugged. "Have you guys never seen the movie Airplane?" He was amazed to see heads shaking a blatant no. "You poor, deprived kids." He went on firing his weapon.

The gunfire continued between the Marines and their Taliban foes. It was unrelenting and tense, but to the point that tense became the norm. Bullets whizzed through the cool Punjabi air with a deadly whistle, ricocheting off the concrete walls and threatening stalemate. A young soldier to Derek's left trembled. He had come to the unit as a replacement just days before. Derek had neglected to get to know him. Friendships had come to run deep. Cliques formed within the platoon. There were those who had been in Pakistan awhile, and those who had not. Then there were the really ancient ones who had seen action in the war with the Republic. This kid appeared fresh, judging by the fear in his eyes and the adrenaline in his heavy breathing. It must have overcome him. He had not fired a single shot in the entire engagement, and now he was leaping into the opening between the two buildings the unit was using for cover. He fired a few shots, and then his chest and back burst open as two bullets ripped into his torso and exited just as quickly.

"Jesus," Derek exclaimed, becoming angry. "Stupid-ass." He looked down at the dead young Marine. "I'm getting tired of these sons of bitches. We've been at it for ten minutes and we have no idea if we've even made a dent. Would somebody please toss a few grenades over these buildings and see if you can take a few of these shooters out?"

"What if school is in session, sir?" a young soldier asked in response. "We don't know if there are kids in those buildings."

"Are you friggin' serious?" Derek snapped back. "That's why you idiots have been holding back? We've been pumping rounds into this school for ten minutes, but you're holding off on grenades because there might be kids inside?" He could see a few soldiers thinking and realizing the errors in their thought process. "Besides, if there were frightened children inside, I'm sure they'd be screaming in terror by now. Now get some grenades over that roof."

Alex, Queens, and two other newer Marines lowered their weapons and shifted their attention to their utility vests. With somewhat of a minor delay and complication, they each removed a standard fragmentation grenade from their vests, pulled the pins, and paused for a moment, still holding the spoon in place. They each then released the spoon, and tossed the grenade over the rooftops of the building that gave them cover, as well as the next, all in hopes of carefully and accurately placing the little fruits of death near the nuisance gunmen.

Gunfire continued—on either side. That was the idea. The Marines did not want things to quiet down enough for the enemy to hear the bouncing of a grenade off a wall or roof, or perhaps thud on the ground beside them. The element of surprise was on their sides. Now there was but to wait for a few moments while the fuse burned, hoping that the gunmen in the school complex were within the fifteen meter reach of the deadly metallic shrapnel.

There was a cluster of loud pops reverberating from wall to wall within the small school complex, followed by the rising of a thin, dissipating cloud of dust billowing up above the buildings. Rifle fire stopped from within and then trailed off amongst U.S. soldiers as all of them waited to see if the fire resumed. All was quiet, except for distant engagements and military vehicles. It was unnerving; the kind of silence and anticipation that causes one's skin to almost separate from the muscle. Shutters of anxiety travelled in painful waves across the body. Hearts fluttered and mouths dried.

"All right." An anonymous new replacement stood up happily, a bright smile stretched across his shaven, baby face.

"Sit down, stupid," Derek calmly said, almost emotionless as he caught a piece of the young Marine's utility vest and tugged him to the ground. "Want to get your head blown off?"

"What?" The young man's exuberance disappeared. "We got 'em, sir. No more gunfire."

"Doesn't mean shit." Derek's face still bore the look of business, strategy behind his menacing soldier's eyes. "They could be trying to draw us in."

"Yep," Queens nodded. "Remember Jordy? That's how his ass got popped. New Orleans. Shot this old-ass house in the Garden District all to pieces. All was still and he went in to confirm his kill. Those rebel boys were waiting for him."

"So what? Wait all day?" The young Marine took an attitude.

Derek and the rest of the troops crouched and waited in silence. Heart rates ran high and everyone soaked in Queens's little recollection. They knew the enemy, should they be alive, could not be left here to attack the next wave of troops that moved through. Live enemy guns meant potential Americans at risk later. Derek toiled inside his head, the work evident on his scowl.

"No," he whispered, using his sleeve to wipe some sweat from his cheek. "There are three rows of these buildings. Alex, you, Voss, and Shepherd go up around the left. Queens, take this moron here and . . ." He searched for a seasoned veteran. "Um, Platt. You guys go up the right. Between the six of you, you should be able to catch a visual and confirm these shooters dead. Now get moving."

The two teams of three brought their weapons up close to their chests and swiftly moved along the back buildings that provided cover, remaining in a cautious half crouch. Their boots quietly and uniformly tamped at the dusty earth as they paused for a moment to peek around the corner of the outside buildings, and then began moving on. They reached another corner of the rectangular concrete structures, looked quickly around the corner, and briskly pushed across the open space to the cover of the next building. Their movement slowed. They were coming up on the approximate location of the shooters. Queens edged along the wall, his rifle at the ready. He approached the corner, and in one lightning flash of a glance, looked around the corner long enough to see the three bodies lifeless on the ground.

Calm swept over his body, and the breath that he had seemingly been holding the whole time exited his lungs in relief. His eyes closed and a grin formed on his deeply tanned, stubbly face. For the other two men with him, looking for themselves was unnecessary. The relief was relayed and now all tense, combat muscles relaxed in unison.

"Shooters are neutralized," he radioed back to Derek.

"Hell yeah," the anonymous young Marine next to Queens sang, and then stepped into the open space for a look. "Do not fuck with the United States Marines," he laughed.

The shot was of the normal decibel level, but somehow seemed louder as it rang out and echoed across the school yard. Blood spouted from the young replacement's upper right torso and he dropped to the dust, writhing in pain while he grunted, and gripped at the wound in futile will for it to stop burning. Queens quickly reacted. He crouched to the ground and reached for the soldier's vest. He caught hold, and yanked as hard as he could, dragging the boy across the dirt with a trail of blood that browned and clumped in the wake.

"What the hell was that? I thought you said they were neutralized," Derek's voice chimed over the radio.

"They are. There's another shooter, but I can't see where the shot came from. Stand by." Queens dropped the radio and turned his attention to the bleeding soldier. "Platt, put some pressure on that wound. Did you see where the shot came from?" he asked the wounded Marine.

"Middle building," he grunted, his eyes tight with agony. "The window."

"Okay," Queens radioed back to Derek. "We have a confirmation on the shooter's location. Stand by." He dropped the radio and turned to Platt. "Are these one-room buildings?" he asked as Platt ran around the corner of the structure behind them and peeked into the window.

"Yeah," he whispered as he ran back around, blood still covering his hands as he reapplied pressure to the wound.

"Drag him around back and get a medic," Queens sent Platt and the other young Marine on their way, and then picked up the radio. "Derek, I'm sending the moron back there with Platt. He's going to need a medic. Can you send me a guy with an RPG?"

"Roger," Derek responded. "On the way."

A few minutes passed. Queens did not dare peek his head around the corner for fear of losing it, but fortunately all was quiet. He sat and listened for the opening of a door or the sound of footsteps in the dirt. No sound was made. He was still in that building, willing to outlast. From around the corner behind Queens, there was the sound of boots on the ground. He glanced over his shoulder, knowing it was a friendly. He could see, in his periphery, the long, menacing missile over the man's shoulder.

"Middle building," he told his comrade. "Aim for the window." He pointed in the direction of the shooter. "I'm going to lay some cover fire to try to keep him out of that window. You bust his ass."

Queens nodded his head with exaggeration, counting to three with each lowering of his chin, and then at the third, he jumped out from the corner, his gun raised and an endless spray of bullets hurling though the air and into the middle structure of the compound sending bits of concrete flying and forming a gray cloud of debris. The RPG appeared from around the corner as well, and loosed in a dramatic whoosh as it flew across the school yard and plunged into the concrete. A massive eruption of fire ensued, blasting apart the small classroom in a brilliantly violent display of destruction. The gunfire ceased, and the two men relaxed. Nothing could have survived. Everyone knew that, and so Queens could hear the celebration from the back of the complex.

It was time to rest; time to kick back. It had been a rough day for Derek's unit. The Marines sat around in the dust, their helmets still upon their heads in precaution, but they were as relaxed as they could be in a warzone. They clung to their weapons, stocks in the dirt, a propping post for them to lean on. Smiles and jokes lightened the mood until someone jumped up to salute the officer that approached. He was a newbie, and the other newbies followed suit.

"Sit down, dumbasses." Alex threw a small rock at one of them. "You don't have to jump up and salute every time a lieutenant walks up," he ridiculed.

"And why not?" Lieutenant Nolan smirked. "It wouldn't kill you guys to show a little respect sometimes," he half chastised, but to a groaning, disagreeing crowd. "Don't listen to these assholes, new guy. They'll get you in trouble."

"Looks like you have some news, sir?" Derek noticed some papers in the lieutenant's hand.

"Yep, that's what I came to tell you guys. Lahore is ours," he said proudly. The troops smiled and cheered, clapping their dingy hands and slapping high fives over seated heads. "It's confirmed," he continued as it got quiet again. "We control most major strategic areas and roadways. There will be a few Taliban stragglers we'll have to root out along the way, but most of the invasion force is again going to move on to the city of Gujranwala as the occupying force moves in."

Faces grew long, an abrupt ending to the short-lived celebration of such a pricey victory. Derek shook his head in disapproval. He hoped that it would remain disapproval—silent and respectful, but in vain. It morphed into anger and he spoke.

"And why can't the 'occupying force' be the ones that move up to Gujranwala?" He tried to suppress the anger in his voice. "Give these guys a break. Let the fresh guys take some hard-core action and let us police Lahore. I saw the map the other day. We've spent weeks taking Lahore, when it only took a couple of days to run the Reds out of Mobile. Lahore and Gujranwala are just the beginning. We're not even close to Islamabad."

The rest of the men and women were silent, but it was unnecessary for them to speak. They paralleled Derek's feelings with the disdain in their expressions. Scowls and frowns were rampant. Grunts and sighs emerged. Restlessness prevailed.

"Stand down, Putnam." He tried to calm the subordinate NCO. "I feel you on this one. I wish it were different. I'd agree with you, but the brass want tough, battle-hardened Marines in the thick of the shit because you guys know what you're doing. You're experienced, cool, calculating killers, and that's what it's going to take."

Disapproval soured further into despair. The troops began thinking of the events of earlier at the school and every other tough engagement they had seen over the weeks. They thought of friends they had just seen zipped up into body bags. The thought that this was but the beginning was a sickening thought that churned the stomach and chilled the skin.

"There's a lot of good news that comes along with this." The lieutenant understood what these soldiers were feeling. "The Commander-in-Chief is disappointed with the time that this is taking and the number of casualties."

"Aw, bullshit," Alex shouted in protest over other less audible negative reactions denouncing the disappointment of the president in their hard-fought progress.

"Wait, wait . . ." The lieutenant stuck out his palms. "You didn't let me finish." Things got quiet. "She's ordered a hell of a lot more aerial surveillance and recon to try to better pinpoint the heaviest locations of Taliban activity and then hit those areas hard with predator drones. She wants to step up the thinning of the enemy forces and make this easier on us."

The mood instantly lightened and smiles again returned. Derek was still unhappy, however. He sat, his chin propped upon his combined fists in quiet contemplation of his growing disapproval for being here. The corners of his mouth sharply pointed down and his thick eyebrows were a mean V. Kendra sat across the group, eyeing him. She longed to walk over and take his side, pulling him close and providing a comfort that only a soft, loving woman could provide. But she just allowed it to be longing and allowed him his troubled state.

Chapter 27

In the deep south, it may not get that cold very often or for very long, but when it does, the combination of the chill in the air and the humidity that naturally fills it gives one the sensation of being doused with a bucket of ice water. Shadows as tall as buildings flickered across the façades of century old creole-style cottages and bungalows. They rapidly flashed against the outer wood panels and front porch posts with eerie opaqueness; walls that had witnessed many triumphs and many heart wrenching tragedies. That is the plague of immortality. The old homes, mainly occupied by college students and professors, stood and watched woefully. Strange, artificial lightning struck in regular intervals causing the thick, ancient oak trees to flash royal blue like some gaudy Vegas mockery of such a majestic piece of vegetation.

The strobes cut blindingly through the night. It was a dark one, and even with the light of the street lamps, the night was almost palpable. It was as if one could reach out and move a hand through the air and the darkness would cause your fingers to glide with a little more drag. It felt heavier in the lungs and clogged the nose. This cloudy New Orleans night was as a great phantom; a black mass of a being casting its frightening cloak over the city and bringing only negative energy to the old colonial town.

"Another one?" someone commented, shivering under flannel pajama pants and sweatshirt. "I've got to get out of this city," she added to another bystander.

People were beginning to emerge from their homes, all wearing similar thick nightwear to combat the dropping temperatures. The yellow police tape flapped in the breeze while the white NOPD squad cars and

U.S. military Humvees drew crowds to the perimeter of the scene like a centrifuge. It was like a porch light that had just been switched on and was summoning an ever-increasing population of flying, swarming insects.

Uniformed city police officers kept watch over the perimeter of yellow tape, monitoring the seemingly docile gathering crowd. At any moment, a distraught parent could burst through the tape or the local news crews would show up trying to push the limits of how close they can get. Some of the officers had small memo pads open, writing down statements and gathering information from the neighbors. They seemed to stay separate from the military personnel, and the military police who obviously were in charge seemed to willingly stay separate from them.

"Jesus, if looks could kill . . ." Lieutenant Clay walked up, glancing over at one of the local uniformed officers on the scene. "These guys hate us."

"I guess I can't blame them." Lieutenant Lopez, his fellow MP glanced at the same cop to see the menacing looks they were getting. "This is their city and we're occupying. But I wouldn't say they all hate us."

"No, you're right," Clay nodded acceptingly. "Just the Republicans. But most of the loyalists on the police force migrated to blue states. So what we get is the leftovers. And those guys hate us. I'd rather not even cover this job—leave crime scenes to the local cops."

"Oh, I feel ya," Lopez agreed. "This isn't what I had in mind when I came here. I liked it better before they had to pull soldiers out to go to Pakistan. Martial law all the way. We police the city . . . no questions asked or we'll shoot . . . and the murder rate was nil." He looked down at the two lifeless young women on the sidewalk growing stiff in cold pools of their own blood.

"Yeah, and of course the colleges and universities all take the lifting of martial law as a green light to open campuses," Clay said. "For all the academic-type people they have in those buildings, they don't have the common since to know that the normal, law-abiding citizens evacuated long before the battle and the dregs are left behind."

There was a silence between them, though the bustling around the scene had increased. More officers were taking statements. Spectators had gathered either to solemnly gossip in order to feel like they were a part of the drama, or to perhaps gain a fleeting and exciting rare glimpse of a real corpse.

"Geez," Lopez spoke with a sigh in his voice. "What is this, the third one this week within a four block radius?"

"Yeah," Clay said. "Something like that." He looked around as if to scan the street names and try to jog his memory.

"No way we're ever going to catch the bastards that did this," Lopez added.

"It's like after Katrina," Clay said. "I did some time here after that bitch screwed this city all up. You wouldn't believe the amount of unsolved murders. There was just no hope in tracking down suspects. Not enough people in the city to actually have witnessed it . . . Not enough cops to handle the number of investigations . . . I wish the coroner would show up so we can get these poor girls off the street."

"Well, until then," Lopez replied, "what does it look like happened?"

"Simple armed robbery," Clay shrugged. "You can smell the booze on them. These are college girls out partying. Clothes are flashy and sexy. The uptown college bars are just a few blocks away. No purses or IDs—looks like they got jumped walking back home."

"Officer," Lopez yelled across to one of the uniforms nearest to a squad car. "Bring me over one of those fingerprint readers, will ya?"

The officer rolled his eyes a little, his movement obedient, but without intending to hurry. He had a visible attitude of disgust for the MPs and the occupying force. He disliked taking orders from these U.S. soldiers, but he also disliked the idea of being arrested for non-compliance. He ambled over to the flashing unit, opened the driver-side door, and reached in to retrieve a gray plastic device that appeared almost like a smart phone. He walked it over to the MPs, rolled his eyes again, handed over the device, and walked away without a word.

Lopez squatted, smiling and shaking his head in disbelief as Clay did the same, silently expressing their distaste for how they had been treated. Without a thought more, Lopez carefully, his hand protected by a glove, lifted the young lady's cold, delicate hand and pressed the thumb to the screen. It flashed and a processing icon appeared on the screen for several seconds before an image from the girl's driver's license appeared and all of her information.

"Okay," he read aloud, "Miss Cynthia Grier. Age twenty. Sarasota, Florida, address. I'm sure that's mom and dad. She probably lives around here and goes to Tulane."

"Why in God's name would any parent allow their kids to return to a city that was a literal war zone a year and a half ago?" Clay said, almost angry. "Regardless of whether or not classes have resumed, my kid would be applying to another college closer to the land of peace and harmony."

"You know young people these days," Lopez smirked. "Throw a little fit to mom and dad, and that's all it takes. Who wouldn't want to go to college in a drinking town like this? I'd be screaming to get back here too. Let's see," he picked up the other girl's hand and pressed it to the screen of the device, waiting a few moments for the information to appear. "Okay . . . Miss . . . Julie Chandler. She is from . . . restricted?" His brow scrunched in the middle with perplexity.

"Restricted? What do you mean?" Clay leaned over for a closer look.

"I get a photo and a name, but no address or other information," Lopez puzzled. "I don't get it. We're federal investigators and this is an FBI database. Why wouldn't we have access?"

"Julie Chandler?" Clay thought hard. "I've heard that name . . ." He paused as epiphany flashed across his face and he breathed deeply.

"I know that name." Clay rose, extending his legs. "I know why it's restricted."

"Why?" Lopez stood as well.

"This is the first daughter." Clay closed his eyes as a sick feeling originated from his stomach and infected the rest of his body. "This is the president's only daughter."

"Are you sure?" Lopez looked back down at the girl's stiffening body.

"Yes," Clay nodded reluctantly, longing to be wrong. "We have to call our CO on this." He stepped away and put a phone to his ear. "Sir?" he spoke. "Sorry to wake you . . ."

"Where is she?" General Bates asked in his same gruff tone as he approached Sandra, the president's chief of staff.

"In the dining room eating breakfast," Sandra responded, but immediately began protest. "General, do you have an appointment?" She stopped him from entering the dining room.

"I'm her top military advisor and this is wartime. I don't need an appointment," he declared as he pushed past the powerless aide.

The room had changed since the last time he had entered it when Republican shelling of Washington began. He could see that repairs had not been completed in this room, as well as with other parts of the White House. Cracks in the walls webbed across much of the room. The ceiling was missing bits of plaster and the elegant floral molding that once crowned the space. Somehow, it felt homey. The smells of sautéing bell peppers and sizzling bacon were stout, bringing with them morning warmth and comfort. The president, seated with her husband at the table enjoying their omelets, would need that comfort.

He approached in the usual fashion, but found himself over thinking it. He thought perhaps his gait was too slow and solemn. He wanted to avoid the president and the first gentleman reacting to some unknown bad news before he could deliver it, so he sped the pace a little. But then he thought maybe he was moving too briskly and he would be perceived as urgently trying to reach them. He attempted to maintain the same old expressionless near-scowl that always characterized him, but drollness was the wrong delivery, as well. For a brief moment, he even grinned, but he rethought. He never grinned. That would trigger an alarm.

"Hello, General." Donny Chandler looked up from his omelet, still swallowing and wiping his upper lip of orange juice. "Coffee?" he offered as Cindy only turned and waved, covering her full, chomping mouth.

"No." He paused a moment to think of how he had rehearsed this on the way over. "No, thank you. Quit drinking the stuff a few years ago. Bad heart, you know?" he divulged.

"Breakfast, then," Cindy smiled, finally swallowing her food. "Javier back there makes a bad-ass southwestern omelet."

"No, thanks." The General sat beside Donny and across from the president. "Um . . . well . . ."

"Yes?" Cindy took an expression of light concern. "You look like something is troubling you. What's on your mind?"

"It's Julie." He hesitated, trembling—something unnoticed to Cindy.

"Julie?" she smiled. "Oh, maybe she will come home for a few days after all!"

"Sweetheart . . ." Donny had a serious look. "General Bates usually doesn't bring us updates on Julie like that. Sandra would."

"Oh God," she realized he was right.

Shivers cascaded from the bottom of her neck down her spine, and branched to her extremities. She could feel cold rush across her body like an ice bath as her breathing grew short and labored. Her eyes widened and pupils dilated while her right hand lifted from the table to cover her gaping mouth.

"What's wrong?" she trembled. "Did something happen to my daughter?"

"I got a call this morning from one of my commanders in charge of the MPs in New Orleans," he began, but was interrupted.

"Damn it," Donny reacted. "Somehow I knew she was giving us a line of crap! She snuck down to New Orleans to see her friends." He looked at Cindy and back to Bates. "So what? Arrested?" he asked as Cindy began to tear, fearing the worst and now praying that her incarcerated daughter was the worst of it.

"I'm afraid not." Bates hung his head, preparing to give it straight. "She was found murdered last night near Tulane—armed robbery."

The last part and some of the further details and explanation were muffled further by the uncontrollable sobs of the Commander-in-Chief. He simply stopped, sitting there silently unable to look at this wounded mother. He had seen many sob over the loss of a son in battle. He was sympathetic, yet immune. He did not want to seem cold, so he simply hung his head in the illusion of grief.

Tears rolled in torrents down the president's face. Her eyes were clenched in a series of wrinkles and swollen tissue. She had trouble breathing in as she leaned further to the left and toppled without control. The sobs became louder as Donny sprang from his seat, tears running his freshly shaven cheeks, yet he held his full emotions back to stand as his wife's rock. He rushed beside Cindy, taking her into his arms. He cradled her agony and embraced her sorrow as his own as she slumped into him and immersed herself in grief.

Chapter 28

Early December

Kyle's hands itched beneath the thick government-issued gloves. Every ounce of flesh and every small bone rattled and vibrated within his hand as the rapid, angry recoil of the fifty caliber rifle relentlessly offered a deadly hail of bullets to the small farmers' villa. It was a day the same as any other. It would have been a nice day in any other setting, but the Humvee ahead in flames and the incinerated bodies of its occupants marred the bright, benign beauty of the day.

Mortars exploded ahead and behind him. He could not see where in the roadside villa they were coming from. All he could do was try to chew through the mud-brick walls of the small buildings, try to take out some of the gunners, and hope his fellow Guardsmen accurately placed their own mortars in the right place.

"We have got to take out those mortars," Kyle screamed to anyone that was listening, briefly glancing to the side where American mortars were being dropped into their tubes and sent hurdling into the cluster of buildings. But he was powerless to do anything. His rank dictated that he simply did as he was told—put his life in harm's way, keep shooting, and never ask questions. So that is what he did.

The rhythmic fire and ejection of brass casings from his weapon were soothing. It was like a mother's heartbeat to her infant son. For such a nightmarish dragon of a weapon, it somehow rocked and lulled Kyle into a numb slumber-like state of dispensing death. And then he was awoken by the lumbering, loud growl of a giant monster from the depths of his fears. The treads of several tanks crushed rock and ground the soil beneath them. They stopped, positioned their commanding barrels, and spouted a barrage that ripped through the small, occupied villa building by building. Chunks of dry beige brick erupted into the air, along with a rising specter of dust as if the souls of these Taliban men were moving into the afterlife en masse. In a matter of minutes, the artillery assault completely dismantled the villa and left no living soul in the smoldering rubble.

Kyle had silenced his weapon. He had stopped and smiled as he comfortably witnessed fire and brimstone unleashed on this compound by the gods of war. It was horrible, but enjoyable. Being fired at will make even the most gentle of hearts sick with anger. He was happy for the break. He was glad for the entertainment. And when the tanks had fired their last shell, he marveled for a moment and then ducked into the Humvee like a prairie dog. The door opened, and Kyle stepped out onto the dusty road. He removed his mirrored sunglasses for a brief time to wipe his face of sweat and dust and then replaced them, scanning the scene and the aftermath as Okie waltzed up still carrying his rifle.

"Goddamned IEDs." Kyle shook his head at the blazing Humvee ahead. He could see the gruesome silhouettes of the men still inside the mangled, burning vehicle. Engineers approached with several fire extinguishers, releasing vast, pressurized clouds of flame-retardant chemicals.

"How would you like to have that job?" Okie commented. "Putting out fires. Dragging crispy, burned corpses out of the Humvee?"

"Might be better than being on the inside of that Humvee," Kyle replied. "Hell, I might like that job over getting shot at every damned day," he half grinned.

"Son of a bitch." Kyle's commanding officer approached, standing next to Okie with his fists typically planted on his thick hips. He never smiled; all business, and his business was devising strategies on how to kill as many people as possible. "We would have been at the gates of Hyderabad weeks ago if it weren't for all these shitty little farming communities. Hell, we're having more trouble with these fuckin' things than we're having with the big cities."

"And still over thirty miles to go," Kyle commented, and then realized that maybe it would have been best to remain silent. But it was too late. It just slipped out and escaped his lips before he knew what was happening.

The captain delayed reaction, and Kyle thought that perhaps he did not hear. The man just stared at the burning Humvee and the attempts to douse the flames. But something registered. He turned his head to the left and drew a direct bead on Kyle, who was trying not to make eye contact. The captain stared for several moments without speaking. He showed no emotion, nor did his eyes deviate.

"PFC Perkins," he finally uttered.

"Sir." Kyle omitted the salute, but his back stiffened and his posture improved in respect.

"I've been watching you on that fifty cal and your leadership abilities come natural to you," he said, and then glanced back at the burning vehicle. "I need a new sergeant." He gestured toward the charred corpses in the Humvee. "Want the job?"

"Sir, I'd be honored sir," Kyle replied immediately.

"Good." The captain turned away and began about his business. "Have your guys start setting up camp for the night." He glanced off at the sun as it approached the western horizon.

"Yes, sir."

He relaxed as the officer disappeared, feeling a slight grin form on his face. Okie just stood there beaming as he shook his head.

"You're trying not to act excited," Okie said. "C'mon, you piece of shit, you know you're stoked."

"Maybe a little bit." He unleashed the smile, but it faded as quickly as it appeared. "But should I be? That's fucked up," he said as he motioned to the dead bodies in the Humvee. "Danny had to friggin' die for it to happen. How can I be happy about that?"

"Dude . . ." Okie held up his hands. "Calm down. Danny signed up like the rest of us. He knew what he was doing. His death's not on you. This shit just happens. It could have as easily been me or you, but it was Danny. You're allowed to be happy to get promoted, regardless of how it happens."

But that provided no comfort. He was pondering deeply at this point, staring at the burning vehicle, and then the smoking, destroyed villa. He took in the guns, the brass casings, and the Humvees. He took in all the mortar equipment being put away and the tanks' still smoking barrels. He reached into a pocket in his vest and retrieved a folded, wrinkled piece of light pink paper. It was worn and a little dingy, but still had been protected in a dry spot away from Kyle's sweat. He held it in front of his nose and took in a whiff. It was faint between the smell of burning material, Humvee exhaust, and dust, but he could smell it. It was the distinct smell of Ashley—specifically her bedroom. He was unsure if it was her carpet or laundry detergent. It could have been her perfume, but he could never really put his finger on it. He could only describe it as the "Ashley smell." He unfolded it for a moment, read a bit, and folded it again.

"Got this from Ashley last week," he told Okie.

"I know," he answered. "I was there."

"She says there's all kinds of trouble at home," Kyle continued. "Clashes between citizens and U.S. occupying forces. Good ol' boys with hunting rifles. Ladies with shopping bags. And the ARA is setting off bombs at state houses and government buildings all over the Republic. Just makes me wonder what we're doing here."

"Getting justice," Okie answered. "Justice for everyone you know in Dallas."

"It pisses me off, yes," Kyle looked at his friend. "I want those bastards to pay as bad as everyone else. But look at the number of lives we're wasting in the process. What are we going to do? Kill the whole Taliban?

And how many men are we going to lose doing it?"

"They ain't dyin' in vain," Okie said. "They're dyin' for freedom. Dyin' for a cause."

"Whose freedom? The Taliban isn't invading. They're terrorists. We should be protecting our people from acts of terrorism, not an invading army that threatens our people and government. Shouldn't we be back at home dealing with our own problems?"

"It's justice, man." Okie couldn't think of anything else to say. "It's just justice."

"Justice?" Kyle asked his friend. "Is that justice? Take a life for a life? Vengeance? When should it ever be an option—an okay situation for you to kill another man? Even in the name of justice?" He walked away to order his men to begin making camp.

Chapter 29

Ashley Dykes's tanned, bare feet strolled delicately across the carpeted floors of her College Station apartment. She was cozy, the heater running and the mid-morning news creating a backdrop of white noise that she could tune in or out at her own leisure. The thick aroma of freshly brewed coffee made the short distance from the little kitchen to the living area, filling most of the apartment. She adjusted her sweatshirt, a once full, red cotton monstrosity, now cut widely around the collar and with the sleeves removed. It hung down off one shoulder, so she constantly straightened it.

She entered the kitchen, boosted herself a little higher on the balls of her feet to open and reach into a cabinet above the sink. She returned to her normal height with her favorite mug, a Disney World coffee mug with a picture of a golfing Mickey and her dad's name on it. She had taken a cup of coffee for the road one day and just never returned it. It was a little piece of home and security she could enjoy away from Fort Worth while living here all alone.

She set the cup down and reached for the glass pot. She tipped it, flowing the deep black steaming liquid from within into the waiting mug, and cutting it off two-thirds of the way full. She placed the pot back on its hot cradle, and moved just a step to the left to open the refrigerator door. The rush of cold, dense air fell out of the appliance, cooling Ashley's arm and part of her semi-exposed abdomen. Chills carried all over as she took hold of the cold gallon of milk and reached over to pour a bit into her mug. She always liked watching the metamorphosis of the deep and dark coffee into the medium tan color it took with the milk. It was a little different with the half-and-half. The heavy cream was so much denser, so it clouded and swirled. But milk just seemed to brighten the coffee as if there were a knob to change the brightness as on an old TV.

She replaced the milk with another little shiver from the cold refrigerated air, and then opened the sugar container. It was a guilty pleasure. She tried to eat healthily, valuing vegetables and organic food. She avoided overeating, tried to limit fatty foods, and stayed away from carbs at dinner time, but a ton of sugar in her coffee was a necessity. Coffee was a new love of hers. It had only been in the last couple of years that she drank it, and only after she had once mistakenly eaten a chocolate-covered coffee bean. Now she would drink it, but it almost had to taste like candy first.

"The RPG attack at the government office building in Santa Fe yesterday . . ." Ashley's attention was caught by the news anchor's statement. ". . . has officially been attributed to the ARA," Ashley stepped gracefully into the living area, holding her cup with both hands and sipping her coffee. "Government and law enforcement officials have always believed that because of the violent nature of the attack, it was the ARA, but a video posted on the Internet by an unknown, masked figure has claimed responsibility for the terrorist act. No one was killed in the blast, as it was conducted after hours. The ARA makes a point to stress in every message that they have no interest in killing innocent civilians, yet Republican Guardsmen are 'traitors' and 'fair game.'"

Ashley continued on into the room, rounding the side of the plush white couch, and slumped into its comforting arms. She grinned a little, as she always did, while she pushed as deep into the backrest as possible, almost consumed by the cushions, and tucked her dainty feet beneath her. The former background noise of the news was now her focus. She sipped away at her coffee, grinning deviously at the topic of the news. Mostly, she was thinking of Kyle. There was a smile at the thought of his baby face, but then a flutter of apprehension at the notion that he might be in danger. She tried to keep those thoughts locked up in a little compartment in her head; far out of sight. She wanted to forget they were there. She wanted to think of Kyle, but not in Pakistan. Instead, she tried to keep memories of him limited to those in the civilian life. He would be wearing cargo shorts and a polo, rather than Kevlar and camouflage. She tried to pretend he was not even in the armed forces; perhaps it was just a long-distance relationship with a boy at a different college.

"In other news, there has been an increase in public outrage over President Crane's announcement this morning that he has signed legislation that would cut the education, healthcare, and public assistance budgets by billions," the anchor continued on to the next story, jolting Ashley from her current thoughts. "Take a look at what the president had to say earlier this morning." The screen cut to an earlier taping of Crane in the rotunda of the Austin state house.

"Right now," he boomed as a fiery Baptist preacher to a sea of cameras and correspondents, "in the sands and cities of Pakistan, our boys—our servicemen—are fighting to preserve the freedom of this great nation. We have to support them. We have to send them weapons and ammunition. We have to give them body armor and tanks. We can't just leave them hanging. They have a job to do, bringing justice to the millions affected by the horrific terrorist attack on Dallas. So if that means we need to tighten our belts back here at home, then so be it. I refuse to raise taxes on the citizens or the businesses of The Republic of America. I promised I wouldn't. It's a basic principle of our founding this country. The common man's bottom line and a corporation's profitability are too important to hinder them with weighty taxes and regulations. So that means we have to cut, if temporarily, certain luxuries."

"What a prick." Ashley shook her head in disgust, continuing to watch as the screen began showing clips of protests all over the Republic and interviews with citizens on the street.

"He's out of his mind," a woman with two children said, standing outside of a supermarket. "My kids' education is one of the most important things I can think of."

"We're already on a fixed income," an elderly man and his wife said. "Both retired. Pension doesn't cut it. The Republic's version of Social Security is crap; it's underfunded. We rely on our 'Red Star' healthcare plan for Maddie's medication," he motioned toward his wife, who was clearly becoming a bit feeble. "I don't know what we'll do if we suddenly have to pay more out of pocket for her pills. They're expensive," he added, concerned.

"They're going to make it to where only the elite can educate their kids," said a college student wearing a multi-colored beanie atop his shaggy hair and beard. Protest signs could be seen in the backdrop. Chants of anti-Crane slogans created a rhythmic mantra of their disapproval. "This is exactly what they want," he articulated quite eloquently. "The public schools will get so bad due to underfunding, that you'll have to send your kids to private school if they're ever going to have a chance to be anything in this country. But only the people with money, and therefore power, will be able to do it. It further widens the gap between the rich and non-rich. This government doesn't want thinkers. They want multitudes of ignorant people who will follow the lead of their educated, elite masters."

"Protests like this occurred in almost every major city in the Republic this morning," the anchorwoman peered into the camera. "The biggest were in Austin, Fort Worth, Tucson, Atlanta, and Memphis. Crane's office, when asked about the public outrage, said the government and the president's office have very tough decisions to make, and ask for the patience of the people while navigating these uncharted waters."

Ashley's thoughts became a bright mosaic of contrasting emotions and images. There were those that were bright and bold. Others were dull and depressing. She felt joy over protests to the president's actions.

There was hope that change would occur soon, but entangled with pessimism that it would happen at all. But the backdrop, at all times, was her beloved Kyle. She worried for him and his safety, as well as his sanity. She knew Kyle did not really want to be there. Yet he risked blood and soul in its name.

And while Ashley sipped her morning coffee, cozy on her couch and bathing in the morning sun that flooded her apartment, Kyle was firing bullets, seemingly into the setting sun. Everything that wasn't on fire was still on fire. The sun, weary from a full day of witnessing the siege of Hyderabad, was now angry. It glowed a wrathful, deep orange, pouring its solar rage upon the city and the combatants engaged there.

"They're not slowing down at all, are they?" Kyle asked, trying to yell over the noise of his fifty caliber and all the rest of the weapons.

"No they ain't," Okie yelled back, closing his left eye and aiming as he fired. "It's gettin' dark," he added, observing that the sun was beginning to sink behind the buildings on the horizon and cast long black shadows across the irrigation canal that separated them from the Taliban defenders. "They should be givin' up soon."

"Don't count on it." Kyle tried to aim for the bright strobing muzzle flashes easily visible in the darkness of the shadows. "These guys know their territory better than us. We would call it a night, but that might give them the upper hand. Just hold the line and we'll choke this city off," he yelled to the men surrounding him.

The Republican Guard continued to close in, tightening their grip on the sprawling port city. The tanks kept blasting and mortars still dropped among the advancing Taliban. Gunfire continued to rage on the part of the Americans, but began to dwindle on the other side. Muzzle flashes grew few while the sun died in the west across the Indus River. The power was still on for Hyderabad. There were no major strikes to the interior of the city, so the lights still caused her to glow in the absence of sunlight. What terror for the children who lived within. To see that everything on their street was normal—no soldiers, no tanks, no guns—but hear the terrible sounds outside of their city. To lie in one's bed, trying to drift into a relaxing and comfortable slumber, but hear the not-too-distant booms of explosions beyond the last home. Would they hope for the Americans to liberate them from the extremists who oppress them? Do they embrace the Taliban? Or do they simply wish it would all just stop, regardless of the outcome?

The battlegrounds surrounding Hyderabad fell silent. No more did the tanks blast or the rifles fire. There were no more tracers streaking through the night air. No more death. No more malice. Strangely, everything was calm. The Americans held to their battlements, keeping a keen eye on the blackness and a tightened finger on the trigger. Eyelids were heavy. Heads bobbed. It was silent, except for the distant sounds of the city, carrying on as if nothing was amiss. The temperature began to drop in the absence of the sun. The long sleeves of the soldiers' combat gear, once too warm in the day, now comforted them in the night.

"See," Okie smirked after a while. "I told you they'd give out as soon as the sun went down. I bet those dumb bastards think every last one of us has night vision goggles," he chuckled.

"I could see that," Kyle nodded. "People in places like this think every last American is a millionaire and we're all educated and elite. In reality, our government can barely keep bullets in our guns."

A silence ensued. It was almost uncomfortable. They had paused, yet were still engaged. It was hard to tell if the conversation was still going. A grunt lingered in their chests, as if loaded and prepared for fire. They each wanted to say something. Kyle feared that he had somehow stepped into a realm of conversation that he should leave alone. He had to watch what he said around these guys.

"You don't like bein' here, do you?" Okie finally asked.

"No, I'm fine," Kyle reassured. "You don't think I'm a good soldier?"

"That's not what I meant." Okie softly closed his eyes for a moment. "You're a great soldier. You're good at this. What I mean is . . . well . . . you don't agree with bein' here."

"I don't know what you're talking about." Kyle spoke in a low tone as he scanned around him to make sure no other soldier could hear him.

"C'mon, man," Okie pressed. "You know exactly what I'm talkin' about. Every day you mention somethin' about the government not taking care of us, only carin' about their agenda, or have some other critical thing to say about the Republic."

"I do?" Kyle tried to play dumb.

"Um . . . yeah," he half smiled. "You're not a true patriot. You're not all gung-ho. That's fine, man. To each his own."

"Well . . ." Kyle paused and stared off at the lights of the city. "Yeah, I suppose you're right. My dad pressured me to join the Guard after graduation. I've never considered myself a Republican. I've never really agreed with the secession. But I've had a duty. I fought in Carrolton with you, but I was mainly defending my home and all the people that matter to me."

"So you don't agree with us being in Pakistan, either?" Okie questioned.

"I was much more enthusiastic about this war," Kyle admitted. "I was kind of excited about it. Revenge for Dallas. It was an emotional thing. But now that I'm here and I'm thinking more rationally, I don't know if being here is the answer. What about just doing a better job of securing our borders against assholes like these sneaking in bombs? Why not quit fighting amongst ourselves—distracted from everything else that really matters? We're not going to 'win' this war in the traditional sense. We're going to take all major objectives and just wait around. But that's not winning . . . not when every day, some insurgent with a vest full of C-4 blows himself up and fifteen of our guys. And what will we succeed at? Getting thousands of people killed and a bankrupt government."

There was a silence and Kyle was worried. He had done this more often since graduating high school. He used to have a light concern for the state of the world, society, and the country. It was more of a conversational thing. Beyond that, he really couldn't care less. But now he did. Maybe it was because he, every day, lived the product of government policies. He experienced firsthand what happens when a government made a decision. And the more he thought about things, the angrier he had become. He had stronger opinions. He felt if he did not voice them, no one else would. Perhaps society would be doomed if he did not speak up. What voice did he really have? Probably nothing he ever said would ever make a difference in the face of legislators who are only in it for their own advancement. But he said them more often anyway. And now he had done just that. Every time he opened his mouth, it seemed, he was offending someone. Was he really that offensive, or were people just that sensitive? He feared alienating friends and family anyway, and now he feared he would alienate his best friend.

"I can see that," Okie nodded, much to Kyle's surprise. "I'm a good ol' boy from Oklahoma. I grew up with traditional values and respect for your leaders. But you know, sometimes I wonder if my fightin' here is for freedom, as they say it is, or if it's just to serve some jackass somewhere up at the top."

A few hundred feet down the line of Guardsmen, in the void of darkness, soldiers sat quietly, staring off into the city. Their eyes floated lazily in their sockets, burdened beneath the weight of the eyelids. They stared blankly and without any particular focal point. But there was a shuffle nearby. A young soldier heard it. Was it the moving of feet somewhere? Then he thought it was heavy breathing. He puzzled for a moment, but then something blocked the light from the city. He raised his rifle, moved his head back and forth and squinted to try and make it out, killing a friendly his biggest concern. Then he saw him—a black-clothed Taliban defender. The soldier jumped up, shouldered his weapon, and unleashed a hail of gunfire that punctured every part of the enemy's body.

Troops leapt to their feet all down the line. Their hearts raced, and they stood silently looking down the way to see what else would happen. No one knew what that was. It was isolated, and there was no gunfire. Hands gripped tight to the stocks of their guns. Their mouths dried. Their eyes were wide and alert.

The young soldier lowered the smoking muzzle of his assault rifle, and crept forward to the battlements. In the deepness of the dark, he could barely detect the outline of a man, bloody and dead in the dust-coated grass. There was no movement. He was sure the man was dead. He began to breathe normally and his heart rate lowered. He moved closer to get a closer view, and then his brow dipped and scrunched in the middle. He noticed something odd—not all his clothing was black. There was something discolored about the torso. He was unsure what it was. And then his forehead wrinkled upward with realization of what he was looking at.

"Bomb!" he yelled, trying to warn the others around.

He tried to scurry away. For the others, what he yelled had not yet processed, and then there was an explosion. Fire expanded from the dead suicide bomber like the big bang. Immense amounts of heat and energy sprang outward, engulfing Guardsman after Guardsman. The shockwave burst outward, sending a dozen soldiers catapulted away, some unconscious, some dismembered, and some aflame.

"Suicide attacks," Kyle yelled, seeing the explosion down the way. "They're using the cover of night." He then led by example, and began firing at nothing.

"I can't see shit, sir," a young recruit yelled to Kyle. "What am I supposed to aim at?"

"I don't care, you dumb son of a bitch!" Kyle yelled over his fifty caliber. "They're coming from in front of us—just aim that way. Light it up."

Every soldier on the siege line shouldered their rifles and began shooting into the darkness. Tracers filled the night like fireflies on a summer evening. They burned and streaked through the air amid a wall of lead. It was a swarm of angry bees attacking an infiltrating badger. But the badger was fierce. With the blazing muzzles illuminating the battlefield, Kyle could see the onslaught of Taliban forces firing back and rushing the line. He could see explosive vests on the torsos of some of the men, and a river of terror flowed through him suddenly and chilled him to the bone.

"You keep those guys far away from here," he yelled out. "Kill 'em out there, and they blow up out there! Stop 'em before they get too close!"

Vests blew apart their wearers all over, mostly in the field. Kyle and Okie shuttered a bit, feeling the intense heat that emanated from each of the explosions. And they smiled. They could see that every time a vest went off, it took several other Taliban gunmen with it. A few got close enough for the blast to knock a few Guardsmen back a few feet with minor injuries.

The fire died down. Kyle could see no more insurgents in the blazing battlefields. He lowered his weapon, as did his men and every soldier in a wave down the battlements. He just stood there for a long moment, marveling at the scene ahead. It seemed almost staged; fake. Dirt mixed with his sweat and rolled down his face. It was chilly, but the heat generated by those suicide vests was great.

"We have any halogen lights?" Kyle turned to Okie.

"Yeah," he motioned behind him. "They're back there with all the supply trucks. I know what you're thinking, but I don't think command is going to let you do this."

"I don't give a shit," Kyle replied, still breathing heavily. "Taliban already knows we're here. There is no element of surprise. Set 'em up because this shit here is not going to happen again."

Chapter 30

The room was not fancy, nor was it spacious. But what else could you expect in a warzone located in a developing country? It was not going to be the Waldorf-Astoria. It was dingy and ill-kept. It might have been nicer at one time; a bit more habitable. It seemed that Taliban control had allowed the place to begin wasting away. Derek imagined hillbillies taking ownership of Buckingham Palace, or some other beautiful abode, and hanging up deer heads and pissing on the toilet seats without wiping it up. He imagined them allowing the place to deteriorate into the shanties he envisioned they came from.

He paused in his thoughts, and realized what he was thinking. He had come from a shanty, only it was in a city, rather than in the wilderness Appalachians. Yet, here he was judging people from poor backgrounds in the southern United States, or what used to be the United States. He realized that it was not a background of poverty or backwardness that he was judging. He was judging the region from which the people came from. He was begrudging the lifestyle and politics of those people. He hated people who came from, supported, and especially fought for the Republic of America.

Jets screamed overhead outside of the base compound, bringing his attention back to his surroundings. He had seen the damage walking into the place. The airstrikes had all but decimated this Pakistani air base. Most planes were in flames and pieces of twisted metal. Fuel burned in what was left of the tanks that held it. The first wave of infantry had slaughtered Taliban-affiliated personnel or taken them prisoner. All that remained was a few hangars and this administrative building.

The conference room was a nice change, as run-down as it was, from the big, loud, open hangars of Lahore. Metal folding chairs sat in rows across the thinly-carpeted floors. Maps barely clung to the concrete cinderblock walls with bits of masking tape scrounged from someone's office desk. NCOs piled in and took their seats. They joked and cut up. Derek remained serious. His game face was on. He sat stiff and erect, attentive to the every move of the general as he strolled up to the front of the conference room. The general cleared his throat loudly and deliberately. It sounded like the gurgling growl of some jungle beast or science fiction alien ready to devour hapless, fleshy victims. It was menacing and commanded the attention of the men and women in the room.

"Welcome to Gujranwala, Marines." His voice resonated within the cold, concrete walls. He paused a moment, taking his time with the briefing. He looked out over the crowd of NCOs, and turned to give the hanging map of the city another quick glance before turning to speak again. "Like Lahore, this is a major objective . . . there's no denying that. In fact, I would say this is a more important city than Lahore. We are here . . ." He picked up a small wooden pointer and marked the place on the map where the air base was located. "We are on the western side of the city. What we will do is fan out north and south along the outer western edge of the city, and move east toward the center here." He pointed to what appeared to be a major road that bisected the city. "This is our primary objective. We will secure most of the major roads and positions throughout the western half of the city, but this road is the most important."

"This is Grand Trunk Road, or GTR, as we'll call it." He then moved over to another map to the right showing a more zoomed-out view of the Punjab region. "GTR runs right up the middle of Gujranwala and connects important cities like Lahore with none other than the capital of Islamabad here to the north," he pointed out.

"Holy shit, I didn't realize we were that close to Islamabad," an NCO commented louder than he planned, and then instantly placed his hand over his mouth in embarrassment while the others giggled.

"Yes," the general confirmed. "We really are that close. Gujranwala is a major industrial center. This was a huge city for the Taliban to take control of because of its importance in supplying their ability to make war and plan terrorist attacks. If we can take control of factory districts and major highways leading out—especially GTR, which runs up to Islamabad—we can make a tremendous impact on the Taliban government and their ability to supply their personnel. Questions?" He scanned the room only to find the slowly-raising hand of Derek Putnam. "Yes, Lieutenant," he called on Derek, noticing the freshly sewn insignia on his shoulder.

"Sir . . ." Phlegm bubbled in his throat. He cleared it quickly and continued. "Sir, is there a reason why we are only approaching the city from the west? Why not surround the whole city and strangle her to death?"

"Very intuitive." The general smiled in a way that he hoped no one would ask that question, but he also seemed impressed that this young Marine had. "I was about to get to that." He paused uneasily as he stared into the podium that he now leaned on for almost total support. "We have a bit of a complication." He now had the dead-silent attention of the men and women in the room. "The powers that be, in their planning this invasion of Pakistan in unison with the Republican Guard, goofed on one of the objectives. We were supposed to take some of the cities and the Guard take the others. We wanted to minimized the amount of contact you loyal U.S. citizens had with the secessionist rebels that we, less than a year ago, were killing in droves. But somehow, both the U.S. Marines and the Republican Guard planned on taking Gujranwala," he announced to the tune of gasps and whispers. "So what's going to happen is we will take the western side of the city and the Guard will take the east. We will meet in the middle with securing GTR from each of our respective sides. We will have no contact, and you will not take any pot-shots at the Guardsmen across GTR. Understood?"

"Yes, sir," they replied in unison.

"Not that I could blame you," he said. "We don't want an incident. Not here. Besides, on the bright side, that's half the city you don't have to worry about. We'll share the responsibility with the Reds.

"How's it looking, sir?" one of the younger Marines looked up from his chatting with Derek's unit.

Everyone turned their focus from the gear they had been preparing. They did not yet know where they were heading, but they knew they were heading for nastiness. That was the way they felt—they always got the tough assignments. Perhaps that was a compliment. This was a high-ly-performing unit. All eyes were on Derek Putnam as he briskly stepped and moved his broad shoulders in a masculine fashion. They dropped ammunition they were loading into their vests and pockets. They put down rifles they were cleaning and inspecting. Their eyes were squinting in the sunlight reflecting off the aging airfield tarmac, yet they shivered as it had turned cold—winter in the Punjab region was unpredictable.

"All right, listen up." He slowed and then stopped before his attentive men and women. "This is not going to be another Lahore. No sweep and clear, so this time, we know what we're after and we're going to get it," he cried as his troops cheered. "Airstrikes and drone attacks have made it easy for us to use this outside loop highway called Gujranwala Bypass." He squinted as he pointed off to a wide highway in the distance. "We'll use this highway to move north—supposedly unopposed for the time being—until we get to Gondla Wala Road. That's in the suburbs—an area called Raj Kot. From there, we follow Gondla Wala Road, or GWR, southeast toward the center of Gujranwala. Expect for us to get some serious flak the further in we get. This is an industrial city. It's very important to the Pakistani economy and the Taliban supply line."

"So we're hitting factories?" Kendra bit her lip at him with a seductive twinkle in her eyes, causing him to trip on the first few words of his response.

"Yeah, um . . ." His mind was momentarily elsewhere. "That's our first major objective. We will follow GWR into an area called Model Town."

"Huh?" Queens puzzled at the name, along with everyone else and their V-shaped brows.

"I don't know." Derek shrugged at the origin of the name of the section of the city. "Our objective is to first secure a major telecommunications and IT company there. Airstrikes have already hit it pretty hard, but they are going to want to reestablish themselves, so we have to secure the area and make sure that doesn't happen. Then we are going to take hold of a major section of the GTR that runs right by the telecom company."

"GTR?" Alex asked. "Geez, send this guy up the ranks and he starts talking in code."

"Funny . . . asshole . . . pay attention," Derek fired back. "GTR is Grand Trunk Road—a major highway that cuts the city in half. All the major industry is along it and supplies Islamabad. We take it and we cut off the supply line to the capitol. Get me?"

"Yes sir," his unit chimed.

"Carry on, then," he nodded. "Queens, come here buddy. You too, Alex." They both stood and walked over to their friend. "I need to have a couple of sergeants I trust under me, and now as lieutenant, I have the power to promote. I trust you guys over anyone else, so you're it." He shook each of their hands. They each pulled in for a masculine hug and firm pat on the back. "All right, get your people's shit together. That's and order." Derek smiled and walked away.

Chapter 31

The room was as a canvas of dull colors. There were nothing but browns and beiges with accents of black, gray, and minute traces of bright colors. It was a dreamlike haze, eyes crossing as if Cindy had gone days without sleep, which was pretty close to the truth. It was like being underwater. Her vision was blurred. Voices droned along, an inaudible pulse of bass tones where the emphasis was in speech. She was drowning in this conference room. Her cheek rested upon her fist with her elbow based at the wooden table. Her glasses had drifted down her nose, resting now near the tip. She was not using them anyway. Her cheeks drooped, the skin a bit looser around the corners of her mouth. Occasional strands of gray were beginning to be visible at the roots along her face. She had aged, and not just since the war with the Republic. It had been the last few weeks. Her eyes were almost permanently puffy from lack of sleep and constant wiping of tears. Now she just stared and tuned out, despite the seriousness of the talk in the conference room.

"Madam President," she finally heard through her mind's fog. "Madam President, what do you think?" She perked up and found the secretary of defense, Jay Shields, staring deeply at her. Everyone else was staring too— the vice president, the secretary of state, and even her husband Donny.

"I'm sorry?" She blinked a few times and shook her head a little to shed the last of her blankness.

"Moving more troops?" Shields said again, though it was the first time Cindy had heard anything about it.

"Wait, move troops? From where? Move them where?" She appeared shocked and agitated. The rest of the room was subtly a bustle with light sighs and silent frustration. Critical eyes remained purposefully off the president. She was clearly somewhere else, and no one wanted to trigger that famous brimstone temper.

"From some of the front lines here in North America," Shields repeated as respectfully as he could. "There are places where the Republican Guard are so thinly placed—Northern Alabama and Missouri, for instance—that we can move our troops holding those lines to places in Pakistan where they can really matter."

Cindy closed her eyes and released every molecule in her lungs in one long exhalation through her nose. She hung her head, drawing in another breath equally as deep and lengthy. There was no response. It was unneeded. She was the president, and she had grown accustomed to not hurrying for anyone. They would have to wait. She removed her glasses, and placed them, still open, on the table before her. She placed her face in her hands and rubbed her eyes before reclining back in her chair. She had opened her eyes, wide and staring off into her own thoughts. Every gaze was upon her, though no one was sure whether she was daydreaming or in grave thought about the decision she had to make.

"So what do you think, Madam President?" Shields pressed, his tone more agitated and impatient.

"I think . . ." she began, and paused, still gazing off into space. Her eyes narrowed and lips pursed. Her cheeks were flushed and brows dropped into a menacing shape. "I think you should stop pushing me and let me make up my fucking mind," she stood and screamed across the table at the secretary of defense.

Heads snapped back and eyes widened to the size of saucers, Shields's especially. Donny closed his eyes, knowing this temper all too well. Only he knew how truly fragile she and her patience were lately. She towered over her staff like a terrible giant of some ancient myth. She puffed and grunted in rage, red as her emotions.

"I'm sorry, Madam President." Shields tried to smooth it over. "I thought it was a simple decision."

"Listen, you condescending prick," she yelled, still furious. "This is never a simple decision. You think it's simple to send a soldier at some boring, lonely outpost in Missouri to an active warzone where he might be killed? You think it's simple to decide whether someone lives or dies?"

"It should be," he rebutted with calmness. "It's tough but it's national defense. That soldier would be fighting for freedom."

"Whose fucking freedom?" She breathed fire. "Pakistanis? What business do we have there? Why not let the Pakistanis fight for their freedom? No one's defending our nation over there! No one's fighting for our freedom."

"You're wrong," Shields said. "They're fighting for our freedom to not have to worry about attacks like Dallas."

"Then we worry about that here," Chandler fired back. "We get our heads out of our asses. That Dallas attack would never have happened if we hadn't been fighting amongst ourselves." She wandered, pacing away from her chair aimlessly. "It would be different if I were ordering troops into Austin to preserve the freaking nation. We're spending billions we don't have in a country we don't need, and you . . ." She turned again toward Shields. "You think it's a simple, easy thing to do to ensure that some mother's child never comes home." She paused, tears rising to the corners of her eyes. "That mother's baby boy or girl . . ." She paused again. ". . . dies cold and alone in some far-off place."

Shields hung his head, feeling foolish. The tone of the room was somber. Eyes were shut, and chins were low. Gulps and lumps filled choked-up throats. Donny's hand moved slowly. His wife stood beside his chair on the verge of a complete breakdown. His outstretched fingers lightly touched hers; a slight caress, and when she did not move her hand, he went ahead and took hold of it. She squeezed his hand as they both, in their own heads, revisited the mourning that neither of them could seem to shake.

"I'm done." She plopped into her seat. "I'm done, so done with this war. I want out. I want out. I refuse to send any more troops to their deaths in the name of revenge."

Unknown to her, the conference room door had opened and in stepped General Bates with his usual folder of papers and intelligence. He calmly waltzed in, having been there long enough to have been able to gauge the severity of the tone within the room.

"You ready to get out?" Bates sat in his usual spot. "Ready to end the war? I think I know how."

"Serious?" Cindy brought her face up out of her palms.

"Remember the conversation we had a while back?" He leaned over the table.

"What conversation?" Shields seemed shocked to be out of the loop. "What are we talking about?"

"The general and I," Cindy explained, "had a very hypothetical discussion last month about handling this war a bit more surgically and with less personnel to put in harm's way."

"And we have some intel," he said as he patted the folder. "Some good intel."

"So what?" Shields inquired. "You want to win the war on what . . . SEAL team strikes and drone attacks?"

"Precisely," Bates confirmed, to Shields's surprise. "Boy, you are living up to your title after all. We have a combination of aerial intel from recon drones and live intel from operatives on the ground. CIA has had agents in the field since long before troops ever got off the boats. We know where the Taliban's biggest outposts are, we know where their biggest leaders are, and we know the location in Islamabad where the acting Taliban Pakistani president lives." He grinned a rare grin.

"We could decapitate the whole monster," Shields pondered.

"We hit with drones, and we hit with special ops," Bates said firmly. "As Shields said, we lop off the head of the monster, and if we do it right, no heads will soon grow back."

"And stick the Republic with the occupation," Cindy nodded. "It's their war; their revenge."

"And we get the hell out of there," Donny finally spoke up.

Cindy scanned the table. All eyes were again on her, watching and imploring. They said nothing, but their faces pleaded. She even thought she saw a slight nod or two. Little thought was needed. She had begun to nod, and without knowing it. Bates was poised like a cat, ready to pounce on the verbal decision and act right then.

"How much time?" she asked.

"We need a couple of weeks minimum to prepare our teams and finalize the strike plans," he said enthusiastically. "We could carry it out in one day less than a month from now. We could have troops out by March."

"Do it," Cindy nodded, her staff nodding with her. "Keep me posted."

Chapter 32

"It's still burning," Queens said, pointing through the Humvee windshield at the column of thick black smoke in the distance down the highway.

"That's the objective," Derek smiled. "I love drones. Drake," he tapped the driver's shoulder.

"Sir." He glanced back, but careful to keep his eyes on the road.

"Bring us in about a quarter of a click closer, and stop. Everyone will go on foot from there," he ordered.

This was no surprise attack. Gunfire echoed across the sprawling city. Jets screamed and helicopter blades beat upon the wind. That business complex at Model Town had been pounded all morning. Resistance at the intersection of Kashmir Road was heavy enough to slow them down, but the smoke rising above the objective was a good sign that most of the resistance was over.

The Humvee slowed, and finally stopped, allowing Derek and his newly promoted sergeants to emerge. He adjusted his helmet on his head and the sunglasses on his face. His boots pounded the dust on the road, undisturbed at the moment. As many businesses and homes as there were, the streets had cleared of any civilians. They likely huddled in their homes, hoping the drones would not mistakenly hit their residences. Soldiers on foot began massing in the location. Vehicles came to a halt, and Derek re-briefed his troops on the assault.

"All right, Marines." He looked around at his unit, all attentive, yet cautious of their surroundings. "Remember, we're sending the tanks up first, followed by fifty-cal support on the Humvees. Try to move low, taking cover as much as you can behind the vehicles. We're moving into Model Town Square, and then right up the middle to secure the telecom building. You can't miss it—it's the one destroyed and on fire. Two more units are moving in—one from the north into Model Town Square, and another on the south side of the business center via Bus Stand Road. This location is dead, but expect that Taliban is attempting to secure the location too, so there may be resistance. Got me?" There were a lot of low "yes sir" responses and nods. "Let's go."

The wheels squealed and treads rattled, sending up a thin haze of dust as the Abrams tanks began to move. This was the only way in, a wider road than the narrow little streets that cut through the neighborhood. Those were more like alleyways, made for foot traffic. The tanks and Humvees moved slowly and cautiously. Marines advanced slightly crouched over behind them, silent and observant. Sharp eyes peered down the little, desolate alleyways where no children played and kicked soccer balls amid laughter. Fifty caliber gunmen stood perched and ready, their eager fingers on the triggers.

The street began to open up further. Derek could see why. The road forked to the left and to the right, emerging into a large, square park surrounded by the aged, crumbling third-world markets and plain concrete boutiques. To the right, beyond the park, the IT building silently burned. The air was thick with the smell of smoldering plastic and melted paint. It crackled and complimented the sounds of the military vehicles lording over the streets.

And then a new sound pierced the rolling groan of the tanks and Humvees. Gunfire popped all along the street behind Derek. He turned, startled, gazing back to his rear as Marines took cover at the corners of buildings and behind the Humvees. Bullets ricocheted from the tanks and concrete and stucco walls. Marines dropped to the ground, bleeding into the street.

"Oh hell," Derek spouted. "They're attacking from the residential streets."

"Grenade launchers," someone screamed over the sound of assault rifles firing down the street at the enemy.

"No," Derek ordered. "There are civilians in those houses. No grenade launchers. No mortars. Hand grenades. Use hand grenades," he yelled from the front of the line. "Fifty cals." He pointed up to the men atop the Humvees. "Pound their asses."

Muzzles flashed and bullets filled the tiny streets, tearing off bits of concrete and mortar as Marines attempted to hit the black shrouded heads that popped from within doorways of private residences. It was like some children's arcade; a deadly game of "Whack-a-mole" on the streets of Gujranwala. Grenades were flung, followed by small explosions—bass notes in the rapid-fire treble of gunfire. And like any song, it wound down to a crawling pace, finally stopping.

The convoy began again, vehicles and adrenaline-filled soldiers moving along, alert and angry. The street emerged into the Model Town Park Square. The trees, once majestic and leaf-laden, appeared to be barely clinging to life. The grass was patchy and wilted, dust having taken over in the neglect. Military vehicles split, some left and some right to move around the perimeter of the square-shaped park. Marine foot soldiers were locked, loaded, and pointing their weapons horizontal to the ground, scanning for more enemies. And the gunfire started again. Derek could see the muzzle flashes ahead.

"Across the park," Alex yelled, pointing straight ahead.

Derek raised his rifle and opened fire, to set the example for his troops. All barrels set the air ablaze as dying trees splintered and the dusty soil of the park spat upward. The fifty-caliber rifles rained death cutting in half everything it touched. "Small resistance—a couple of dozen at best!" he encouraged. "Tear 'em up and let's move on."

The skirmish ended long before Derek predicted. No special weapons were needed—just rifles and rage. And then the dead were left behind, the convoy moving around the perimeter of the square without further resistance.

East of the park, beyond a strip mall of sorts; dirty, rundown shops in one long building, the convoy passed to the north and the south, splitting and skirting the perimeter of a large, tree-filled lot, at the center of which there was the concrete rubble of perhaps Gujranwala's newest and nicest office complex. Dense smoke billowed up, partially concealing flickers of deep red flame.

"Amazing, isn't it?" Kendra asked Derek as they walked past.

"What?"

"The precision of those drones," she gaped, wide-eyed in amazement. "Not one mortar crater. Not one bullet hole in a tree. The building is the only thing destroyed. See the school on the far side across the street? The homes over there?"

"Yeah, if this were 1942, those would all be leveled, and every kid inside," Queens added. "We've come a long way."

"And not necessarily for the better," Derek commented.

"What, you want to bomb schools and houses?" Queens seemed appalled. "That's no better than these assholes we're fighting."

"That's not what I mean," Derek back-pedaled. "It's just a different world. A different kind of war. Precision is great. I don't want to see dead kids in the wake of this war, but you know . . ." He paused a moment. "Carpet-bombing in Germany and Japan were meant to destroy morale. The people feared for their lives—wanted it all to stop. So the hope was that they would turn their backs on the leaders."

It was silent for several moments, and uncomfortably so. The troops moved along the street past the first of a series of destroyed buildings in the vicinity. Eyes were wide and heads alert. Taliban soldiers were bad about sending two or three blazing guns on a suicide collision course with Allah, and taking out several Marines in the process.

"Okay, there's the IT company up there on the left," Derek pointed ahead. "Keep an eye on it, but really watch this big bus station over here on the right. We'll secure the area, and hit the next objective. That road on the other side of these buildings—that's Grand Trunk."

A deafening thunder of heavy weaponry rang out across the area, echoing through the arched awnings of the bus station and off the shops and office buildings. Derek and most of the Marines knew that sound—artillery, though at first, they hoped it might be their own. Derek popped his head up higher, scanning out across at the Grand Trunk horizon, and then his blood went cold.

"Tanks," Derek called out, alerting his team. "Al-Khalids." He motioned ahead.

"Damn it." Alex looked up and saw them crossing the medians of Grand Trunk. "Had to be the big ones."

They rolled ahead, apex predators of the Pakistani-Taliban ground military forces. They rumbled and shook with a metallic ferocity, aiming their smooth-bore cannons ahead and loosing deadly 125mm shells against the advancing Marines. Buildings behind them erupted with brick debris as some of the shells missed their marks. Others demolished Humvees in one shot or sent bursts of dirt and concrete upward along with pieces of American soldier. From atop the Al-Khalids, machinegun fire spat hot 7.62mm rounds across the battlefield, along with fire from Taliban ground troops advancing from the highway.

Marines scattered and scrambled for places to take cover behind cars or buildings, fleeing the machinegun fire, and praying to God that the cannons would not target them. They popped up occasionally to fire a few bursts at the advancing forces while Abrams tanks moved in from the north, west, and south, firing off their own cannons at the approaching mobile artillery pieces.

"What's the plan, Captain?" Queens slid in next to Derek, who had taken cover behind a beat-up abandoned car. "My guys are handling the foot soldiers okay, but those gunners up on top of the Al-Khalids are tearing us up."

"I know," Derek nodded. "Make sure the fifty cals are focusing on them—not the foot soldiers—until our tanks knock them out for good."

"Yes sir." Queens ran off to command the Humvee gunners.

Derek slowly raised his head and weapon to point through the broken windows of the old sedan, firing as many rounds as he could before attention was drawn to him and he took on a heightened level of fire. Bullets popped and clanged as they punched dozens of holes into the metal doors and fenders. He crouched to peer beneath the car to the other side to see that enemy bodies were piling up, yet a few feet were drawing close. He pulled a grenade from his utility vest, pulled the pin, and threw it over the roof of the car. He listened as it exploded and shrieks of pain rang out amid the droning of machinegun fire.

He looked across to see Kendra crouched, her back against a concrete barricade. She seemed focused, but as she fired over the top and drew a few enemy shots, ricocheting around her, she sunk down as if she would meld into the ground and the barricade itself. She curled into a ball, tucking her helmet down in fear. He watched as she tightened all her muscles, and then looked up, breathing deeply. She picked up her weapon and opened her eyes, now burning with rage, rather than apprehension. She lifted her rifle again, and took aim at a couple of advancing enemies, which she calmly and coldly dispatched with only a few well-placed shots.

The Humvees that remained intact sat idling as fifty caliber gunners pivoted their weapons, aiming them at the gunners atop the Al-Khalids. They sent an endless chain of rounds that popped and sparked around the small metal shields surrounding the enemy gunners until they silenced and slumped over. Queens crouched next to one of the Humvees, firing his rifle at the oncoming foot soldiers. He watched as the Abrams tanks shook and recoiled with each shell fired. Al-Khalids burst open, shrapnel and paneling riding the waves of fire outward into the bus stand parking lot and into the middle of Grand Trunk.

The fifty cal gunner above Queens grunted as bullets clanged around the shielding. He looked up to see the young man slumped over, and then peered out across the field of battle to see that it was still raging. He opened the door of the Humvee and crawled inside, his hands sliding across the blood-slicked floor. He sat up and removed the dead gunner, pulling him down into the cab, and then took up the post, grabbing the triggers and firing at the gunners atop the Al-Khalids.

It was a much better view than the dusty ground below. He could see the broad spectrum of the skirmish—the dug-in Taliban soldiers in the boulevard ahead, the Al-Khalids taking a pounding from the Abrams on his side of the line, and of course, the dead lying in dark pools of their own blood. He continued to fire at the tops of the enemy tanks, tearing apart gunners piece-by-piece. He could see up Grand Trunk to the north and down the major highway to the south. There were skirmishes all over, coming from both sides of the road.

Below, Derek tried to keep an eye on his Marines, especially Kendra, while still taking active part in the battle. He continued to pop up and fire three or four rounds at a time through the windows of the bullet-shredded vehicle. And then there was an explosion. Another followed. Derek's sight was obscured at the moment, crouched behind the car. But he knew that its sound was unlike the boom of the tank cannons. They sounded chunky, like the blasting apart of concrete. He listened closer and could faintly hear distant thumps of mortar rounds popping out of their tubes.

He looked up at the field of battle and witnessed the explosions of concrete and asphalt in the road and bus stand parking lot. Taliban soldiers rode the geysers of destruction upward in pieces of flesh and bone. He dipped back down, facing the opposite direction, and searching for mortar squads behind his lines. He could see none.

"Queens," he yelled up to his friend, firing from atop the Humvee, but his friend was unable to hear. "Queens." He finally stopped firing and looked down at Captain Putnam. "Queens, where the hell is that mortar fire coming from?"

Queens gazed out across Grand Trunk, squinting and attempting to pierce the haze of dust and smoke. He could make out the main highway and the enemy there, but there were other muzzle flashes twinkling through the smoke on the eastern side of the road, as well as small squads sending mortars into the middle of the road and the enemy defenses.

"Across the road," he yelled down to Derek. "It's an attack from the eastern side of Grand Trunk."

"Eastern side?" he confirmed, pausing to puzzle a bit. He could not remember any units being briefed on attacking from the east, and then it hit him. He knew who the force was. "That's the Reds," he yelled to Queens. "The Republican Guard is securing that side of the city. GTR is the dividing line. We've got the Taliban sandwiched," he half smiled.

The onslaught continued for several more minutes, and then sharply died down. The number of enemy barrels blazing decreased and the tank fire was nonexistent. Soon, only a few sporadic shots persisted, and then there was nothing. Derek's lungs filled with dust and smoke. He could hear grunts and screams of the wounded and dying. He stood, and looked out across the bus stand. It was demolished and filled with craters. The area was littered with body parts and bleeding corpses; mostly Taliban, but a sickening amount of Marines. He could see two Abrams tanks ablaze behind him, and several Humvees that had met the same fate. Queens dipped into the vehicle, and exited the side door holding his right shoulder.

"You okay, Queens?" Derek walked up to him.

"Yeah." He removed his hand to reveal a gash on his upper arm. "It's okay. Just grazed me."

"Damn, that was a close one," Derek smiled, and patted his shoulder. "Go see the medic."

Derek turned back to the battlefield to see Marines canvassing the area. He began out that way, walking through the rubble and stepping over bodies. Over a dozen soldiers checked over the Taliban soldiers lying in the dirt, occasionally putting an extra round into the still breathing. He continued walking past what used to be the awnings of the bus depot, and stood at the edge of Grand Trunk Road amongst dead Taliban soldiers and destroyed Al-Khalids.

He could see movement of soldiers on the other side, something that alarmed him at first. But he could make out the twenty-nine-star red flag of The Republic on the shoulders of the soldiers. He watched as the soldiers checked through the dead on that side and canvassed the little residential streets. Alex walked up beside him and stood viewing as both watched Guardsmen raise their weapons and push around Pakistani women in robes and veils. Derek's mouth dropped open in horror, his hand reaching out helpless to do anything. He could hear the women crying; begging for their lives in the only language they could speak. And then the shots rang out, sending the women lifelessly to the ground. Children stood crying over their mothers, begging them to wake up as Guardsmen laughed and shouted faint claims of revenge for Dallas.

"We have to do something," Alex said, imploring his captain.

"Can't," he replied. "We have specific orders to not interact with the Reds in any way, and especially not to engage them."

"Captain," Derek could hear from behind him.

He turned, almost thankful to be freed from having to watch the scene on the eastern side of Grand Trunk. The scream seemed frantic and imperative. He jerked his head around looking for the source, and then caught sight of Queens kneeling down beside a concrete barricade. He recognized that barricade, and began toward it, first at a trot, and then as a full sprint. He arrived in a matter of seconds, kneeling beside Queens, and then removed his helmet. His mouth hung open and his hands slowly moved downward. His eyes puffed up underneath, and then he closed them, finally placing his hands gently upon Kendra's paling body. Her eyes were wide and face was turning blue with just a bit of blood still rising from the hole in her neck, and down to the large pool upon the ground.

He held her for a moment as several men, including Queens and Alex, stood over them, silent and somber. Derek pulled Kendra close to him as if he would get the same warm feeling from her in death as he did in life. That was in futility. She would not hug him back or caress the back of his neck. He laid her down in the dust, and just stared at her, not allowing a single tear to flow down his face. He saw a little white corner sticking up from a pocket beneath her utility vest. He went for it, slowly tugging at it until it was released.

"Envelope," he said aloud. "Death letter to her parents. You guys move along. I'll take care of this."

He flipped the envelope over to its front to see that it was not addressed to a mother and father somewhere in the States. It had a single word: "Derek". His lip quivered as he read it, and then reluctantly opened the sealed envelope, removing the folded letter. It smelled like her. He could pick up her scent even through the smoke and sweat. He unfolded it, a tear forming in the corner of his eye, and then began to read.

Derek,

If you're reading this letter, one of two things has happened. Hopefully, it's just that we have parted ways and shipped out to the States. But it's also possible that I'm dead. Either way, we'll never see each other again, and you'll go back to your girlfriend and your baby to live a long, happy life. I don't want you to feel guilty or bad about it. Don't worry for me, and don't feel that you're abandoning me. I knew what I was getting myself into when I went after you. I knew I could never have you forever, no matter what. But at least I got to be with you for a little while, and for me, that was totally worth it. Loving you for this short period of time and having your love to warm me at night was enough to last me for the rest of my time on Earth, regardless of how long that might be. All I want is to occupy some little corner of your heart—just a piece—for the rest of your life. Think about me from time to time and remember what we had. I love you, my captain, and wish you the best life anyone could ever have.

Love,
Kendra

Derek loosed a few more silent tears as he folded the paper. They rolled out of his eyes, dripped onto the ground and onto Kendra, soaking into her dirty garments. He placed the letter back into the envelope, and tucked it away in his own vest, and then sunk into the ground—or he wanted to—continuing to mourn as the troops cheered upon word that Grand Trunk had been secured all over the city, and Gujranwala was conquered.

Chapter 33

January

Joe Crane leaned his head to the side. The reflection of his head emerged from behind his plate, mirrored in the reflective polish of his great, solid wood dining room table. He moved it left again, obscuring the reflection, and then peek-a-booed out from it again, smiling childishly. The aromas rose from his plate and were consumed greedily in his nostrils. His eyes momentarily closed in ecstasy. The clang of a fork against the china rang out from across the table. He watched his wife sparing no time in consuming the hearty breakfast, and then looked down at his untouched plate, finally ready to strike.

He cut into the sausage patties with the side of his fork, flavorful grease seeping onto the plate as he applied pressure enough to break it apart, and then hoisted the first bite into his eager mouth. Not one to eat one thing at a time, he showed equal attention and love to the two over-easy eggs sprinkled with Kosher salt and pepper, and to the two homemade biscuits doused in a country cream gravy made from the grease the sausage had been cooked in.

He was comfortable here. He hated the idea that he had to go downtown to the capitol. He had gotten used to taking a break for the holidays. A week and more into the new year and he was still reluctant to go back to work. It was a welcome break. The warmth and smell of burning wood in his fireplace was just too comfortable. He shuttered at the thought of having to change from his sweats and hoodie, and don the same old stiff executive suits he wore nearly every day of his adult life.

And then to further interrupt his comfort in simple pleasures, sometimes work found its way to him at home. It sought him out. The door-bell rang, jolting him from his concentration on the wonders of country cooking. It was tantamount to a rude and annoying squeal of the alarm clock invading the most wonderful of dreams. Neither Crane, nor his wife moved an inch; only looking up briefly to hear the housekeeper shuffling down the hall to answer. The next sound was the creaking open of the door, and then muffled speaking. Crane prepared himself. The guards only let his closest staff past the front gate. Soon leather soles clapped against the hardwood floors, and there was a presence in the dining room.

"Señor Wallace . . ." The housekeeper announced Zack, already in his governmental best attire for the morning.

"Jesus, Zach." Crane waved away the maid, his mouth still chewing on biscuit. "Can't you let a man have his breakfast before you jump right into business for the day?" he half smiled, attempting to hide the food in his mouth with his hand.

"My apologies, sir . . ." Zack bowed a little, his hands clasped together. "But there is something that requires your attention."

"Breakfast?" He half ignored his chief of staff. "I can get Pedro, or Paco, or whatever the hell his name is to fix you up some of this. It's amazing." He took a big bite.

"Um . . . no sir . . . I don't eat breakfast," Zack shook it off. "Um, an announcement . . ."

"You don't eat breakfast?" Crane was shocked. "That's the most important meal of the day."

"Um . . . I just kind of do the coffee thing," he said, and then shook his head, a little frustrated. "The TV—"

"This gravy is—"

"Sir." Zack immediately regretted interrupting, and in such a matter that Crane was now frozen in place staring at the young man. "Sir," he said more gently, "Chandler is about to announce something big any minute. Every news agency in the western hemisphere is at the White House waiting her conference. I don't know what it is, but I think you should see it."

Crane just looked down at his breakfast, and nodded silently. He picked up the deep red cloth napkin from beside him, and clamped it on his mouth from both sides, wiping heavily, and then placed it again at the side of his plate as he stood. He led the young man from the dining room and his continuously dining wife, and started down a dark hallway into the study where he did much of his business. He passed the large cabinet that housed the television, and opened the double doors, letting them swing open with ease as he circled a coffee table and plopped down into the leather upholstery of one of the couches. He watched as Zach stiffly seated himself in an armchair. Crane picked up the remote control, and clicked on the TV and the cable box, not bothering to change the channel as it was already on the Republic's main news channel.

"Sad that our new agencies know something's going on before me and my staff," Crane scoffed as he reclined back a little.

"If you're just joining us, we're covering the live press conference at the White House in Washington, DC, where President Chandler is about to make a major announcement," the anchor stated from behind a newsroom desk. The picture-in-picture at the bottom was of the ballroom in the West Wing, a podium in the foreground and the red carpeting of the inner hallways in the back. Suddenly, as she was about to say something else, she stopped and the main screen was that of the press conference as Cindy Chandler stepped up to the podium.

"Thank you, ladies and gentlemen," Chandler began. "Today is a turning point; a new day in America. We have been at war for too long. We've seen too many young men and women die. Too much destruction. We've strained the economy and drained the treasury. We have to learn to, when necessary, fight wars smarter and more efficiently. We have to the technology. We have the expertise. We have to stop fighting twenty-first century wars with twentieth century methods. For the last few months, we have been compiling greater intelligence on the whereabouts of top Taliban leaders in Pakistan, as well as better knowledge of where the most important installations are. In the last two weeks, drone strikes and surgical special operations strikes have been focused on the hideouts, headquarters, and even homes of the most important of Taliban Pakistan's leaders. We are particularly focusing, of course, on objectives in the capital, Islamabad."

Crane's eyes widened and his jaw hung as he leaned forward in shock, listening to what was said more closely.

"Today we have confirmation that the Taliban's hold on the government of Pakistan is splintered. Communications with their bases in Afghanistan and other surrounding areas are broken, and activity at known planning centers is nonexistent. My military advisors, as well as the CIA, are now confident that the Taliban's grip on the Pakistani government is broken, and complete control of the country is eminent. In essence, we have won the war," she said as thunderous applause erupted in the room and she paused to take it in.

"What?" Crane leapt from his seat, his hands on his head. "When the hell did this happen? Did anyone from the U.S. government let us in on this? Am I the only one out of the loop?" He was frantic. Zack just sat, shaking his head in disbelief.

"We have done our part in taking down this terrorist entity and shaking their grip on a nuclear country," Chandler continued. "We have assisted our neighbor, The Republic of America, in avenging the horrible attack on Dallas last year. Now it is our time to bow out, and turn control of the occupation of Pakistan over to them. I will, in the next day or so, give the formal order to retract all U.S. forces from Pakistan. And with that threat now neutralized, perhaps both our countries can rest easy and enjoy the comfort of peace. Thank you." She stepped away as the inevitable onslaught of questions spewed from the mouths of journalists. They would be unanswered as Cindy backed away from the podium, to smile and wave to the tune of endless cheers and applause.

"This is bullshit." Crane stomped in rage. "We had an agreement. Islamabad is ours. And we share the conquest. Now they're going to duck out and leave us holding the bag. Let us sit there occupying the country for years? Draining our treasury? Damn it."

Chandler's smile faded as the cameras were far behind her and she was making her way down the hallway back into the West Wing. The applause became less audible and her step increased as Weaver joined her side, as did her chief of staff, Sandra.

"They love ya," Weaver grinned. "You're an employee of the people, and you gave the people what they have been asking for."

"I agree, Madam President," Sandra added. "It's the right move."

"I just wonder if it's enough." She kept moving swiftly, the general and Sandra trying to keep up. She stopped suddenly to look out one of the windows that viewed across the White House lawn. Coat and scarf-clad crowds were gathered and surely building along the fence line separating Pennsylvania Avenue and the north lawn. They were cheering and chanting joyful messages of peace, as well as approval for the president. Chandler grinned slightly, and then it faded. "They want an end to war, I know. But I wonder if what they want more is a unified nation," she said, and then kept moving.

Chapter 34

Kyle and Okie stood guard affront the traffic police station, their eyes scanning the motor and foot traffic coursing through the busy square, an intersection of five major streets in the very center of Hyderabad. It was a major objective during the conquest. Not one concrete wall was without bullet scars. Across the intersection, an electronics store lay blackened and gutted by fire. Dark red stains still marked the concrete sidewalks and asphalt, testaments to a deadly encounter here in the previous weeks.

Otherwise, it appeared almost as nothing had ever happened. The air was heavy with exhaust fumes, mostly from motorcycles, mopeds, and rickshaw taxis shuttling people around about their business. They seemed to pay little attention to the armed Americans outside the police station and scattered around the square. Kyle looked up at the sign and awning of the station. It was the first time he had ever seen a police station with advertisements for the local brand of bread on the sign.

"Corporate-sponsored police," Kyle said, prompting Okie to look up at the sign. "Scary. Glad we don't have anything like that back home."

"Yet . . ." Okie grinned.

In fact, this must have been Hyderabad's version of Times Square. Of course, it lacked the jumbotrons, glitz, and neon, but it was one of the city's biggest intersections. Aside from the bullet holes, sandbag bunkers, and blood stains on the ground, it was a prime location for advertisement. Entire three- and four-story apartment buildings were painted bright colors, standing as giant billboards for flavored milk and Japanese pickup trucks. Signs hung along the storefronts marking tech schools, tutoring, security, and clothing shops. The astounding thing was that, even as some street signs were in Arabic or Sindhi, most of the signs and advertisements were still in English.

"Been quiet for the last few days," Okie said. "Eerie. The Paks are actin' like everything's cool. They don't even notice us anymore."

"They're just used to us," Kyle replied. "Ever get something for Christmas, and you're all excited to get it, and in just a few weeks, you don't even notice it lying on the floor?"

"You're assumin' these Muslims were ever excited to see us invadin' their land," Okie scoffed.

"I imagine they were," Kyle smiled, to Okie's surprise. "Most Muslims hate these Taliban and al-Qaeda assholes. They're extremists, and most Muslims are just normal people like us. Taliban gives these folks a bad name. So I'm sure they were happy to see us show up."

"Maybe," Okie shrugged. "Whatever. Maybe the slowdown means we're out of here soon. Did you hear anything at briefing about the drone attacks and SEAL strikes in Islamabad? I've been hearing the war is over. Are we out of here?" He began to get a bit excited.

Kyle grinned, hung his head, and began to chuckle. "I was wondering when you'd ask me about that."

"Well sure," Okie sparked up. "Shit, everybody's talkin' about it. Everybody thinks we're goin' home."

"I'm not supposed to say anything yet," Kyle responded honestly.

"Dude," Okie pried. "I'm your best buddy. I swear I won't tell anybody."

"All right," he said. "But don't tell a soul."

"Swear to God . . ."

"We're not going anywhere," Kyle said. "The U.S. got tired of the same old tactics and sending tens of thousands of troops in and tallying up the casualties. So they spent months doing recon and gathering intel, and they hit some key locations, took out some key leaders, and the Taliban regime in Islamabad is in shambles."

"So the war is over . . ." Okie tried to clarify.

"Yeah, kind of," Kyle said. "The U.S. wanted out, so they ended it, and now they're out. But winning the war always requires a period of occupation."

"Oh." The excitement melted from Okie's face. "And so we get stuck here while the Blue boys get to go home."

"Makes sense."

"How do you figure?"

"It's not really their war," Kyle replied. "It's ours. They were helping us out, and now that it's over, they're leaving the occupation to us."

"Geez . . ." Okie hung his head. "That sucks. You mean U.S. forces are going home and we're staying here?"

"Yup."

"I hope that doesn't mean what I think it does." Okie became distraught.

"What?"

"Everything back home . . ." He tried to leave it at that, thinking Kyle would catch on, but Okie just shook his head and continued. "All those U.S. servicemen back in America, and all of us still here in Pakistan. What if . . ."

"They attack the last Republic strongholds?" Kyle finished the sentence. "It's a thought. But I don't think it will happen. The liberals in the U.S. get tired of war easily. They are all gung-ho in the beginning, and then when casualties start happening, they all freak out. They're tired of war. I wouldn't be surprised if not a damn thing happens once the Blue boys get back home."

A chorus of vehicle horns blasting out their annoying monotonous reveille pierced the air to the point that Kyle almost jumped. The two men, as well as other troops in the area, turned their attention to the traffic in the square. An old pickup truck was stalled in the middle of the intersection, smoke and steam billowing up from under the hood as the driver emerged from inside to open it. The motorcycles and mopeds zipped around the obstruction with ease until other cars and rickshaws began piling up into a quickly growing traffic jam. People walked along the sidewalks and stopped to gawk and investigate.

Kyle scanned around the square for any local traffic police. They had been standing outside a police station, and had not seen an offi-cer come or go in hours. The confusion was mounting, and the horns were increasing exponentially. Shouts of anger arose, likely cursing one another in Sindhi. Crowds were expanding and frustration thickened. Two soldiers across the way looked around for any sign of local police, and realizing there were none to be found, began moving for the truck at the center of the confusion. Kyle watched as the driver, a simple-look-ing local man, threw up his hands, explaining that he was unsure as to what was wrong with his truck. The soldiers moved in for a closer look as the driver moved away. And then the driver backed far away. He began sprinting away, and Kyle's eyes widened. He spotted some large canisters in the bed of the old truck.

"No," he tried to yell out to the soldiers digging under the hood. "Get back," he screamed, waving his arms, but they could not hear over the yelling and horns dominating the sounds of the square.

In a panic, Kyle grabbed the still oblivious Okie, and threw him down behind a sandbag bunker. They crouched as low to the ground as they could, their hands over their heads as a surge of heat filled the dry air. The temperature increased by dozens of degrees, followed by the deafening sound of the ignition and explosion. Kyle could feel the air rush over the sandbags away from the center of the square, and then back in to fuel the flames. Bits of the truck and surrounding vehicles fell, raining fire on the whole intersection. He could hear the raging crackle of the flames as sweat rolled down his face in streams. He could hear moans turn to screams as life became death.

"You okay?" He looked at Okie's bewildered face. He nodded, but said nothing.

Kyle hesitated, and then grew enough courage to raise his head above the sandbags for a peek. He slowly lifted his chin and peered out across the intersection. At the center was a bonfire of ripped-apart vehicles, raging with flames. The metal was beginning to melt, and no sign of anything human was recognizable in that core of the inferno. Cars and trucks lay overturned and damaged all over the square. Ash was beginning to snow down, coating everything in a gray wintery-looking blanket. The streets were littered with people. Men and women lay on the pavement, some completely still, and some writhing in their own blood. Arms and leg were placed haphazardly atop cars and the curbs. Debris was strewn about, blackened or burning. Women clung to bloody, lifeless children, while others screamed in pain, their legs or arms trapped beneath vehicles or large chunks of metal.

"Command, do you copy?" Kyle spoke shakily into his radio as Okie's head popped up for his own look. "Command."

"This is command," the radio crackled back.

"This is Sergeant Perkins at Chandni Cinema Rd. and Thandi Sarak. There's been a suicide bombing. Over," he reported.

"Damage? Dead?" the voice sighed.

"Don't know." Kyle looked across the intersection. "A lot. I don't know how many Americans. At least two. The whole square is blown away. Requesting reinforcements in case Taliban ground troops show up." He scanned carefully for shooters.

"On their way," the radio squawked one last time.

Neither Kyle nor Okie knew what to do. They were dumbfounded and horrified. All they could do was watch. They dared not leave their cover. Aside from the thunderous flames and screaming civilians, the square was quiet and unnerving. They just waited and took in the horror until reinforcements could arrive.

Chapter 35

Derek, seated on his Kevlar helmet, his rifle propped on his knee, dug into his pocket, excavating with dirty, gyrating fingers. The black-framed fingernails emerged, his fingers clutching a small plastic package of paper tissues. He fumbled around into the package, retracting one of the scented sheets, and began digging and blowing out the elusive junk that had come to permanently live in his nostrils. He had felt sick the entire time he had been in Pakistan. His mucus caught seemingly pounds of dust, exhaust, and powder fumes. He had come to really appreciate these little tissue packets for getting rid of the black tar that gummed up his breathing passages. Can't be doing good things to my lungs, he thought as he put away the package and tossed the tissue on the ground.

The bus stand around him was ruined. It and the telecom building across the way had long ceased smoldering. Enemy bodies had been hauled away, the wounded treated, and prisoners taken. For all the damaged vehicles and equipment removed, and all the bodies taken away, the damage was staggering. Almost nothing stood. Rubble and blood stains were common sites. Derek spotted a finger lying on the cracked pavement a few yards away. He just stared at it for an extended moment, unaffected, and then looked up at the military trucks being packed with supplies and moving away.

That's what the rest of his unit was doing. They sat and relaxed, watching it all happen. They just observed the destruction, as well as the detraction. Black-smudged faces sported days old stubble and deepened lines. Their skin had become almost leather; miles away from the youthful complexion of normal young men. Their eyes were panes of glass;

windows into a kaleidoscope of pain. It turned and churned, mixing and combining into new combinations of negative emotions. Cigarette smoke swirled and coursed between them, speaking for the silent troops.

"Captain," a voice called out, startling the unit. "Men. Get your gear." Major Dokka's deep, baritone voice accompanied his Paul Bunyan stature.

"Sir." Derek began scrambling as he and his unit frantically tried to stand at attention.

"Forget it." He raised his hand, half smiling. "You've earned the rest," he said as they slowly and cautiously seated themselves. "But you need to get your gear together and get ready to push out. We'll move south down Grand Trunk Road, back into Lahore. Grand Trunk then cuts east, and then it's only about twenty-three clicks east to the Indian border." He paused for a moment, watching the attentive men nod. "You did good, Marines. You've earned your ticket home to your families. It's almost over." And then he walked away.

Derek, nor the rest of his unit said a word. Mouths remained clamped; their eyes unmoved to watch the major off, they just stared as they were; as if the major had never even dropped by. Grunts packed crates onto the trucks. Troops loaded up on personnel trucks. Lines of tanks and Humvees trailed up and down Grand Trunk. But Derek's eyes were glued to one sight. He watched as light wooden boxes were loaded upon one of the trucks. They all caught sight of it, and they all slumped, watching and mourning. Coffin after coffin was hoisted upward, stacked into the covered bed of the truck. And then one with black stenciled letters on the side: "Voss, Kendra." Derek stared at it, heavy-eyed for several moments until it too was lifted and loaded. A tear lined each eye. A heavy, supportive hand appeared on his shoulder, and then he blinked, shaking his head.

"All right, guys." He stood, giving the coffin truck one last glance. "You heard the major. Get your gear and let's get the hell out."

Chapter 36

February

Caught somewhere between light and dark, the room slowly and dully bubbled with a jumble of almost whispered conversations. They rolled, folded, and kneaded along, sometimes dotted by the unexpected shrill peak of laughter somewhere across the space. Through the blunt, artificial dimness provided by lamps lowered to nearly off, the occasional wine glass or diamond ring gave an instantaneous flash of brilliance. Glasses dinged with a pleasing tone, accenting happy, carefree conversations taking place all over the seating area. Gourmet aromas of fresh herbs and tender cuts of the finest meats filled the nostrils. Finely-crafted flavors pleasured taste buds. Top shelf wines and liquors warmed bellies as tuxedoed servants bustled about with trays and libations, ensuring that no one was to want for anything.

It was a nexus of upper-class surrealism; a world separate from the harshness of reality. It was a darkened parallel dimension where gravity and physics were the same, and so were all of the foods, drinks, languages, and fashions, yet nothing existed as it did for normal people. There were no twenty-five-dollar-dinner-for-two specials. No one used gift cards given to them as a birthday present. No one was on a budget or worried about how they would pay off their sons' medical bills. The amount of money to be spent on groceries filled no one's mind. The greatest area of concern was whether to order the steak or the fish, and what was to be the perfect accompanying wine. Cocktail dresses paired with high-end suits. Valet tickets were clutched by gold- and platinum-laden fingers.

Most patrons were couples—wealthy young businessmen wooing gorgeous women with an eye for financial security or seasoned executives out for a high-priced dinner with their trophy wives. But in the back corner was a larger table of half a dozen men, smiling arrogantly and sipping their after dinner martinis. Laughter erupted from time to time and the other patrons trying to enjoy a warm, wonderful meal with their dates and spouses were almost forced to glance back each time, mostly out of reflex, but not without some level of disdain for the commotion.

"Joe, don't let those damned moderates get you down." An aging businessman slapped his knee, laughing as the President of the Republic of America smiled and nodded politely.

"The moderates keep me sane." Crane wiped a few beads of vodka and vermouth from his upper lip. "It's the radicals at the capitol that worry me. They seem to have no rhyme or reason to what they're always squawking about. I'm no moderate—trust me—but some of these guys just keep going further and further off the deep end."

"The social conservatives?" another businessman asked.

"Usually," Crane turned, nodding. "Guys that only seem to worry about abortion and what gay people are doing. Some congressman from Arizona, the other day, tried to get support for a bill that would outlaw birth control and contraceptives. I didn't even realize this was still an issue."

"You let them have those issues," the first businessman nodded, and smiled almost deviously. "Keep him distracted with his crusade against whatever. You need his support, and you need his supporters. You show them you stand for what they stand for—wholesome values, gun deregulation, and prayer in schools—and you will have their support in doing what you and I want."

Zach Wallace sat at the far end of the table, quietly enjoying a drink, and hiding in the shadows. He was a listener; a watcher, yet ready to advise President Crane as soon as the vultures took flight from the bleeding carcass that attracted them. He cast his gaze across the table now, leaning forward in anticipation of Crane's response. It took an uncomfortable moment or two, worrying Zach.

"Let's talk for a moment about what you and I want." Crane cleared his throat, and took another sip of his clear martini. "You want to make money. I want to solve the government's growing deficit and debt problem."

"This charade can't last forever," the businessman calmly said. "You can't run a war and occupation and cut taxes as you've done."

"That's what the people wanted, and that's what our legislators gave them," Crane replied.

"That's great and everything, but the average constituent isn't a tax economist. That same guy also wants to eat cookies every day and lose weight."

"I hear there's a diet for that," Crane joked. "No, I know. Trust me, I know. We have some money issues. But I think there's an endgame here, and that's why I wanted to see you gentlemen tonight." Crane poised for the attack, straightening himself comfortably in his chair. "We privatize," he simply stated.

There was no response at first, only a few confused looks around the table. Some were unsure that was the end of the statement. They waited for many moments for any further explanation, but nothing followed. Crane just sat back, watching amusedly as the executives awkwardly fumbled about, unsure of what he meant. Zack leaned back, pleased, smiling, and crossing one leg over the other, eager to see this unfold.

"Privatize what?" one of the men spoke up.

"Privatize everything," Crane grinned, folding his hands.

"I don't know that I follow," another spoke.

"Gentlemen, we've been talking about this for years—even back in the U.S. Congress," he began. "We've always talked about how government has no place in the business world. We preach Adam Smith and the invisible hand. We talk of government as a laissez faire entity that only decides disputes. And that's what it used to be until Teddy Roosevelt and the antitrust laws and his nephew and The New Deal screwed everything up for businesses like yours. Now you're stuck with all these damaging regulations we've carried over from U.S. policy, simply for the convenience of starting our own government. But that's just it—we have our own government now. Now we can remove all of those barriers. Now we can privatize all of these things that are a drain on our government. We can keep the taxpayer happy with low rates, and take that fiscal burden from the Republican government. We privatize."

"Privatize the . . ." a businessman began to name some things, but was beat to it by President Crane.

"Fire departments, police, all healthcare," he listed. "All schools become private schools."

"Jesus," one man commented. "So how do people pay to send their kids to school?"

"They just pony it up. They'll have to," Crane said. "Everyone should pay their fair share—no free rides. Then maybe they'll learn to appreciate it. They won't take it for granted when they're paying for it out of pocket. And if you can't, then the burger joint is hiring people to wash the lettuce. Gentlemen, this is capitalism at its finest. It's something we pride ourselves in. Free enterprise! People being responsible for their own futures and well-being. You and your companies could take over funding the schools and charging tuition. You could run the fire and police departments and charge for services. And most importantly . . . take over the military."

"The military? Are you nuts?" a man remarked.

"Why not? That's how the Romans did it. Privatized armies."

"Yeah, and that's how Julius Caesar got his army to march on Rome," a man said.

"But it's a good idea," another executive rubbed his chin. "Can you imagine how lucrative? Corporate-run armies taking over weaker countries and exploiting their resources? Coal, oil, natural gas. Metals and shipping. The possibilities are endless."

The table fell into silent contemplation. Every businessman, with the most analytical of fiscal minds, sat calculating and pondering. Wonderment cultivated while Crane and Zach awaited reactions and responses.

"How soon can you propose a bill?" a man asked.

"We are in session," Crane said. "We can be voting by next week."

Chapter 37

Derek shuttered as he pushed open the aluminum door with a clack of its push-bar lever system. He should have known what to expect. The metal was freezing to the touch, just a split second before he opened the airport door. His sense of realty was that of Pakistan. Now he broke the virtual vacuum of the Cleveland airport and found himself nearly in shock with these below freezing temperatures.

It was momentary. Suddenly, the cold was irrelevant. He was home. The cars were of a certain make and newness. The air smelled the same. He realized conversations that could be overheard were not in Punjabi, but in English. It rushed back to him, this environment, and immediately he was searching for a familiar set of faces. Carly and Olivia. Jake. Then a sudden jolt of sadness struck his gut as he realized he would not likely see Jake today, but surely he would see him soon as his unit was pulled from duty.

He adjusted his issued duffel bag, heavy on his right shoulder, and continued to look with mounting excitement, and perhaps some anxiety. He was afraid he might cry to see that Olivia had aged drastically or that Carly had dyed her hair something completely different. And then he saw the car. Carly leapt from the driver's seat and hustled around the side, her breath heavy on the freezing air. She ran toward him as he dropped his bag and darted over to meet her. He caught her in a swift, punchy embrace, their bodies clapping together like two football players. Arm muscles tightened and bodily warmth was shared between them. Derek could hear sniffling by his ear, and wondered if that was winter or her emotions in action.

"I missed you so much." She pushed back and reached out to touch his face.

"And I missed you, babe," he grinned, sort of glad that she had not changed. His head moved toward hers and she closed her eyes, eager to touch his lips with hers. Standers by, unseen by their passion-closed eyes, clapped and cheered to see the reunion, and then he released her lips. "Where's my other baby girl?" he beamed.

"In the car," she said excitedly.

She rushed over and opened the back passenger door to reveal Derek's own flesh and blood, sitting in the car seat gnawing on some plastic toy. She first looked strangely at the man, examining him with his military gear. There was no emotion, but Derek was all smile; bright and wide—gaping even. He removed his cap, and moved closer in. Finally, neutrality turned to joy and excitement on the little girl's face. Her little nose crinkled and her eyes squinted while Derek moved in to embrace her in her restraints. It was not enough. He frantically fought at the buckles and straps, unfastening his daughter, and finally yanking her from her car seat and taking her into his warm, safe arms. And there she stayed for several minutes. The little girl laid her head on his shoulder as he swayed with her, tears welled up in his eyes.

"Hey . . . um," an unfamiliar voice uttered. "Welcome home, Marine," Derek heard, and turned to see an uneasy smile on the face of an airport security officer. "I hate to break this up, but I gotta get your car out of here to make room for other people picking up passengers."

"Okay." Derek's smile was gone, but he understood, moving for the running vehicle draped in the noxious fume-steam pouring out of the exhaust.

"Sorry, Captain," the man gave a brief and sloppy salute. "And again . . . welcome home," he said.

"Thanks." Derek returned the half-salute and then set his child back into her seat, strapping her in before climbing into the front passenger side of the old station wagon.

Soon, they were driving along Cleveland's snow-lined highways and streets, making their way back home. It was silent for a bit, from time to time. There were large gaps between dialog. So much time away, yet so little to say. Derek could never understand it. He would be away on duty for months at a time with only a handful of letters in between, and upon reuniting, there would be silence. But what would they talk about? The number of people he had seen blown to pieces?

"Did you see Olivia's outfit?" Carly suddenly perked up, smiling giddily as she drove.

"Yeah," he grinned, glancing back over the seat at his content young daughter. He was unsure if Carly was excited about the outfit or the opportunity to break the silence. "Pretty. Where did you get it? That place at the mall you like?"

"No, I made it," she beamed.

"Made it? Really?" He looked back at Olivia, quite shocked, and then back at Carly.

"Yeah!"

"You're joking . . ."

"No, really. I made it."

"That's amazing," he gushed. "How?"

"Easy, really," she said. "I just buy the fabric, sew it, decorate it, and there it is."

"That's awesome." He was still stricken. "When did you start doing this?"

"A while back," she shrugged. "Halloween. I was making Olivia's costume, and it was so cute that some other moms in the neighborhood and some of my sister's friends loved it. They said I should do it for a living. So I started experimenting with other clothes for Olivia and came up with some cute stuff. So now I make all her clothes. It's cheaper anyway."

"Woah," he smiled. "You should start selling this."

"I'm starting to," she nodded. "A few local stores have ordered some outfits, and my sister's husband is going to help me set up a website people can order from. I think it's a great way to make some extra cash, and it gives me something to do. All of my sister's friends have ordered clothes, and they pay well, so what the hell?"

The conversation, as exciting as it was that Carly had kept herself so busy with such an industrious hobby, unfortunately faded. It sputtered and slowed. There was only so many times that Derek could congratulate and praise her without redundancy. He began to just nod his head in the silence. He looked around the car and out the window, nodding and smiling. Even with the still awkwardness, he thought that perhaps he could seem as if he were still excited and upbeat. He was happy to be home, but not at ease.

"Any word from Jake?" he spouted, suddenly discovering a treasure of a topic that he could use to break the silence. "He go to Pakistan?"

"Um . . ." Her eyes darted his way a few times. She gripped the steering wheel a little tighter and focused on the road. "Um, I don't know. Nothing big. He went to Pakistan a while back . . ." She squirmed in her seat.

"What?" He dropped his eyebrow.

"What?" She looked at him and snapped her eyes back to the road.

"What was that?" His mouth hung open.

"What?" she maintained.

"You know what." He cocked his head over. "You're acting funny."

"Um," she uttered, and then her eyes began to turn pink and the skin around them to inflame. "Well . . ." Tears began to form along the bottoms of her eyes, rolling along into the corners, and finally down her face. "I was going to wait until later—not right after you got off the plane—but I guess I have no choice now. Jake . . ." She paused. "Jake was killed . . . early January . . ." The tears continued to fall. She sobbed too hard to continue, trying her best to pay attention to her the road.

Derek said nothing for a moment. He saw it coming. It was her body language. He already knew. He closed his eyes tight with anger and pain. His head shook left to right and back slightly as he listened to the sounds of Carly sniffling.

"I knew it." He kept his eyes closed, and laid his head on the dashboard, shielding his face on each side with his hands. "I knew it. I knew you were acting weird. I knew it," he kept repeating. "I should have known it from the letter you sent me months ago—the one where you told me he was going. Somehow I told myself he was going to be okay, but I knew that wasn't true. Life isn't sacred. It's cheap. It doesn't matter how wonderful or how shitty of a person you are. They all go out there and die. Shot up. Blown up. Fucked up . . ."

Carly had stopped crying for a moment and listened to Derek. She looked over at him, his head still buried in the dashboard, hopping up and down with every bump in the road. She watched as clear liquid drops fell, soaking into the carpeted floor. She started crying again, placing her hand on his hunched back and stroking him. But comforting Derek would not be as easy as a loving hand, and she retracted it for the time being, focusing on the road ahead.

Chapter 38

Two solid raps sounded out from the heavy door, carrying into the office. It resonated through the Oval Office, finally soaked up by the fine blue carpet and the exquisite furniture. President Chandler looked up from her desk, silently droning on through an endless stack of papers, bills, and reports. She peered over at the door for a moment, suddenly jolted from her work and unable to process beyond it for a few seconds.

"Um . . ." She shook her head, snapping out of a momentary daze. "Yeah . . . come in."

The door swung open, and in walked a familiar face—one as welcome as her own husband's. General Bates and his usual green uniform; his usual gait and trying-to-smile crotchety scowl. It was the best he could do. He strolled across the office, seating himself in front of the desk where his president sat.

"Hello, General," she said with a formality in her voice. "How can I help you? You have a report? Something to consult with me about?"

"Nope," he replied.

"Then what?" She appeared confused, and perhaps a bit annoyed, glancing back down at her papers and reports.

"Just checking on you." He put it simply.

"Checking on me?" She half laughed. "I'm fine," she scoffed. "It's not your job to check on me." But he just stared at her with no change of expression. "Really . . ." She raised a brow, but still there was no response, or even movement. And then her face softened. "Really." She seemed to admit something unsaid. "I'm doing okay. It's getting better . . . easier . . . or not. Maybe I'm just coming to terms. Numb?"

"You know . . ." The general leaned forward a bit, repositioned himself, and shifted back again. "I lost someone close to me when I was young. Well . . ." He thought again. "I guess I've lost a lot of people since then. That's just getting old. But when I was about twelve, me and my friends one summer went down to the creek nearby our farm in North Carolina. That's where the whole family swam. We even had Fourth of July barbecues down there with friends and family. The water was cool and shaded by the trees. It was way back in the woods. There was a rope swing and a deep spot we could jump into without getting too hurt. But I went down there one day with my friends, and my little brother Jacob went with me . . ." His expression softened. "I begged Mom not to make me take him. He was five years younger than me and my friends. He was a brat. But she made me take him and watch out for him. So he tagged along. And I shooed him off as soon as we got there. I played with my friends, and poor Jacob had to play alone . . . until I didn't see him again. I noticed he wasn't around, and I panicked. I looked and looked, and found him under a clump of heavy downed branches in the creek. I don't know what happened or how he got trapped underneath, but . . ." He trembled. "We couldn't get him back. Mom never forgave me. Neither did Dad. Hell, it took a long time before I forgave myself."

The president said nothing at first, staring into the wood grains in her desk. She was somber and attentive. She was soft and vulnerable. "How long?" She seemed to swallow a growing lump in her throat.

"Years," he nodded. "I spent years blaming myself, and even to this day, I wish I could go back and tell my idiot, selfish, twelve-year-old self to take care of his brother. But at some point in my life, I realized I couldn't go on defining myself by tragedy or by my mistakes. As much as it hurt, I had to move on. I had to realize . . ." He leaned in to connect directly with Cindy's eyes. ". . . that I can't control everything in the world. Even if I had been paying attention, there's a possibility Jacob could have died that day anyway."

"I could have . . ." Tears rolled down the president's face as she tried to wipe them away as soon as they set into motion. "I'm her mother. I'm supposed to protect her. I could have done something."

"You told her not to go to New Orleans," Bates interrupted. "You did all you could, but Julie was an adult, capable of making her own decisions. She was in charge of her own fate, and she had made up her mind. She was going to find a way to go, no matter what."

Silence again followed. Cindy reached for a tissue popping up out of the top of the box on her desk. Bates just looked at it, sure that it was the first time he had ever seen a box of tissue on her desk at all. He wondered how many boxes she must have been through over the last few months. She wiped her tears and cleared her nose, though it did no good for her appearance. Her puffy eyes were marked by smeared black eye makeup. She would have to visit the bathroom and fix that problem.

"I suppose you're right," she finally said.

There was another knock at the door, but there was no waiting for a reply or a presidential permission to enter. The door swung open, almost with sound of friction with the air. Sandra had her urgent face on, carrying a clipboard, as usual. Distress was in her voice.

"Madam President," she barked. "You have to see something. It's all over the news. Turn it on." She searched all over the desk for a remote.

The president, with a face of near annoyance, picked up the remote control, almost jerking it away from Sandra's reach. Sandra knew that expression of a territorial mother dog defending her den. Cindy looked at the device for the power button, and extended her arm toward the TV and cabinet to the left. The set warmed up and picture faded on, already a news channel and coverage of the breaking story.

"It's not a decision our government came to lightly," Joe Crane spoke with confidence and conviction from inside the rotunda at the capitol in Austin. "We struggled and grappled with history and ideal. We debated the changes in paradigm and culture. But in the end, we did what we thought would be in the best interest of the people of our young Republic. It's no secret that America is the greatest place on earth, and that the Republic of America represents the purity of our once unified nation's vision and message to the world. And from the days of Truman and Eisenhower battling the evil ideals of socialism around the world, it is capitalism that has always made our American economy a shining beacon of righteousness and opportunity. I feel now that we are the final stewards of such an ideal. Our neighbor to the north and east is slipping further and further into the darkness of Marxism. So we must now carry the standard for free enterprise. We must purify the market system. It is government interference that has always hindered the market economy. They have disenfranchised those just trying to make an honest dollar. And with that power comes corruption and cronyism. I believe in our decision. I believe in our fervor. I believe we have done right. And I am proud to announce that all government programs will now be turned over to private industry, where they belong."

The three stared at the television, Sandra's hand over her mouth and her arms clutching her clipboard for comfort. Bates's face never changed for really anything, but Cindy seemed the most affected, physically. Her face was still flush and her eyes puffy. They looked like that a lot lately. It was commonplace to her staff and advisors. Shock now set in as she shook her head.

"Dear God," she uttered. "Someone finally did it."

"That's what their voters asked for," Sandra said, an unsympathetic scowl crossing her face. "That's Capitalism in its purity."

"That's what they were told they wanted by the Republic's propaganda machine," Chandler corrected. "I think they're going to find out that they had no idea what they were asking for."

Chapter 39

"You have to admit, this is pretty nice." Okie smiled at his friend Kyle Perkins as they walked their patrol near the center of Hyderabad. "I don't feel nearly as naked." He tugged at his new gear comprised of new body armor, a high quality utility vest, and the newest technology in head gear.

"Yeah, thank God for Telaco, huh?" another soldier responded in Kyle's silence. "No more government corner-cutting. The best gear from here on out."

"Come on, admit it," Okie prodded boyishly as Kyle tried to remain serious and scan the streets for anything out of place. "This is working out pretty well. They should have done it a long time ago."

Kyle still said nothing. He just continued looking around at the store fronts and traffic. It was still so hard to tell civilian from foe. The remaining Taliban operatives had gotten even better at blending in. It was becoming impossible to predict attacks and insurgency. One had to keep a keen eye at all times. But he was beginning to grin, wavering slightly from his duty.

"I'll tell you what," Kyle finally spoke. "It is pretty nice having a full belly and a few extra clips." He felt the added weight of ammunition in his vest. "This thing has been way too light for way too long. I hate having to scrounge for ammo like I'm looking for loose change in the seat cushions. It's nice to have some extra for a change."

"That means they actually care about us," the other soldier said. "I was starting to feel like the Republic didn't." He paused. "This is really the best thing they could have done for us. I just wish the damned Telaco logo wasn't plastered to everything." He tugged at a patch sewn to his utility vest, looking it over and running his fingers across the raised threads.

"Yeah, what's up with that?" Okie agreed, watching Kyle smirk cynically and shake his head.

"To let you know who owns you," Kyle scoffed. "When you find yourself in doubt; when you think you might be questioning your loyalty, that there is to remind you of who signs your paychecks—Telaco." He chuckled, though deep down, there was nothing humorous.

"Forever the cynic," Okie said. "Why can't you just admit this is a good thing?"

"Because it's not," Kyle replied. "It's just not. There is a reason some things have to be government funded." He paused. "I mean, come on . . . the city of Karachi fell months ago—during the first wave of invasion—and just now are occupying forces being ordered to take complete control of Pakistani State Oil Corporation, headquartered in . . . you guessed it . . . Karachi. And in a few days, our own unit is pushing out a few clicks west of here to secure an oil field."

"Sounds like a conspiracy theory," the other soldier said, with a grin in his voice.

"The Republican Guard is a corporate entity, run by one of the biggest oil companies in North America, and just now we're ordered to take hold of the oil industry here . . . after the fall of Islamabad. Does that sound like just another conspiracy theory to you?" Kyle snapped at the man.

"Okay, I get it," Okie said. "Don't get your panties in a wad."

"Maybe this is just war in the twenty-first century," the other soldier said as they continued to walk along. "The new normal."

There was nothing startling to the men about a single gunshot. It was almost dream-like. They each recognized the sound. Two years ago, that sound would have prompted an extreme response. They would jump, startled, and search for cover. Heart rates would elevate and survival instincts would kick in. Thoughts of dying would flood present thoughts. Now there was a delayed reaction; looking for the source. It was calm and slow, yet all this happened instantaneously.

But as Kyle's brain failed to react the way it used to, he reeled in a more exaggerated way than Okie. A warm mist showered his right side. He could feel it spray his face, neck, and hand, and then grow cold. The soldier to the right of him slumped to the ground, falling against Kyle's right leg, and pushing him off-balance.

More shots followed as Kyle was still dealing with the initial horror of being covered in another man's blood. Civilians screamed in terror, scrambling to get off the streets and protect their children. Okie found a parked car, sliding in behind it, while Kyle pulled himself together, and followed, looking back at the young man as the blood poured from the hole in his neck.

"I heard two guns." Okie peeked up through the dingy windows of the parked car, scanning for any sign of a shooter. "What about you?"

"Two," he breathed heavily. "Maybe three at most, but definitely more than one. I didn't see anyone on the street with an automatic. They must be holed up somewhere. Look at the store fronts and in windows."

They scanned the entire area for a gunman. The busy street had gone from bustle to dead silence in a matter of minutes. Cars and scooters were abandoned for the moment. People crouched behind vehicles and inside shops. The occasional cry of a baby or terrified weeping of Pakistani women could be heard in the square, but all else was still and dangerously eerie.

"Great," Okie rolled his eyes. "Stand-off. They're not just going to let us walk out of here."

"And they're not going to fire and give themselves away until they have a chance to hit one of us," Kyle said. They continued to kneel and think for a few more moments. "We need them to screw up." Kyle rolled back off his knees and onto his feet, still crouched. "Watch for muzzle flashes." He got ready to move.

Okie readied himself, positioning his feet beneath him, clutched the trigger of his weapon, and sharpened his focus. He raised his head slightly to see a bit more of the street through the car's windows, and then Kyle bolted down the sidewalk. He ran in a crouched position as fast as his boot-clad feet could carry him as shots again erupted and rang out across the square. They echoed from building to building as bullets struck concrete and metal panels of the car Kyle slid in behind.

"Ah," Kyle yelled. "Dammit, I'm hit." He groaned from behind the car, clutching his left calf.

"Bad?" Okie tried to be quiet.

"It's not bleeding all that much." Kyle lifted the left leg of his pants, struggling to get it high enough to see how bad his wound looked. "Grazed. Burns like hell, but it looks like a Band-Aid will do," he sort of joked as he rolled the pants leg back down to grab his gun. "You see the shooters?"

"Yeah," Okie replied. "Third story, right above that little café thing over there. Two windows side-by-side, one of them with the blue curtains."

"I see it," Kyle looked up. "What's the game plan? I've got no radio. No way to get reinforcements."

"Blow 'em out?" Okie suggested.

"I don't want them switching rooms," Kyle answered. "Don't fire yet. I don't want to indicate that we've spotted their positions."

They waited, both of them trying to imagine an ingenious plan that did not simply consist of blasting away at the two windows. These brick and concrete walls were thick—too thick for anything less than fifty caliber rounds to be effective. It would be a waste of ammo, and the enemy would switch rooms if they hadn't already. The gray of futility was setting in and Kyle needed medical attention.

And then there was a terrible and familiar sound. The thrust of a rocket-propelled grenade, and then another right behind it engulfed everything. It was menacing. Kyle and Okie looked up from their positions behind the cars briefly, knowing they should keep their heads down. There were two rockets in the air, and two of them in two separate positions. Kyle's face flushed cold as he fully prepared to see an RPG headed his way, and then the positions of the shooters exploded. In a huge double burst of concrete and brick grit, the two windows erupted into the square with fire at the core of each. The deafening explosion rained debris and a thick cloud of dust and smoke filled the area as silence returned and the two men slowly removed their hands from the backs of their heads, lifting up slowly to assess the damage.

There was a gaping hole in the side of the building where the two windows were, flickering flames within the smoking, smoldering rooms. Nothing could have survived that, yet they rose to their feet, unsure if the shooters had still been inside. With each moment devoid of new gunfire, they became braver, and more relieved.

"We get 'em?" someone yelled out. Two soldiers appeared from around the corner a block away. "Did we get the right windows?" They drew closer to Okie and Kyle.

"I think so," Kyle said, shaking the man's hand. "Goddamn, I'm glad to see you guys," he said.

"Our pleasure, sir." The man noticed Kyle outranked him. "We heard the first shots from a couple blocks away," he said as Kyle pointed to the dead man on the sidewalk to indicate the result of those first shots. "We came a-runnin'." He glanced at the corpse. "And by the time we took cover at the corner, we saw you runnin' across drawin' their fire. That's when we got a bead on the sons of bitches."

"We owe you guys one," Okie smiled. "Thanks."

"All for one," the man said. "You're hit, sir." He motioned toward Kyle's wound. "Let's get you to command."

"How's your leg?" Okie walked into to the medic's tent, and up to Kyle, who sat up on a padded table.

"It's fine." He winced a little as the medic cleaned it with alcohol.

"Doesn't look fine," Okie grinned as he watched Kyle continue to grimace in the face. "Looks painful. Maybe you need to go home and get some rest."

"It's fine." Kyle raised his voice in annoyance.

"Maybe get a little Superman Band-Aid," he laughed, "and Momma to kiss it better."

"It's fine," Kyle shouted over Okie's outright laughter. "Besides, for your information, it hurts like hell."

"Dude, it's a scratch," Okie pestered.

"Hey, have you ever been shot?"

"No."

"So shut the fuck up," Kyle snapped.

The medic inserted the needle again and again, stitching back and forth and closing the wound. Okie continued to watch, and giggle every time Kyle made a face, but their attention was drawn by something else. A stretcher rolled by. It was draped by a blanket, but the lumps underneath were unmistakable—a nose, forehead, feet. They knew who it was. Neither of them could even remember his name. He had not been in the unit long—maybe a month. It was hard to get attached to the new guys.

"Sergeant Perkins," a corporal strode up.

"Yes?" Kyle spoke up.

"Here you are, sir." The corporal handed Kyle a message, saluted, and turned to walk away.

"Looks official," Okie smiled, reading Telaco letterhead. "Maybe you are going home," he chuckled.

"Shut up, it's fine." He winced again as he read over the orders. "Holy shit. I am going home."

"No friggin' way." Okie rushed over.

"Not over this leg," he clarified. "And guess what. We're all going home. The whole unit." He slapped Okie's outstretched hand, grasped it, and pulled him in for an awkward, yet masculine hug.

"Well, I'll be damned," Okie laughed out loud. "Finally get a break and get out of this shit hole."

"For now, at least," Kyle said. "Looks like it's temporary. A couple of months at best?"

"Better than not at all. When?"

"A few days from now—Thursday."

"We just have to stay alive until then," Okie smiled.

Chapter 40

Somewhere outside Derek's direct vision, the television flickered, switching rapidly from edited shot to shot. He was not paying attention. Differences in scenery or clothing flashed erratically, to his mind, imitating some sort of strobe with a lack of rhythm. He was not even sure what the program was. It just provided a backdrop of light in the dim.

His mind was elsewhere. There he sat, his chin propped and his elbow on the armrest of his mother's favorite chair. He stared into his leg, as if Christ would appear miraculously in the pattern of lighter and deeper blue threads of his jeans. Golden liquid filled his mouth, an ice-cold, watered-down blend of malt flavors and hops. It fizzed and foamed in his mouth, engulfing his teeth and tongue, before his throat opened and it found its place in his stomach. Every mouthful felt better. I wish more of me felt better, he thought as he set the much lighter brown glass bottle amongst its fallen, empty comrades gathering on the end-table.

He spoke not a word on his own, sometimes watching the ever-running television, and sometimes not. He answered when spoken to, but only with brief response. He had had a shower the day before, when he needed to. Carly felt he should get out. She needed diapers, and it could not wait. He wandered around that store for twenty minutes before he found the diapers, and then stood, staring for an eternity at the various brands, sizes, colors, and packaging. He hoped what he picked was correct, and then he was appalled with the price. His frustration was visible in his face and body language, though he said nothing. But the cashier saw it. She felt it, and then saw his dog tags dangling from his neck, and gave a little "Uhhh-huh . . . ," rolling her eyes as if it was typical. That frustrated him even more, and he stormed out, back to the car. He had trouble crossing the parking lot from the store. Cars just kept zooming through the pedestrian crossing, disregarding the fact that he was awaiting a chance to cross. There was no more leaving the house. That was one of the few instances he had in weeks.

He slept a lot, and at strange times. He used the bed some, but mostly fell asleep in the chair. He watched TV, and drank beer, and then would dose off for a few hours. Carly tiptoed around him, in an attempt to keep Olivia from waking him. She kept making noise, banging toys around, or wanted to crawl into his lap. But Carly did not want him to be startled. She had seen him awaken suddenly, and for no reason. His eyes would be wide and his breathing labored. He jerked violently, looking around himself as if he were unsure as to where he was. There was an un-ignorable risk that went with Olivia suddenly awakening him. He had now only been awake for an hour to have dinner, and surely he would again stay up most of the night watching mindless programming and swilling bottle after bottle.

"Was dinner okay?" she asked him from where she was cleaning the dishes.

"Yeah," he mumbled.

"Yeah," she continued. "I got the recipe from the neighbor. I wasn't sure if it would turn out okay."

"It was fine," he said without enthusiasm.

She could think of nothing else to say. She struggled to. She wanted conversation. She craved it. It was not quite the same with a toddler. Her eyes grew a bit heavier. Her body slumped, and her mind darkened, tired of trying. She only sighed, continuing to keep herself busy with the dishes as Olivia played on the floor near her father. He ignored her, or perhaps did not notice. Every muscle was relaxed and motionless. His breathing was faint, and his eyelids hung low. He felt nothing—no response to stimuli. Only numbness and the endless wandering through fields of open consciousness without organization, or even substance.

Without him noticing, Olivia had abandoned her toys for the moment. She had toddled over by him, and had begun reaching up to the top of the end table, grasping for the empty bottles atop it. She caught hold of one, and recognizing its purpose, tipped it up to her mouth.

"No, no," Carly shouted from the kitchen.

"Oh, Jesus," Derek snapped out of the trance, and removed the bottle from the child's hand as Carly rushed over.

She took her child by the hand, leading her away. "Those are Daddy's drinks." She shot Derek a sinister, disapproving look.

"What?" He suddenly sat up straight. "It's my fault?"

"Derek . . ." She raised her voice in response. "You were right friggin' there. You didn't see her?"

"Well Jesus." He became defensive. "Aren't you watching her?"

"I'm doing the dishes," she yelled. "I'm doing everything. I've spent months upon months holding down this household and raising our daughter. I can't do it all."

"And I've been getting shot at every one of those days." He stood up. "Don't I get a fucking break for a while to do what I want to do?"

Olivia started to cry with the sudden loud noises. Carly stopped immediately. Her expression changed. She had opened her mouth to say something, and his words stopped her cold. She just became sad. Her eyes drooped as she picked up the crying child, and carried her off to a bedroom room to console her, head shaking in disgust.

Derek sat down again. He felt he was right. His mind still frowned and grumbled. But as he listened to Olivia cry, and Carly's sad face remained semi-permanent in his immediate memory, he lowered his head. He closed his eyes. Shame set in.

Chapter 41

This place felt foreign—as foreign as that God-forsaken desert death trap, Hyderabad. It was all surreal. The cars along the street or in the driveway were familiar, but distant somehow. Memories of walking down the sidewalks to school seemed almost from a dream. They were happy, or happier at least. They were never perfect, but disposition was positive. All that was gone. So was the appearance of the neighborhood. It was spring. Flowers were blooming in the well-tended gardens. Grass thickens and turns deep green with professional fertilization, ramped up watering, and careful manicuring. It no longer looked that way. Nothing appeared as it did. The flower beds had all been invaded by weeds. The lawns were patchy and unkempt, often sporting For Sale signs—more than he had ever seen in a neighborhood.

"Up here, sir?" the private driving the little single-cap pickup asked.

"Yeah," Kyle replied. "Right up here. Two more on the right," he pointed.

The little truck crept up a few more houses, before it slowed to a halt affront the familiar house. Kyle yanked on the plastic handle, and hopped out onto the concrete street. He hoisted out his duffel bag and walked back to the open passenger side door.

"Thanks for the ride, private," Kyle nodded, and adjusted the heavy bag on his shoulder.

"You bet, sir," the young man smiled uneasily as his superior officer closed the heavy door with force.

That was weird, Kyle thought to himself as the truck drove off. He did not know that kid. He only met him on the flight into DFW. He said he had a truck waiting in the parking garage, and that would save

Kyle's mother or Ashley the trip. The whole thirty minutes was awkward, bumming a ride from a subordinate stranger. It felt so civilian being back in the Republic, but things still had to be somewhat formal with the young man. They were still in uniform.

And now here he stood in the driveway of his home. The old Corvette he never got running was still covered and parked there beside him. It had been there for years now. It was a monolith—a monument to the regrets and mistakes he had made.

The yard looked bad, much like most of the other houses. And then there was something new. Even his house had a For Sale sign in the yard. He stared at it for a long while. It was tall and white, with some guy's picture on it. He hated it from a deep place, from the cheap paint to the toothy, veneered smile on the agent's face. He leered at it as if he were trying to send it flying away through telekinesis.

Finally, he was able to pull himself away, adjusted the bag, and moved for the door. He stopped, and considered knocking, and then decided against. But then he just tapped as he opened the door. It made that sticking sound it always had made, like the pulling apart of Velcro. It could be heard all over the house, and from the family room across the house, two figures appeared.

Ashley sprinted down the hallway as if she were competing for a medal. Kyle saw it almost in slow motion, a blissful smile on his face. He dropped his bag, and forgot about everything else as he opened his arms. She was stunning, her shiny long hair whipping back and forth behind her as she ran. She dashed into his arms and he grasped her tight, lifting her off the ground while she planted a long, hard kiss upon his lips. She retracted, and kept pecking at his face like a starving hen. He set her down. Every muscle in her face was being used in smiling as she allowed herself to just take him in, stepping back a bit, unable to believe he was really there. She would never tell him, but she thought about him dead every day, almost to the point she expected that to happen.

And now she was surprised he was standing before her, handsome and strapping in his uniform.

"I've missed you so much," Ashley barely uttered, and pulled him in for one more embrace.

"I never want to leave you again." He held her a bit tighter.

"Kyle . . ." Angela walked over with pride in her son.

Ashley stepped aside for a moment to let her in to cradle Kyle's face in her hands. She looked him over, proud of the man he had morphed into. She was silent, taking him in. He was so much more of a man now—even more so than coming home from his first tour against the Marines north of Dallas almost a year before. She was proud, wrapping her arms around him for a brief hug.

His smile left him, and he looked around. Confusion was now the expression. The walls were bare. The art, mirrors, and wrought-iron pieces were now on the floors, leaning up against the walls. A few nails and hangers remained. Others had been removed, leaving holes; scars. It was as if makeup had been washed away, revealing a badly blemished real self. Boxes were stacked two and three high in various random spots throughout the rooms. All was in disarray. Nothing was the same.

"What the hell is going on here?" he puzzled, bringing his attention back to his mother.

Her eyes began to glisten. She placed her hand over her mouth, and just nodded at first, confirming what she knew he would notice immediately. She said nothing. She just turned and walked back toward the family room. Kyle took the cue and followed, with Ashley. The hall opened into the kitchen and family room. Open boxes piled up with kitchen appliances and silverware. Newspaper lay stacked and ready to wrap glasses and vases. Kyle followed as his mother took a seat on the couch, and he came in next to her.

"Where is Dad?" he asked. "Where's Dylan? This is crazy."

"Kyle . . ." Angela paused, but her mouth remained open and her gaze elsewhere, searching for some sunshine-bathed way to put it. Ashley gripped his hand. "Drew's gone. Your father is gone."

"Dead?" Kyle reeled.

"Oh, God no," his mother shook her head. "I think he has an apartment over in Watauga. No, I'm divorcing him. I asked him to leave."

Kyle just stared, his brow sharpened high above his nose. He leaned in on his knees, hunched over, and unable to relax. His head shook in disbelief, unable to rationalize. Reality was no longer.

"Where did this . . ." he began but stopped short. He only sort of chuckled with his breath. "Why?" He looked up at her. "You and Dad were one of the happiest couples around."

"I know." She allowed a few tears to well up at the bottom of her eyes. "I know we were. But these last couple of years, something changed. I don't know if I changed, too, but your father is not the man I married. Not anymore. He's angry—angry about everything. The economy. The U.S. The wars. The bomb. All he does is fight when there's nothing to fight. So he ends up just fighting me."

"Hit you?" Kyle's chest puffed out and his shoulders broadened.

"Oh no," Angela responded swiftly. "Jesus, no. But verbally, we fought. We fought all the time. And I just felt so down all the time. Unhappy is no way to live. He couldn't seem to be happy or find peace, and that unhappiness is like a cancer in the relationship. And sadly, it died."

"Oh, Mom." He hung his head. "I'm sorry . . ." He paused for a moment. "I hope none of it was about me. I don't want to—"

"I'll be truthful," she nodded. "We disagreed about how we felt about you in the service and his pressuring you and everything. But in the end, it was about a great many other things. We just grew apart."

"And so now you have to move out."

"Can't afford to live here," she said. "I have my job, but I don't make as much as your father did. He's been ordered to pay alimony, but when all is said and done, the house note is too much. Everything's privatized now. The government doesn't regulate interest rates anymore, and so the bank pretty much doubled rates overnight. I have to sell. There's a little rental about a mile from here that I'm getting."

"I saw the signs in the other yards," he said.

"Everywhere," Ashley chimed in. "Even my parents' neighborhood. And with so many houses on the market, your mom will be lucky to get rid of it . . . at least with any equity left over."

"Ashley has been wonderful," Kyle's mother gushed over her. "Coming in from College Station to help me with all this mess." She motioned to all the boxes and things. "She's helping me all weekend."

They both smiled, but Kyle hunched over some more. His face was obscured by the big masculine hands that covered it. He took some comfort in the moist warmth of them. It was something he remembered from when he was little. It always seemed to help. But it was not helping this time. His mind was jumbled with too much thought to organize. It was a trippy hallucination of a whirlwind in there, unable to be tamed. He had never felt so close to actual madness, not even in Pakistan.

"And where's Dylan?" he spoke through his hands, muffled and hindered.

"He's . . ." Angela stopped. She hesitated to say it. Kyle removed his hands from his face when she balked. Her expression implored him not to force the answer from her lips. "He's at basic training."

Kyle leapt to his feet, and turned to look at his mother through piercing, evil eyes. They were wide and vicious, engulfed with deepening red skin. His hands stiffened and locked into a curved position as his every muscle tightened. And from his lungs came a great vibration. It shook his chest, escaping out from his mouth as he looked toward the ceiling as he roared like a savage predator out of the wilderness. It ended, and his breath became rapid and animal-like. He loosed another longer and more powerful roar, and as his body relaxed and his breath escaped him, he slumped onto the coffee table, and back into the safety of his hands.

"You never knew," Angela wept. "You never knew how much he looked up to you, but he did. You know how much more like your father he always was—more so than you. All colleges are private now. And they're expensive. But Telaco would pay his way, and he always talked about how proud he was of you that you were off over there avenging the people in Dallas. He turned eighteen and wanted to be part of it."

"And it's my fault," Kyle yelled as he jumped up. He began to pace about. "My fucking fault." He beat his chest. "If I'd never joined the Republican Guard . . ." He paused, but continued to rage. "On one of my last patrols, I saw a kid right next to me—no older than Dylan—get shot through the fucking throat," he screamed almost yelling at himself. He seemed to ignore the two women. "Fuck the Republic. Fuck the Guard. I'm done."

"You mean done-done?" Ashley looked at him. She saw him calm a bit as he paced off the rage, and then sit. Now he just rocked back and forth on the coffee table. "You mean AWOL?"

"Yeah." He stopped and thought about it. It occurred to him that maybe he had not thought about this long enough. It was an emotional decision. He silently asked himself if that was what he wanted. "Yeah," he confirmed. "I think I'm done. I don't know what I'm going to do or where I'll live." He shook his head.

"I don't think you can live with me," Angela said. "Or your father. They know where we live. If they were to look for you, it would be with us."

"I'd never live with him. But with you? Even in the new place?"

"They would surely have access to rental records or all my mail being changed to the new address," she said. "They would find you."

"Come with me." Ashley grabbed his hands. "Come down to College Station. They don't have any record of my being connected to you. I have my apartment off campus. You could just sit around all day and relax—watch TV. My dad pays all the bills. You'd be set. They would never find you."

"There would be no way to contribute," he balked at the idea. "I couldn't get a job. I would have to have no record of my presence. I'd get no paycheck from Telaco. They'd be looking into my whereabouts. I couldn't use my debit card. No paper trail of me."

"Don't worry," she smiled. "All will be taken care of. You'll see. And before you know it, all this will be over with and life will go back to normal," she said calmly.

It was strange. There was something in her voice. There was something in her smile. He believed her, and without question.

Chapter 42

"Good to see everyone." President Chandler greeted the select advisors and cabinet members seated along her end of the long, rectangular table. Everyone smiled back at her. Each of them had prayed over the past several months that she could get through it all, and it appeared that those had been answered. She was in higher spirits than usual. Her eyes were not as dark and puffy. Her complexion had improved. There was light in her voice again. "It seems like these status meetings keep getting shorter and shorter. Thank goodness for that."

"Means we're almost done." Bates cracked a rare grin.

"So hit me," she said. "What's going on?"

"We're down to just shy of two thousand troops left overseas in south Asia," Bates cited the file before him. "Most are out of harm's way—they're in India. There are a few companies still in far eastern Sindh region, but we should be getting them out soon. They're in contact with Republican Guard quite a bit and there have been some little fires to put out concerning that."

"Bad stuff that we're going to have to do damage control with?" Cindy asked.

"Not too bad," Bates said. "Fights. Taunting. No shooting yet. But it does seem to be getting worse. My guys keep reporting some horrible things they see the Reds subjecting Pakistani locals to."

The president said nothing. There was just a raising of one of her eyebrows as she leaned forward and propped her chin on her fist. Her blazing eyes cast out at the general through her small, cat-eye glasses. He had her full attention, and so he continued.

"You name it, and it's happened," he sort of shrugged. "I don't know how much of the truth has changed as the story gets reported and then re-reported, but there have been beatings of civilians. Rapes. Guys shooting people and claiming they saw a weapon. They break into stores and shops and loot the place . . ."

"Oh my God, and we handed those poor people over to the Guard." Cindy shook her head and removed her glasses.

"It's not our fault," Bates said. "The Republican Guard would be present in Pakistan regardless of whether or not we are."

"Revenge," Secretary of State DeLaune said. "They're still getting revenge for Dallas. And they don't distinguish between Pakistani civilian and Taliban extremist."

"Ignorance, plain and simple." Chandler put her glassed on. "It was the same after 9/11 with all the people that just wanted to go nuke every Muslim country on Earth over the actions of a few terrorists. I'm just glad we're getting our people out of there."

"Those are just the individual things that soldiers are doing," DeLaune added, shaking her head. "What Telaco is directing the Guard to do on a state level is atrocious, blatant and greedy."

"Oil?" Chandler guessed.

"Oil, chemical manufacturing, textiles . . ." she listed. "They've taken over large-scale food production and large service industries. All of it will be controlled by Telaco. And they're using Republican Guard to enforce it, control it, and basically enslave the people that work in these places."

"Spoils of war," Bates shook his head. "True imperialism. All they have to do is pay tribute to Austin in order to operate militarily under the Republic's flag. Honestly, I don't know how much longer those Republic boys are going to fight for this."

"Why do you say that?" Chandler asked.

"Trouble at home," Vice President Coffman said. "It's all falling apart. Those boys are all out there in Pakistan fighting for corporate greed while the Republic has taken away every public service available to their families—well, all families—back home."

"Protests are ongoing at Republic state houses and offices of their representatives," DeLaune continued. "People are having to pay a monthly bill to fire and police departments, and expected to pay again when they use those services. It's like insurance. The elderly have their government pensions and medical coverage cancelled. Veterans benefits could be cut at any time by their corporate employers should they need to cut costs. The government provides no services. Everything is corporate and subject to the whim of maximizing profits."

"Jesus . . ." Chandler again removed her glasses and rubbed her eyes with her index and thumb.

"The people down there are fed up," Bates commented. "They don't feel like they're a priority anymore. Why do you think The ARA has been so active lately? Blowing up Republican Guard convoys and front-line outposts. And the public has just stopped caring."

Chandler continued in her deep thought, her eyes closed by her finger and thumb. Her head hung as if she was fighting off the onset of a migraine, but she was just thinking. She tried to focus on the domestic side; concern herself with only U.S. business. But the Republic's very existence still just bugged her. And then she suddenly looked up, her eyes wide and bright, as if light would beam from them.

"So would you call the Republic disunified?" she asked.

It took a moment as her cabinet and advisors sort of looked around at one another without a word. Nothing really had to be said. Slow, slight nods began, each chin out of sync with the others, and then they became prominent. The whole room nodded a resounding yes without a word, and Chandler smiled.

"So maybe this is our opportunity," Chandler suggested.

"Maybe," Bates agreed. "I mean, that's why the CIA has increased funding, training, and weapons to the ARA to help undermine—"

"Wait, wait, wait," Cindy interrupted him. "The CIA?"

"Yes, ma'am," he nodded. "The Central Intelligence Agency."

"Don't be an ass," she snapped. "I know what the hell it stands for. What are they doing involved with the ARA? And why is this the first time I've heard of it?"

"It's not," Bates responded. "I told you this months ago."

"You did not," she railed. "I think I would have friggin' remembered something like . . . you know . . . our CIA funding an anti-Republic fucking terrorist organization."

Silence followed. Only someone's sniffles resonated within the room. And there were some shifting papers. It was a slow, conscious attempt not to disturb the silence and the cutting look President Chandler was slaying the general with. Tension was almost visible in the room, and the anger upon the president's face displayed primordial malice. Her eyes themselves threatened a demonic glow.

"My apologies, Madam President," Bates conceded, hanging his head.

"You get me," she began lowly and calmly, "CIA Director George Gawain." She closed her eyes and tried to continue calmly. "On the fucking double."

Chapter 43

Uniformed men in beige fatigues and Kevlar moved through the streets, crouched and aware. They scanned the area with keen eyes and aimed assault rifles as they sought cover behind whatever they could find on the street. They fired off shots across the way as brass casings ejected to the side. The air was constantly hazed with loosely drifting dust. Explosions rocked buildings, sending debris piling into the streets. Smoke and dust plumed upward over the city like a frightful column of hate.

Derek had no reaction. The sound was on, but it was unheard. The right side of his face distorted, the skin rearranged with it leaning against his propped hand. His eyes were heavy and his face slow. He was pretzeled in his position in the easy chair. He just stared into the screen as some correspondent tried to describe what had happened that day in some distant Pakistani city. All seemed quiet where he was, but the picture-in-picture continued to loop footage of the fighting between Republic soldiers and some unseen Taliban foes.

Carly sat across from him on the couch, plucking clean garments from the load of color laundry in the basket at her feet. She kept a close eye on Derek, watching his being; his inaction. She studied him, glancing down at the shirt or pair of boxer briefs in her hand to make sure she folded it correctly. She glanced with increased interest at the violence on the TV. He said nothing, and neither did she. She found herself doing that of late—not talking to him. Or was it he that was not talking to her. He seemed to pay attention to nothing but that television. He just glassed over and stared all day and evening, oblivious. She was afraid that if she said something to him other than to ask what he wanted for dinner, he would snap at her. She could handle it somewhat, but feared that her opinion of him would change. He was gone so much that she had to keep the concept of Derek constant in her head. She was afraid that the more time she spent with him, that concept would change. Did she really know him? She noticed Olivia playing on the floor. She was looking at the television more and more.

"Don't you get tired of this?" She let words escape almost by accident. She regretted it for a moment, but that faded as she watched her daughter viewing the barrage of violent acts. "The news, I mean. It's always negative stuff—nothing happy anymore. It gets depressing." She continued folding, presenting the subject as small talk. There was no answer, or even movement. "Maybe we could find some cartoons for Olivia." She leaned forward to reach the remote.

Derek snapped to life, suddenly, his hand grasping and guarding the controller as his head turned and his eyes met hers. She braced herself for wrath and anger, but he said nothing. His eyes projected pain rather than rage. She looked into those eyes for several long moments, searching them for some kind of meaning. He turned, but he was still animated.

"I like to stay on top of what's going on there." His voice was coated in phlegm, unused for so long. She hesitated to respond for a few moments, trying to think of just the right thing.

"I understand," she finally said. It was all she could think of, and it was a lie. Again, there was no response from him. He seemed to be slipping back into his news-coverage coma. A sadness crept into her thoughts, and then he again spoke.

"This is so pointless," he uttered, his eyes still on the TV.

"What?" she asked, realizing that she sounded too eager and excited, afraid to lose him again.

"These tactics," he pointed. "These guys are all greenhorns—newbies. They have no idea what they're doing," he sort of giggled, but without play or happiness. "Oh hell! The whole thing is pointless anyway. They're never going to get out of there."

"What do you mean?" she burst as she attempted to hide the growing smile. She wanted to keep him talking.

"Do you think these guys are ever going to completely defeat the Taliban?" Derek asked the rhetorical question. "Hell no. Taliban has been around for decades, and they will continue to thrive as long as they can control and oppress people. And they'll keep throwing guys into these Pakistani towns and cities. And the Reds will keep fighting them. They're like the Viet Cong. They blend in with the crowd, and when you least expect, they come at you. I've seen it."

"So you think these troops will just stay there forever fighting, thinking they will eventually win?" She was intrigued.

"I don't think these soldiers or their brass know anything about the politics down there," Derek shook his head. "I don't think they know anything about the culture or history. I read up on it on the way out there. These guys don't give up. But as long as the Republican Guard thinks they're the biggest bad-asses on the block, they'll keep fighting. And as long as the execs that run that army keep getting their profits, there the soldiers will stay."

"And keep fighting," she said. "And keep dying."

"Needlessly." He again stared into the television. His demeanor and face softened as tears began forming at the bottom of his eyes, but stopped. "And no one cares. Names on a placard on some memorial eventually forgotten. No one remembers what they did or sacrificed. No one sees the name and wonders what kind of person he was or what his talents were. No one will care. And the fighting will continue until troops eventually—a decade later—go home. And the Taliban just continues . . . regroups. And we're back to square one. And all we had to do was pay closer attention to what was going on at home. Stop attacks from happening here."

She watched him as the tears formed again, this time rolling through the stubble forest on his cheeks. His eyes remained unmoved from that screen, and as Carly looked also into that screen, she understood. This was not only grieving and mourning. If she had for weeks thought of this TV as his home, she realized that was accurate. Not the easy chair, but the content on the screen.

He continued to gaze into it, the tears beginning to dry. And then a tiny hand appeared on his knee. It was barely a quarter the size of his own calloused and scarred hands. He studied the delicate appendage. It was milky white and soft with little dimples for knuckles. He could not help it. A smile formed on his face, and grew like a sponge suddenly exposed to water. His daughter stood between his knees, slapping them playfully with her little hands. She looked up at him, her eyes squinting as her smile filled the majority of her face. Her arms extended upward to him and his heart melted as he picked her up and took the child into his embrace. He wrapped her in a father's love, holding her firm, but gentle as Carly buried her joyous face in her hands, praying that he was back for good.

Chapter 44

The upholstery of the plush, luxury sofa swallowed Kyle. It was soft and inviting, yet still he found it difficult to get settled. His flip-flops lay on the floor before him, and his hair-covered legs felt naked and cold in his cargo shorts. He fidgeted and scooted around, feeling trapped by the soft support of the sofa. His t-shirt was too thin. He was too comfortable. Everything in the small living room was white and bright, despite the darkness pouring in through the glass sliding door that led to the apartment's balcony. The newest model television rested across the room, complete with a DVR box and sound strip. Modern art prints hung perfectly level on the walls. The carpet was bright and completely devoid of stains or spots. It was immaculate.

"Here you go." Ashley emerged from the kitchen area and rounded the sofa. "I'm sure you've been dying for one." She handed him a beer.

"You have no idea," he replied as he took the cold bottle from her and twisted off the metal top. She sat there with hers unopened. She waited with a sweet smile until he got the message and twisted off her top as well.

Beer was still not a flavor Kyle had gotten used to, even in his time stationed on the outskirts of Dallas before the nuke. He did a lot of drinking in those days, but beer remained something new to him. The taste of the barley malt and the bitter hops was almost soapy to him. But he was amazed at how easy it now went down. He drank it like a runner gulps down water after a jog. He did it to actually quench thirst, but there was no thirst. It just somehow was the right thing to drink at the moment. It actually made him feel better for a bit.

"You're right." She looked into his eyes. "I don't have any idea."

"That's probably for the better." He took another gulp.

"No, I want to know," she implored.

"It sucks." He grinned a little, trying to make light of it. "You get used to seeing dead people eventually." He became more solemn. "You have to. Their dead; your dead—all lying there spilling blood out on the dirt. That is, if it's a bullet wound. It really takes a long time to get used to seeing dismembered corpses." He talked about it nonchalantly to Ashley's horror. "What's strange is those are the things you get accustomed to." His grin faded. "Women and children, even. What you don't get used to is watching your own guys acting like savages—shooting some woman in the face for no reason. Spitting on her body after. Cursing her for what 'her people' did to Dallas." He shook his head. "Call her a 'raghead piece of shit.'"

"Oh my God," Ashley grimaced. "No one did anything?"

"Commanding officers didn't care," he said. "I've seen commanders order civilian executions. It really got bad after Telaco took over. Guys were getting orders to go into homes and seize private property; loot homes. And they did, for the most part, gladly."

"Are you glad to be done?" she asked.

"I'm glad to be home," he answered.

"But I mean, are you glad to be out of that? Done with Pakistan. Done with the Guard," she said. "You seem to be having a hard time acclimating."

"I feel like Anne Frank hiding from the Gestapo," he said. "Can't go anywhere. There are going to be people looking for me. I can't be seen— can't go out," he said. "And I wouldn't want to hide out with anyone else." He leaned over for a peck on the lips. "But yes, I'm glad I'm done with the Guard. You know, for a while I had a renewed sense of pride in being a part of it. For a while, I thought it was the right thing to go over there and avenge Dallas. And it happened, and I really don't feel any better about it. I got to express my anger. I got to let out the frustration. I got my fill of killing," he sneered. "And then what? I realize I fight for and represent a set of ideals that I don't hold as my own values. Private armies. Greed. Control. Lack of regard for average people and citizens. I saw how our people treated the Pakistani civilians. And I see how our government treats its own citizens. And it sickens me. It's all about the power and the greed. Never about the people it all affects. So yes, I'm done with it. And good fucking riddance."

Ashley just took it all in for a moment or two, nodding and comprehending. She could feel the anger radiating off of him and filling the room. She could not imagine, but she understood. She understood his conflict between duty and belief. Bitterness had taken him.

"It's been bad here," she finally spoke. "Once everything privatized, government retirement pensions went away. There's no Republic Social Security. Old people. Poor people. They have no healthcare assistance. They can't get their medications and treatments. It's private insurance and private healthcare. People's houses burn down if they can't pay the fire department. You have to make a monthly payment to the police departments if you want protection. And education," she said in disgust. "Education is all private now. Parents have all gotten a letter in the mail saying that the schools are all private entities and that tuition is expected for the child to return in the next school year. As for college, no more government grants to help students out. No more subsidized student loans making it easier to go to school. I'm lucky I have a scholarship and a rich father. But what about the other ninety-eight percent of the people? Now you can only go to school and college if you can afford it. The few at the top will be the educated lords, and the rest of the uneducated peasants will work for them."

"And all the while," he shook his head, "I've been fighting for that. I represented that. That ideology," he shouted.

"Not anymore." She placed a soft hand on his. "This is not who you are. I know it's not what you represent."

"Still doesn't make me feel any better," he grumbled, taking her hand.

"What if you could represent something better?" She leaned over and gazed into his eyes.

"Like what?" he asked, confused. "Protest?"

"Even bigger than that. Something that takes action," she said softly. "The ARA."

"The ARA?" He jerked his hand back in reflex. "You're in the ARA?" He seemed appalled.

"Yes, but—"

"It's a terrorist group, Ashley. You see what they did at that speech."

"It's not a terrorist group," she assured him calmly. "We only target military and government—no different than the U.S. military."

"No civilians?" he asked cautiously.

"Never," she shook her head. "It's the resistance to the secessionist government. Come with me to meet our chapter. See what it's all about," she pleaded, grasping his hand. "We could use ex-military like you."

He was still taken aback. He was having a tough time assimilating the new information about his girlfriend. He was unable to yet look at her, but then he raised his eyes. He sighed deeply through his nose, a stern expression on his face. He blinked, and spoke.

"Okay," he nodded.

"Good," she smiled giddily. "But for now, let's just have a few more beers."

Chapter 45

The leather seats were soft, the cushions cradling, but supportive. The climate control set perfectly. The BMW rode over the suffering asphalt of South College Avenue like it was a hovercraft skating on a pocket of air. Yet Kyle was uncomfortable, and unable to remedy it. His stomach churned as he leaned his face toward the window and peered out at the neighborhoods as they passed heading into the town of Bryan. Some were old and run-down, and others very nice. Burgundy A&M flags hung from the porches outside. It was a college town, adjacent to College Station to the south. It carried the same loyalty, as well as some likely alumni and faculty.

"You okay?" Ashley lowered the radio for a moment and smiled, taking her eyes off the road for just a moment to look over at him.

"Edgy," he said honestly. "I little bit."

"You're going to be fine." She reached over to grasp his hand.

The car slowed, and Ashley turned right off into a neighborhood. It was a picturesque little place where the houses were all old early-twentieth-century family homes. They were all wood—no modern brick grandeur or vinyl siding. Each one's paint job was within a few years old. Nothing chipped. Nothing was out of place. They were neither big, nor small. The yards were manicured and cut, finally reviving the green from the slumber of winter. Flowers were in bloom. Sprinklers slung water all over. People walked their dogs and children rode their bikes as if the place were in a bubble separate from the rest of the world.

Another right, and then a left a few blocks over, and finally they were slowed. Ashley pulled the car over to the side of the street, parallel parked with ease against the curb affront a pristine little suburban gem painted a light yellow with white trim. Kyle reached for the handle, ready to open the door, but he paused, and then shrunk into himself at the sight. From a pole extending out from the house by the front door, a bright red twenty-nine-star flag of the Republic gently waved from side to side. His eyes widened and his face lowered, as if he were to hide behind the lower part of the door.

"Are you coming?" Ashley walked around to his side, her face puzzled. He said nothing. His eyes were fixed to the house and the flag. "Come on," she motioned, and then turned to see what he was staring at. "It's okay." She opened his door, and pulled him out by the hand. "It's a front."

He still said nothing, but allowed himself reluctantly to be helped to his feet. He lazily stood and walked forward a few steps, closing the door behind him. Ashley took his arm in hers, linking to him and leading him up the concrete pathway to the front steps. Kyle eyed that flag the whole way, watching it sway with the wind and praying Ashley had the right address.

She stopped at the bottom step, and relinquished Kyle's arm for a moment, taking out her phone. She flicked on the screen with a button and unlocked it with one motion, and then began typing on the touch screen keypad. She pressed send, put it away, folded her arms, and stared at the door.

"Are we going to knock?" Kyle puzzled at her.

"No," she said to his surprise, but then the door opened and he understood. "Fries their nerves. I can just text 'open up,' and it's less stressful on everyone. Trust me, this is an ARA house."

The man stood in the doorway, leering at the two on the steps. He was stern; his steel blue eyes cutting. Dark, loose clothing and a wallet chain decorated him like a skater soldier. His head was buzzed and as stubbled as his face. He slowly shifted his gaze from Kyle to Ashley and back many times without a word. He analyzed and judged as Kyle kept his hands in his pockets, rocking back and forth with increasingly frazzled nerves.

"This him?" he finally spoke, and gestured toward Kyle with his hand.

Ashley just nodded meekly and watched the man cautiously step aside. She began up the two concrete steps, followed by Kyle. He could feel the man's eyes scanning every inch of him as he passed into a house that seemed some ten degrees warmer on the inside. It was immediately stuffy. The lack of circulation was stale and staggering. It was well-kept, though. There were vases with flowers and framed pictures on the mantle. The furniture was quality varnished wood and upholstery. The real hardwood floors were cared for and produced that classic hollow, creaky sound when a step was taken.

But the feeling was not as inviting. Kyle could feel the man's eyes still, and so could Ashley. She had been in this house dozens of times and never felt this way. Kyle saw a few people moving about in the kitchen beyond the den he was standing in. There were voices jumbled and muffled further in the house. Out of the corner of his eye, there were another two faces. He turned his head to see they were familiar. It took a moment. He glanced and then away. But after another look, he was able to make the connection. It was the girl and one of the men at the coffee shop before he shipped out—the ones with disdain for the Republic and its military. He hoped they did not remember him, but it appeared they were making the connection, too. Moira's mouth gaped and her lungs gasped. Her carefully manicured finger raised and she pointed at him.

"You're the Guardsman. From the coffee shop," she yelled.

Ashley shuttered as her eyes moved all over while Moira and Brice stood from the couch. A few men emerged from down a darkened hallway and from the kitchen. The house was silent of speech for a moment, but screaming with activity and eyes of impunity. They converged in the den, nudging Ashley to the perimeter as they surrounded Kyle. He spun and observed. He was trapped and his arms raised, attempting to show no threat.

"Guard?" the man who opened the door yelled. "You brought fucking Republican Guard in here?"

"Aaron, wait." Ashley tried to tug at his arm to get his attention, but he paid no mind.

"Is that true?" He reached into the small of his back and retrieved a sleek black handgun, which he cocked and aimed directly at Kyle's head.

"It is true," Brice yelled and pointed. "He's a Guardsman. He's Ashley's boyfriend." All eyes briefly cast hatred at her and then back to Kyle. "He met us for coffee once."

"Do it, Aaron," someone yelled from across the room. "We can't have him here."

A dozen voices filled the stuffy air and joined together into some ugly Frankenstein's monster of malice and verbal assault. Fingers flew out from bodies. Eyes narrowed atop angry gaped mouths. A chaotic chorus of urging surrounded Aaron as his finger slowly tightened on the trigger.

"Aaron. Aaron," Ashley screamed, her voice powerless in the mix of shouting. "Aaron, no." She suddenly became frantic and jerked on his arm, unable to think of what else to do.

She pulled on his arm as hard as she could, and the gun waved from right to left and back again, pointing all over the room until his tension and reflex resulted in the firing of a shot up and to the right, sending the bullet through the drywall near a window. Aaron composed himself enough to lunge to his right, knocking over Ashley and sending her to the hardwood.

The people in the room reeled from the unexpected shot, but Kyle watched his girlfriend hit the floor. His body trembled and his heart raced. He could feel his face heat to what seemed to be the boiling point for the blood that filled his cheeks. He burst forward and with all his strength released a swing that landed his tightly-closed fist directly into

Aaron's left eye. He fell to the ground, dropping the gun as a couple of the larger guys in the room took hold of him and another pummeled his face. Kyle dropped to the ground, his arms shielding his face from the further barrage.

"Stop," Aaron said calmly as he again took up his weapon and slowly rose to his feet. He drew a bead on Kyle's head, ready to pull the trigger, but looked over at Ashley on the floor, tears rolling from her eyes. She tried to get his attention. He stared and implored her to finally be heard.

"He's AWOL," she sniffled. "Done."

"That doesn't mean shit," Aaron said, still aiming his weapon.

"It's true," Kyle spoke.

"So what, you just suddenly changed your mind?" Aaron raised his voice. "Just overnight? You just decided you weren't loyal to the Republic anymore? I don't buy it."

"I never was loyal, asshole," Kyle yelled back. "I was supposed to just go to A&M with Ashley." He calmed his tone again. "My best friend joined the guard right after we graduated high school—right after the invasion of Mobile. My father pressured me to join the Guard and I caved." He spoke to a silent Aaron and a silent room. "Ended up at a post north of Dallas. I was there when . . ." He paused. "I was there when the Marines came in—my first time to pull the trigger. My first time to shoot at another human and they were fellow Americans. It sickened me. But then the bomb . . ."

"Jesus." Aaron lowered his weapon and clenched his temples with his thumb and middle finger. "You see time in Pakistan?"

"Just got back," Kyle replied. "I was at Hyderabad. At least there, I felt like I was doing the right thing . . . like I was doling out justice for the poor people of Dallas. But the brutality . . ." He paused, shaking his head with recollection. "The shit I saw, and then the Telaco privatization . . . I'm done."

"You fought for the Reds and claim never to have believed in the

Republic?" Aaron shook his head, still having a hard time believing.

"Never," Kyle said.

"It's true," Ashley joined.

"My father," Kyle said. "I've had this lifelong obsession with pleasing him. I justified it. I was just a kid, for God's sake. And then the bomb and Pakistan . . ." He took a moment. "But I never believed in secession. Democrat. Republican. It doesn't matter. I don't give a shit where someone's politics fall. But secession is not an option. Unity must be preserved. I truly believe that. And I'm willing to do anything to reunify this country."

The crowd was silent, standing close in a circle, awaiting Aaron's reaction. His gun had long been lowered. His eyes were narrow and contemplative. He stared into the floorboards, away from Kyle, willing a solution like they were tea leaves. Then, slowly, his head moved with a nod up and down in confirmation. His face was still stern and almost interrogative as he extended a hand to help up Kyle. Someone handed him a dish rag to dab the blood from his lip and nose.

"You're in good company, soldier," Aaron said. "We could use more trained guys. A lot of these boys have training," he gestured around. "Some have seen combat. See the old man over there?"

"I'm only forty-two," the man said.

"See the old man over there?" Aaron repeated to the tune of the man's extended middle finger. "He served in Iraq back in the day."

"And you?" Kyle asked.

"Republican Guard. Served on the front lines out in the Carolinas early in the war," he said as Kyle sort of smirked. "Took off. Couldn't bring myself to kill another American. That's when I decided this whole thing was wrong."

"So you just up and decided you weren't loyal to the Republic anymore?" Kyle said, the smirk still there.

"Precisely." Aaron smiled for the first time. "Let's get you cleaned up

. . . and myself." He lightly touched his swelling eye. "We have to get you up to speed. We have a hit on a military parade in Fort Worth coming up, and you're going to help us bomb it." He patted Kyle's shoulder and led him away into the house.

Chapter 46

The Virginia suburbs of Washington, DC, were a strange place. One crosses the bridge south of the city into Arlington, which is just as urban, in many respects, as the District of Columbia. But then driving to the northwest into the hills that line the Potomac River, it becomes suburban and rural all at the same time. The area is riddled with affluent neighborhoods occupied by diplomats, lobbyists, and Pentagon personnel. The nearly consistently two-story federal-style homes are worth millions. They sit on one- and two-acre lots. They have heated pools and pristine landscaping painted with bright pastels of the flowers in the gardens.

Yet, they are concealed away from the roads that snake between the neighborhoods. To the average driver moving down the two- and four-lane highways and roads, it is the country. The homes lay stashed aside in a nest of large trees away from the asphalt. A veil of greenery separated them from motorists like a stage illusion.

The black SUV turned off of Dolley Madison Boulevard and onto Potomac School Road, finally reaching a side road that was unassumingly marked as Georgetown Pike. There was another sign indicating what was down the road: the FHWA Turner Fairbank Highway Research Center and the Claude Moore colonial farm. The SUV turned. Cindy Chandler snickered, and General Bates knew why. There was something else down this road that was not so widely publicized. They slowed and approached a gate and a guard station occupied by two young soldiers, who stepped out and up to the opening driver-side window.

"Special clearance for a ten a.m. appointment," the suited agent in the driver's seat said as the soldier approached.

"Um . . ." The young man checked his clipboard. "You're not on the list."

"Oh, we're on the list—just not your list," the driver said with a grin.

"What is the purpose of your visit?" the soldier pried.

"The national security kind," General Bates said, rolling the darkly-tinted pane down just enough to reveal his face. "Top secret. Now stand aside."

"Yes, sir." The young man's hand snapped to his brow the moment he saw the four bright stars on his shoulder.

He motioned to the other soldier to open the gate. With the push of a button, the chains began to move and the gate swung open to allow the unmarked SUV to pass through past the fence and the razor wire and into the compound.

"Couldn't we have just brought the director to the White House?" the general asked his Commander-in-Chief. "It's a haul to come out here to Langley. And they always give you hell to get into the place, especially when you make it secret."

"Couldn't risk it," she said. "Not with the media's ever-watchful eyes around the White House. Bringing in the director of the CIA would have gotten us some buzz on the nightly news."

"Sad, isn't it?" the general shook his head. "Sad that the White House isn't the most secure place in Washington. If you want privacy, you have to come all the way out here to Fort Langley."

Cindy grinned as the vehicle drove around the perimeter of the massive parking lot that surrounded the headquarters. The road led them to an entrance at the side of the building where the SUV stopped, and out jumped the two Secret Service agents in the front seat. They opened the doors on the side to allow General Bates and President Chandler to exit. They were escorted to the side, which was guarded by armed personnel who opened the unconventional entrance and escorted them into the building.

The entourage travelled the seemingly narrow, beige-colored hallways with ease. It was cleared of any wandering cubicle workers or analysts. It was an endless row of locked offices and corporate-looking carpet leading into the building. They turned a corner or two and finally the president and her chief military advisor were being ushered into a random office devoid of any color, character, or personality.

But there in a chair across a small, cheaply made desk, sat the CIA director, George Gawain, and another man that was perhaps in his late thirties. He was not in a suit, but rather casually dressed in jeans and some light brown leather shoes. Parts of a military tattoo peeked from beneath the sleeve of his t-shirt. Cindy knew who he might be, but she said nothing as she walked in and sat alongside the general as the door to the small office shut and they were alone.

"Madam President." George half stood and shook Cindy's hand. "General." He shook Bates's hand as well.

"And this must be . . ." Cindy sat, motioning to the other man in the room.

"Wayne Dupuis." He reached for the president's hand, but she sat, warily eyeing him. She shot scrutiny from her eyes, watching and cutting him with the dropping of her brow. "A pleasure." He sat, visibly dejected.

"You've got some explaining to do, George," the president spouted pointedly. "Serious explaining. For months and months, I've been pushing serious investigations into who the damned ARA is and how to take down these bastards who took out a Republic president willing to work with us, as well as almost taking me out."

"For the record, we never targeted you," Wayne commented, but was silenced by the president's raised hand.

"I didn't ask you a thing," she cut him off. "I'll get to you soon enough."

"Wayne is ex-army and all loyalist," George defended the man to his left. "He's a patriot—a good man."

"I'm sure he is, but that still doesn't account for the CIA funding and training a terrorist group," she said. "Christ, we're no better than the Goddamned Taliban or al-Qaeda."

"They're not a terrorist group," George rebutted respectfully. "They're a paramilitary group. They don't target civilians; only military and the occasional government official. They fight other soldiers—ones on the wrong side of this conflict. Sending them off to inflict damage on the domestic force of the Republican Guard is no different than you giving the order for Marines to invade Mobile."

"Okay, so explain to me how this came about." She folded her arms and prepared for the story. "And why I wasn't consulted."

"It happened after the first time our guys tried to take Austin and couldn't," George began. "I started wondering how long this was going to last, and then it occurred to me that even if Austin fell, there were several other states out there still a part of the Republic that war had left untouched. Those states had to be won, and those people had to be won over. So it got me to thinking. What if we generated a Red-side resistance? It could reach all corners of the Republic and be carried out by civilians undetected."

"Our own personal Viet Cong," Bates sneered.

"Precisely," Gawain pointed at him. "And then I found out that such a group already existed. They were ex-military and loyal to at least the concept that the United States was indivisible. And so I asked to see their founder, and operatives brought me this man." He motioned to Wayne. "We had a long—very long—meeting, and came to an ideological agreement. I felt comfortable enough to offer Mr. Dupuis funding, training, and protection as long as they waged war on the Guard, and that they did . . . successfully. And they've done it in most red states. Even the ones out west that have been outside the theater of war." He paused a moment. "And to some degree, we're seeing people in these states change their minds.

"Look, I get it," Cindy said. "I'm sure you were justified. But I have to also worry about the economy, pass budgets, and read books to school kids—not just send people off to war. So I rely on my people to make good decisions . . . and freaking inform me. She leaned forcefully. There was a momentary pause. The two men across the desk waited patiently for blessing or condemnation. "Is it working? Do you have a plan for an endgame?

"Yes," George answered. "We have groups in every red state, and they are putting pressure on state governments and the Republican Guard. They want an end to this thing and reunification as soon as possible."

"Can't argue with that," she lightened up. "So how?"

"We can infiltrate Austin." Wayne leaned forward, folding his hands almost deviously. "We hit Austin from within its very core, and the U.S. military overwhelms it from the outside."

Cindy rocked in her seat while the general just stared at her. He willed her silence to end and for her to voice her thoughts. Her lips smacked and her eyes darted side to side. She stared into the grains of the wood desk, and then she spoke.

"Tell me more," she said.

Chapter 47

May

Joseph Crane stood tall, the light pouring through the window from the blue Texas sky shining his face and flawlessly pressed suit. It darkened his back like he was a half moon phase on a black country night. His hands rested in his pockets, his arms ruffling his jacket a bit above. His eyes, from beneath fresh brow wrinkles, cast his gaze out across the Texas State House lawn and beyond. He was greyer. His hair was thinner. The lines at the corners of his eyes were sharper. His eyes were somehow softer and more elderly; grandfatherly. Sternness eluded him. He stood contemplative and free of any tension, something rare of late.

The crowds across the street had grown over the weeks. He saw them grow every day, really. He watched them gather every morning and stay through the evening. The metal barricades had become permanent; the Austin police had stopped hauling them away at the end of the day. They reassembled over and over again. Telaco Republic troops lined the streets around the State House, attentive, yet nonthreatening. Shouts had grown from solid protest to cuttingly angry. Signs evolved from expressions of dissent to ones of defiance, bearing slogans accusing of the Republic government of "Selling Out the People" and "Enslaving the Citizens" with their policies.

The light knock at the door did nothing to draw Crane's attention. He heard, but without reaction. He did not glance or turn to see Zach entering the room. The young man inched across the floor and stepped light and deliberate to try to soften the sound of his leather soles on the floor. He slunk up behind his president, who heard him; knew he was coming.

Zach came to a halt to the left and behind Crane, placing his hands in his pockets, almost purposely mimicking the president. He looked out across the lawn at the same crowd, delaying any words for many moments. They silently examined, studying them. They let it soak in.

"Nothing but a distraction," Zach spoke. "I wish we could just haul them off or make them carry on this bullshit someplace else."

"I don't." Crane convulsed once with a soundless, half-hearted chuckle and pitying smirk. He waited for a moment, watching from the corner of his eye as Zach formed a confused expression. "They represent democracy—the will of the people." He paused for another several moments. "Probably the purest form of democracy. Mob mentality."

"They're doing this all over the Republic," Zach noted, but Crane knew that. "We can't have this kind of dissent. Something has to be done about it."

"They're not doing anything wrong," the president replied. "They're voicing discontent with us. They don't like the decisions we've made on their behalf. They are wavering in their view that we represent them here in Austin. What we've done here, they don't want."

"Maybe they don't know what they want," Zach suggested. "That's why you and the legislators are here. You're the elite. The fate of our republic can't be entrusted to them—the ignorant, uneducated masses. So people like you make decisions on their behalf. The proxies of the populous. Do what's best for them. And I think you have. They'll thank you in the long run for shrinking the size of their government—taking out all the fluff and socialist spending. Getting them off the tit of the government. And now maybe they'll learn to do things for themselves. No more government help."

"Hmm . . ." He nodded and then glared out the window. "That was a nice speech. But I'm not sure they would agree with you. And they outnumber you and I." He crossed this arms. "With most of our troops overseas and this government becoming so unpopular, I'm not sure what the future holds. I don't know how much longer I can hold this together."

Chapter 48

June

Hoards of sweaty civilians assembled along the black paved streets of the Fort Worth Stockyards. They coursed within the complex of old livestock pens that once punctuated the southern end of the old Chisholm Trail, but now was filled with high-end barbecue and Tex-Mex restaurants and little Western boutiques. The young clung to their parents clad in cargo shorts and sunglasses as they bought fudge and cowboy hats for them. New and old country music oozed from within the neon-lit restaurants and concocted in the scorched streets to the north of downtown. The faintest hint of manure drifted on the light, ineffective breeze.

The crowd was thicker today by a lot. Police kept the streets clear, forcing the thickening masses to clutter along the sidewalks, beneath the awnings affront the old honkytonks, and in the touristy shops. They came from all over Texas to visit the Stockyards, but the area was as much of an attraction to locals across the Metroplex as it was for out-of-towners. Young families gorging on the teat of consumerism walked and fed, draining their wallets, running up their credit card balances, and filling their arteries with saturated fat.

The paved streets began to bustle and liven beyond the police barricades. First were the clack of bovine hooves and shoed horses. The longhorns ambled and mooed down the street in the cowtown tradition, mounted cowboys in Wranglers and Stetsons poking them along toward the stables. They were followed by the sounds of trumpets, trombones, and oboes. The big bass drums thundered, the cymbals clashed, and the snares laid down a traditional marching beat. The Republican Guard

Band sang with the old standards of Sousa, leading in the marching fighting men, many of them fresh out of Pakistan.

The crowds, filled with loyal Texas patriots who came out specifically to greet the triumphant army, cheered and clapped for their heroes. Little boys and girls, perched upon the shoulders of their fathers, smiled innocently as they waved to the troops. Tan combat boots stamped the asphalt in unison as they paraded, straight-faced behind the band.

The hum and grumble of an engine followed. A big green John Deere tractor, personifying the lingering agricultural spirit of Fort Worth and the surrounding areas, tugged along pulling a brightly decorated trailer float. White ruffles and deep reds complimented the twenty-nine-star flag and the insignia of Telaco emblazoned in the mobile spectacle. Aboard, locally-born or stationed colonels and lower officers, along with a couple of minor generals smiled and waved. They sat tall and straight, basking in the praise that rose up from the crowds. They sat as living statues of glory and valor that avenged the tragedy that occurred just forty-five miles away. Behind the float rolled a Humvee and a whole company of troops marching behind.

In the sea of joyful patriots, a few dark specs floated along. They blended well with their thin, airy t-shirts and cargo shorts. Their hair was brushed and flip-flops left tan lines, yet they were foreign. They eyed the procession as it passed, silently lurking. They remained straight-faced and neutral, trailing through the throngs unnoticed. They were phantoms moving through the walls of family fun, ready to cast their menacing shadow.

The Humvee behind the officers' float rolled along, its diesel engine gurgling as it rumbled ahead of the company of soldiers. It was fully manned with four fatigue-clad troops inside and one up on the fifty caliber. The driver slowed the vehicle slightly and reached into his pocket. His finger touched a little button on a little black plastic device, and suddenly the engine shut off.

"Shit," Kyle said as he threw up his hands behind the wheel of the Humvee. He looked at the dashboard and then at the sergeant next to him. "What the hell happened?"

"Why did you stop, Private . . ." The sergeant paused to read the name on his shirt. "Kessler. Why did you stop the Humvee?"

"I didn't, sir," Kyle continued the act. "It just died." He got out of the vehicle, as did the others. Kyle peered around the side and grinned briefly to see that all the troops behind had stopped, slaves to their marching protocol. The men exiting the Humvee began opening the hood to try to diagnose the problem as the officers' float ahead continued to roll into a wide intersection.

From between two individual metal barricades darted a small flash of brown and black, scampering across the pavement. The miniature Doberman quickly dashed out in front of the tractor pulling the float. He stopped, barked, and jumped about, deeming the big John Deere a threat worth challenging. He hopped around in front as the driver of the tractor clutched and shifted down, grinding the brakes to a halt. He was alarmed, but wooed by the tiny bark and the short legs. He grinned as the soft-looking mini warrior attacked the monstrous contraption. Laughter dully emanated from the crowd. Children giggled and pointed while their mothers oohed and ahhed over the wayward pup.

And then out popped his owner, pushing slyly between the same metal barricades and into the street. Her brown cowboy boots knocked solidly on the blacktop, one foot directly in front of the other. Her tanned, sculpted legs sprouted up from the leather in a gradual, wonderful muscular thickening that peaked high above with a pair of tight denim shorts that barely covered the bottom curves of her butt cheeks. They were nearly painted on, and displayed covertly every enticing curve and inch of feminine allure that she possessed. Above, her chiseled abs flexed with every deliberate, hip-swinging step. A plaid half button-down blouse was tied together at the tails just below her supple breasts, which shook and moved in unison with her hips to catch every male eye on the parade route. Ashley strutted her stunning physique and dark flowing tresses as she moved into the street unchallenged to retrieve her dog. The tractor driver, as well as the officers, gawked as she bent down to pick up the little canine and rose again to throw a wink and a smile up to the driver before trotting off back into the crowd. Wives snarled at their husbands' glances. The officers and driver lingered with her, still trying to catch another glimpse of her even as she disappeared into the masses.

By then, the band and the troops affront were far ahead. The Humvee behind was still stopped as the men tried to figure out the problem with the engine. From a storm drain on the far side of the street where no spectators gathered, a small object emerged unnoticed. A toy tank buzzed across the street, its sound drowned by the bustle of the crowd and the roar of the engines. The silvery metal tip of an antenna barely gleamed from within the storm drain as the toy meandered across the intersection and disappeared underneath the float.

On the other side of the street, hidden deep behind the crowd, a man sat innocently at a patio table of one of the barbeque restaurants. He could see the float past the backs of the parade goers. He grinned and inconspicuously picked up his smart phone. Pressing the icon for messaging, he brought up the cue for the sending of a new message. He scrolled through his address book with the tip of his index finger until he saw the contact name he wanted—J.J. Evans. He selected and cued the field for typing a message and then typed in the word "dy-no-miiite!!"

An inaudible electronic chime occurred under the stationary float and then it was lifted from the street in a sudden flash of heat. A shock wave pushed out from the intersection knocking onlookers back. They turned and darted away from the sides of the street. Screaming and confusion ensued as the float broke apart, splintering and charring wood. The metal frame bent and twisted. The men on the float were lost to the fireball, obscured and engulfed by flames and immediate death. The tractor was blasted forward several hundred feet, rolling and tumbling like a child's toy misused. The debris of the trailer crashed back to earth in a pile of destruction and heat as the troops amassing behind the stalled Humvee rushed forward with the intention of helping, though there was really nothing to do. All rushed over except one man. Kyle paused a moment to take in the scene, unsure of whether he took pride in this act. Finally, he smiled. The thought of every atrocity he witnessed in Pakistan. This was karma. They deserved it. And he walked off the street in anonymity, heading to the meeting point.

Chapter 49

Laughter resonated through the house, the sound waves bouncing from one wall to the next and vibrating the very structure of the expansive living room. It was a beautiful room and a beautiful house in a neighborhood just past its infancy. It was completed just before the secession, enjoying all the underwriting funds of the U.S. financial sector. Granite countertops and top-of-the-line stainless appliances crowned and complimented the tall, darkly stained cabinets. The living room sprawled with rust-colored scored, stamped, and stained concrete floors and large expensive rugs topped with solid wood and leather couches, chairs, and ottomans. Bookshelves neatly held a wealth of literature and displayed little trinkets and conversational pieces. The dark brown of the walls sharply contrasted with the gleaming white of the molding and chair rails. High-dollar chandeliers and recessed lighting set a comfortable ambiance in the room as joyful voices added substance between the walls.

"God, I'm glad that dog did what he was supposed to do," Brice burst. "We would have been screwed."

"I told you," Moira pointed at him. "I told you he'd attack the float. He's a little bitty bastard, but he thinks he's a friggin' pit bull." She raised her beer bottle to her lips and gulped down a big sudsy load into an already flooded stomach.

Kyle grabbed more dark brown bottles from the refrigerator. He gripped them by the tops of the necks, clinking the glass together at the bottom, and pulled them from the cold. He shut the door and paused a moment, peering through the doorway from the kitchen to the living room where everyone was gathered. He listened to the talking, cutting up, and laughter filling the room, and battled the gauntlet of mixed emotions. He had proven himself, yet he had remained quiet all night, afraid to say anything. He hesitated to walk into the room, still an outsider. But he walked in anyway, feeling the eyes on him as he sat next to a more conservatively clothed Ashley. He handed beers to her and Brice before opening his own and placing his arm around his girlfriend.

"And I think we should have a toast," another man said across the room, raising his bottle into the air, saluting. "To Ashley and her hot little ass," he toasted as everyone erupted into laughter and raised their glasses and bottles in unison. "The star of the show. That would not have been possible without her. Those old geezers on the float had one last thing of beauty to look at before they were dispatched."

Kyle's grip around her tightened a bit. He looked around, his temper threatening to flare, but he was outnumbered and her receptiveness as a compliment spoke to her relationship with this group. She felt his arms pull her closer. She understood. She placed her hand on his knee and massaged. She glanced up at him and grinned, watching his tightening forehead relax in her eyes. There isn't a person in here that wouldn't jump at the chance to screw you—even the girls, he thought as he looked at her. But you're mine. And he smiled.

"And to our new associate," Aaron said from his chair in the shadowed corner across the room. He raised his glass of scotch. "You have definitely proven yourself, my friend. Well done," he nodded.

Kyle looked around at the silent room. The group was solemn, approving with their eyes and slight grins. They all nodded at him, raising their glasses and bottles, then imbibing the alcohol they held. Finally, he felt comfortable, his muscles and joints loosening as he sunk a little deeper into the leather upholstery.

"How do you feel?" Aaron asked.

"How do I feel?" Kyle raised his eyebrows.

"Yeah," he said. "You just committed an act of terrorism. How do you feel about that?"

He paused a moment, choosing his words carefully. "I'm not a stranger to killing people," he began, but paused a bit once more. "I've never been a supporter of secession. It's treason. I'm solid in that belief now. And not only did those officers betray their country, but I've seen the things they've ordered done in Pakistan. Karma's a bitch."

Aaron nodded approvingly. "Well said."

"Hey, who lives here?" Kyle randomly asked, feeling comfortable enough that he had the floor.

"No one," Brice answered with a chuckle.

"I mean . . . the pictures." Kyle motioned to the family portraits and random pictures of people on the mantle and shelves.

"Ha-ha," Aaron laughed. "Pretty convincing, huh? All staged. It's a CIA safe house."

"CIA?" Kyle had no idea.

"Yeah, we're CIA backed and funded," Aaron confirmed. "And this is one of their safe houses we use when we're up here. Looks like a real family lives here. All the bedrooms have clothes in the drawers. The bathrooms are stocked with toiletries. The bedrooms upstairs are painted in pastel blue and pink with gender-appropriate toys in the playroom. There is food in the pantry—" He stopped abruptly as his cell phone rang. He took it out and looked at it. "Speak of the devil . . ." He put the phone to his ear and walked into the study adjacent to the living room.

The room continued on without interruption. A few briefly lost that gleeful smile as they eyed Aaron walking out of the room, but they returned to the giggling and drinking characteristic of a celebration. Not Kyle. His eyes were fixed on their leader muffled by his proximity and pacing back and forth across the study. Kyle could only see him for a moment at a time in the darkness of the next room when he paced within view through the doorway.

And then he returned, crossing the threshold back into the living room. One by one, the people in the group caught sight of him and his decision not to sit. He stood there as if to address them, but said nothing. His hand rose to his mouth as he rubbed it and his cheeks, contorting his face for a few moments while he collected his thoughts. The conversation and the decibel level lowered surely, as if someone were turning the volume knob.

"That was Dupuis," he said, making eye-contact with every person in the room.

"Dupuis?" Kyle whispered to Ashley.

"The ARA's leader and founder," she whispered back. "Our connection to the CIA."

"He wanted everyone to know how proud he was with today's hit," Aaron continued. "He's very pleased." He paused for a moment before providing the rest of the news. "And he wanted to give us the order for the next one." All was completely silent; no movement, no drinking of beers. Even breathing was shallow. "Austin," he said, exhaling as people suddenly squirmed in the leather seats and whispered in excitement to one another. "The capitol building. He wants us to execute in two months, so enjoy yourselves now. We have a lot of work to do." He made his way back to his seat, plopped down, and polished off the last gulp of his scotch in silence.

Chapter 50

The thin brown carpet was very uncomfortable. It lacked padding underneath and had endured decades of hefty foot traffic, but no matter. Olivia was a drug that dulled the ache in Derek's back, and he was addicted. Surrounded by cheap plastic toys of an assortment of bright, child-like colors, Derek lay there between his easy chair and television. He hoisted his young daughter into the air above him, straightening his arms and locking the elbows. Above, the toddler grinned and giggled with an open mouth. Her lips were wet with drool, which occasionally dripped in a clear stream directly onto Derek's face, but he was strangely okay with it. He made goofy faces and silly noises at her, and all the while she knew what was coming—just not when. At odd intervals of time, he suddenly dropped her from her lofty position. She fell a short distance before Daddy stopped her plummet just before impact, and hugged her close, mimicking a growling dog and pretending to gnaw at her neck. Then he started the process over.

It never got old. The television rarely saw use anymore. He would play with her for hours. Sometimes he would just lie there beside her as she sat on her diaper-padded bottom playing with her toys. He observed her every move as she attempted to figure out what goes inside of what. She experimented with shapes and sorting colors. She occasionally put something in her mouth for a moment to test its level of harmfulness or benevolence. She tapped and banged hard plastic items on the floors or the legs of chairs to see what noise would occur. She was a wonder, full of curiosity. He watched before him the miracle of his daughter's discovery of everything that adults take for granted, but for her a treasure of a brand new find.

Carly kept her distance. She said nothing when he was spending time with Olivia; getting to know her. And Olivia was getting to know him, touching his face and interacting with him. She would mill about the house smiling at them as they cut-up and laughed. She watched from her duties cleaning up after Olivia as she always did. She wiped the applesauce splatter from the high chair or cleaned some dishes. She folded little shirts and shorts or emptied the dirty diaper pail from Olivia room.

And then there was an interruptive electronic tone. It pierced the joy and laughter like a booster shot needle into the tender thigh of a screaming toddler. It jolted Carly a bit, awakened from her trance in watching Derek and his daughter. Derek simply looked over, his smile weakening only for an instant, but then returning to his parental silliness. Carly looked over at Derek's cell phone chiming and vibrating on the counter. She placed the sippy cup she was drying in its respective cupboard, and then leaned over to read the screen and the caller identification.

"I don't recognize it," she said as she picked it up and walked it over to him. "It's not a number in your contacts list."

"Probably another damned sales call. You'd think getting on a national do-not-call list would cease and desist all sales calls." He sat up and put his daughter down to sit on her butt. He kissed her soft, baby-plump cheek and took the phone, pressing the answer button. "Hello?" He paused for a moment as a muffled voice on the other end identified himself. "Yes sir." He physically became more rigid—Marine rigid. His voice changed and his eyes hardened as he stood and briskly walked out of the room.

Carly's mind raced with thoughts on who that might be, but she knew quite certainly who it was. The question was why they were calling. Her eyebrows turned upward, and she danced a bit in discomfort, almost as if she were about to urinate down her leg. She leaned to the right, trying in vain to get a view of him in the other room. Her gaze darted from that doorway to her oblivious child playing quietly on the floor. She could hear the conversation abruptly end, and in trudged her man, his hands firmly in his pockets. The look on his face was not the one she wanted. In fact she briefly dreaded it just before he entered the room.

"The Marines?" She ripped he bandage off.

"Yeah," he confirmed as he removed his hand from its pocket and scratched his head. "Combat duty."

"Combat? But I thought U.S. troops withdrew from Pakistan," she clarified frantically, her stability decaying. "You're home . . . for good."

"Not Pakistan." He hesitated. "Um . . . down south." He paused for several long moments. "Texas." He stopped again, watching Carly's eyes become glassy. "We're making a move on Austin."

Tears rolled from the bottom rims of her eyes. She shook her head in disbelief, wiping those silent tears and dancing from foot to foot in mild panic as Derek helplessly watched her melt down.

"That's bullshit," she said calmly. "You just got back a few months ago. You've done your duty," she declared, her voice raised.

"Hey . . ." He raised his finger to his lips to indicate that she should calm and lower her tone. "Let's go out on the porch."

"Olivia . . ."

"She'll be fine," he whispered, and motioned her for the door on the other side of the kitchen. They stepped out and pulled the door almost closed, easily able to look in on their toddler if they needed to. "I don't have a choice." His voice gained normal volume and tone. "It's my duty. I'm an enlisted Marine."

"You've done your time," she yelled. "You've bled more than once for them. Watched men die."

"I'm fucking aware of what I've sacrificed," he yelled back. "Trust me. I was there when I sacrificed, so you would think I'd remember it happening." He stopped, closed his eyes, and lowered his tone. "I know I've done my part, but it doesn't matter. I took an oath. I go where they send me—any time they want. It's what they pay me for. It's what pays the bills. If I don't go to combat, than I'm not earning my paycheck. It comes at a price. Unfortunately, my paycheck often involves people shooting at me."

"Fuck that," she said. "I'd rather you go back to being a mechanic."

"And what about what I want, Carly?" He raised his voice. "Huh? I left that job as a mechanic for a reason. I like being a soldier."

"No," she shook her head. "I forbid you to go."

"Oh, so you're forbidding me?" He seemed appalled. "Really? That's just wonderful. Sure, pick my career for me. Forbid me to do whatever. Why don't you just go ahead and comb my hair for me and pick out my fucking clothes? Iron my tighty-whities." He paused for silent fuming. "No one forbids me to do what I want to do. Or what I need to do. Or decides for me what my duty is."

"You let the Marines decide those things," she calmly said.

He tried to rebut, but nothing came out of his mouth. He was unsure what to say for several moments. "I don't like the idea of going back to battle, not because I'm not good at it. I am. And I like it. I feel at home in it. But I'd rather be with you and Olivia. And even though I'd rather stay, I need to go. This is a chance to end this whole shitty mess once and for all. You can forbid me all you want, but I'm going. I have to pack. I leave in a few days." He stormed off into the house with a mission and a purpose, leaving Carly still tearful and in shock on the front porch.

Chapter 51

July

Clouds blocked any hope for starlight or the crisp brilliance of the moon. Instead, city-wide orange street lights shined upward in a rapture of artificial luminance and lit the bottom of the clouds for a dingy urban glow that blanketed Austin with an ominous heft.

The grit in the damp dust ground and crumbled beneath several sets of feet as they trudged through the lot. They dodged small craters in the dirt and gravel where rain and truck tires had eroded away the soil. Patches of weeds grew tall at the perimeter and in junk piles garnishing empty drums and whole engine blocks stripped away of the essentials that once made them run. The chain link rusted and decayed along the borders of the yard, links popping open to create small, yet expanding gaps in the fence. A dog barked in the distance, suddenly reminding Kyle that dogs often roamed these kinds of places. He was already on edge, but now more so. But he managed to giggle more audibly than he intended.

"What's so funny?" Ashley asked as they pushed on, following Aaron's lead.

"I was just thinking," he said, "that this is more like it." He smiled at her and the others.

"How so?" she took the bait.

"I mean seriously," he answered. "What paramilitary resistance group meets in a fully-furnished, five-hundred-thousand-dollar garden home to plan their next strike?" he grinned. "Give me an abandoned auto repair shop and a single hanging light over a map on a table any old day of the week."

Ashley smiled, and then it grew into a little chuckle. Kyle looked around at a few of the others to make sure he did not just say something stupid and out of place, but all were grinning as well. He was sure Aaron was not, though. He never really did smile. Kyle liked to think that in this moment Aaron wanted to, though. He just forced himself not to. He had to play the part of the badass, fearless leader.

"Stow the jokes once we get in, Perkins," he grumbled from in front. "Have your game face on. Goliath doesn't fuck around. He's all business."

They approached the corrugated aluminum structure and stood affront the single giant rolling door as Aaron moved to the heavy steel personnel door to the right of the vehicle entry. He stood for a moment, staring at the rust on the outside, and then he knocked. The metallic bang was hollow, and almost mechanical. It resonated in the shop, vibrating the whole structure. A few moments went by, and then finally the knob turned and the door pushed ajar, smartly snapping to a halt at the end of the security chain. An eye was barely visible through the crack. It moved up and down, analyzing every inch of Aaron's stubbled and stern face. The door shut, and then there was a metal-on-metal grinding or sliding. The door flung open and the man stood aside. Aaron motioned for the others and they crossed the threshold one by one.

Kyle rolled his eyes as he entered the shop. He sneered as the bright flood from the large halogens above fried every inch of the interior with blinding, unnatural light. There was no mystique of ambiance—darkness to the vast edges and corners of the metal building. There was no unknown beyond some singular light illuminating a stained map held down on a table with grenades and tank shells. Dusty, scarred wooden shelving in a couple of corners of the shop were stacked and cluttered with grime-caked spare parts and rusty tools. Chains that once hoisted engine blocks from underneath the hoods of vehicles still hung loosely from the steel rafters. Haphazardly placed assortments of mechanic paraphernalia littered the shop from one end to another.

At the center stood the out-of-place element. An old gray painted metal desk, surrounded by people in various assortments of street clothes and dressed-down combat gear, stood as a centerpiece of the room. A laptop computer's screen glowed crisply with a variety of regal-toned colors. Beyond the desk was a huge rack with shelving to the side. It was fully stocked with assault rifles, grenades, metal ammunition canisters, and stacks of explosives. Kyle was unsure which of the thick, burly individuals in the group ahead was Goliath. He was leaning toward the one in the hole-ridden tank top and the scar down his cheek.

"Glad you made it in," a skinny, stubbly man with jeans and a little blue t-shirt pierced the air with his shrill, squeaky voice. He shook Aaron's outstretched hand, placing his other hand on top.

"Goliath," Aaron greeted. "Good to see you again. It's been awhile."

Goliath? Kyle raised his eyebrow and cocked his head. I'm disappointed.

The College Station group walked up, completing the present half dozen Austin ARA semi-circle. They all stood silently sizing one another up, yet taking comfort in the solidarity of alliance. A few even nodded sternly. It was silent for some time. Eyes met but words failed to emerge, to the point that it verged on awkwardness.

"So this is it, huh?" Goliath placed his hands on his hips and looked around at everyone, finally locking his gaze on Aaron. "All this time, and we finally got the call."

"I don't know what took so long," Aaron commented. "Presidential approval. I wonder how long it took before they grew the balls to even tell Chandler about the CIA connection to the ARA."

Goliath just nodded initially, taking the statement in, and considering it, but generally uninterested in answering. "I'm ready. It's time to put the last nail in this Republic coffin. Preserve the union at all costs," he nodded some more, his hands still on his hips. "At all costs—even that of Joe Crane himself."

"That's the plan?" Aaron asked. "Take out Crane?"

"Take out the whole Goddamned capitol building in Austin," he said. "And with Crane inside it. Come take a look," he motioned for Aaron to come closer to the computer. "Blueprints to every level of the capitol building. Can you believe this shit? Didn't even have to steal them. They're right here on an old Texas state website—public information," he smiled.

"So this is another demolitions hit," Aaron commented.

"Yeah, but we're not blowing up dignitaries' cars or floats full of Guard officers," Goliath corrected. "This is large-scale. An entire building. Stack over here," he said as he pointed to the large man with the scar, "has studied every bit of this material, and he's come up with a plan."

"If we want to take down the whole building," Stack spoke up with his baritone voice, moving over to the screen, "we're going to have to get access to the basement. There are some key concrete-and-steel supports down there that run upward through every major level of the building," he said, pointing to the locations on the screen. "If we hit each one of the eight simultaneously with enough of a charge, the supports should fail all the way up, and the structure will implode."

"Okay, sounds good," Aaron nodded. "Simple. But how do we get in?" He paused for a moment, nibbling the inside of his lip. "The place is going to be crawling with Guard"

"Maybe not," Goliath interjected. "The Marines are going to be knocking on Austin's back door. It's all hands on deck for the Guard in the city. They'll all be out on the front lines—and they're coming hardcore. We've been watching the updates on the Internet all evening. Marines pushed past DFW today, pretty much unchallenged. Estimated ten thousand strong," he said excitedly. "We'll sneak two men in—sorry ladies. We'll dress them as Republican Guard. No one will be the wiser. The rest of the team will monitor by tapping into security cameras in the capitol, and check reports of everything from where the U.S. forces are to when Joe Crane goes to take a shit."

"Just two?" Aaron asked.

"It's easier to get just two in. Any more and it will get hard to move quickly or think on the fly."

"Do we even know Crane will be in the building?" Kyle chimed in as Aaron shot him a look to shut his mouth. "I mean, the Marines are up to a month from reaching this area. They'll have Fort Hood to deal with on the way. What if Crane bugs out?"

"What's your name?" Goliath peered over at him.

"Kyle Perkins," he answered with his chin high.

"I like you," Goliath smiled. "Always thinking ahead. The truth is we don't know for sure. But we think he will stay in that building until Uncle Sam himself drags him out by his dick. We've studied his moves extensively. He's a creature of habit. Leaves home at the same time every day. Eats lunch at the same time, at the same restaurant every day. Meets with his advisors, generals, Zach Wallace, every day. And he doesn't leave the office until late. We're pretty sure he's screwing a girl in record-keeping, by the way," he said. "He'll be there, and we're going to make him go down with the ship."

"But why even take down the ship to begin with?" Kyle pushed, watching Goliath appear to get annoyed. Aaron gave him a look that implored him to shut his mouth, but Kyle ignored it. "With the Marines coming in, won't they take the capitol? Take Crane into custody?"

"We've been waiting for this—planning for months," Goliath said. "We were just waiting for the opportunity. We execute as U.S. military forces roll in to take Austin. Sure they'll take the capitol building, but we—the powers that be, even—don't just want it taken. They want it crushed . . . destroyed." He pointed downward. "It will implode from within. We need this public and dramatic. The other twenty-eight states will get the message that this is a sure thing, and if they don't surrender to the union, they will suffer a similar fate."

Goliath's words bounced off the walls of the building with an almost metallic twang. They were not loud, but elevated, and filled the room. And when the sound had run its course, it left all silent. Kyle understood. His lips, glued together, offered no challenge. No one did. Aaron's cutting eyes willed him to die by them. He then turned his attention to Goliath, who was still soaked with the passion in his rant. His eyes were wide and wild. His breathing was shallow and labored.

"We'll do it," Aaron said, perhaps to calm the man down. He needed to draw the man's attention and bring him down from this amped-up state. "We'll set the explosives. We have had a lot of good fortune when it comes to that department."

"I don't know." Goliath snapped out of it, and then set to pondering the notion. "This is my town—my territory, and I'm a bit of a control freak." He was silent for quite some time, staring down into Aaron's pant legs. He was lost in the deep blue for an extended period, as if he would not resurface.

"You guys monitor," Aaron broke the silence. "I'll take one of my guys." He paused for a split second. "I'll take loudmouth there," he pointed to Kyle. "He may be a dipshit, but he's got a gigantic set of balls on him, and on top of it, he has conviction."

Goliath continued to think on it, his eyes beginning with Aaron, now staring into this face in contemplation. He then suddenly cocked his head to the side, and shot his eyes over to young Kyle, sizing him up. His mouth hung ajar slightly as he attempted to look right through the young man.

"Okay," he jerked to attention. "Fine, you and the loudmouth get the most dangerous job—the one that includes plastic explosives and sneaking into the enemy capitol. We start training tomorrow." He pushed past Kyle, patting him firmly on the shoulder. "Tonight we get drunk."

Chapter 52

The cheap black plastic was malleable between the near perfect white teeth within Cindy Chandler's mouth. She dented and maimed the pen cap, causing it to flatten somewhat before rotating it and chewing it back closer to its original round state. She covered it in saliva and lipstick, mangling and disfiguring the hapless object while she looked over the map laid out before her in the situation room.

"Are you sure?" She looked up at General Bates. "Are you sure we have to take this objective? The Reds can't have many men here. Can't we just push on past them and move for Austin."

"Fort Hood is a must, Madam President," he nodded insistently. "Can't leave it behind. Aerial recon estimates that base at about seven thousand armable personnel. We're only hitting it with about ten thousand, and while we outnumber them, they aren't exactly going to let us just walk in there and sit down at the dinner table and start hogging the cranberry sauce. They're going to hit us with a few tanks we see on the recon pictures. They also have an airfield there with quite a few choppers. This is going to be a tough one."

"Again, why don't we just bypass Hood and move for Austin?" she asked.

If we do that," he said," we're leaving an entire base full of reinforcements, tanks and reinforcements. What are we going to do once we get into Austin, and then suddenly those Red bastards from Hood come back to haunt us? We have to take that base and secure that airfield—especially that airfield. It will be a hell of a lot easier to launch airstrikes and drone recon out of Hood, rather than fly it in from Fort Polk in Louisiana, or from Carlswell Naval Air Station up in Fort Worth. We need this victory."

The president did not remove her spectacle-jacketed eyes from the map. She studied it over, her eyes always returning to Fort Hood. She pursed her lips and silently pored over it before speaking. "Okay, if you say so, Bates," she conceded. "I just don't want too many casualties before we move on Austin. We need everyone we can get. Austin is weak. I still think we're wasting troops on a stronger base when we could be focusing on taking the capitol."

"I understand, ma'am," he nodded. "But I think this is the right move in the long run. We can always bring in reinforcements out of Polk if we need more personnel for the Austin assault."

"Okay," she sighed. "When?"

"Tonight, after dark," he said, and then pointed to the map. "They surely know we're coming, just not when. We've set up about ten miles out in the hills and patches of woods to the north and east. They haven't had the firepower or equipment to try and come out and thin us out by air. And they sure as hell ain't comin' out to meet us outside their comfy little base. So the ball's in our court. We'll start moving just after dusk and attack out of the countryside under the veil of night. No airstrikes. Tanks will be there only to battle with any tanks they may have at Hood. We want minimal damage to barracks and buildings. And we sure as shit don't want to crater up that airfield or destroy all the choppers. We may need them to take on Austin."

Derek watched as the western sky slowly faded from a bright gold to a deepening orange color. A few clouds were whipped and spread into cotton candy that turned pink against the orange horizon and the baby-blue above it. Little hindered the view of the metamorphosis of day to evening. The trees were to his back. A few shrubs and mesquites dotted the field ahead of him. The nearest neighborhood of the town of Kileen was over a mile away, a small military base town prosperous with middle-class and good schools. But no building was in sight, and so Derek held tight to his gun and savored the final rays of sunlight before the terror was to begin.

Soon, all light was gone and the stars were there to bear silent witness to the events unfolding. Derek noted that there was no moon yet, and smiled. He looked out across the solitary highway that led into the base, and beyond that into the open field leading to the airfields. His stomach turned somewhat and a chill of nervousness covered him, but only for a moment as he focused and waited for the signal.

"Jesus," Queens whispered from behind him, and then moved up to his side. "We've gotta cross all that to get to an even more wide-open airfield?"

"Yup," Derek nodded. "But at least we have darkness. See over there? The airfield is lit by solar lamps. The sun's down, so they just came on. But I think without a moon overhead that we can cross most of this field without being seen and drawing any fire." He looked at his friend to see him nodding. "Remind your guys to stick to their formation. We have gunners in this tree line. Tell your people to stay clear of their line of fire."

"Yes sir," Queens acknowledged, and turned back into the tree line to talk to his men.

All eyes were fixed on that somewhat distant patch of lights. They could see the paved slab where the helicopters took off and landed. They could see the two big arched hangers beyond, and all was quiet. Nothing stirred in the night or on the base. And then there was a slight click on Derek's radio, like someone pressed the button to talk, said nothing, and took their finger off the button. It caught his attention, and he looked down at it, waiting. Another click followed, and then another distinctive one. Derek looked up and took a deep breath, allowing the shiver of nervousness to begin and then die as quickly.

"Let's go," he said, whispering as the used his hands to indicate forward motion. "Remember—trot across that field. I know it's dark, but it's wide open, so you need to cross as much of it as you can before they get wise to our being here. Watch for holes and shit. Don't break an ankle."

The men began moving from the tree line, their dark green and brown camouflage perfect for the darkened wooded area. In a mile and a half line, the men pushed forward, slowly and cautious at first, and then as confidence built, their legs felt a new rush of energy, and the pace increased. Soon, thousands of men were crouched and trotting across the road leading in, and traversing the high grass, ever approaching the lights of the base. Derek could see his arms and his weapon slowly become more visible. His hands bore the color of flesh in the brightening night, and then there was a sound he recognized all too well. In the distance, yellow-orange flower-like bursts popped and echoed over the field as Marines all around began taking bullets to all parts of the body. Blood erupted from their limbs and torsos as shots rang out from Guardsmen around the corners of the buildings and from a few apparent machine gun nests in the shadows of the hangars.

"Shit," Derek yelled, still moving as swiftly as he could toward the deadly fire.

"They were waiting on us." Alex pushed along with his platoon in tow.

Muzzle flashes lit in the darkness like a terrible candlelight vigil, but instead of bringing peace and remembrance, there was death. The Marines swarmed toward the illuminated airfield like moths to a porch light. The machine guns behind them in the tree line sprang to life with the mechanization of slaughter. Phosphorus-coated tracers streaked through the night, marking the path of death to any Republican Guardsman unfortunate enough to be in the path.

Derek could see men ahead of him moving ever closer to the base, and each of them fell to the ground. And then he stopped, looking around at the assault. His eyes widened, and his brow arched upward as the epiphany struck him like an enemy bullet.

"Stop," he yelled out. "Stop and hit the deck!" He continued to see men push forward and meet their demise. "Stay back and hit the ground. Back where it's dark. They can't see you as well. Don't give them a target."

Finally, others to the side and behind him followed as he fell to the ground. Down the line, a chain reaction of men slowed, stopped, and went to their bellies, continuing to fire from the veil of tall, wild grass that surrounded them. The gunners in the tree line continued to tear up the corners of the buildings, as well as the two machinegun nests in the shadows beside the hangars. Dirt popped around Derek like random exploding popcorn kernels. Bits of soil and grit rained down on him while he continued to put rounds into that defensive line. Tracers streamed like deadly fireflies overhead, and one by one, each machinegun nest fell silent.

"Got the big guns," he yelled out, trying to carry his voice over the gunfire from both sides. "Start crawling forward."

Elbows dug into the dry dirt and bits of rock, each man and woman inching closer to the light, and closer to the enemy. They moved some, and then stopped to continue to put a few rounds into the enemy defense. The machineguns on the ridge released a staggering amount of fire into the line, sounding off like a nonstop typewriter in the night. The enemy fire dwindled, and as Derek noticed, he lifted his head a bit, looking forward at the Guard defense, and then to his men.

"That's it," he called to his men. "Get up and charge."

Marines rose from the darkness and the grass like a hoard of monsters springing spontaneously from the earth. Swift legs carried booted feet quickly in from the fields and into the glow of the halogen lights above the forward helicopter pads. Marine fire continued as long as there were muzzle flashes coming from the buildings and hangars. Derek watched as a few more of his men and women fell in the charge, but the numbers poured in and soles began clapping on the concrete pads. They were now overrunning the airfield. By the time he approached the white building ahead of him, enemy fire had stopped. He slowed, as did the others, cautious as to what was on the other side or around the corner. Two men sprang from around one of the walls, and Derek quickly put a close-range bullet into one man's head as the other was dropped by another Marine.

Marine fire slowed and stopped at the airfield, but could be heard in the distance across the base as other units carried out their objectives. Men pooled along the protective walls of the large building they had come to. As everyone in Derek's unit began gathering, he assessed the situation and started to give orders.

"Okay, get those gunners up here closer," he said. "That was probably the toughest part of it. But we have one more long line of buildings across this helipad here on the other side of this building. I don't know how the defenses look over there, so we're just going to have to take it slow and cautious. Get the gunners up on the roof of this building and give us some cover."

The machinegun teams packed up their large weapons and ammunition, and moved them ahead through the night and onto the halogen-lit tarmac. They came upon the large building where all Marines of this unit were gathering.

"Get up on this roof—all of you," he said. "A few of you grunts go with them in case you need to clear out a few stragglers hunkered down inside. This airfield is huge, so all the other units will take the other parts of this section of Hood. We're focusing on those few small administrative buildings over there and the big white hangar directly across the parking lots on the other side of this building. Go."

The gunners, accompanied by some other troops, found a glass door forty yards down. A few shots were fired into the door, causing it to spider web, and then shatter into thousands of light blue shards. The men stepped in over the bottom section of the aluminum door, cracking and crunching the glass beneath their feet. In the dark, lit only by the faint intrusion of the halogens through cheap plastic blinds, a receptionist desk with a little plant on top was silhouetted across the room. They carefully proceeded down a hall, weapons drawn, scanning for any movement.

Flashlights clicked on to light their way as they got away from the windows in the front, and at the end of the hall they found a stairway. Without a word, a Marine carefully peeked around the corner and up the stairs, his flashlight illuminating the top of the stairs as he carefully inched forward, followed by the other soldiers and the gunners. They began to make their way up the stairs, bypassing the second floor, and moving up and beyond until they reached a door. A boot lifted up and a swift kick to the doorknob unlatched the metal door from its jam. It swung open and the teams walked out, crouched and poised for attack. They swept the roof, clear of any enemy, and then allowed the gunners to move cautiously for the edge of the building facing the next set of buildings.

Crouched and inconspicuous, they set up their weapons, feeding in chains of ammunition and deploying the bipods for easy positioning. The other soldiers quickly made their way back through the roof doors and down the staircase. They sprinted down the hallways and out the doors, exiting the building to rejoin their unit.

"They're in position, Lieutenant," they reported back to Derek, who simply nodded in acknowledgement.

He looked around the corner and lifted the infrared binoculars to his eyes, scanning as much of the next line of buildings as he could. He could see minimal movement, but there were Guardsmen there. He grimaced and winced, almost in pain as he looked, and then lowered the binoculars, deciding in his head the best possible solution.

"They're there. I'm sure they fell back from our current position and solidified with the secondary line," he said to anyone within earshot. Queens and Alex walked down to hear what he had to say. "I just don't know how many, and I doubt the gunners can gauge it in the shadows of those buildings either." He paused, looking out across the parking lot again.

"It can't be many," Queens said. "Or they'd be more liable to make an advance on us right now."

"Shit, we might not have made it this far in by now if that were the case," Derek replied. "They're waiting to draw us out. We're going to overpower them by sheer numbers, I think. I just don't know that I want to sacrifice anyone just to get that ball rolling." He looked down at the ground, again silent. "Fuck it, let's do this." He raised his eyes and developed a sour, menacing look. "You." He poked his finger into the chest of a young private. "Haul ass back up to that roof and tell the gunners that I'm going to fire once and that's their signal to light those buildings up. From that point, we fan out around both sides of the building and into the darkness. You tear those buildings and that hangar up," he growled. "Move slow and steady, and don't let up. We won't give them a chance to counterattack. Got it?" he looked around.

Everyone nodded, and clutched their weapons close. The lower NCOs trotted down the line of men to deliver the orders as Derek peered out again around the corner of the building. God, I hope this works, he shook his head with doubt. He gave it several minutes, assuring that the gunners had gotten the message. This would not work without covering fire from up top. He gave it another few seconds for good measure—almost as a superstition. And then he shouldered his rifle and fired a single shot into the shadows of the hangar across the way. With that the aerial sound of what amounted to a very dangerous storm began churning out lightning of the gods. Round after round was pumped into the enemy's defenses, drawing some fire, but not much.

"All right, move." Derek led his unit out and around the corner and pushed forward toward the parking lots.

Soon, a steady stream of soldiers were advancing and firing into the direction of the hangar and administrative buildings ahead. Every muzzle breathed fire as the tracers rained down from above, combining for a deadly assault and advance. Spotty fire erupted from the enemy side, but it was inconsistent. Derek watched as clips fell to the ground and new ones were jammed in to replace the old. A soldier in front of him fell, blood spraying out from his body like a geyser. But the Marines pushed further across the lots and into the vicinity of the hangar. The fire from the top of the building ceased, yet the infantrymen continued to pump huge amounts of lead into the buildings.

Fire slowed as they approached. Derek motioned silently for men to move around the buildings and secure the perimeter. They obeyed, and Derek could hear a few shots ring out as they circled the hangar. He moved through the pitch darkness of the inside of the empty hangar, his rifle shouldered as he scanned. Shots began to echo within the building as he watched a couple of men on the right drop to the ground and into a pool. Quickly, Derek spun and fired a few shots into the shadows where he saw the muzzle flash, and then walked over to check the man's status. But as blood poured out of the Guardsman's head like a spilled gallon of milk, he knew that man would die. Fuck him. He shouldn't have joined the Republican Guard, Derek thought to himself as he watched the life drain from a young American.

"Airfield, north end secure," Derek picked up his radio and spoke into it.

Lieutenants all down the line began to chatter on the radio that their areas of the rather large airfield were also secure, and eventually commanders all over the base confirmed that their part was secure until the entire base fell into submission. Derek and his men began taking off their helmets and taking seats wherever they could find them. Cigarettes lit up and smiles peeked out of the cloudiness of exhaustion and toil

"What now?" Alex found Derek.

"Start cleaning up and regroup," he said. "And I'm sure briefing will start tomorrow or the next day for the move on Austin." His men just stared at him blankly and exhaustedly. They needed a break. He saw that. He needed one, too. He took off his helmet, and sat down on it for a moment, rubbing his head and propping himself up on his rifle. "Austin," he shook his head and grinned slightly. "Can't fuckin' wait."

Chapter 53

August

Derek's lungs filled with a mixture of air and smoke, and he promptly released it. He leaned against the beige brick wall, his helmet at his boot-clad feet. He lifted the lit cigarette to his lips again, drawing another mouthful of smoke as the cherry glowed a deep orange. He dialed a number on the unit's cell phone, and then placed it against his ear, listening to the digital ring. He waited and it continued to ring until it halted with the recorded outgoing message. "Hi, this is Carly. I can't answer right now, but leave a message and I'll get back to you as soon as I can," the message sounded. Derek grinned a bit at the end as he heard Olivia in the background babbling as toddlers do. But he frowned again, jamming his thumb into the end button and closing the phone.

He leaned his upper back against the wall again, relaxing as much as he could while he took another drag. He looked forward at the boulevard and across the street to the homes and the small real estate offices and medical clinics. He turned his head and viewed down the street, and then looked left the other way. Humvees and military vehicles moved up and down the street, as well as soldiers carrying out various tasks. They moved about from place to place. They loaded and unloaded equipment, trying to get ready to make camp. They escorted prisoners to their place of incarceration. They looked tired. Even Derek felt as they looked. Dirt and grime mixed with sweat on his face. His short spiked-out hair was wet and dripped with perspiration from the ends.

He watched as columns of smoke rose in the distance. A tank down the street to his right burned in bright orange flames, the paint and rubber melted and fried, thickening the air around it with black, dense smoke. He could see a few craters in the pavement. Blood pools remained on the asphalt, still wet and deep crimson. In the distance, bodies, possibly friendly, possibly enemy, were hauled off the street. He took another drag, and reacted as he saw a familiar face.

"Ready?" Queens walked up with Alex.

"Yeah." He drew another mouthful of smoke, inhaled it, and blew it out as he dropped the cigarette to the concrete and stomped it out.

He pushed off the wall and joined his friends as they rounded the corner and walked down the breezeway between the buildings. They came to the glass double doors beneath the Round Rock High School sign and pulled them open. They entered the school's common area where officers, commissioned and non-commissioned, gathered and chatted. Aside from that, it was normal. It smelled like a school—a mixture of pencil shavings and stale milk. Small bulletin boards covered with colorful butcher paper and giant cutout letters decorated the walls. World flags hung from the high ceilings. Tables in the lunch area sat empty, waiting for adolescents to sit and socialize.

The officers all herded in through the doors to the fine arts center— the auditorium connected to the common area. Derek looked ahead of him at the range. He saw those who were soiled and red in the face. They walked with lag and ache. They were sluggish and shuffled forward. Others were very clean and pressed. They were shiny and military perfect—higher officers that had no intention of getting their hands dirty. Still, everyone pushed into the fine arts center all the same.

It was as the entering of any theater, but was lit with almost blinding overhead light. It had that quality of a movie that had just ended. The color of the seats and the walls were dark and able to absorb light. It starkly contrasted with the brightness, creating almost a level of discomfort and imbalance that struck Derek unfavorably. They filed down the aisles and percolated into the seats to the side, settling into the comfortable fold-downs as they waited.

"Look at 'em." Queens gestured to the left at a large group of higher brass. "Fuckin' colonels and generals. All tidy and clean. I bet they were having a wonderful breakfast and coffee this morning while we were storming downtown Round Rock and getting our asses shot off."

"I'm sure," Alex grinned, as did a couple of other dingy NCOs.

"Those guys have put in their time," Derek said. "Most of them probably served in Iraq or Afghanistan at some point way back. They got their hands dirty. Now they get to sit back and send in all the grunts into the shit. They earned it, and right now, we're earning it."

The other guys nodded, leaning forward on their knees. The room filled with the rumble of conversation. It grew dense, unable to bounce from wall to wall. It absorbed into the fabric covering the walls, the seats, and the special ceiling panels. And as if a mute button were pressed, the talk ceased with the repetitive knock of boots on the hollow-resonating stage. Every back straightened a bit. Every eye was on the general and the screen behind him.

"Here we are." He stopped ahead of the large projector screen. "On the enemy's front porch. We've been waiting for this. It's been almost two years since the twenty-nine states seceded and almost that long that we've been at war with our fellow Americans. And now we're here, just about twelve miles outside of their primary defenses of the capitol city of Austin." He pointed a laser dot at their position on the map. "It's time. It's time to put this to rest. We hope that by taking Austin, we shatter the Republic and the secessionist states will all surrender to the United States in a short time. So we have work to do."

"Here are the primary defenses." The general pointed with his laser. "Highway 183 runs in a half circle to the east. The Republican Guard is concentrated along this line. It's heavy. It's everything they have, and still, they're outnumbered. Something we're going to have to deal with is artillery. We believe they've evacuated everything just to the outside of this 183 defense line for about a mile or so. Up in the hills here to the west, heavy artillery is going to be pounding us hard on the way in. We're going to do some drone reconnaissance to try to pinpoint most of their positions and try to take them out from the air. But I can't guarantee it will totally be wiped out. So this is going to be old school. Here's a heavily defended city along a defined line complete with large caliber machineguns and tanks. And they're going to have artillery on the high ground deep behind the line. We have no choice. We hit that line with all we have. And we break through. Austin's not a huge city. It won't take weeks to take like Lahore."

A hand raised, and the general recognized him. "We lost about a thousand at Hood," he began. "We're getting that back in reinforcements, plus another two thousand. So that puts us at about eleven thousand. Is that going to be enough?"

"Good question," the general nodded. "We do outnumber them, but again, we're on their turf, and they're dug in deep. They also have the artillery advantage. They're going to have about eight thousand. They have staffing problems—always have. They had them in the beginning of this war. And they gained numbers going into Pakistan, but the problem for them is they're still in Pakistan. And now they're serving a corporation more than the Republic. As long as they're supporting the exploitation of Pakistani resources, we think Austin is going to suffer. And I also think that being a corporate army is going to be the demise of the rest of the secessionist states—even the ones out west that the war hasn't touched. They're employees of Telaco, but there's still that connection to the government and serving their country. And once there's no government, there's no government contract. Hopefully, they start jumping ship and defense is done. Any more questions?" he asked, but no hands went up. "Okay, we'll brief you further once reinforcements arrive. Expect to roll out within the week. Start prepping your people." And he walked off the stage.

"Ready for this?" Derek smiled, almost excited.

"To put an end to this shit?" Alex answered. "Hell yes."

"Brief your platoon." Derek stood up along with his friends. "Let's get it done."

Chapter 54

Kyle stood still, allowing his body to be jerked about somewhat as Ashley reached inside his urban camouflage BTUs. She looked up at him lovingly, yet somberly, her brown eyes big and full as she fastened wires to the inside of his garments. The plastic click of keys in the keyboards fired off in rapid succession, accompanied by low-decibel mutterings about frequencies and signal. It was background noise. He paid little attention. He looked around the room at his Austin counterparts, people he barely knew, intermingling with his own group. Monitors lit up and equipment glowed to life. The cubicles and trappings of a small business office were all about, but were abandoned in the wake of an impending battle literally on the horizon.

The sounds that really got his attention were elsewhere. They were distant, but distinct. It always sounded like the Fourth of July to him. It was a fireworks show somewhere across town. Heavy booms sent giant tsunamis of sound across the area, shaking even the largest buildings to their very foundations. And in between, there was a fierce, wild crackling or gunfire amid the chopping of helicopters overhead and the roar of jet engines.

His heart fluttered just a bit. It was familiar, and hearing it again at home was far different than hearing it across Hyderabad. It brought sourness to his stomach. He had seen that before. He knew what those sounds looked like. They looked like rubble and fire. It looked like blood. Even as he geared up in his familiar garb, a strange comfort came with knowing he would not go near it; not the front.

He felt Ashley tug and button. He looked down, watching her close his uniform, and even sneaking in a few soft caresses of his torso as she did. She adjusted the microphone at the top of his collar, allowing it to be only slightly exposed, but unnoticeable to anyone not paying attention. When she was satisfied, she leaned over and picked up another small device from the table, and placed it carefully in Kyle's ear, securing it comfortably, and obscurely. He stuck his finger in his ear to adjust it.

"Careful, it's fragile." She began to reach out, as if to stop him, but cut herself short.

"Feels weird," he grinned, looking over to Aaron, who nodded sternly as he finished his setup.

"Let's test," Goliath said from across the room as he walked over to a table and put on a hefty set of headphones. "Test, test," he spoke into a small, slender microphone stem erect on a table. "Test. Do you read?"

"Got you," Aaron said, nodding in affirmation.

"Yeah, I got it," Kyle said, reaching up and slightly touching at his earpiece.

"And I have you on my end," Goliath said as he removed his headphones. "Excellent. You guys ready for this?"

"Yeah," Aaron simply said, no emotion on his face.

He and Kyle continued to gear up. It felt natural to Kyle. He swiftly slipped on his vest, fully loaded with extra ammunition, and placed the sturdy Kevlar helmet upon his head, fastening it down below his chin. With the sounds of fighting in the distance, he slipped back into a state of mind he thought he would be free to forget. But his demeanor changed, rigid in the back and legs, and stern in the face as he was handed a rifle to match his Telaco-sponsored combat gear.

Ashley moved back from him a few small steps, without even realizing she was. Space grew between her lips and her brow raised to crinkle her forehead. This was not her Kyle. It was something she knew that he was in some other place at some other time. It was something she tried to ignore in his identity. She hoped she would never have to see Kyle the Republican Guardsman, and it had previously seemed that she might get away with that coming true. But here he was, standing before her, and she was frightened somewhat.

"Charges are in your packs," Goliath said as Brice handed them each a Telaco-issued backpack. "Four in each. Aaron's has the radio detonator. Blow it as soon as you get enough distance between you and the capitol. Can't wait. We can't risk them finding the charges while you try to get back here," he instructed, and then paused, becoming somewhat softer and more compassionate. "Be careful out there," he nodded as some sort of half salute. "Last I checked, there were a lot more Guardsmen on the capitol grounds than I anticipated. Good luck."

Ashley's heart sank into her gut while tears immediately welled up in her eyes. She rushed over to him, throwing her arms around him and his gear as best she could. He ignored the bulky clips of ammunition in his vest. She overlooked the assault rifle at his side. She held tight to him, burying her head into the camouflage. He leaned down and kissed her on the top of her head. She pulled her head away from his torso and silently pleaded for one on her lips, perhaps the last one before she pushed away from him, dried her eyes, and allowed him to embrace his mistress, fate.

The two men made their way from the back of the office, turning a corner and heading toward the front. They could see the sunlight far ahead of them across a sea of office droll. Cubicles lined the thinly carpeted walkway, gray and veiled in dimness without the fluorescents on overhead. Calendars themed with puppies and tranquil scenery hung on the plastic walls above the tight, individual work spaces. Family photos sat framed near computer monitors, reminding the employees why they would willingly walk into this hell every day. Trinkets of individualism attempted to brighten the cubicles. Candle warmers were there offering some pleasantry. But as none of these things really comforted the employees that normally occupied the office, neither were the two decked-out soldiers walking through the corporate cave.

They reached the front door, a small, plate-glass portal to the outer Austin world, and they paused to look outside and across the empty parking lot. They could not see the actual capitol building from their vantage point—not through the large building in between. But it was somewhat active out there. Few civilians could be seen. There were a few stragglers—adventurous younger people who likely lived downtown and decided to weather the incoming assault perched high in their condos and chic apartments near the excitement of 6th Street. Kyle grinned a bit as he knew they had no clue what was coming, and they may wish they had taken refuge. But most of the activity was from Republican Guardsmen and military vehicles.

They gave each other one last look, almost trying to transfer confidence to one another through sight, and then they waited until they were sure no one was passing or watching before pushing the door open and moving out into the Hill Country sun. Immediately, they gasped for breath. It was like the sensation of bending over and opening an oven positioned low below the countertop. The suddenness of soft room temperature on one's face becoming a cinderblock of heat is staggering. The sun immediately began frying any exposed skin. The convection of heat rose almost as wind from the parking lot blacktop. But they pushed across it.

They reached the street and crossed quickly, almost as a trot, carrying their M-4s across their chests. The sounds of artillery and gunfire persisted, much louder outside. They felt it in their chests as they approached Colorado Street, the western bordering street that formed the loop around the capitol grounds. Covered personnel vehicles loaded with soldiers passed on the street behind them, along with Humvees and troops on foot. Suddenly, the anxiety mounted. Almost all people that passed them along the sidewalk that lined the black cast-iron fence that surrounded the grounds were fully equipped Guardsmen that appeared as they did. They avoided eye contact. They spoke to no one.

They reached the gate and cut sharply to the right and into the capitol grounds. It was a step into another world—from the streets of a city like any other and into a park as green and manicured as any could be. Concrete walkways and clean asphalt drives snaked through the greenery, all lined with hardwoods of various species. Bronze statues, informational and historical markers, and monuments dotted the complex, yet instead of serene and stately, it was chaotic. It crawled with troops, all filled with purpose and wearing their duty on their faces. Kyle kept his eyes on the concrete before him, his mind working overtime. He was, at moments, sure that these troops knew something was amiss. They would be stopped at any moment.

"Hey . . ." Kyle stopped, jerking to attention almost in terror with the sudden voice.

He recognized that voice—perhaps not specifically, but that was some sergeant or lieutenant with a hard-on for barking orders. Could this one see right through him? Aaron stopped, too, and both of them turned to the aging NCO whose leathery, aging face was full of stress and business.

"Where the hell is your post?" he snapped. Aaron stuttered.

"Capitol, sir," Kyle replied calmly. "East wing."

"Well, what the hell are you doing down here? Taking a break to jerk each other off?" he barked again. "Get your asses to your post. Move."

"Yes sir." They both turned and trotted toward the building.

They glanced at each other briefly as they made their way toward the steps. It was a look of stress and relief. It was a look that visibly indicated elevated heart rates and the sudden sensation of a filling bladder. They reached the concrete steps and tan and dark reddish checkering of the walkways, and with their packs secured on their backs, they proceeded into the building.

Chapter 55

"Keep it moving," Derek instructed his unit as they steadily pushed forward along a high, institutional-looking concrete cinderblock wall.

The median in the middle of East Dean Keeton Street erupted, sending large chunks of dirt and asphalt into the air. They seemed to stay suspended for an unusual amount of time, defying physics before beginning their descent, raining down in the same vicinity. Derek and his troops shielded their eyes from bits of dirt and debris as more shells found their mark sporadically around them. A house on the other side of the street suffered a direct hit, as did the greenhouses on the other side of their wall. Derek watched helplessly as chunks of concrete landed atop hapless soldiers in other platoons. Another unit took a direct hit, sending soldiers and their removed body parts hurled into the bright, hot Texas air.

"Jesus," Queens gaped.

"Keep moving," Derek urged on. "The closer we get to that highway, the lighter this is going to get." He pulled the radio from his vest and began talking into it. "Central . . ."

"Central," it returned.

"Word on that airstrike?"

"Inbound," the voice stated simply.

In fact, he could already hear it distantly as he pushed closer to the overpass across the next lot. The F-16s screamed in from the north out of Fort Hood. The pilots, coolly navigated in, calmly confirming location of the targets. The six jets tore through the sky over the thousands of U.S. infantrymen, losing their missiles toward the hills to the west. Trails of vapor left their marks as the projectiles soared over the city, followed by the full-bodied sounds of explosions on the other side of Austin. Soldiers smiled and screamed, and then stopped and fell silent, waiting to see if the shelling continued. Though the sounds of thousands of gunshots and blasting cannons rang out all over the area, it seemed quiet as the troops waited. Then another shell fell nearby, throwing more dirt and grass into the air.

"Damn it," Alex cursed, a scowl on his face.

"It's not going to stop completely," Derek said. "Without somebody to paint each target—without laser guidance—those F-16s just can't be accurate enough. They're moving too fast," he explained. "Just keep your asses moving."

Above, another wave of jets passed over, firing more air-to-surface missiles, followed by more explosions. Queens looked up, bearing witness as an F-16 roared across the sky, yet was intercepted by a patriot missile. The direct hit caused the aircraft to break into many small and large metallic chunks, propelled outwardly by a brilliant flash of orange fire. Pieces rained down over some unseen area of the city, crashing into businesses and apartment complexes.

The Marines moved, stunned, along the wall as long as they could. The shelling was less frequent as other units moved down the street and along fences leading toward the highway. They opened into a parking lot next to some kind of shop or garage. The overpass was mostly obscured by the trees, but they could see gunfire up there, coming from two separate directions along the elevated highway. They slowed their advance to a creep, watching the skirmish along its course until one side fell silent.

"Overpass is clear," a voice chimed on Derek's radio.

"Roger that," he replied. "Get your gunners in position," he said, and then turned again to his troops. "Get moving. Quickly. Get to that highway."

The Marines picked up their pace, yet moved cautiously ahead across the parking lot and past the line of trees on the outskirts. They stumbled into an unexpected graveyard with an unimpeded view of the overpass and the shaded areas beneath. As they dodged headstones and elevated marble plot borders, gunfire erupted nearby. Derek could see the muzzles flashing on the other side of the overpass as dirt kicked up around them. Pieces of marble and granite chipped and flew as bullets ricocheted off the monuments and Marines began to fall to the ground mid-stride. They dropped their weapons and lay bleeding and dying in the green cemetery grass.

The others began diving behind whatever they could find for cover. Most tried to find a larger headstone or one of the several large trees, but space was limited, and many had to make due with just lying face-down in the grass as everyone raised their rifles and began returning fire.

"God damn it," Derek yelled in frustration. "There's a chain link fence keeping us penned in!" He pointed ahead toward the frontage road and the elevated highway.

"There's an open gate over there to the right, sir," a soldier pointed out before returning to his trigger.

"We're not doing that," Derek said. "Those sons of bitches know that's the only way out. We'll bottleneck and they'll mow us down as quickly as we can get men through the gate."

He began to panic as dirt kicked up around his tombstone and he watched his men—men he led into this slaughterhouse—die. He calmed himself, becoming steel-eyed and cold. He jerked the radio off his vest and spoke into it.

"Gunners," he called to the men and women on the overpass.

"Yeah," they answered.

"I need a little help."

"We've got our hands full up here," the gunner said. "We have the northbound overpass, but the southbound is still hot. We're trying to neutralize it for you guys."

"Do you have any grenade launchers?"

There was a momentary silence, and Derek started to believe he would not answer. "Yeah," he finally said. "M203s and a few high explosive rounds."

"We have to get through this fence," Derek called out. "I need to you blow the son of a bitch apart."

"So . . ." the gunner said. "So you want us to fire grenades toward you?"

"Yes," Derek returned. "Put a few holes in this fence. We're sitting fucking ducks in here, and we have to get to that highway."

The radio fell silent as the exchange of gunfire continued. A minute or two passed as Derek eyed the top of the overpass with fading hope. Dirt and grass continued to fly upward. Chips of marble bounced among the thick green blades. And then he saw a silhouette, and then two more at the top of the northbound overpass. He yelled to his troops to take cover as the gunners up top aimed the grenade launchers at the chain-link fence affront them. They fired and the rounds shot down across the frontage road and into the dirt at the base of the fence where they delayed for a moment, and then burst, sending a series of massive explosions of dirt and metal into the air. It silenced everything, or at least drowned it out. Ears rang and specks of grit fell in all directions. The dust produced a sort of aerial film that lingered for a few minutes, and when it had cleared enough, Derek could see a large chunk of the fence open. He smiled.

"Go, go," he ordered his men and women. "Get across while we still have the dust."

Marines lifted themselves from the pocked and cratered cemetery ground, bits of dirt rolling off as they stood, clutching their rifles and moving forward. It was a sprint through the open gap and the gate to the right side of the burial ground. They hopped over smaller monuments and dead comrades as enemy fire again commenced and more soldiers fell injured or lifeless.

They leapt through the openings and reached the blacktop of the frontage road parallel to the two separate overpasses and the HOV lane on the ground level in between. Marines scurried across and dove for the angled concrete embankment below the northbound overpass. Some took cover behind the pylons that supported the overpass. The rest set up on their bellies, hoisting their muzzles over the tops of the embankment, and continued to lay down fire, along with support from the gunners above them.

A new sound became audible on top of the deafening, relentless gunfire. It began distant and muffled, but grew fiercely and Derek and his unit were now able to see a pair of inbound AH-64 Apache helicopters appear over the oblong white dome of the University of Texas practice facility.

"Oh shit," Queens cried. "Get down. Get down," he motioned toward everyone within earshot.

The Apaches approached as they unleashed a fury of bullets upon the gunners atop the overpass. It was a steady, unbroken stream of fire that no one on the ground could see, but could only imagine the carnage.

"They don't see us yet," Derek pointed out. "Look, they can't even get in position. The street lamps are in their way. What kind of firepower do you have down there?" he yelled to his lower-ranked officers.

"Just fifty cal," Queens yelled.

"Fifty cal, I think," Alex also replied from the other end.

"Okay." Derek thought for a moment. "That'll do. Get 'em to move up to the guard rail and take down those Apaches."

Suddenly they heard the unmistakable swoosh of a rocket from nearby. Derek's heart froze. It was not a pleasant sound without expecting it or knowing where it was coming from. His head ducked down in reflex, but out of the corner of his left eye, he could see the Stinger missile propel away from one of Alex's men. It roared through the sky and found its mark with one of the Apaches hovering over the practice field. The aircraft exploded into a thousand olive drab pieces, sending the main rotor tearing into the domed football facility and other debris raining down upon the Republican Guard defenders.

"Why didn't you tell me you had Stingers?" Derek yelled down to Alex.

"Didn't know," he replied. "And I didn't order it. He just did it on his own." He paused and listened to the anonymous soldier say something. "He says that was his only one."

"That kid's getting a medal," Derek muttered. "Okay, get the fifty cals going before that other Apache circles around."

Two young men set up their bipods as quickly as they could, propping the heavy barrels up on the concrete guard rails. They aimed as the Apache seemed to be attempting to pull away and reposition. The large-caliber rounds began barking from the muzzles with flashes of fire. Sparks of super-heated metal flew from the sides and rotors of the Apache and holes began to appear in its windshield. It moved erratically, swaying from side to side before finally plunging ahead into the side of the southbound overpass. The rotor broke apart as troops on both sided ducked for cover. The helicopter broke apart, and fell to the asphalt below, mangled and maimed before exploding and sending debris shooting about in all directions.

It took a few moments, but Derek and a few other troops peeked up over the guardrails to assess. There was no enemy gunfire, yet they could see Guardsmen scurrying away. Derek opened fire at the retreating enemy, as did they others. They mowed down the opposition as Derek motioned for all personnel to move ahead across the HOV lane and into the receding enemy line. They crossed over, bypassing the helicopter wreckage and reached the opposite frontage road before traversing a dismantled fence line and reaching the outskirts of the University of Texas campus.

They proceeded unimpeded across the practice fields and around the large domed structure, still smoldering and littered with helicopter wreckage. Bodies of the enemy lay strewn about in haphazard positions, most dead, and others close to it. Their advance was brisk, moving in a calculated, professional way with their weapons up and ready to fire.

As they came to the other side of the practice facility, they found themselves either coming down a slight incline toward the gate to Red River Street or upon a raised area overlooking it. Enemy fire resumed from across the street and across a large tree-lined parking lot. Muzzle flashes began anew from the long white building across the way—the Lyndon Baines Johnson Library.

Atop the raised wall overlooking the street, troops began taking position along the screen-covered chain-link fence, poking their muzzles through the gaps and unleashing relentless fire across the library parking lot. Derek could see northbound up the street at the next intersection as more units came in, some with Humvees and mounted fifty-caliber rifles. He could see the Abramses moving in from the north. They stopped, positioned, and began blasting away at the enemy force across the parking lot. Derek smiled confidently, and continued pulling the trigger as they tightened the noose.

Chapter 60

The door shut behind Kyle and Aaron, almost as a vacuum seal, as they rushed into the air-conditioned capitol building. They rushed without rushing, briskly walking side-by-side across the red, white, and blue granite floors with the names of all Texas counties inlayed. It was both southern and western, a classic nineteenth century state house with large off-white Roman columns and wide, ornate archways. The bottom quarter of the walls and major doorframes were deeply-stained hardwood which seemed to support the plaster walls and the expansive ornate coffered ceilings.

They avoided anyone who came near, clinging tightly to their rifles and retaining the look of seriousness, they could not be bothered. Others would perceive that these young Guardsmen had their duty cut out for them today. But no one bothered with them. Every office employee and lingering statesman or judge had their own skin to save. The blasts and rapid gunfire to the north was getting louder, and anyone ordered to stay behind in defiance was now disobeying orders and fleeing. Secretaries clacked across the gray and tan stone floors of the rotunda in heels and skirts. Men in suits scrambled past the watchful and judging eyes of governors past, their portraits remaining along the walls of the rotunda.

Most were not office workers, though. Surely the majority had been evacuated long ago. Even if the president had thought the city impenetrable, surely he would not risk putting any civilians in harm's way. But was he really still in the building himself? Did it really matter? Kyle became nervous to see that the majority of the people he saw inside were Guardsmen. His gut twisted a bit as they passed through the rotunda, with its bright lone star overhead, and into the north wing where they would access the stairs downward into the basement.

"Okay, are you in the building?" they both heard Goliath in their earpieces. "Raise your left hand if you hear me." He scanned the different security camera shots on the monitors. Aaron raised his left hand, and Goliath reacted. "Okay, I see you."

They reached the black lacquered staircase, giving a quick glance around to see if anyone was really paying attention to them, then they made their way down with quick, choppy steps. The clacking of boots and their echo from the plaster walls sounded the rhythm of their descent into another world altogether. The classic multi-colored granite floors above became a shiny gray sealed concrete in the basement. The word basement really was an inaccurate word; only in the sense that it was below the main floor. Perhaps in earlier years, it may have been used for storage, but what they saw was restored and revitalized. There was no dust-coated clutter. There were no cobwebs or rat droppings. The floors were polished and the white plaster walls were adorned with framed composite photos of legislators past. The old, plain ceilings were fitted with modern track lighting.

"There they are," Aaron motioned toward the giant copper-colored columns along the corridor.

"Charge number one," Goliath commented as he watched the two on the screen. "Be careful."

They were careful to look around and make sure they were alone. Why would anyone be down here? There was nothing important. Their footsteps echoed and squeaked on the polished floors as they hurried down the eastern corridor, coming to a halt at a column at the end. As Kyle kept a close eye on their surroundings, Aaron knelt before the column and reached into his pack, retrieving a large square device with a small keypad and screen. He pulled from the bag what seemed to be a gun. Pressing the device against the obscured side of the column, he pressed the gun into a hole atop the device and pulled the trigger. A pressurized carbon dioxide canister built into the handle released a quick burst of gas, driving a steel bolt through the hole and into the concrete, fastening the device to the column. He swiftly pressed a button, bringing the screen and keypad to life, and then typed in a code. With a subtle chime, the screen read "armed" and Aaron looked up at Kyle with a nod of confirmation.

"One down, seven to go." He stood, picking up the pack and moving for the next column to their rear.

They visited column after column, following the same protocol each time. They were sure to try to mount the explosives on the side that would be least likely to be seen by someone happening into the basement. Finally, they had made their way, in a short time, to the western end of the corridor and Aaron began mounting the final charge. A new sound could be heard. It was the sound of boots on the staircase. Aaron stopped for a moment, edging his head around the side of the column. His blue eyes were wide and alert as he and Kyle watched to see if anyone would emerge.

"Hey." Goliath began to panic as he noticed on the screen that someone was heading into the basement. "Hey. Heads up. Guardsmen heading into the basemen," he yelled as Ashley watched the monitors, her hand over her mouth in terror.

They saw a pair of camouflaged legs, and then another pair. Two Guardsmen stepped off the lacquer and onto the lustrous basement floor. They seemed oblivious at first as Kyle stood silent and motionless in hopes they would be ignored and the men would disappear.

The Guardsmen ambled about for a few moments, not really looking around very attentively at anything. Who knew what they were looking for? It was probably nothing. Then one of the men noticed something as he was about to lead the other man back up the staircase. He spotted something on the column to the left of the stairs. He crept in for a closer look, first seeming puzzled, and then alarmed. His head jerked around, scanning the hallway, and then he spotted Kyle.

"Hey," he pointed. "Hey, what the hell are you doing? Who are you?" he yelled as Kyle froze.

"Do it," Aaron silently pleaded from his crouched position. He watched as the Guardsman raised he rifle. "Shoot him," he tried to say quietly, and then yelled. "Shoot him."

"What?" Kyle was still in shock. He looked at the Guardsman and back at Aaron with confusion.

"Shoot him."

Kyle raised his rifle, and fired a few bursts, striking the soldier in the torso. He continued to fire at the other man, as well, and in the end, they both were face-down on the polished floors. They twitched, but there was no longer any life. Large amounts of blood spilled and spread across the concrete as Kyle gained a sick look about his face.

"Aaron," he said. "Hurry, man. We're going to have company."

Aaron frantically worked on mounting the bomb to the column as more boots could be heard on the steps. Kyle slid into a recessed door-way alcove, hiding most of his body, but allowing his eyes around the corner to look down the top of his rifle barrel, which was fixed upon that staircase.

Three men trotted down onto the basement floor, looking around for what could possibly have made the sound of gunfire in the capitol basement. Then they saw the bodies, and as an automatic reaction, they hoisted their guns and scanned for any enemy shooters. Kyle wanted no chance of being spotted. He opened fire, cutting down one of the men as more Guardsmen descended the stairs. They began to exchange fire as bullets ricocheted off the concrete and chipped large white chunks out of the plaster walls.

"Almost," Aaron shouted over the deafening amplification of the shots in this confined space. The column before him was getting divots and craters by the dozens as Kyle held them off, dropping another Guardsman. "Got it," he stood, keeping the column a shield from the return fire. He lifted his rifle, and began firing as well, killing one of the Guardsmen.

"Get the hell out of there," Goliath ordered as he watched helplessly.

Kyle ripped a grenade from his vest, pulled the pin, and allowed the spoon to pop away. He delayed for a second or two, and then rolled it across the floor as he and Aaron took complete cover. It came to a rest by the staircase, and before anyone could react, it detonated, sending shrapnel in all directions. Guardsmen dropped to the floor all over as Kyle peeked around to see that it was clear. He made his break from his alcove and ran for the exit doors behind them. Aaron followed; running for the door as another soldier came down the stairs, took aim, and fired, sending several bullets into Aaron's back. He dropped, his momentum keeping him moving as he slid a couple of feet and bled out onto the basement floor.

"Aaron." Kyle stopped shy of the door, reaching out for him in vain. A look of hate formed on his face as he raised his rifle, and fired back. He missed, but it gave himself a chance to break for the door and exit the building. He raced up the steps outside to the ground level, trying to appear calm. Perhaps everyone up there would still just take him as another Republican Guardsman.

"God damn it," Goliath screamed, still able to see Aaron's dead body on the monitor. "Kyle, more Guardsmen are entering the basement. They're moving slow, but they're going to eventually make it your way. Get far away. Don't run, but don't fucking mosey, either."

He walked along, ever separating himself from the capitol and the scene of the skirmish. He defied his instinct. Adrenaline coursed through his body as quickly as his rapidly-beating heart would carry it. He was short of breath, but everywhere he looked, he saw potential enemies, and they were all carrying weapons, so he had to appear calm. His lungs ached as he willed them to slow their function. Sweat poured down his face from his brow as he scanned the grounds nervously, occasionally glancing behind him to see if he was pursued.

"Why haven't you blown the charges yet, Perkins?" Goliath yelled frantically, transmitting into Kyle's ear. "I can see them on-screen. They're investigating one of the charges. Detonate them now. Do it now before they evacuate."

"Why is that such a bad thing?" Kyle spoke calmly in reply, yet a wave of doubt and fury came over him. He stopped moving and looked down at his feet. He looked at the uniform he was wearing. There was a change in his eyes. He shook his head. "You really want all the civilians stuck inside to die? They're innocent."

"I don't give a shit, Perkins," Goliath screamed as tears rolled from Ashley's eyes. "They're traitors. They deserve it."

"He's right, Goliath," Ashley spoke up. "This is wrong."

"Hitting soldiers or military supply lines—that's one thing," Kyle said, still walking away. "I'm not killing civilians. Not even Crane. Someone will deal with him later."

"You selfish, idealistic, bastard," Goliath barked at him. "Both of you," he snapped violently at Ashley. "You just watched Aaron give his life to place those charges, and now you don't even want to use them? Are you insane?"

"I think you might be the one that fits that description," Kyle said. "Aaron made his own decisions, and he reaped the consequences. He knew what he was getting himself into. And I'm finally making my decision. I'm done. I'm done with all of this shit." Ashley smiled, still wiping away tears and nodding.

"Seriously?" Goliath threw his arms up. "Fine. You don't have to be the one to do it."

"I have the detonator, genius," Kyle smirked.

"Are you retarded?" Goliath laughed out loud. "You think I would give you and Aaron the only detonator? What if both of you got killed? I'll blow the Goddamned thing."

"Goliath, wait."

But as Kyle protested Goliath was already jamming down on the button of another radio detonator. The sound and the sensation were simultaneous for Kyle. Though he knew it was coming for half a second already, he had no time to prepare for it. He was still on the property when he felt a great rumble of the ground beneath his feet. With the loud burst of an explosion, he fell to the earth, immediately looking back from his position face-down in the lush grass to see a cloud of smoke and dust plume from the east wing of the capitol. And a small portion of the east wing crumbled and sank inwardly, but the rest held true as soldiers and a few civilians all over the property lay reeling in terror in the grass all around. People began filing out of the building covered in dust. They stumbled in a disoriented fashion, pushing into the sunlight and distancing themselves from the capitol as best they could.

"Yes." Goliath celebrated amid other cheers in the room as he felt the shock waves. He watched the security camera feed from the basement of the capitol go to static. But as he monitored the screens, his smile faded. The security cameras transmitting from the far north end of the grounds were still sending a feed. "Damn it," he screamed, throwing his headphones across the room. "You've got to be joking. Fucking joking. What happened?" he yelled to some of the other men in the room.

"I, I don't know," one of them answered from his position seated in front of the electronic equipment. "I can't see anything from the basement, or anywhere inside the building, but if I had to guess, I'd say maybe only one or two of the charges blew. Look," he pointed to the screen. "See how only one part of the capitol is really damaged and partially imploded?"

"This is bullshit," Goliath screamed again as the others in the room cowered. Moira stepped back a step as he seemed to stagger toward her. "He did it on purpose. Didn't he?" he jerked his head around, looking for Ashley. "He rigged them wrong," he raged, Ashley was nowhere to be seen.

"Dude, you saw Aaron set all those charges," Brice reasoned. "Kyle didn't touch them."

"He did it, I tell you," he ranted. "Must have fucked with them on the way to the building or something. And where is Ashley?" He looked around but she was nowhere to be seen.

The dust cloud spread, and thus grew less concentrated. The bright August sun illuminated the thinning blanket haze as civilians fled south and soldiers moved north. Kyle stood, a little disoriented, and watched through the veil of dust as the damage settled and the capitol building stood maimed, yet firm. Gunfire grew louder; closer. Tanks blasted their volleys as F-16s continued to occasionally fly over, sending missiles into the hills to the west. They were coming.

He took out his earpiece, and flicked it like a spent cigarette butt across the lawn, surely to be lost in the millions of blades of grass for years. He ripped out the microphone and wire, smiling as he removed his helmet and threw it to the ground. Confidence filled his step as he tossed the rifle. The rebirth of pride straightened his shoulders. He breathed freshly and un-conflicted as he walked through the gate and off the capitol grounds. He immediately headed back in the direction of the headquarters. He had no idea what he was going to do as he walked in there for Ashley, but he would do it with a concise idea of who he was and what he wanted. In retrospect, he thought he should have held on to the rifle. But no matter. He crossed the street. There was no going back, and he did not want to anyway.

But as those thoughts rolled around in his mind, he saw Ashley emerge from around a corner, her long dark tresses tossing from side to side as she looked for him. He smiled and trotted to her, taking her into his arms. They smiled into each other's eyes as the explosions grew closer and the gunfire grew louder.

"Let's go," he said.

"Where?"

"Wherever you want," he grinned. "For as long as you want." And they turned and pranced down the sidewalk away from the incoming assault.

Chapter 61

Derek Putnam stood looking around him at the once great and proud institution of higher education. He could see to the left of him down West 21st Street. Smoke pillowed upward from a crumbled portion of the football stadium. The tree-shaded lawns, sidewalks, and pavement were littered with camouflaged bodies spilling crimson blood onto the ground. The university churches were punctured with bullet holes. The halls of learning were scarred, a few with sections blown out with 105mm tank rounds. The walkways were cratered, and the campus forever scarred.

He peered down University Avenue at the dome of the capitol building, smoke rising above it as U.S. forces charged it from the north, sending the Republican Guard into retreat toward the river. He smiled a little. There was no denying his emotions about it. A hand landed on his shoulder, lightly, but firm. He swung his head and acknowledged Queens to his right. They both turned their attention to the fountain, still cascading within itself in the shadows of the infamous University of Texas clock tower. But the water cascaded red, and mostly submerged in its waters was Alex, their friend and comrade. Derek patted Queens's hand on his shoulder, his smile turning to grimace. He shook his head in denial, and closed his eyes in acceptance. He looked again down University Avenue as the city fell, and all he could think of was Carly and his young daughter Olivia.

Republican Guardsmen swiftly moved south down the streets of downtown Austin, reeling from the onslaught of U.S. assault. Occasionally, a shot would be fired back at the invaders, but there was no hope, and most troops saw that. U.S. forces began to find it easier to move along.

They became comfortable and even giddy as they rode into town like cowboys, playfully conquering the fallen presidio.

Joseph Crane stumbled out of a side exit, disheveled and dirty. The jacket of his suit was unbuttoned, and his shirt untucked. He immediately raised his hand to his brow to shield it from the sun. He watched as his troops retreated toward the river to the south. He witnessed the incoming hoard but remained still. A disappointed, yet accepting sort of expression appeared on his face as he took a seat on the concrete steps. He leaned forward against his bent knees, locking his fingers around his shins. He did not shy in the face of gunplay or tank blasts. He just watched as the invaders chased their prey down the streets.

Several figures appeared on the on the grounds. They looked like soldiers, but without soldierly movement. They wore the same Kevlar helmets and camouflage BDUs. A few carried rifles, but one very imposing figure walked ahead of them. As they drew closer, Crane could see what this was, and he knew it would come eventually. The obviously older soldier in the middle strode forth, four stars lining the tops of his shoulders. His lips were thin and his skin fair. His mouth was as a straight line with a slight curve downward. He came to a rest before Crane's seated body.

"Joseph Crane," the general said, casting a shadow over the silent president. "With the power given me by the President herself, I hereby place you under arrest for crimes against the United States of America."

Crane just looked up at the general silently, his hands again shielding his eyes. He stared for a moment, and slowly helped himself to his feet, brushing his behind and then the rest of his suit and his hands. No one laid a hand on him, nor did anyone speak. Crane followed his captors with a defeated, but proud gait, accepting his fate.

All over the twenty-nine secessionist states, the masses arose. The images of the defeated and captured Republican Guard spread across the Internet. Photos and videos of the crippled Texas State House blanketed social media awash with a message to the people of the Republic of America— change is coming. It is sweeping, and this was just the beginning.

It started in Santa Fe. Soon it happened in Lincoln, Nebraska. From there the whole western half of the twenty-nine was in revolt. The people of those states, whether they once supported the Republic or not, began gathering outside the state capitols. They were armed first only with signs and voices, telling their elected leaders that they, who had put these men and women in office, demanded a return to their rightful union. There was little resistance, and when they did, the people solidified, reaching for their own arsenals, and took back their sovereignty by force.

Soon, Tallahassee, Florida, was experiencing the same, as well as the rest of the deep south that was not already occupied U.S. territory. Angry people tired of being misrepresented took matters into their own hands. They wanted to close the growing gap between the wealthy elite and the common masses. They cried again for education and equality to be reinstated. They called for the return of programs that promoted greatness and growth. They called for a return to their rightful place in control of their own government, its place under the Constitution, and a restoration of the United States as the greatest nation in the world, indivisible under law. And one by one, secessionist regimes fell.

Chapter 62

"Today is a great day," Cindy Chandler spoke, her eyes still weary, and her face with a few more lines than she had on election day. Carly and Derek snuggled on the couch, their darling little girl nestled in between. They watched as the president addressed the nation. "Today we see the promise of a restoration of our country's greatness. Even before this terrible and tragic conflict, we had lost that status. People lied to themselves. They proudly stated that the United States of America was the greatest nation on earth, bar none. But no one really believed it anymore—not in the deepest corners of their hearts. We clung to an era long past. My mother's father was wounded on the shores of Anzio, Italy. He bled for liberty. So did my father's father at Normandy. That was a great generation. The "Greatest Generation." But not because they invaded the world and kicked people's asses. It's because what they ultimately were defending for the oppressed people of Europe, and for their families back home, was the freedom to lead a decent life without having their rights trampled by an elite few with an agenda. And when they came home, they began a time of prosperity. It was a country of opportunity—of decent wages and high standard of living."

"And somewhere along the way, that changed." She spoke softly as Angela Perkins watched, sipping her coffee alone on the couch. "Greed struck us ill. Power among our elected officials corrupted them. They no longer represented the people. They represented their own aspirations. They favored not the masses by which they were elected. They favored lobbyists and corporate millions. They would sell out millions of average people in the name of Capitalism almighty. And there's nothing wrong with capitalism—nothing wrong with making a profit. But there is something wrong with ripping people off to get it. You add ideology and ignorance, and there's where you get the notion to secede—to throw a temper tantrum because something didn't go your way in the way our government does business. We're not a perfect system, but if we work hard and compromise with the well-being of all Americans in mind, we can get pretty damned close."

"And today, we are the phoenix," she announced, Kyle watching intently, but alone on the soft, white sofa. "We give our great nation its opportunity to rise again. We accept the twenty-nine secessionist states and their citizens into the union once again, but under these circumstances. They must denounce the Constitution of the Republic of America, and draft a new state Constitution that reflects the system and values of the United States Constitution. They must include in those state constitutions a law prohibiting ever seceding from the United States again. They must submit to a level of military occupation for an undisclosed time period. Citizens of voting age must re-register to vote and at that time swear an allegiance to the United States of America before being reinstated as citizens, along with their children and dependents. Furthermore, no former Republic political or military leader shall have citizenship granted to them for the rest of their lives. That is the merciful penalty of treason. All Republic corporate contracts are null and void. All Republic debts are null and void."

"You're missing it," Kyle called out to Ashley, peering down the hall for her, and turning his eyes back to the television.

"And since all twenty-nine have already passed resolutions beginning the process of complying with the United States's demands, I hereby declare that the U.S. is now reunited forever and all time."

Kyle smiled and gaped at the TV as he leaned forward, absorbing the joy as he watched and heard thousands cheer from the audience the president was addressing. His fists clenched and his eyes welled up with tears as his mind thought back through all of this. He thought of Ryan dead on that training field. He thought of his father. He tried to imagine his brother was back from Pakistan safe and sound, though he had heard nothing from him. He thought about Aaron. He thought about all the people whose deaths had been his responsibility. And then he saw Ashley emerge from the shadows of the hallway, nearly staggering and her hand over her mouth as if she felt faint.

"You okay?" Kyle stood, turning his attention from the TV.

"Kyle," she looked up at him. She paused for a moment. "I'm pregnant . . ."

She grinned slightly, watching Kyle's ever emotional expression. His previous reflection turned to perplexity, but as the notion sunk in, his eyes widened and heart rate increased. His palms trembled, and Ashley began to worry. But the smile started forming, and then into an expression of overwhelming joy as his mouth hung open with exuberance. He began screaming in a manly way, jumping up and down before pulling her into his arms and nestling her into his strong torso.

"I'm going to be a daddy?" he affirmed softly.

"Yes," she nodded, her eyes closed in her feeling of comfort and safety. "The best daddy ever."

"I'm going to be a daddy," he reminded himself, again taking in the cheers on the television. Sure, they could be for him.

About the Author

J.M. Richardson is a native of southeast Louisiana where he studied education and social sciences, earning his degree from Louisiana State University. He has been writing for leisure nearly all of his life, wrote competitively in high school, and had intensive writing coursework in college. He now resides in the Fort Worth, TX, area with his wife and two daughters where he teaches geography, history, and sociology.

www.ingramcontent.com/pod-product-compliance
Lightning Source LLC
Chambersburg PA
CBHW030619250626
47154CB00006B/1857